SURVIVING DEATH

SURVIVING DEATH

SARAH GRIBBLE

Would you like to be the first to hear about Sarah Gribble's latest news?
Please go to http://bit.ly/sarahgribble to sign up to her author newsletter.
They're packed full of free stories, giveaways, and general horror and dark
fantasy chatter.

ALSO BY SARAH GRIBBLE

The Hike

For family gone too soon.

No fame of them the world permits to be;
Misericord and Justice both disdain them.
Let us not speak of them, but look, and pass.

DANTE ALIGHIERI

PURGATORIO

In the beginning, when the World was empty, the sun and the moon fell in love. They chased each other around the World, neither able to catch the other. The moon, in her distress, cried every night. Her tears filled the valleys and made the oceans, lakes, and rivers. The sun, in an attempt to comfort, shone his light down on the World to dry her tears. Every day, he tried his best to purge her tears, and every night the moon cried another river.

Then came an eclipse, and the two lovers were finally able to be together. They embraced and children came forth. The moon was happy, content to watch over her children every night.

But, as siblings will, her children fought.

And the more they populated the World, the more they fought.

Unable to intervene directly, she decided to take seven of her children and put them in charge of the others.

She led them to a magical and sacred tree that served as the doorway to the World and the immortal realms. Upon touching the tree, the seven were imbued with powers and knowledge of magic.

This was how the gods were born.

The Disciplinary Building loomed before Tilly. It was identical to the rest of Between with its dull gray façade. Squinty-eyed windows glared down as if they knew what she'd done and didn't approve.

They're going to send me to Hell.

Tilly repeated the sentiment to herself to quash the seed of defiant hope that bloomed in her mind. *Third strike. I'm going to Hell.* The idea seemed surreal, but so had everything else she'd experienced in the months since her death. Tilly shuddered.

Naveen gently placed his hand on the small of her back and urged her toward the door. His touch was a shock at first, but then comforting. She wished she had the nerve to hug him, to let him hold her. If he would.

"Is there anything you can do?" she whispered, staring straight ahead. She couldn't look at him; she didn't want to see the disappointment in his dark eyes.

"You didn't kill those kids, Tilly," he said. His voice was clipped, hard. She couldn't tell if he was angry or sad, though she rarely could. Naveen, like this place, this death, was an enigma

She knew she hadn't killed them, but that truth provided no comfort. The teenagers had made it out alive, but they wouldn't have if it weren't for Naveen. He'd saved them, not her. And the truth was they wouldn't have needed saving if it weren't for her foolishness.

The heavy steel door slammed closed behind them. Tilly inhaled sharply at the hollow ring. Her lungs no longer served a purpose, but breathing—like sleeping and eating—was a habit stamped on the soul, a wishful imitation here in the afterlife. Tilly and Naveen stood in a drab and colorless lobby. Large double doors on the opposite wall shielded the judgment room from view.

Tilly risked a sideways glance at Naveen. He was staring ahead, no indication of his emotions written on his face. She wished he would yell at her. She wished he would say *something*. It was worse, this torture of his silence, than the idea of the panel of judges behind those doors.

The door they'd just entered opened and someone whooshed in beside them. The person wore a dark cloak with a hood pulled forward and moved swiftly toward the double doors. Tilly felt Naveen tense at her side, his fingers, still on the small of her back, turning hard.

"Hello, Death," Naveen almost whispered. His deep voice echoed off the bare lobby walls, causing the hooded figure to pause and turn.

"Naveen," he said, his voice affecting surprise at finding the two of them standing there. A line of straight white teeth flashed in the dark hole of the hood. He reached up with one pale, skinny hand and pulled back the hood. Tilly cringed, fully expecting a skeleton head with red orbs for eyes.

What she saw instead was just a man. At first glance, she would have said he was old. Upon closer inspection, she realized timeless seemed a more apt description. His unlined skin was pale, almost translucent. No hair graced his head—not even eyelashes. His face was angular, with high, razor-sharp cheekbones. Thin lips smirked at her. He could have been a hundred or twenty.

He unsettled her. Not because of the eerie baldness or the slightly sinister expression that had settled on his face. It was his eyes. They were a light blue, so pale they seemed translucent, and looking into them was like looking into the depth of an ocean trench. He studied her, those eyes probing her soul, reading her like a book, searching out all her secrets. She wondered if he would be kind enough to share them with her if he found any.

"Is it your protégé then that we're judging today?" Death asked Naveen, his voice false innocence. "I had no idea. A ward of the great Naveen in front of the committee?" He *tsk*ed. "What *is* Between coming to?"

"I'm sure you're enjoying this," Naveen said.

"More than you know, old friend," Death countered. Those unsettling eyes moved to Tilly and trailed up and down her body. Again, she had the sensation of being cut open for the world to see, all her secrets exposed. "We meet again, Matilda," he said.

Tilly suddenly wished she had the ability to be sick. "Have we met?" she managed to ask after a moment.

That grin again. Those teeth were almost blinding. There was something familiar about his smile. "Of course we have, dearie. I was there when you died." He cocked his head to the side and continued to study her.

"I don't remember anything about it."

He searched her face intently, as if he were trying to

5

decide if she was lying. After a long moment, he said, "No one does, dearie. At least not at first. And some would be better off forgetting forever." He gave her a pointed look, but if he meant for her to understand his meaning, he was disappointed. A second later the grin was back and he swept his hand toward the double doors. "Shall we?" He locked eyes with Naveen, his face conveying a mixture of smugness and defiance. Naveen's jaw clenched and he held the stare for several moments before marching through the doors. Tilly shuffled after him, pulling herself up to imitate his defiant posture.

The double doors slammed behind, a jail cell crash signaling the end of freedom. Tilly hesitated, but Naveen's hand returned to her back and gave her a little push to the center of the room. Tilly's fingers went to the mangled scar on her wrist and she dug at it as she stepped forward and looked around. It was a cavernous room, probably taking up the entirety of the first floor of the building, save the lobby they'd just exited. The angles of the walls seemed off, just slightly askew, giving Tilly the unsettling impression of walking through a funhouse—always a bit off balance.

A high bench stretched along the far wall, five chairs behind it. Metal of course. Everything in Between seemed to either be cement or metal, a characteristic Tilly associated with a morgue and assumed that was the point.

Three men—identically craggy with long beards—were already seated, looking bored. The leftmost man's chin rested on his chest, eyes closed. A lithe woman with long ebony hair caressed the large ruby-colored pendant around her neck as she paced behind the bench, her eyes never leaving Naveen as she walked. Naveen stared back at her, his eyes dark with emotion, almost heated in their intensity.

There was something about the shared gaze that screamed intimacy and Tilly felt a pang of jealousy.

Death glided across the room, his cloak billowing behind him, to take the rightmost empty seat. As he sat, he swept his cloak to the side in a dramatic gesture and Tilly snorted a laugh before she could catch herself. All eyes snapped to her and she felt like shrinking down into the gray floor. *Not the time to appear nonchalant, Tilly.*

"Something funny, Matilda?" Death demanded.

"No, sir. I—just something in my throat." A bald lie, seeing as how she was dead. She braced herself for a lecture or just straight up damnation without the trial or whatever this was supposed to be. Miraculously, the only reactions she received were a small smile from the leftmost old man— the one who seemed too sleepy to be here—a grunt from Death, and a sharp glare from the woman who still paced behind the bench. Tilly pulled herself up to her full height and met the woman's gaze. The woman's eyebrow cocked upward.

"Let us begin," the woman said and flung herself down in the last empty chair. She shared a look with Death as she settled into her seat. Tilly marveled how the woman could look so comfortable, so regal, in a chair Tilly knew had to be about as comfortable as a rock.

Naveen's hand finally slid from the small of Tilly's back. Immediately she missed the touch and she gave him a questioning look.

He leaned in and whispered, "You'll do fine," in her ear. He hesitated before pulling away, his lips still parted as if he wanted to say more, and Tilly got the ridiculous notion that maybe he was going to kiss her—on the cheek, for luck, of course, nothing more. But then he abandoned whatever he'd been about to say and gave her an awkward pat on the shoulder before stepping backward, away from Tilly, too far. Tilly suddenly felt exposed, even more than when Death had studied her in the lobby.

Unconsciously, her right hand stretched upward a few inches, wanting to grab him back like a security blanket. He shook his head. "I can't," he said simply as he continued to back away. Hysteria crawled around her abdomen. The only reason she'd been so calm was because he'd been there. Now he was backing away, toward the door. He was leaving her, abandoning her to this soul-hungry tribunal. He hadn't said he was going to leave her. He hadn't warned her.

But he didn't leave. Not completely. He stopped his emigration a few feet from the door and gave her an encouraging nod. She lowered her hand and immediately her left fingernails found the scar and dug in. She turned to the panel and set her chin. They were going to condemn her, Naveen seemingly wasn't going to help her, but she wasn't about to beg.

"Tilly," the woman began, "you've reached your third strike—"

"You'll not be running these proceedings, Eris," one of the bearded men interrupted.

Eris's face tightened and she clamped her mouth shut. Tilly was beginning to like these weird bearded men.

"Tilly," the bearded man said, his voice harsh, all business. Tilly noticed he had a rather large mole on his lower lip that waggled when he talked. "You've reached your third strike. Between cannot function if every soul does not do their part. If a soul wants to reside in Between, they must acclimate to a job. They must! If said soul cannot acclimate by their third assignment, there simply is no room in Between for that soul."

"All of this is stated in section one-one-three of the Inter-

Realm Rulebook and Manual you were given when you first arrived," Death added.

Tilly closed her eyes briefly. She hadn't read the damn rulebook. It was a tome at least as thick as a concrete foundation slab and just as heavy. She'd skimmed it at most, and that was just to see if she could find a map of Between so she'd stop getting lost. No such luck.

Even so, she was aware of that particular rule. Naveen had drilled it into her head, along with a few other rules, namely no traveling to the World without supervision and only using magic associated with your job.

"Do you know what that means, Tilly?" the middle bearded man asked. His tone was much gentler than his colleague's, kind even.

Tilly absently rubbed her scar. "It means I'm going to Hell."

Kind Beard nodded slowly.

"For the record," Death said, "let's review the tapes."

Tilly shot a confused look over her shoulder at Naveen. Infuriatingly, he shrugged. She gritted her teeth and returned her gaze to the panel before her. She felt like a fool. All this time and she'd thought she meant something to Naveen, that she wasn't just the same as every other protégé he'd had over the course of his tenure as a mentor. He'd made her feel like she'd had a connection here, a family even. Which was especially important because she couldn't remember her actual family. And now he just stood there shrugging as if he didn't give a damn.

A jerky picture appeared on the wall to her left, projected from somewhere unseen, and the murky light that came from nowhere and everywhere all over Between dimmed to movie theater darkness. She saw herself in the projection, lurking in a bedroom with a dolphin nightlight and glow-in-the-dark stars pasted on the ceiling and a little bundle tucked tight in a race car bed.

She looked away. She knew what the projections would show. First, Tilly as Nightmare Inducer, scaring the hell out of a four-year-old when she was meant to frighten his older brother. From what she'd heard, it took the boy months to stop wetting the bed.

Next, Tilly as Possessor, taking over the body of an elderly man, only to be surprised by the extreme effect gravity had had on his testicles. She'd taken the man's body on a naked run around the park, laughing maniacally. The poor grandpa had been booked for public indecency and given sex offender status. Not exactly the traditional projectile vomiting and speaking in tongues the possession was supposed to bring.

As the projector jerked through her first two failed assignments, Tilly's eyes returned to Death. She should have asked him how she died when they'd been in the lobby; she probably wouldn't get another chance. Naveen had said her memories would come back eventually, but she'd already been in Between for months with no more than vague flashes of her life and not one hint at the cause of her death.

She studied Death as the light vacillated between dark and light, willing her mind to associate him with a memory. Nothing came to her, but she did realize with a vague curiosity that he wore no pendant. Everyone but those in training wore a pendant; having magic was essential in the afterlife.

There was a long pause where dark reigned, and Tilly could feel the tension rise. Hers was fear. But what emanated from the panel seemed to be excitement. Was she imagining that? Or were they really out to get her?

Finally, the projection reappeared, at first a white light

showing nothing. But then eventually shapes took form and she saw the rundown house. This little clip started before she'd screwed up, before Naveen had left her to her own devices in the house, when he was still teaching her the ropes.

She supposed that was fitting; she'd really messed up inside that house. They probably wanted to make sure she was trained properly, that Naveen hadn't neglected his duties. She told herself that was all, and that it wasn't because they wanted to rub her nose in her failure like a puppy who'd pissed on the clean carpet.

A Harmless Haunter's duties include such things as moaning and groaning, creaking floorboards, and slamming doors. Tilly had mastered every trick Naveen had taught her within the first few nights. After he'd left her to it, she grew bored quickly. She'd been curious what else the pendant could do, so she held it and concentrated, pressing her thumb against the hardened jelly-like red bead in the center. The power was there, enormous and intoxicating, but just out of her reach. It made her feel as if she were standing at the edge of a pool, only able to dip her toe in when what she really wanted was to dive in the center.

The recording showed several nights in staccato of Tilly alternating between wandering around bored and experimenting with the magic in the bead. Finally, it paused on an ever-brightening light bulb. She'd figured out how to control electricity. The recording slowed down as the bulb got brighter, its glow murky through the years of dust accumulated on the bulb. Tilly stood in the background, her initial shocked expression settling into a mirthful grin.

Tilly wondered who'd edited the recording. The pause was theatrical and she could almost hear the *dun-dun-*

duuunnn that should've accompanied it. She caught Death and Eris sharing a smug look before the recording sped up.

Tilly stopped her pantomimed breathing as the teenagers appeared on the screen. She wanted to look away, to hide from what was coming. But she was also curious; maybe it wouldn't look so bad on the screen.

The projection showed the teens as they barreled through the broken door and set up a little party in the living room. Two girls, four boys. Tilly had migrated from upstairs, the bulb fizzling back to darkness as soon as she stopped concentrating on it. She now stood on the stairs in the background, watching as the kids pulled out flasks and sloppily rolled a joint. A couple disengaged from the group and retreated to a corner to make out.

Another wave of jealousy rolled through her, the same as it had the night before when she stood in that rundown old house: this time over the teens, of their life, their memories. She'd hated them, even if it was just for a second. She wasn't much older than they were, yet she'd been robbed of everything they still had.

On the recording, she went about her business. She creaked the floorboards, but no one heard over their half-stoned laughter. She moved on to slamming doors. One girl noticed, but a boy quickly reassured her there were no ghosts. Tilly had begun to feel that hate again, this time because they were ignoring her.

The recording zoomed in on her—*Seriously, who was behind this supernatural camera?*—as she clutched the pendant once more, her face screwed up in concentration. The bead had pulsed under her thumb, responding to her command, and now in front of the Disciplinary Board, her thumb itched with the urge to press the bead again, to feel that power underneath. But of course, her pendant had been confiscated as soon as she'd set foot back in Between.

The bulb in the entryway flickered briefly, then stayed on, emanating an increasingly bright light. The girls screamed. The bulb grew brighter and brighter until it popped. Everyone stared at the ruined glass, mouths agape.

The popping had been unexpected, but Tilly finally had everyone's attention. She smiled onscreen.

Then popping sounded all over the house, small explosions like backyard firecrackers, as every ancient bulb in the place ruptured. The girls screamed again and huddled together. Straight lines of fire appeared on the walls: the wiring had caught.

Tilly shut her eyes. She didn't want to see this part after all. It was burned into her memory: the small fires springing to life in every room she could see from the stairs. The flames growing, and fast. Within moments, what was left of the moth-eaten curtains in the living room were in flames. The fire spread to the wood trim, giving the flames an expressway throughout the house.

The screaming echoed throughout the room and Tilly opened her eyes again in time to see her projected self freeze as the flames grew higher. The recording showed her lips moving as she stared into space; she seemed to be mouthing the same phrase repeatedly, a mantra, a spell . . . she couldn't remember. She studied it closer. Come back? Was that what she was repeating?

The teens' frantic screams echoed throughout the room for a few more minutes before the recording cut out.

"That was fairly self-explanatory," Death said. "As you can see, Matilda violated several rules in that house last night. I don't think any of us have any objections to damning this girl, so let's get on with it."

Tilly hugged herself and waited for the swishing whoosh of a portal to open. Would she be able to hear the screams of the damned before she was shoved through? Would she be able to see the flames, feel the heat? Ever since she messed up with her first assignment, she'd imagined what it would be like to be stuck in Hell, wondered what part of it would be the most unbearable. Everything seemed equally terrible, but deep down she knew the answer.

For her, the intolerable aspect of Hell, no contest, would be the flames licking at her. Her left fingertips dug into her scar compulsively. There was a burning twinge there, a sensation that had been more prevalent as she stood in the fire with the teenagers. It was deep. She rubbed harder, hoping to quash it.

Steady footsteps came up behind her and Naveen appeared at her side. Tilly almost melted with gratitude: he hadn't abandoned her after all. He cleared his throat.

"The children were all extricated successfully by Risk Management," he said, his voice clear as it echoed through the chamber. The panel paused, all eyes on Naveen.

Then Eris, her eyes narrowed and sharp as pins, said, "You are *not* allowed to participate in these proceedings, Naveen."

"I'm simply acting as Tilly's advocate," Naveen said, spreading his arms wide, an innocent gesture.

"There are no advocates allowed!" Death bellowed, rising from his seat. His words slammed off the cement walls, but when they reached Tilly's ears, she thought she heard a hint of petulance there.

The old man with the mole on his face—Mole Beard, as Tilly had come to think of him—vibrated a hand in Death's direction like he was trying to shoo a fly. Death plopped back down in his chair with a heated glare.

Mole Beard sighed at Naveen. "Unfortunately, my not-so-esteemed colleague is correct, and you know it, Naveen. No advocates. Not anymore."

Naveen didn't argue, but smiled widely instead. "I thought you might be curious."

"No one gives a corner of a bead what happened to those children," Eris scoffed.

"I do." It was Kind Beard, to her rescue yet again, if only for a few moments. "I'm curious," he said. "Continue."

Naveen gave the man a deferential nod, which was returned in kind. Death and Eris clamped their lips shut and scowled. Death's eyes were locked on Tilly, no longer exploring, no longer curious. He looked like he wanted to set her aflame.

"As I said, the teens were extracted by the heroic members of Risk Management. They were shaken up, especially given that from their view, invisible hands removed them from the burning house." He paused. "But maybe this will spawn a small renewal of belief in Guardian Angels. God would be happy about that."

Kind Beard nodded rapidly, rolling his lips in and out of his mouth as if he were trying to solve a particularly difficult puzzle or chew a piece of meat without teeth. But he said no more, and the little seed of hope that had begun to bloom in Tilly's mind retracted to a cold corner of despair.

"Well, if we're finished with *that*," Death said, "we can get on with it."

"Hear, hear," Eris agreed. "We all saw the tapes. This girl has been disobedient, incompetent, and a general pain since the tunnel dropped her into the Pit. Let's send her on her way."

Tilly's body clenched in fear. She thought she might start convulsing in panic. A fire flashed through her mind, but not the one she'd been in last night. This was different. She was outside a house watching the flames. A wave of intense sorrow washed over her.

Naveen took a few steps forward, planted his feet as if ready to take a blow. He was partially blocking her from view of the panel now. Protecting her?

"Tilly is not at fault for any of these incidences," he said. "If anyone is to blame, it's me. It was my responsibility to ensure that she performed her job well and acclimated to life here in Between. As you all must know, I could have interfered during any of these jobs, but I chose not to. If you must punish someone, punish me."

Tilly's eyes widened in shock. Had Naveen really just volunteered to go to Hell in her stead?

"I'd condemn the both of you if I could," Death said, "but I don't think Lucifer would take kindly to you going past the gates, Naveen."

"Hell is overpopulated at the moment." Everyone started at the unexpected voice of the bearded man on the end, the man who'd been half asleep for most of the proceedings. He spoke slowly, enunciating every word with care and obsessively caressing his beard.

"You have to be joking, Ret," Death scoffed. "I remind you that the purpose of this panel is not to judge, but to cut the fat. Our goal is to ensure Between runs as efficiently as possible, not to listen to any defense or excuses. *This* is exactly the reason we banned advocates eons ago!"

"If Naveen feels she should not be damned, I am inclined to trust his judgment." Ret looked pointedly at the others, each in turn. "As should the rest of you."

Eris inhaled through her teeth with a sharp hiss. A

moment later, the entire panel had jumped from their chairs —including the sleepy man on the end, Ret, who'd done so with astonishing ease—and were at each other's throats.

So quickly that Tilly could barely register what was happening, Naveen turned, grabbed her by the waist, and rushed her back through the double doors that had seemed like the seal to her tomb only an hour or so before.

WHEN NAVEEN HAD FIRST LAID eyes on Tilly, he saw nothing but hair. Wild and a soft red, it covered her face completely as she was lifted out of the Pit. She was holding her hands out as if balance was something needed when floating through the air courtesy of magic. He smiled a little at her uncertainty, but by the time she had ungracefully plopped down in front of him, he was grinning full on. She had a scattering of pale freckles and her green eyes held a glint of mischievous glee as she landed. She had spunk, and he was pleased to see someone with a little bit of life left in them.

Now he looked down at her as she clung to his arm and pictured her in Hell. He couldn't bear the idea. Hell would break her.

They listened to the commotion going on behind the doors. Screaming, banging, the crackling whiz of what Naveen recognized as lightning. Eris was the loudest, but then she always had been a banshee.

Tilly caught him looking at her and self-consciously released her grip on his arm. She stayed close, though. "Thanks," she mumbled at the ground. "You know, for standing up for me." She chuckled. "I thought you were going to abandon me there for a minute."

"Of course not," he said, which wasn't the truth. He

hadn't precisely planned on defending her, or saying much of anything for that matter. Being in the same room with Eris made his skin crawl and the less he was the center of her attention, the better. And, if truth be told, he was a little mad at Tilly for the entire mess with the teens. He'd been training souls in Between for centuries, and no one had had as big of an issue acclimating as Tilly.

He'd surprised himself, stepping forward like that. He'd thought any semblance of caring about his charges or the afterlife bureaucracy had long left his mind. But Tilly was different. Interesting to say the least. She'd brought out a seed of humanity he didn't realize was still inside him.

Pissing off Death and Eris was never a bad thing, either.

"What's going on in there?" Tilly asked. Her gaze skipped to the other door in the lobby, the one that led to the outside, to what she probably saw as freedom. What she didn't know was there was no freedom in the afterlife, no matter what realm you were in.

He shrugged. "A little argument. I'm sure they'll be finished in a moment or two." A lie. He knew from experience a fight like this could last for millennia.

That would be inefficient, though. And wasn't that what this was all about now? Efficiency, smooth operation, all the damn *rules*. He smirked to himself. If they didn't stop soon he'd go back in there and tell them all they were a bunch of hypocrites for delaying their precious proceedings with this childish nonsense. Not that that would make much difference. He didn't have any power over their decisions.

Of course they could just send him to Hell. Doubtful, but they could. And he would put up a fight if they tried. *Probably*.

Tilly had begun pacing around the room, only pausing to look at the double doors if a particularly large crash happened inside the room. He watched her walk, studying her. Trying to find why. Why?

Why had she been able to use magic in a way she wasn't taught?

That was the question the panel should have been asking.

There were really only two options. She was either a reincarnated soul and remembered magic from a former life. That was the more unlikely option, since reincarnated souls tended to remember their lives much quicker than average souls. Tilly had been in Between for months now with only infrequent flashes of incomplete memories.

The other option was that she was a descendent of a god.

It would have to be pretty far back, as no god he knew of had mated with humans in eons. The act was illegal now, like so many other things. He tried to do some math. How long had it been exactly? Was there a chance there had been a drop of divine blood in Tilly's living veins? He shook his head. Highly unlikely. Highly.

Either way, she was talented. And intriguing.

The chaos behind the door came to a crescendo and then abruptly ceased. Tilly stopped pacing and stared at the door as if she were facing down a hungry lion.

The minutes ticked by. Tilly started to fidget with impatience. Naveen didn't move a muscle. Minutes meant nothing to him, not like they did to Tilly. She was too young yet, too unused to the unceasing monotony of Between.

His heart did pound in his chest, though. He couldn't remember the last time he was this nervous.

The truth was he had no idea what this panel was going to do. Eris and Death hated him—maybe for good reason.

And Ret, Rho, and Ren had no reason to have any loyalty to him whatsoever. Not really.

Would they send him to Hell? Was that even possible? Would Lucifer *allow* it?

His heart wasn't pounding because of nerves, he realized.

He was *excited*.

The door swung open, smashing his thoughts and making his heart skitter. Tilly jumped, then shirked away as if she could melt into the wall furthest from the door.

Death and Eris emerged together. Death marched through the doors and exited the building without making eye contact, but Eris paused to whisper to Naveen, "One of these days, you're not going to get your way, *dear*."

Naveen took the first full breath he'd taken since Tilly had returned from the teens and managed an insolent grin. Eris's eyes glowed like embers and her fists clenched. Naveen, still grinning, shook his head and clenched his own fists. He could feel the power just waiting to lurch out. "You don't want to do that."

Ret cleared his throat from the doorway. He was flanked by his brothers and all three looked ready to resume their fight.

Eris took a deep breath and slowly relaxed her hand. Her eyes returned to their normal coal color. She turned to leave, paused at the door. "Good luck on your new job, Matilda," she chirped loudly, flashing Tilly a sickening smile.

Tilly mumbled a confused thank you and Eris cackled as she glided through the door.

"Don't pay her any mind," Ret said after she'd gone. The three old men abandoned their fighting stance and were once again the harmless, wrinkly codgers they normally were.

Ret held out a manila envelope. Tilly took it with a relieved smile. Ret gazed at her with a pitying look, then said to Naveen, "It's the best I could do. And I won't be able to save her again."

Naveen's excitement turned to dread.

The three men shuffled out the door and into the gray streets of Between without a backward glance.

"I CAN'T BELIEVE WE WON," Tilly said. She was gripping the envelope outside the Disciplinary Building. She playfully nudged Naveen with her elbow. "We won! Why aren't you excited? Was it something that woman said to you?"

Naveen's jaw clenched, but he shook his head.

She flipped the envelope over and went to rip it open. Naveen placed a hand on hers. "Wait a moment. There's something I should tell you first. About your new job."

She barked a laugh. "You don't even know what my job is yet."

"I do."

The tone of his voice took all the excitement out of her and replaced it with trepidation. "Naveen, what's going on?"

Naveen's mouth opened and then closed again.

"This is ridiculous." She ripped the envelope open in one fell swoop and dumped the contents to the ground.

"Tilly . . ."

Crouching, she sifted through the contents. A pamphlet entitled "Your Death: How to Make the Most of It." A map she'd long since learned was useless in the ever-changing city. She'd seen it all before. Only one thing caught her interest: an index card with her job title on one side and a brief job description on the back. It was bright red, the color of freshly spilled blood.

Naveen tried to grab it from her but she darted away.

On the front, centered in a plain black typeface, were the words ESCORT TO HELL.

"Calm down."

"How could anyone be calm in this situation?" She flicked the index card at him. "You have to get me out of this." She pointed to the pendant around his neck. "Isn't there something useful in that thing? Couldn't you take me away somewhere?"

Naveen instinctively grabbed his pendant. Technically, yes. He could spirit her away, somewhere in the World. But they would track them down easily, and then Tilly would definitely be damned.

"You don't actually have to enter the gates of Hell," he said, "just stand outside and check the souls in." He hoped this would make her feel better, but he knew it wouldn't. Not after her reaction to the fire earlier. She may not have to stand in the flames, but she'd be close enough to feel the heat.

She paused, taking in the new information. "I don't understand," she said. Her voice was still tight, but no longer frantic. "Doesn't Death have Acolytes to help him?

Why can't they take the souls? Or a tunnel like the one that picked me up?"

"Death and his Acolytes cull the souls," he explained. "They don't have time to escort them. And the tunnel is only for people assigned to Between. It was more of an afterthought than anything."

Naveen remembered a time when each individual soul had their own personal Escort. Someone familiar, who would stick with the nearly departed for days before the death, coming to them in dreams, appearing at their vision's edge. It was all somewhat romantic and made the transition easier. But with the population boom, the system had to be rethought. Death needed helpers—his Acolytes—and a tunnel was magicked into being to vacuum up the souls assigned to Between, as if those souls weren't worth the time it takes to escort. The lack of respect sickened Naveen, but he could do nothing about it, so he ignored it as much as possible.

"The souls assigned to Heaven or Hell stick around," he continued, "attached to the body until an Escort picks them up."

Tilly chewed her lip and dug at the scar on her wrist. He watched her, wishing she could remember how the injury happened. He knew charred flesh when he saw it.

When she spoke again, she sounded resigned. "I don't have to go into Hell?"

"No," he said. "I promise you will never have to set foot inside the gates." He closed his eyes briefly, hoping with all his soul that it was a promise he would be able to keep.

"And I don't have to hang around with Death?"

"I'm going to keep you as far away from him as possible." He paused, letting her have a moment of relief. "There is one thing, though."

Her eyes snapped to him and he saw panic rising again. He held out his hands in a calming gesture. "It's not a big deal, really. It's just that you'll be able to feel the heat in Hell."

She furrowed her brow. "I can feel heat in the World."

"It's not the same. Hell is set up for punishment, so everything is tenfold down there. Souls can feel ravenous hunger that's never satiated or extreme fatigue without being able to sleep. It won't be like that for you, as you'll just be on the platform, but you *will* be able to feel the heat."

He watched her face closely, but what he said didn't seem to register. He didn't think she fully understood how different it was down there. While she could feel physical sensations in Between, they were dulled, like touching someone through several layers of clothing. The World was similar. In Hell, however, pain was commonplace. He wished there was some way to intimate to her the shock that would come, the unexpected pain, like a sleeping limb waking all at once. He couldn't find the words to fully describe it. Unfortunately, she would just have to experience it herself.

TILLY WALKED past the Pit on her way to her room. Naveen had offered to port her home, but she'd wanted the walk to clear her head and, for some reason, the Pit always calmed her. She supposed it was something to do with memories, of which she had very few before the Pit.

She paused at its edge, watching the throngs of souls packed in like sardines, new ones arriving every second. Confusion and panic skittered over their features. She felt sorry for them. A few minutes before, they'd been floating in an infinite black space with no memory, weightless and disoriented. Once they finally began to get used to the emptiness, a tunnel showed up to bring them here.

Tilly remembered the tunnel well, the pinprick of light at the end, growing bigger by the second, holding promises of Heaven. She remembered the excitement as it sucked her along, how she'd thought she was going to meet her maker. All hopes were dashed when she came to the end and was dumped unceremoniously to the ground, just another soul banished to Between.

She remembered thinking she'd been sent to Hell. She'd panicked, shoved her way through the crowd trying to find a way out.

"No cutting!" a man beside her had said, then gave her a little shove on the shoulder. She shrank away from him.

"Don't worry, dear, your turn will come." An ancient woman stood at her side. Her face shriveled in on itself, like a dried apple doll. She made Tilly uneasy. Had she been waiting there that long, or did she die that old?

"Do you know where we are?" Tilly had asked.

"We're in a giant hole." The woman gave a big toothless smile that took up her whole face.

"Helpful," Tilly mumbled, turning back around.

"Oh, I'm only joking with you, dear," the woman said, patting her on the arm. "I'm not exactly sure where we are, but I know it ain't Heaven, that's for sure."

"Hell, then?"

"No, it ain't Hell, neither. I have a feeling we'd be in a lot more pain if it were."

"It's purgatory." This came from a blue-haired, over-pierced teenager on the other side of the old woman. He turned toward Tilly. His eyes were the same striking and unnatural color as his hair. "I heard a rumor." He shrugged and looked straight ahead again.

Hours passed without anyone else talking to her. She wondered what she'd done to cause her soul to end up here instead of Heaven—or what she didn't do. Most of all, she wondered how she died. Try as she might, Tilly couldn't remember anything before the darkness and the tunnel.

Tilly shook off the memory and sighed in frustration. She didn't have much more information about her life now than she did then.

IT HAD TO BE HER, Death thought. The way Naveen had looked at her. Hell, the way he'd stood up for her. In all the years Naveen had been haunting the four realms, Death had never seen him stand up for someone like he'd done today.

There was only one solution: Death had been right and Tilly was the one.

But he had to be sure. The Fates would go straight to God if they found out he'd overstepped again. He knew they were watching him . . . from somewhere. It surely wasn't where he'd found them to begin with. The thought made him feel sick.

Eris sat in Death's office, across the large desk, unenthusiastically picking at her nails. He could hear the dull click each time she pulled one back. His jaw clenched.

Eris hadn't left him alone for long since the coup. One would think he would've gotten used to her by now, would have possibly even come to care for her, but no. His annoyance with her increased exponentially like a boiling plague.

He thought to tell her to find something to do, something elsewhere, preferably. He even opened his mouth to do so. But then a thought struck him and he changed his mind. If she wouldn't find something to do on her own, he'd give her something to do. Something that maybe would solve his problem without having to get involved personally.

"You should do something about those two," Death said.

Eris stopped her incessant nail picking and looked at him through the tops of her eyes. Her perfect left eyebrow cocked up.

"Surely you noticed the way they looked at each other," Death continued. His head was bowed and he shuffled papers on his desk as he spoke. The perfect mask of disinterest.

Eris snorted. "You can't mean Naveen and that *girl*."

Death shrugged at her and went back to his papers. She sat up a little straighter, leaned forward in her chair.

"You cannot be serious. Naveen could never be seriously interested in some simple soul."

Her words were emphatic in denial, but Death heard a bit of a waver there, a bit of oncoming hysteria. Eris had always been one to fly off the handle easily. Death felt his lips upticking toward a smirk and schooled himself.

"I'm just saying I thought I saw something between them."

Eris waved her hand dismissively and returned to picking her nails. Click, click, click. The picking was happening faster now. Death waited.

"And so what if it's true? It would only be a minor dalliance." She sat forward once more.

Again, Death shrugged. "There's a prophecy, you know."

"What do I care about something some babbling child said?"

"This one happens to mention Naveen, but if you don't—"

"No! Tell me this instant!" Eris stood in a burst of upward movement that threatened to propel her across the desk and into Death's lap.

This time he didn't hide his smirk. If his amusement angered her more, so be it. It wouldn't be him she'd be taking it out on.

"Let me see," Death said, tapping his chin. "It said something about Naveen falling in love with a girl. 'A girl scarred by fire,' if I remember correctly." Death remembered correctly. He remembered every word of that particular prophecy. It haunted him, the remaining words, the ones he wouldn't tell Eris—or anyone.

He watched with satisfaction as her face darkened. Ah, that temper. It could be beautiful when aimed in the right direction. He turned away from her. "As I said, you should do something about those two."

He heard a large huff as she stormed from the room. His smirk died on his lips. If Tilly was really her, the girl from the prophecy, Death would have to get rid of her. Immediately. He couldn't afford a wrench now, not when he was so close to a new life.

He just had to be *sure* first.

THE MURKY STREETS of Between were deserted, as usual. There was nothing to do in this wasteland, so there was no reason for any soul to be out of their rooms when not on duty.

Naveen wandered aimlessly, his sandaled feet shuffling over the never-ending pavement. The streets wound around nonsensically, like a toddler had thrown blocks together from mismatched Lego sets. He hated it here; it was more of a half-place that never really seemed tangible. Overcast always, but no clouds. No sun, no moon, no wind or weather changes—as if everything was waiting for something. Always waiting. He supposed he was waiting too, but wasn't quite sure on what.

Normally he would have done his waiting in his room, tuned out, staring at the wall. But the day's events had left him restless. He wanted to do something, but he was powerless. The feeling left him angry, and he didn't want Tilly to see him this way.

He let out a derisive chuckle. Why did he have this insane urge to protect her? She was just another charge and they wouldn't see much of each other after she assimilated. Yet he'd put his neck out for her. She made him feel things he hadn't felt in eons.

She made him feel alive again.

He hadn't always been this way. Once, he'd been passionate. He'd lived by one rule: do anything and everything as long as it felt good. It wasn't necessarily the best rule to live by, but no one would stop him. No one *could* stop him. The people he'd surrounded himself with even encouraged him. Death, for instance.

Naveen had known Death for so long, he couldn't remember meeting him. He was always there, lurking in the shadows, ready to pounce any moment. On enemies, on neighbors, on loved ones. Death had no qualms about killing, and at one point, neither had Naveen.

They'd been friendly, once, a long time ago. But that was long gone. Now Naveen was washed up and powerless in Between, far from home and alone, while Death strutted around like he was in charge of the entire afterlife.

"Penny for your thoughts?"

Naveen froze mid-step. "What do you want?"

Eris slunk from beside a nearby building. "I'm sorry about Tilly's misfortune," she said, her voice low and breathy. She moved toward him until she was close enough to reach out and touch him. And she did, placing her hand on his shoulder and sliding it over his back as she walked around him. He recoiled.

"I'm sure you feel bad for her," Naveen said, his voice dripping with sarcasm.

The woman pouted. "Of course I do, dear Naveen. Not as much as you do"—her eyes darkened at that—"but I do have compassion for the girl. I don't want her to go to Hell." She batted her eyes, a ridiculous gesture, but one that used to work on Naveen.

He glared back at her.

Her pouting lips took on a harder quality and her eyes flashed. "I don't understand what you see in her, Naveen," she spat, her saccharine attitude completely gone, replaced by the temper Naveen knew all too well.

Naveen didn't respond. Even if he had the urge to justify himself to Eris, he wouldn't know what to say.

"She's going to fail again, you know," she said, smiling as if the thought gave her satisfaction.

"She won't," Naveen said, "not this time."

Naveen could see Eris's brain working, trying to come up with the best plan of action. The best plan to get him on her side again. They'd had nothing to do with each other for centuries—his decision, not hers—and he was having trouble imagining what her sudden renewed interest was.

"I want to go home, Naveen," she whispered, again trying to be sweet. Naveen knew she didn't mean back to her room here in Between. He knew she meant *there*, the place they used to live. The place where they had power. She'd always loved the power.

31

"I don't," he said bluntly. But he was tempted. He was nothing here. But there . . .

But that was no longer an option. It couldn't be, not for him. Not anymore.

She stared at him, her eyes wide in disbelief. Then she narrowed them and smirked. "You do, and you know it. After all, you offered to go to Hell today. You can't tell me that was purely for her sake."

Naveen clenched his jaw. Had it been only to save Tilly from the torment? He wasn't sure.

"It was you, wasn't it?" he demanded. "That suggested she escort to Hell?" He needn't have asked; he knew the answer.

Glowering, he gripped her toned biceps and squeezed. "Why would you do that to me?"

Eris giggled, an annoying, high-pitched sound that had always made Naveen's skin crawl. "One day, my dear Naveen," she said, her voice slithering from her lips, "one day, you'll return to what you were meant to do, and stop being a slave to idiotic souls like your precious Tilly."

III.

Tilly dreamed of fire.

It was night, the full moon shining with inappropriate cheerfulness down on the horrific scene unfolding in front of her. She stood on the grass in her bare feet, her thin nightgown twisting around her small body as she thrashed. Someone larger, stronger than she restrained her as she watched the house burning across the yard. She was bawling, frantic to get away from her captor. The more she struggled, the more the burn on her wrist screamed with pain, but she couldn't stop. She needed to get free.

They'd left something inside. Something important.

Tongues of flame lapped out the windows and up the pale blue siding, hungry for more. The smell was sickening: all burnt hair, rubber, and a slight tinge of charred meat. It coated her nostrils and stung her throat. Still she screamed. "Come back! Come back!" It was a chant, a mantra of horror and desperation.

The fire engulfed the house before the fire trucks arrived. It was too late.

"I'm sorry, Matilda," a man's voice whispered in her ear.

She became still at his words and slumped against his strong chest, completely exhausted from her struggles and her grief. His heart pounded against her head like a frantic drum. He tried to turn his restraining embrace into one of comfort and love, but she resisted. He'd let this happen. She didn't know how, but this was his fault. "I'm so sorry," he repeated. His voice cracked at the end.

Good, she thought. *You should be sad. You should feel guilty.*

He turned her to face him, his face close to hers as he bent to her height. He had dark hair, slightly receding, a face just starting to show worry lines. "I only had time to get you out," he said, his gaze pleading, willing her to forgive him, to validate his decision.

"You let her die," she said, her voice low and full of menace. The firefighters were busy behind her, trying to keep the fire from spreading to the neighboring houses.

The man shook his head weakly, tears streaking down his face. For a moment, Tilly felt sorry for him. She knew it wasn't really his fault. She knew, but he was the only one there to be mad at.

"You had time!" she screamed. "You had time and you let Mommy die!"

Tilly jerked upright as a knock exploded on her door. The knock grew louder. She rolled off her futon, struggling to remember where she was, what was happening. She could still smell the acrid smoke from her dream, still feel the heat of the inferno on her skin. She struggled against an overwhelming sadness as she rose. The pain of remembrance was intense. Her wrist tingled, the scar a bright pink. Her mother had died, but something was there she wasn't quite remembering.

She squinted her eyes closed, picturing the house on fire, feeling the breath hitching through her little body as she screamed for her mommy. What was it? She was missing something.

Another knock. Slowly, she took in the sparse furnishings—cheap particle board desk and creaky chair against the wall; one small window through which the depressing bland haze of Between filtered through; small, worn futon she used as seating and as a bed—and realized why someone was knocking at her door. The dread in her chest doubled, chasing away the last frantic wisps of dream, as she remembered what she had to do today.

She swung the door open to a smiling Naveen. He took one look at her and his smile faltered. "What happened to you?"

"Nothing."

He cocked an eyebrow.

"It was just a nightmare."

"About?"

"I don't want to talk about it." He glared, his eyes too intense, reminding her of Death the day before. She held back a shudder. "Not now, at least," she added, hoping to appease him. Then she immediately felt guilty for feeling such things. Naveen had saved her hide not twenty-four hours earlier. She was not afraid of him.

"Later, then," he said, pulling the familiar red pendant from under his white linen shirt. "You ready?"

She struggled against the wave of panic, managed to nod.

There was a sucking sound and the portal opened in the floor, bluish and swirling. Naveen shot her an odd look: pity, worry, sadness. Then he saluted her and jumped through. Tilly hesitated. She'd never liked porting; she didn't understand the exact mechanics of it, and the feeling of floating nothingness inside reminded her of the tunnel when she died. She wasn't solid inside the portal, somehow. But so far, she'd always emerged intact, so she scrunched up her face and squeezed her eyes shut as she stepped in.

She emerged in a giant circular room, ports with scrolling signs above them positioned every few feet. They looked to be permanently open, which made the walls seem like a roiling ocean. People milled about, laughing, fighting, chatting. Naveen pulled her close. His lips moved toward her face and she was reminded of when she thought he was going to kiss her before the disciplinary hearing. The idea didn't seem as ridiculous today.

He moved his mouth to her ear, shouting over the commotion. "Welcome to the Escort Dome." He released her, and she immediately missed his hand on her arm, wanted to cling to him.

"Naveen!" a man's voice called from across the room.

The crowd parted to make way as a man strolled through, his smile so beautiful it almost glowed. He was tall with side-parted blond hair so slicked back it looked like a helmet. He wore a dark suit without a jacket, sleeves rolled to the elbows; the complete opposite of Naveen's flowing linen clothes. He sauntered up to Naveen and Tilly with a cocky smirk on his face.

"Luke! How have you been?" Naveen and Luke embraced in a manly, back-patting hug.

"Everything's jake," Luke said. His voice sounded as slick as his hair looked. "Can't complain." He turned to Tilly and looked her up and down, whistling softly through his teeth. "And who do we have here?" he asked.

Tilly hung her head and rubbed her scar.

"This is Tilly," Naveen said. "She's a new Escort."

Tilly wished he would stop saying the word *escort*. It made her feel dirty.

"Oh, that's great! You're going to love escorting, Tilly. You get to meet some of the most interesting people, and the hours are great on account of fewer and fewer folks getting into Heaven nowadays—"

Naveen cleared his throat. "Actually, Luke, she's an Escort to Hell."

Luke's face fell. "Oh," he croaked.

Tilly dug her nails harder into her wrist.

Luke recovered quickly and gave another million-watt smile, waving a hand in front of his face as if he were swatting away the awkwardness. "Well, that's good, too! A very important job, escorting people. No matter where you're taking them."

Tilly nodded and tried to think of something to say. She wanted to keep him talking, draw out this reunion as long as possible so she didn't have to go to Hell.

Luke's eyes widened and he snapped his fingers. "Wait a second. Aren't you the little lady who caught all those kids on fire?"

That wasn't the topic of conversation she had in mind, and she didn't particularly care for being called a "little lady."

"I didn't catch them on fire, exactly," she snapped.

Luke didn't notice her peevish response. "Well, what did happen?"

"Luke's a bit of a gossip," Naveen said disapprovingly.

Luke winked and tapped his temple. "I know everything about everybody."

"That's nothing to be proud of," Naveen said. "Think you could do something useful and help me show Tilly the ropes?"

Tilly relaxed somewhat, glad for the change of subject,

but still not too keen on Luke hanging around. Still, it had to beat Hell.

"Oh, sure," Luke said. "No problem." He put his arm around Tilly's shoulders and spun her around, pointing with his free hand at the ports. "Those ports take us close to where we need to be. They're always open, so you only need to use the pendants when you want to come back."

"When those signs above the door list a name," Naveen chimed in, "the next available Escort goes through. A name scrolling in red means Hell, and green means Heaven."

Luke kept his arm slung casually over Tilly's shoulders. Tilly resisted the urge to throw it off.

"Where are the pendants?" Tilly asked as she squirmed out from under Luke's arm.

"You like to get straight to it, huh?" Luke said. "I like that in a lady." He grabbed her hand and led her to the far side of the circular room, leaving Naveen in their wake. Tilly looked back at him for help, but he waved her on. She did notice his lips were pursed, though.

The pendant kiosk looked like a jewelry armoire, covered in pendant-laden hooks. "You won't get your own until Naveen is done training you. I assume you know these are to be returned after your shift?"

"This isn't my first day in Between."

He cocked his head and narrowed his eyes, leaning in conspiratorially. "Well then, smarty pants. Ever stolen one?"

Tilly shook her head.

"You know you can go anywhere with them, right?" Pulling his own pendant from around his neck, he took a quick look around the room, making sure no one was watching, then opened a port in the floor and dragged Tilly through it.

They popped out in a large city next to a giant bull.

38

"Welcome to New York," Luke said, holding his arms wide and spinning slowly in place.

Tilly looked around, amazed. She hadn't been in the World much since she died—at least not outside the jurisdiction of her jobs. She wanted to walk around, check out the sights. Evidently, Luke didn't want to sightsee. He pulled out his pendant and brandished it in front of Tilly's face like a prize. "Where do you want to go next?"

She hesitated. "We should probably get back." She thought of the recordings at her hearing. They were watching her.

Luke's left eyebrow twitched upward. "Don't tell me you're a spoilsport. Come on, just think of a place."

He shoved the pendant in her hand. She hesitated for a moment. In order to port, all a person had to do was think of where they wanted to go as they pressed the pendant. The thought directed the magic. She concentrated on the Escort Dome as she brushed her thumb across the bead, reaching with her mind into the magic inside. The bead was like any other she'd touched: unnaturally warm and soft, with a tiny jolt of something that felt like electricity pleasantly zapping the pad of her finger.

Another thought wheedled its way in, overlapping—and for a moment overpowering—her thoughts of Naveen and the Dome.

Home.

Then came the familiar whooshing sound and the portal opened at her feet.

"I HAD no effect on him whatsoever," Eris whined. "He hates me. I can see it in his eyes."

She threw herself into the chair opposite Death's desk, her shoulders slumped, tears brimming. Death clenched his jaw and willed control. He couldn't stand crying women. He sighed and reached into a drawer, pulled out a large book. Eris's sniveling immediately stopped. She stared at the book in wonder.

"That's been missing for the better part of a decade," she said.

"Lucifer had it." Death caressed the spine absently. "I never understood what the attraction was with this book. It's just a bunch of fairy tales." He slid it toward her.

She reached forward reverently and took it in her lap. "They're not fairy tales, and you know it." Flipping it open to the back, she shuffled through the last few pages. When she found the spot—the one where the last prophecy should be, but where she only found frayed edges of paper—she snapped the book shut again. "Where is it?"

"You don't need to concern yourself with that. I already told you what you need to know."

"Then what exactly am I supposed to do with this?"

"Am I the only competent one around? You give it to the girl."

Eris's look was blank; he would have to spell it out for her. "What's at the beginning of the book, Eris?"

"History. Well, slightly embellished history."

"And if Tilly finds out who Naveen really is, what do you think would happen to their relationship?"

A slow smile crept up Eris's face. Finally, she understood.

"Now get out of here."

When she left, Death reached back into his desk and pulled out a sheet of paper. He read it again, for the millionth time, hating every word, then folded it back up and tucked it away.

TILLY POPPED OUT, not in the Escort Dome, but on the steps of what looked to be an old courthouse. A dozen or so people spread out on the steps, enjoying the sunny day as they tucked into greasy sandwiches bought at the sketchy food trucks lining the street. Men and women in meticulously pressed dark-colored business suits and product-laden hair scurried past, yapping into their cell phones. Tall buildings rose around them, dwarfing the much older courthouse, their bland gray coloring reminding her a little too much of Between.

"I made a mistake," she told Luke. "I meant to take us back to the Dome but I thought of something else right as soon as I jumped."

"Home?"

She nodded, feeling a little guilty.

"Yeah," he said, looking around, "I would've done the same thing if I were you. Of course, my home isn't anything like I remember it." His gaze softened and he looked far away. He gave her a wan smile. "Don't remember much yet?"

She watched the buses going by, the people jostling each other on the sidewalk. "I don't recognize anything here." The fact saddened her more than she would've thought. How can you miss memories you don't remember ever having? "We should get back." She looked eagerly at the pendant he'd placed back around his neck, willing him to open another port, get her back to the Escort Dome. He didn't.

"You know Naveen used to be my Teacher."

The statement wasn't exactly a shock to Tilly. Naveen had obviously had other wards before her, and she'd assumed their chummy attitude upon meeting meant they'd had a previous friendship. She found herself wondering if she'd still be friends with Naveen after he'd taught her how to escort. The idea of not seeing Naveen every day wasn't a thought she wanted to hold on to.

"Naveen has been a Teacher for a long, long time," Luke continued. "I had a hard time of it when I first came through. Naveen helped me through it."

"I find it hard to believe you have a hard time with anything."

"Well, that was then, darlin'," he said, winking. He waved his hands over his body. "Now I'm better than ever. You just let me know when you want to see for yourself."

Tilly shifted and looked away, her hand instinctively moving to the scar on her wrist. "I really think we should go back."

"Oh relax. If they were watching us, they would've been here by now. No one cares."

"They care about me. They're watching me. Luke, I'm on my last strike here."

He laughed. She couldn't believe it. She was begging to go back, to follow the rules, to *not be sent to Hell*, and he was laughing at her. She lunged at him, grasping for the pendant at his neck. He was too quick and sidestepped her, holding out his hands, palms out. "Whoa there, little lady. Let's calm down, okay?"

"I don't want to calm down. I want to go back!" Flames leaped into her mind. "I could be sent to Hell, do you understand?"

"No one's sending you anywhere," he said, his voice low as if he were talking to a spooked animal. "I promise if those goobers from the administration show up, I'll take the blame. They can roast my ass for the rest of eternity. Okay?"

"I don't understand why you just can't take me back." She hated the childish petulance that had crept into her voice.

He shook his head and sighed. "Look, I'm trying to be friends. I know what it's like to be new in Between, and it doesn't seem like you're having such an easy time of it. I mean, you're wound so tight you look like you might implode. I thought maybe hearing my story, or maybe asking me some questions about life in the afterlife . . . I don't know. You can't be going around picking up damned souls looking like you're about to jump out of your skin." He reached for his pendant. "But if you're not interested, that's fine. We'll go back. I was just trying to help you like Naveen helped me."

Tilly groaned. "Wait." He had a point. No one had come to carry them away. Maybe they never would. But the bigger appeal was maybe finding out more about Naveen and his past. "You promise you'll take the blame if they come? Scream from the mountaintops that you kidnapped me?"

"Scout's honor."

"Okay. Let's sit."

Luke grinned.

IV.

Luke died in 1918 at twenty-five years old. He fought briefly in the Great War, but was injured early on and sent home. Tilly thought he seemed bitter about it; he kept saying it wasn't that bad of an injury and they should've let him stay with his buddies. A few years later his sisters caught the Spanish flu, and he followed suit.

"I'm sorry," she told him.

"Don't be. It was a long time ago, and it was quick. I missed the flappers, though." He looked up and shook his hands at the sky, crying forlornly, "Why, oh why, God, did I have to miss the flappers?"

"You're kind of a douche," Tilly said with an eye roll.

He considered that. "I think that's a new one. 'Douche.' Nope. Don't think I've been called that. I kind of like it."

Tilly couldn't help grinning. He was a bit of a douche, but after hearing his life story, she'd thawed a bit toward him. He seemed like a decent guy, deep down under all that suave exterior.

"There we go! A smile from the ol' girl."

They sat for a moment in companionable silence,

watching the living move about their daily lives. Tilly envied them. They weren't thinking about death or Hell or even Heaven. They would finish their day without seeing torture, go home to their loving families, and fall into a comfortable bed.

"How long has Naveen been dead?" Tilly asked. The people milled by. Their chattering and footsteps seemed overtly loud, like a stampede of monkeys. Sound didn't carry well in Between—it was like the air ate your words almost directly out of your mouth—and Tilly had gotten used to the cotton-like quality of the atmosphere. She supposed she should be glad the sun wasn't out today; she definitely wasn't used to that.

Luke gave her an odd look. "I think that's a question for Naveen."

"I thought you wanted to talk."

"Naveen is . . . complicated."

"Well, uncomplicate him." She was getting antsy. The noise and the people and Luke were wearing at her.

Luke's smirk slid into a frown. The facial expression didn't suit him and aggravated Tilly even more. He reminded her of a pouty little boy who hadn't gotten a treat.

"Never mind," she said shortly.

"We should probably go soon," Luke said, but his voice held no conviction. Tilly barely heard him anyway. She was too busy watching a woman sidle over to where they were seated.

The woman looked remarkably like Tilly. Her red hair was swiped back into a low bun and she was about a decade older, but the similarity was there. There enough to flame the fire of envy in Tilly's heart.

With a shock, Tilly realized exactly what she was missing out on. She'd spent so much time in Between worrying about remembering the life she'd had, she'd forgotten about the life she *wouldn't* have. She would never reach the woman's age. She would never marry, never have children, never have a career. She'd never go to another concert, cry on a friend's shoulder, or bring home a puppy from the pound.

She wouldn't live.

The woman settled on a step near Tilly and Luke. She placed her bag beside her, pulled out her phone, and began scrolling through some social media site. She smiled, tapped the phone a few times, smiled wider.

Tilly closed her eyes, wishing the woman would go away. Luke said something to her, but she didn't hear. He was far away. The only thing that was close was the envy. The anger. Eventually, the rage.

Tilly launched herself off the step and marched over to the woman, fists clenched. She wanted to smack her, pummel her even. It wasn't fair. Why should she have to die so young while this woman—this woman who *looked* like her—got to sit here on her lunch break smiling and chatting with friends? Why should this woman get to live out her life, oblivious, for years, possibly decades, while Tilly trudged around in Between, or Hell, for fuck's sake, shuffling souls to and fro, wondering about the life she'd left behind, while slowly going insane from boredom?

It just wasn't fair.

Luke called her and she ignored him. She prepared to bring all her might down on the woman's head, erase that smug, happy look right off her Tilly-like face.

The woman jerked in her seat before Tilly had the chance to bring her raised fist down. The woman's eyebrows met and she squinted straight at Tilly.

Tilly jolted to a stop. A second later, Luke's hand was

wrapped around her wrist. "What in the hell are you doing?" he hissed.

"She sees me," she whispered.

Luke kept hold of her arm as she lowered it. He was glaring at her, the calm and collected look now missing from his face. "She can't see you and you know it."

She did know. She'd been told almost as soon as she floated out of the Pit. Living souls could sense the dead, but they couldn't see them. It was impossible.

But this woman looked like she was looking right at them.

Luke let go of Tilly's arm and waved both hands in front of the woman's face. He hooted at her. He danced from foot to foot. Finally, he turned, bent over, and wiggled his butt inches from her nose.

The woman shuddered a little, then turned back to her phone. That was it.

"See?" Luke said. He was grinning, but that quickly faded when he saw Tilly's face. If she could muster up some tears, she would be bawling. As stupid as it sounded, she'd kind of wanted the woman to see her. She'd gone unnoticed for too long. Her existence seemed useless. She looked at the woman again. Happiness. That's what death was supposed to be about. That's what her dad had told her when her mom had died in the fire: *She's in a better place now, Matilda. She's happy.*

"It's a little tough seeing them, isn't it?" Luke said.

She ignored him again, trying to hold on to the memory. It was slippery. It went in and out of focus until it faded completely. She was left with one burning image in her mind: her dad. Balding, slightly portly. He smiled in her memory, turned, laughed. A woman appeared. *The Bimbo*, Tilly thought with disgust. The woman he found not long after Mom died. He was happy with her. Her mom was happy in Heaven, supposedly.

The only person who wasn't happy was Tilly.

"Will I ever get to go to Heaven?" Tilly blurted. It was a question that had been on her mind since the day she'd arrived. At this point, Heaven was more of a pipe dream, given her failures. But she'd heard souls sometimes got out of Between, and she could still hope. And if her mother was there, maybe she could find her and have someone again.

Luke looked much more comfortable with this line of conversation. He brightened again and launched into a speech like he was giving a museum tour to elementary school children.

"Ah, the big question! No one knows, really. Sometimes it seems the rules around the afterlife change daily. And then there's always the possibility you'll go to Hell instead, but I think you know that already."

She glared. He didn't notice.

"I heard that if you get sent to Heaven," Luke continued, "and you mess up, you can still get sent down." He chuckled at the look of surprise on Tilly's face. "If you remember anything from your Bible, Lucifer used to live in Heaven. No one's ever off the hook."

"That's very comforting." She crossed her arms and kicked at the side of a step. Her hope took a nosedive. Even if she got out of Between, it didn't sound like they'd take to her in Heaven either.

Luke shrugged. "The big man has rules. You break them, you go down. That's just how the system works. No exceptions."

Tilly paced. "What's it like? Heaven, I mean." She didn't look at Luke, wanting the question to seem nonchalant, but on the inside, she was dying for the answer.

"Personally, I think I'd rather be reincarnated." He reclined on the step, a wistful look on his face. "So many women to date."

She hadn't realized reincarnation was an option. Could she manage that? Would she want that? The idea made her nervous. The only thing she knew was this: death, Between, the afterlife. She didn't know what kind of life she'd lived. If she'd been happy. If she'd been loved.

What did it matter now? She was stuck here and she had a job to do. "We'd better go back," she said, trudging down the steps. Able to see or not, she really didn't want to open a portal right next to a living soul. Even if nothing happened, it was weird.

A little girl darted in front of her and she almost collided with her. Both the girl and Tilly stopped. The girl was around ten and wore an overlarge white t-shirt that hung off her body as if she were a skeleton playing dress-up. Her dark hair puffed around her head in a natural halo. She was smiling, revealing one missing front tooth, and looking directly at Tilly.

This time, Tilly didn't panic; she knew the girl couldn't see her. Then the girl slowly cocked her head and winked. Then she ran off, darting in and out of the crowd, eventually running across the street and disappearing into an alley.

The whole incident happened in an instant. So quickly, Tilly couldn't be sure it *had* actually happened. It was possible the little girl was winking at someone else. She looked over her shoulder, but all she saw was Luke using the magic in the pendant to toss rocks at people. When one hit, the person looked around in confusion and Luke chuckled.

"Hey, did you see that?"

"See what?"

"Was there anyone near you a second ago? Maybe a little boy or something? Kids playing?"

"Just me, little lady. Why? You look like you've seen a ghost."

He descended the stairs as Tilly pointed toward the alley the girl had run down.

"Did you see that little girl?"

Luke looked, shook his head.

"She was just here. She winked at me . . ." She couldn't have though. Tilly scolded herself for being stupid. Luke had just proven the living couldn't see them. Luke was looking at her like he thought she was crazy. "Never mind," she said, trying to smile. "Let's just go."

Before Luke had a chance to open a portal, another one opened at Tilly's side. Naveen emerged, jaw and fists clenched. For a second, she could have sworn his normally black eyes glowed with a red tinge. She took a step back, right into Luke, who immediately put his arm out to steady her.

Naveen grimaced. "Getting cozy, are we?"

"Oh, come on, Naveen, I was just showing her around. Like you said."

Naveen closed his eyes and breathed deep. Tilly noticed how much his chest moved up and down when he did so. She thought about her own "breathing," tried to force air into her lungs to make her chest expand that much. It didn't come close. Naveen calmed and his chest slowed, almost as if he really had been taking deep breaths. Tilly thought breathing was just a habit, something a soul lost after a while. Luke's chest barely moved at all.

Without opening his eyes, Naveen opened another port. "We've got a soul to pick up. Go back to your playtime, Luke."

Luke gave Tilly a conspiratorial wink and took his pendant back. "See ya soon, toots." And then he was gone.

Tilly approached the open port at Naveen's feet. "I thought we needed to use the ports in the Escort Dome to get souls."

Naveen looked surprised for a moment, then scowled and looked away. "Just get in."

THEY MATERIALIZED in a rundown urban neighborhood: houses with busted windows, graffiti, trash clogging the gutters. No one was in sight, but the streets had the feel of abrupt abandonment. A wheel on an overturned bike still rotated slowly. The air was thick with tension, as if the entire street was holding its breath, waiting for something to happen. Tilly spun around, looking for life in the neighboring houses. Her eyes landed on the face of a little boy in one of the windows. A second later, a woman snatched him up and yanked the curtain closed.

Naveen popped out of the portal a few seconds behind her. Tilly stepped toward him, needing his confident presence to reassure her she was safe.

Men yelled nearby, followed by the harsh pop of several gunshots. Tilly ducked, holding her arms over her head, terror pumping its way up her throat.

The gunshots stopped, replaced by the squeal of tires. "I'm guessing our dead guy is over there," Naveen said flatly. He looked back at her. She was still ducking. He sighed. "There's no need to duck. No human can harm you."

Tilly lowered her arms and returned his gaze. She hated how he was looking at her: pity, amusement. Maybe a little loathing, or was she imagining that? She stood up, aiming a little loathing back at him. "Being dead takes a little getting used to, I guess," she muttered. But he was no longer looking at her; he had turned back in the direction of the gunshots. The look on his face puzzled Tilly. His eyes were intense, the rest of his features set and hard, like he was ready to attack. Like he was starving and was looking at food for the first time in a long time.

"Are you ready now?" he snapped.

She nodded, but she wasn't. She didn't want to be here. She didn't want to see what lay around the corner.

And she no longer wanted to be next to Naveen and his intensity.

But she followed him anyway as he stalked confidently down the deserted sidewalk and around the corner. She paused before turning the corner and closed her eyes, hoping this was all an elaborate dream and she would wake up, wake up . . .

Wake up!

When she opened her eyes, she was on the same dingy street corner, still listening to the heavy silence of the neighborhood. Now there was an undercurrent of voices muttering. She peeked around the building, fingers digging into the brick, and saw a group of men circled around something on the ground. They were shaking their heads and talking in hushed tones. Naveen was approaching, his stride slowing like an animal stalking prey.

Something whooshed at Tilly's head and her vision was filled with black. She cried out and slammed herself against the building. The black flapped away—becoming just a dark robe, an Acolyte's robe, nothing sinister, nothing evil, she told herself—and revealing a snarling face. The man was pale like Death, but not him, not those deep Death eyes. This man tilted his head side to side, slowly, decreasing the distance between his nose and hers with every tilt. His grin was wide and looked painful. Absurdly, she had an image of his face splitting in half, and still he would tilt his head side to side, his teeth slowly falling to the ground as they dumped from their skull container. She wanted to puke, but what came out of her mouth was a little shriek, a kind of crazed cackle of fear.

"Leave her alone," Naveen said. She'd missed him returning to her side.

The man stopped. His eyes rolled to Naveen, then back to Tilly. His tongue came out, poking between those teeth, reaching, reaching.

He wants to taste me. He's going to eat me.

Tilly had a feeling this was the end, that she'd died before, sure, but there was another end, a more permanent one, and this man was about to send her there. She felt light, like she could float away and watch this scene unfold from above her own body.

"I will *not* repeat myself," Naveen growled.

The tongue wiggled.

Sirens wailed in the distance and the men in the circle scattered. The man in front of Tilly gave one last thrust of his tongue. Then he jerked away and a portal opened almost simultaneously. A moment later, he was gone.

Tilly was shaking. A weight landed on her shoulder and she jerked away. Naveen pulled his hand back quickly, looking like he felt guilty for touching her. "What the hell was that?"

"Acolyte."

"I know that. What the fuck is *wrong* with him?"

Naveen shrugged. "Some people can't handle all the death." He regarded her for a long moment. She struggled to regain her composure. Her fear had turned to anger and she wanted to pummel someone, but the only person here was Naveen, and as weird as he was acting, she didn't think he deserved an attack. She set her jaw and stared back at him. He nodded once, an approval. "I think you'll do all right, though."

He stepped to one side, revealing a man standing over a body. Sweeping a hand out, he said, "After you."

She shook her head. A small frown tugged at Naveen's mouth, but he didn't scold her. "Follow me and pay attention," he said instead.

Tilly rubbed her scar as she followed him. She found her anger dissipating with each step, anxiety creeping into its place. This man was damned. She was approaching someone who was destined for Hell.

Her mother's worried face popped into her mind. *Stay away from that man, Tilly. He's dangerous.*

A memory. A small one, but this was no imagined encounter. Her mother had always told her she had a sixth sense for evil people. Her dad had told her her mom was full of it.

She'd say the same thing now, Tilly knew. *Stay away, Tilly. He's dangerous.*

Would these words of warning apply only for this dead man? Or would her mom have been leery of Naveen as well?

Naveen put his hand on the man's shoulder. "Hector?"

"How do you know his name?" Tilly whispered at his shoulder. He waved her off.

The man looked up at them. "I'm dead, man."

"Yes," Naveen said gently, "you are. We're here to escort you." He was so gentle, Tilly felt guilty for thinking he was dangerous a moment before. He was probably just as uncomfortable with this whole thing as she was. He hadn't looked well when she'd gotten the assignment.

Hector's face contorted in a confused grimace. He shook his head and stared blankly in the direction the other men had run. Tears shone in his hard eyes. "They just left me here. We were friends, man. And they just fucking left me here."

Tilly's eyes lowered to the corpse on the ground beside Hector. It was his exact twin: red bandanna tied around the shaved head; flannel shirt covering a white undershirt; cross tattoo on the neck. Everything was the same. The only difference was a growing bloodstain on the front of the corpse's shirt.

Tilly didn't know what she was expecting, but this wasn't it. She hadn't realized she would have to look at the body—at least not a murdered body. Dead while lying comfortably in a bed, maybe, but not covered in blood.

Even more surprising was the sorrow she felt for Hector. He was damned, and probably for good reason, but as she looked at the anguish in Hector's eyes, he didn't seem evil, or even creepy. He was just a normal guy, upset over the abrupt end to his life. She could empathize with that.

Police cruisers and an ambulance turned the corner down the street and barreled in their direction, sirens blaring. Tilly had to steel herself against her body's reaction to move out of the way. It was an instinct that was hard to overcome, but she managed it. She snuck a glance at Naveen to see if he noticed her little act of bravery, but his eyes were still on Hector's soul.

Hector glanced at the cop cars and shook his head again, more violently this time. "I'm not leaving," he said. "Not until they do something with my body. I want to see my funeral, and my girl one more time, and I want to make sure Mom puts me in the ground next to my brother . . ." He trailed off as he looked at Naveen's face. Somehow, Naveen was conveying a look both harsh and sympathetic.

"You can't stick around for that," Naveen said. That was all. Simple and matter-of-fact and no room for argument.

Tilly thought she would've argued if she were Hector. It was Hector's death, after all. Didn't he have the right to see it through if he wanted?

Naveen put his hand under Hector's arm and gently tugged upwards. Hector stood, his eyes never leaving the still-open eyes of his corpse doppelgänger. He was a rag doll, the shock of the events clearly written on his face. He muttered something about wanting to stay, but gave no physical protest.

Two EMTs hopped out of the ambulance and dragged a gurney over to Hector's body. They checked his pulse and closed his eyes. Hector's spirit body slumped and he began to moan, a sound that escalated into a tormented wail. Tilly shuffled from one foot to the other, unnerved at the sight of the tough-looking man crumbling beside her. She wanted to comfort him, maybe give him a hug or something, but Naveen, as if he knew exactly what she was thinking, shot her a hard look of warning.

She scowled back at him. This man was in pain. It wasn't right that they'd just shuffle him off with no compassion at all.

"I'm Tilly," she said, forcing a smile and holding her hand out to Hector. He sniffed and stared. Naveen's eyes widened. Tilly's smile faded and she slowly dropped her arm. She cleared her throat and tried to think of something comforting to say instead. "At least it was quick," she blurted, then winced. It had sounded more comforting in her head.

Hector did seem a bit cheered by the sentiment though. He gave her a weak smile, which she hesitatingly returned.

Naveen pulled the pendant from under his shirt with one hand. The other was still clamped around Hector's bicep.

Naveen sighed and looked up at the sky, as if he were pleading with an invisible force, then pressed his thumb to the bead. The portal opened and he nodded to it. "After you," he said to Hector. "Make sure the souls always go through first," he added in a low voice to Tilly. "You don't want one getting away from you."

Hector crossed himself while looking at the heavens and muttering one last prayer—an eerie mimicry of Naveen— then stepped into the whirling portal. His faith amazed Tilly. How could he still believe at a moment like this? Although, given the circumstances, it couldn't hurt. She thought about praying as well, but she wasn't exactly sure how, so she decided against it. She didn't even know if God would listen to someone like her, someone who escorted souls to Hell for a living. Or even someone who resided in Between, for that matter.

Did God hear the prayers of the dead as well as the living?

She stared at the port for a few seconds after Naveen passed through. The EMTs were all packed up. No more sirens. No more lights. No more body.

There was nothing on this side of the portal for Tilly.

But Hell was on the other side.

Maybe it wouldn't be as bad as the rumors. Maybe it would just be hot and not full of souls screaming as demons ripped them to shreds. She dug at her scar to calm herself, remembering what Naveen had told her the night before.

She didn't have to go in. Only to the gates. No need for the innocent to enter such a place.

Tilly was slightly comforted by the thought, but as she jumped through, the words *abandon all hope, ye who enter here* ran through her mind.

V.

Tilly felt the heat before she even finished porting. She felt *everything*, and it was torture.

When she emerged on the platform, she couldn't move for several seconds. The heat was intense and consuming. It penetrated her head, her lungs, her bowels, areas of her body she hadn't been aware of in all her time in Between. Her eyes felt like they were shriveling in their sockets, drying out like raisins.

Water ran nearby—a steady whoosh providing the bass line to the cacophonous screaming all around her, so loud—and she wished she could see the source through the dark haze. She wanted to run to the water, dive in, quench this fire burning in her depths.

All around, ports popped like firecrackers, each dropping off the next unlucky soul to join the queue. People pushed and shoved, jostled for space. There was little room for movement, adding to a general feeling of suffocation. A strange smell filled her nostrils: a nauseating combination of sulfur and decay. On her wrist, her burn scar hurt badly enough to be fresh. She glanced down to see if it was seeping. It wasn't, but there was an odd pulling sensation in her arm, like a puppeteer was yanking her strings. Her body wanted to move forward, toward the screams, toward the heat.

Her mind reeled at the idea of so much physical sensation as she silently cursed Naveen. He hadn't told her it would be like roasting from the inside out, like the growing spark before spontaneous combustion. But he had told her she wouldn't be in the fire, and that was true. She wasn't standing in flames; she couldn't even see any in the vicinity.

Naveen's jaw was set and he stared at the giant gates in front of them. The heat didn't seem to be affecting him. He had a firm grip on Hector's upper arm. Hector was sobbing, barely able to stand as Naveen patiently pulled him forward, one trudging step at a time.

A surge of panic crawled up Tilly's spine. Where was he going? They had brought Hector. Couldn't they just leave now? Her wide eyes looked toward the gates, horrified. The rolling cacophony came in screeching waves of horror. She stared at the looming gates, hypnotized by the noise, the heat, and her own shock.

Suddenly a hand grabbed her own and tugged gently. It was Naveen, giving her a small, pained smile. His hand was cool, she realized, and relished in her ability to feel the sensation and the relief it provided from the heat, however miniscule. She wanted to pull him back, crawl on him, cover her overheated body with his and let his coolness seep into her. But he kept moving forward, and she had no choice but to grip his hand and follow for fear of being abandoned outside the entrance to Hell for eternity.

Dark brown goo covered the platform. It stuck to the bottoms of her shoes like chewed bubblegum as they moved slowly, painstakingly forward. She was thankful she'd died in tennis shoes—anything open-toed here would have been awful. Every few steps, there was a crunching noise under her feet, like small bones cracking. She shuddered, imagining tramping over the skeletons of small animals or babies.

The gates of Hell loomed impossibly tall. A massive wall flanked either side, stretching off into the distance to disappear into the thick, watery-blood-colored fog. On top of the wall, thin, sharp spires stabbed toward the gloomy sky every twenty feet. Some of them were topped, shish kebab-style, with what looked to be heads—some skeletonized, some with carrion birds picking at leftover flesh, all screaming in agony. Alive. They were alive. Tilly's stomach roiled.

The gate itself was made of massive, dinosaur-sized bones, and was open wide with a steady stream of people flowing inwards. Sick curiosity overcame revulsion and Tilly glanced inside. She couldn't see much past the enormous three-headed dog standing just inside the gate. If the dog shifted, she caught a glimpse of the throngs of people and mountains burping fire every few seconds. The pulling sensation in her arm intensified. The more she looked at the fire inside, the more the feeling increased. Quickly, she dropped her eyes. If she concentrated on what was on this side of the gate, the fear seizing her wasn't as bad, even if the heat was.

Two booths, elevated atop a pile of rocks and some sort of goo Tilly didn't want to think about, flanked the gate. Inside one was a haggard man dressed in tattered clothing with a long, scraggly beard and sunken cheeks. A woman sat inside the opposite booth. Both surveyed the crowd from their perches like kings watching gladiators in the Colosseum, barking instructions to the newly arrived damned.

Tilly thought the woman looked in better shape than

the man, and was glad when Naveen adjusted his course to head in her direction. Then the woman turned her head and Tilly saw her full on. Half her face seemed to be slowly sliding off her skull like a melting candle. There was no eye or eye socket, just charred flesh. Her lips on that side were nonexistent, exposing her broken and rotting teeth. Every few seconds she inhaled sharply through her teeth, trying to suck the drool back into her mouth. Tilly held back a gag and stopped short. Naveen tugged her toward the woman, but she pulled back. "I'd rather go to the man," she said. She had to lean in close so he could hear her over the screaming souls.

Naveen shook his head. "No. That's Charon. He's a little cracked in the head after eons of being down here. Dealing with Martha is much easier, trust me."

As if sensing they were talking about him, Charon shot a snaggletooth grin in their direction. Naveen ignored him and towed Tilly and Hector up to Martha.

"Why does she look like that?" Tilly asked as they approached. "No one in Between looks like that."

"This is Hell, Tilly." His voice was hard and his gaze stuck on Martha. Was it her imagination, or was Naveen avoiding looking through the gates as well? "It's a little different from Between, if you hadn't already noticed."

"That's the understatement of the year," she mumbled.

Martha held a clipboard with a huge stack of papers and a pen made from what looked to be bone. There was still blood and a chunk of some sort of viscera on the top of the pen. Tilly didn't want to know what species the bone came from.

"Next," she crowed from her perch. She looked down at Tilly with her one good eye and gave a sickly, yellow-toothed smile. "A young girl! They'll have fun with you in there, missy!" She laughed until she went into a coughing fit, which ultimately ended in a golf ball-sized chunk of phlegm shooting out of her mouth and landing on Tilly's shoes. Tilly shook her foot in disgust, but the mess stuck.

"This is Tilly," Naveen said. "She's a new Escort. I'll be with her until she gets the hang of it."

"Ah, Naveen," Martha said. "Haven't seen you for a while. I've missed you." She attempted to make a kissy face at him, but it ended up looking more like she was trying to chew her own lips off.

Naveen yanked Hector forward, presenting him like a prize pig. "This here is Hector Hernandez. He's the one on your list."

Martha had been looking Tilly up and down, smacking the lips on the good side of her face as if she wanted to eat her. At Naveen's pronouncement, she gave a little huff of disappointment, then said, "Hmm. All right," as she looked down at her clipboard. "Hector Hernandez, Hernandez . . ." She drew the bone pen down the page. "Ah! Got him right here. Blasphemy, adultery, fornication, murder. All the big ones."

Tilly didn't see how blasphemy was a "big one," but she didn't think it was her place to argue. Murder was probably what got him here in the end, anyway, and there was really no arguing with that one.

Martha checked his name off and pointed to the gate with her pen. "Go on in, Hector. Don't be shy." She grinned like a jack-o'-lantern.

Hector had stopped sobbing and now wore a glazed look as he stared through the gates at what awaited him. He joined the line of damned souls without a backward glance. Tilly watched him walk, his back curled over and his head tucked. A squealing wail of pain floated through the air from somewhere inside the gates. Tilly thought of nails being yanked from fingers, of hot pokers going through eyeballs, of weeks of waterboarding. What would happen to Hector in there, Hector who only wanted to see his mother and girlfriend one more time? Hector who wanted to be buried beside his brother? Hector, the man who sobbed over his own dead body?

Martha's words came back to her: *blasphemy, adultery, fornication, murder.*

Murder.

Hector was a murderer. *Don't forget that.*

"We're getting a little overcrowded in here," Martha said to Naveen in a stage whisper that carried across the platform. She'd leaned over the booth, her massive bosom swaying over the side. Tilly got the impression the woman was deliberately showing Naveen her cleavage.

"Lots of escapees lately," Martha added, nodding seriously. "It's all gotten to be a little much for old Cerberus, here." As if in response, Cerberus whipped his snake-like tail around and smacked it into a group of newly damned souls, sending them flying every which way. His three heads grinned at Naveen and Tilly in a sloppy, slobbery way and he whimpered. Tilly cringed and hoped she never had to come closer to the dog than she was at that moment.

Naveen pursed his lips at Cerberus, who jerked toward them and bowed as if he wanted to play. A chain at his ankle kept him from poking more than his heads out onto the platform.

"Let's go," Naveen said, and pushed his way back through the crowd. Cerberus whined pitifully as they walked away.

The tugging sensation in Tilly's arm lessened once her

back was to the gate. The heat did not. She walked quickly, mumbling, "Almost done," as she hurried.

They were out of the worst of the crowd when a loud explosion rumbled through the air. Tilly's arms shot out for balance and she looked wildly around for the source. Everyone around her did the same, craning their necks to see inside the gate.

Once the ground stopped trembling, the cheers of a billion damned souls went up. The sound was deafening and Cerberus answered with three equally deafening simultaneous howls. Naveen quickly opened a port and they were back in the Escort Dome a second later.

Tilly collapsed to the floor. The heat had subsided as soon as she reentered Between, and she reveled in the relief. She glanced at her shoes; the mess was gone, evaporated with the heat.

"Unfortunately, you'll get used to what you saw today," Naveen said. His voice was oddly hollow. "You'll be doing more runs than you can count. It'll be like an assembly line." His eyes were fixed on the wall of open ports, a longing written in his gaze that Tilly couldn't understand. Abruptly, he turned and walked toward a port opposite the pendant kiosk. Tilly quickly stood and hurried to catch up. She had a million questions for him, but mainly she wanted to hold his hand again, to see if she could still feel his cool skin. She knew it wouldn't be the same here, but still wanted to try.

He spoke before she could do anything. "I think that's all for today. We both need rest."

The idea of going back to her room and pretending everything was normal seemed ludicrous. "I don't think I'll ever rest again." Naveen answered her sentiment with a wan smile.

The scrolling sign above the port read EXIT and Tilly had a fleeting hope it would be the exit from this world, not just the Escort Dome. Once again, she wondered if this was all a dream and she'd soon wake up, safe in her bed, the memories of her time here fading faster than she could remember them.

NAVEEN COLLAPSED ON HIS FUTON, cradling his head in his hands. Shudders cascaded through his body as flashes of Hell ran on a loop in his mind. He was tired. He was on edge. Mostly he was pissed.

He hadn't seen Hell in a long time. Even the name *Hell* set his teeth on edge. It was a ridiculous name Lucifer had invented, along with the system of punishments and a rather dramatic redecorating. All of it an attention ploy, a final fuck you to old Dad.

Lucifer had ruined the underworld.

At least Cerberus was still there, though he wasn't fond of the chain. He'd always been a good dog. There was no need to keep him tied like that.

Naveen took a deep breath. Damn Eris for sending him down there. He had no doubt it was *him* she'd sent. Not Tilly. She gave no shits about Tilly, not really. If she thought his relationship with Tilly went further than mentor/mentee, she was mistaken. Naveen had never crossed that line.

And even if she wasn't mistaken, so what? They'd both had their dalliances over the years. That was the deal. Getting married to a living human was one thing, but when you considered a lifetime stretching for millennia, things got a little looser in the adultery department.

Maybe he would take Tilly as a lover, just to piss Eris off. It would serve her right for invading his privacy after all these years apart. Maybe he would just do that. He stood up, ready to go to Tilly's door, but sat right back down.

He couldn't do that to Tilly.

He's seen the way she looked at him. He really wished she wouldn't. If she knew who he was, what he'd done . . .

He could tell her. That would take the sparkle out of her eyes when she looked in his direction.

He groaned. The thing was, he didn't *want* to see the sparkle go from her eyes. He liked it when she looked at him like that. Once people found out, they never looked at him the same, no matter how much they claimed to be okay with his past. Except Luke. But Luke had his own demons to wrestle.

Two weeks. That was all he had to train her. He could handle two weeks. There was no need to tell her, no need to get attached. He would get her assimilated and then move on to the next soul plucked out of the Pit. He would be done with her.

And he would be done with Hell.

Just two weeks.

IMAGES OF LICKING flames sputtering from Hell's mountaintops haunted Tilly as she shut the door to her assigned apartment behind her. The dim light of Between peeked into the lone window, barely illuminating the few pieces of furniture stuffed into the small room. The sparse furnishings in her room were the only things Tilly could call hers. And she supposed those weren't technically hers; she doubted the worn pieces would follow her to Hell if that was where she ended up. She doubted there were apartments in Hell anyway. No creature comforts for the damned.

"I guess this room is one thing Between has going for it," she muttered, trying to see the space with a new appreciation. She cocked her head to the side; something sat on her desk.

It turned out to be a wooden box, deep brown with carvings on the top. It was about two feet wide and a foot deep, with a hinged lid. It looked like a large, ornate humidor. She sat at her desk and ran her fingers over the carvings. She recognized a few of the symbols: an ankh, a cross, a few others. She noticed a swastika-like symbol with dots in all four corners, as well as an elaborate eye, and one that looked like a ship's wheel. A symbol in the center, much larger than the rest, and deeply etched into the wood, looked like three interconnecting oblong ovals.

The hinges squealed as she lifted the lid. Red velvet lined the inside, faded in spots to a pinkish color. A book— leather-bound and covered edge-to-edge with the same symbols as the box—was nestled in the center. The book's pages were trimmed in gold. The book itself was about five inches thick.

Expecting more instructions for escorting or some new Between rulebook, she flipped through nonchalantly. Her fingers slowed as she realized the words on the pages had nothing to do with Between at all. Instead, she skimmed sections devoted to the World's mythology. The Bible, the Quran, Celtic stories, ancient Greek and Egyptian myths, pictures of many-armed Hindu gods, others she didn't recognize. She grinned. *Reading material.*

She hefted the tome from the box, crossed the few steps to her futon, and began to read.

"In the beginning, when the World was empty, the sun and the moon fell in love . . ."

THE GOD of Death ruled the underworld with an iron fist. His queen sat beside him, their thrones a smooth silver, as they imprisoned the souls under their rule. There was no escape for these souls. The gates to the underworld were high, patrolled by a legion of lesser gods and a giant, three-headed dog named Cerberus.

The God of Death was fond of visiting the World of the Living as often as possible. Though he had long ago made a minion to help him with his work, he preferred to perform the deed himself. There was a pleasure in it for him, one that could not be matched by any amount of ambrosia.

Bringing death to the living was his duty and his passion.

When the mother moon brought the gods to the sacred tree to receive their magic, she did so with the hope that those seven children could bring peace to the world. Instead, they sowed chaos, and none of them so much as the God of Death.

He was an angry god, prone to fits of rage. If his queen angered him, he would take to the World of the Living, rampaging through the small towns and villages, bringing death without purpose. His helper would often accompany him, and between the two of them, they could demolish a dozen cities in a single evening if they so chose.

The God of Death would eventually retire to his place in the underworld, satiated and spent, and the World of the Living would be safe from his rampages for a time. But not from the fury of his helper, who was always on duty. Often the helper would go on rampages of his own, leaving a wake in his path. This amused the God of Death and his queen.

The people of the World began to sacrifice their own in order to appease the gods. More sacrifices were made to the God of Death than any other god. But he did not accept these sacrifices as intended. Instead, he demanded more, bloodier. Pain was the way to appease him, he told them. The sacrificial lamb must suffer for me to know you worship me properly!

The living began castrating, ripping beating hearts from babes' breasts, slowly removing limbs, keeping the body alive as long as possible. They ate their sacrifices. They bathed them in their own blood and chanted their pleas for the God of Death to keep away from their door.

And he was fascinated with their creativity. He watched them from afar, marveling at the myriad ways the human body could be killed . . .

Tilly heard footsteps in the hall of her building. She paused in her reading and listened carefully. The footsteps stopped outside her door. For a moment, she had the notion it was the God of Death, there to torture her, rape her, carry her off like he had Persephone in the Greek myths—she'd skipped that part in the book, mainly interested in those myths that hadn't stuck in her mind after her death. She clutched the book with white-knuckled fingers and didn't move.

When the inevitable knock finally came, she jumped like a shot had gone through her. She waited, hoping whoever it was would simply go away. An image of a vacuum salesman came to mind. *Hello there, young lady, is dust ruining your afterlife?* The thought made her relax a little and she almost giggled. Then another knock boomed against her door, louder, more insistent. She gripped the book tighter, steeled herself, and decided she had to see who was there. The knocking might wake her neighbors. From what? And what neighbors, for that matter? She hadn't seen anyone actually living in this building since she'd arrived. She'd barely seen anyone at all, save for Naveen and the people in the Escort Dome.

"I'm an escort to Hell!" she called. She'd risen with the book still in her hands—it was really the only heavy thing in the room—and approached the door. "You don't want to mess with me. I'll take your ass straight down." She swung the door open with one hand while brandishing the book like a weapon in the other.

Luke was leaning against the frame, arms crossed and grinning. "Well, you've sure gained some confidence in the past few hours."

Her arm fell quickly to her side, carried by the force of the book. "What are you doing here?"

He stuck his bottom lip out in an adorably cute and aggravatingly immature pout. "If you don't want me, I'll go." He slouched and turned like a scolded puppy.

"It's not that I don't want you," Tilly said. "I mean, not *want* you, want you, but . . . ugh, you know what I mean."

Luke stood straight again and puffed out his chest. Tilly braced herself for more flirtatious teasing, but he let it go. "I just wanted to see how your first trip to Hell went."

Tilly grimaced.

"That bad, huh?"

"You have no idea." She gestured for him to come in and placed the book back on her desk.

"I can imagine." He sat down and crossed one leg over the other, propped an elbow on his knee and his chin in his palm. "And how does that make you feel?"

She shot him a glare.

"Sorry. I know it can be hard. I had a rough time of it the first couple of days."

Her eyes narrowed further. He escorted to Heaven; there

was no way he could understand what she'd been through today. She didn't even quite understand it. When she tried to remember events in the order they happened, all she saw was fire and three giant dogs' heads. The rest was a blur of fear and disgust.

He cleared his throat and changed the subject. "What do you have there?" A nod toward the desk.

"Oh. Just a book."

He cocked an eyebrow. "Where did you get a book?"

"Just showed up," she said with a shrug. Looking down at the cover, she thought of the story she'd been reading about the God of Death and gave a little shudder. "It's got some pretty gruesome descriptions in there." Luke had made his way to the desk and was staring down at the book's cover, his fingers lightly trailing the symbols.

"Like this God of Death guy, have you heard of him?" Tilly continued. "The stuff he was doing was royally fu—" She stopped. "Something wrong?"

Luke's stare had turned into a deep frown and his jaw muscles were clenching.

He turned to her, and with visible effort, rearranged his face into his normal wry grin. "Nothing at all, darlin'. Just wondering who would've given this to you."

The idea of entertainment in this gray-washed place had filled her with such relief that she hadn't considered who might have gifted her such a thing.

"Tell ya what," he said. "I'll ask around for you, see if I can find out."

She nodded, but couldn't fathom why it was so important to him. It was just a book, after all. A bunch of bedtime stories filled with magic moons and wrathful gods.

Luke gave one more wary glance at the book and then

bounced on his toes. "I can't be trapped in this room anymore. Let's go do something."

She gestured toward the window: at the gray light and the confusing streets lined with never-ending skyscrapers that should house millions of souls but were always vacant.

"What's there to do?"

"There's always something to do when you're with me," he said, slinging his arm around her shoulders.

VI.

Tilly and Luke wound through the empty streets of Between. Tilly brought up the God of Death again, but Luke simply told her she shouldn't believe everything she read and she decided to drop the topic of the book entirely. She was beginning to wonder if Luke had some sort of issue with women reading or something. He did come from a different time, after all. It was possible he was a sexist pig. It really wouldn't surprise her, given his obsession with and inappropriate comments about women. She'd known him for less than a day and he'd already managed to at least minorly offend her no fewer than half a dozen times.

So why are you out with this guy, then? she asked herself. *Simple answer? There's nothing else to do.*

But that wasn't exactly true. She had reading material now, didn't she? But did she really want to stay home with a book when a guy had asked her out? *Had* she been the type of person to do that? *You don't have to go out with everyone who asks,* she heard her mother say. That was after she'd gotten her first kiss on the bus. Some guy named Cory. Or was it Cody? She couldn't remember, but she did remember her mother making a face when she told her she'd only done it because he'd asked.

"Hey, are you in there?" Luke's voice chased the memory away. She realized they had stopped walking and he was smiling at her, his head half-cocked. "What are you smiling about?"

She hadn't realized she'd been smiling, but now she felt the small curve of her lips grow. "I was remembering my first kiss," she said.

Luke nodded in appreciation as he rapped an intricate knock on the metal door of yet another drab building. "Maybe later I can see if I can make you forget all about that guy." At her scowl, he added, "I'm just poking fun," but she doubted that was the truth.

The knock was answered in kind and the door swung open. A young girl sat inside the door. She lifted her chin at them and Luke started down a short staircase. Tilly said hello to the girl, but only got a dead-eyed stare in response. She followed Luke down the few stairs to a dimly lit hallway. Tilly instinctively grabbed Luke's starchy white dress shirt as he led the way.

"Easy, honey, there'll be time enough for that later," Luke said.

"You really need to stop that shit," Tilly snapped, "or I'm out of here."

Luke's hands went up in surrender. "I'm sorry to have offended the lady."

Sarcastic, but she'd take it for now. She promised herself if he said one more smartass remark about getting it on with her, she'd deck him.

The hall dead-ended at another door. Luke cleared his throat and bellowed, "*Patefacio*." The door instantly dissolved into a portal. "Shall we?" he asked, giving her a deep bow.

"What the—? How did you do that?"

He winked in answer and swept his arm toward the portal.

"No way," Tilly said. She crossed her arms over her chest. "Naveen was pissed enough about our little jaunt earlier. No way am I going back to the World."

Luke's smile wavered. "We're just going to a party."

"We can't. I'll go to Hell."

"Who said the party's not in Hell?" he said with a wiggle of his eyebrows.

She took a step back from the portal so quickly she almost stumbled. Luke laughed, but it was uncertain. "I'm sorry. It was a joke. A joke! We're not even leaving Between."

Tilly turned to go. "I've had about enough excitement for one day, I think."

He jogged a few steps to catch up to her. "I *am* sorry, you know. Sometimes I just . . . I don't know." Tilly kept walking. To his credit, Luke didn't grab her arm or try to block her path. He simply walked beside her.

"I really wasn't all that popular with the girls when I was alive," he mumbled. "I'm not very good at this."

She hesitated. Dammit. Now he was going to go all human on her? She stopped to look at him. "Another joke?"

He hung his head. Shook it once. "I just thought you'd like to go to this party to take your mind off today, you know." He met her eyes with a half-grin and a one-shoulder shrug. "I suppose I should have asked you out properly instead."

Tilly rolled her eyes in the dark and groaned. "Okay, let's start again." She stuck out her hand. "I'm Tilly."

He looked at her, a bit bewildered, then finally shook

her hand. "Luke Hastings," he said. His old self was coming back, she could tell. The confidence in this man basically oozed out of him.

"Well, let's see about this party, Luke Hastings."

THE ROOM TILLY and Luke materialized in was the size of a football field with a red velvet carpet slicing through the center. Stanchions laced with burgundy rope cordoned off the carpet. A long line of bored-looking people waited to be let in by a large man holding a clipboard. The man's face looked like he had been disappointed too many times in his life, turning his expression into a permanent scowl. He blocked yet another door that was painted deep red and had a symbol that looked like three interlocking ovals—the same as on the book sitting on her desk—etched into the paint. The room held the silent air of a wake.

"Are we on the list?" Tilly asked, eyeing the long line.

"Honey, I'm always on the list." Luke slung his arm around her shoulders and guided her toward the bouncer. Tilly flashed apologetic smiles as they brushed by the people in line, which were returned with indifferent stares.

"Hey there, big fella," Luke said to the bouncer. "I'm Luke Hastings. I think you'll find me on your little list." He winked at the man, who grunted and scanned his clipboard.

"Sorry, no Luke Hastings."

Luke blinked. "There must be some mistake. Check again. Where's Tony, by the way? I've never seen you before."

"Tony's gone. He hasn't worked here in years."

"Well, what is your name, good sir?"

"Carl," the man said. "You'll have to leave if you're not on the list."

Luke flashed Tilly a tight smile. "I'm a friend of Vernon's," he told the man, his voice lowered to an almost-whisper. "Just give me the riddle, and you'll see I'm allowed in."

Carl grunted. "If you're a friend of Vernon's, then you know your name has to be on the list. Then you get the riddle. No name, no riddle."

Luke continued to argue with Carl and Tilly tuned them out. She looked around the room, noticing other symbols carved into the stone walls. Some she recognized, some she didn't. There was an ankh, a cross, a Star of David, a clover-leaf, a scythe. There were also weird symbols she assumed were runes, but couldn't be sure. She noticed a staff with wings and snakes, and knew it was a medical symbol, but couldn't remember the name. She'd seen them all squeezed into every available square inch of the book sitting on her desk.

Luke's voice had grown loud enough to attract attention from the people in line. Everyone was staring and whispering. Tilly gently laid her hand on Luke's arm and was about to say, "Let's just go," when the red door flew open and a short, bald man stormed through, accompanied by a quick burst of music and laughter. "What the hell is going on out here?" he bellowed. A hush fell over the room.

Carl was the first to speak. "Vernon, this guy claims to be a friend of yours, but he's not on the list."

Vernon squinted at Luke. Luke gave a shy wave. "Didn't I ban you?" Vernon asked.

"Yeah you did," Luke said, throwing a sheepish grin at Tilly before turning his attention back to Vernon. He lowered his voice once again. "It was a fifty-year ban. And it was up yesterday."

Vernon scowled. "I'll check my records, but for now, go ahead and give him the riddle, Carl." Vernon disappeared back through the door.

Carl sneered at Luke. "Well, here it is, smartass. How does the blackbird fly?"

Luke laughed. "You're not serious?"

"As a heart attack," Carl said, his sneer growing, "which, coincidentally, is what took me out."

Tilly's brain was working overtime, trying to solve the riddle. Wings? Feathers? Aerodynamics?

"They don't until someone lets them out of the pie," Luke answered.

Tilly coughed a laugh. It was the most ridiculous answer she'd ever heard. She expected to see a grin on Luke's face, but he was serious.

Carl's face fell. He cleared his throat as he stepped aside and jerked his head to the side, indicating they could go in.

Luke gave him a pat on the shoulder as they passed. "Thanks, Carl. I'll be seeing you again." He slipped something small and red into Carl's hand. Carl nodded, a surprised look on his face, and resumed his post.

A bewildered Tilly followed Luke through the red door.

The months of quiet living in Between hadn't prepared Tilly for raucous noise inside the club. It reminded her of Hell and Cerberus howling at the screaming masses. She ducked her head and rubbed the scar on her wrist, wanting to escape.

Luke, on the other hand, was in his element. He laughed and greeted most everyone with a slap on the back and a "How have you been? It's been ages!" People flocked to him; he was obviously the star of the show. Tilly found herself

79

sinking back a couple steps, hiding behind Luke as she followed him through the crowd. No one seemed to notice her, and she was trying to decide whether she was offended or preferred it that way. Had she been this shy in life? Had she ever been to a party like this? Maybe she was the sort of person who wasn't invited to parties at all.

Luke paused to talk loudly with a group of people sitting at a table and Tilly took the time to take in her surroundings. The club looked like a former cathedral or meeting place for a secret society. Large stone pillars spaced fifty feet apart held up the vaulted ceilings. Curved stone beams ran from pillar to pillar. Faded murals covered the ceiling and large, two-tiered wrought iron chandeliers hung around the room, each one covered in low-burning candles, giving the room an eerie low glow.

A dance floor was in the center of the room, full of people grinding and swaying. Most of them looked half out of their minds—giddy and exhausted. They looked like they'd been there for weeks.

In the open aisles running alongside the main room, intimate seating lined the walls, each table donned with a single candle centered on a short white tablecloth and flanked by leather club chairs. Large bookshelves covered the entirety of the sidewalls. The image of the bookshelves among the swarms of clubbers made Tilly think of a library taken over by hordes of teenagers. The thought of teenagers made flames and screams leap into her mind and she winced.

Just when she thought Luke had completely forgotten she was there, he turned to her with a mile-wide grin on his face. He leaned in, having to yell over the noise. "We're heading over there." He pointed to an empty table behind the nearest arch, then shook hands with a man in a tuxedo.

Tilly followed him over and sat down. She was on the edge of her seat, fidgety, wondering if she would be required to dance. She didn't remember if she knew how to dance and talking in the loud room would be near impossible. She found herself wishing for Naveen, for his cool skin and calm manner.

Instead of sitting, Luke walked to one of the bookcases and leaned in closely, skimming his index finger along the large leather tomes and frowning in concentration. With an abrupt grin, he tipped a book forward. The bookshelf groaned and slid open, revealing a secret room. Luke swept his hand out and said, "After you." Tilly hesitated, but obliged. Anything would be better than sitting in this noise.

The bookshelf door shut behind them, letting out a sucking noise and a small cloud of dust as it did so. It blocked out all outside noise. Tilly exhaled a grateful sigh. This room was more to her liking, even if it was on the small side and smelled dusty and unused. Sheer white curtains were draped over gray stone walls, the decoration livening the sparse room, but not much. The only furnishings were a table and chairs identical to the ones outside and two red chaise lounges. Luke reclined on one and nodded toward the other. Tilly sat but didn't recline. Nerves coursed through her. A moment ago, she wished to be alone, and now she wished to be back in the throes of people.

She looked at Luke, whose eyes were closed, and cleared her throat. Luke opened his eyes and looked at her expectantly. Her mind swirled as she tried to think of something to say.

Luckily, she didn't have to think long. A knock sounded on the back wall, followed by a man entering through a door hidden behind a curtain. It was the tuxedoed man from earlier. He had a white towel draped over one arm and held a bottle of champagne with his other hand. A small woman followed him in with drinkware and an ice bucket. She was in and out in such a flash, Tilly barely had time to register her presence.

"Shall I pour, sir?" the waiter asked, his voice deep and soothing with a tinge of a French accent.

Luke nodded and stretched on the chaise, looking like a little boy waking from a nap. The waiter poured the champagne, gave a little bow, and left the way he had come.

Luke stood and grabbed the champagne flutes off the table, handing one to Tilly. She took a sip. And then another.

"Take it easy," Luke said. "I wouldn't want you to claim I got you drunk and took advantage of you." He winked.

Tilly sat her glass down immediately.

Luke laughed. "Don't worry, I was only joking. You can't get drunk. Not on this stuff, anyway. This is purely for nostalgic reasons."

Another silence fell. Tilly squirmed in her seat. Luke refilled his glass. "What do you think of the club?"

"It's very, um . . ." She hesitated, trying to come up with the right word, one that wouldn't offend him but would also make it clear she wouldn't want to come back.

Luke came to her rescue. "Not your thing, is it?" he said softly as he sat back down.

"Not exactly."

"I didn't think so. This is my favorite club, but I could see as soon as we walked through the door that you didn't like it. That's why we're back here, in this rather claustrophobic room."

Tilly smiled at him. "I didn't realize you were being so attentive."

Luke didn't return the smile. He met her eyes. "Of course I am."

He continued to hold her gaze as Tilly reached for her wrist. She dropped her eyes and mumbled something noncommittal, then grabbed her drink and took a gulp, all while trying to avoid Luke's piercing stare. Her mind flew, trying to come up with something to change the subject.

"What were all those symbols on the walls out there?" she blurted. "I knew some of them. Like the Christian cross and a few others."

He shrugged. "They're just symbols from the various cultures of the world. You'll find them on most things having to do with the afterlife."

Tilly thought of the book. "There was one symbol I was particularly interested in. It's on the door here. Do you know what it is?"

His brows met.

"It was like three ovals interlacing?" She tried to make the symbol with her fingers.

"Oh, you mean the triquetra," Luke said, laughing. "The trinity knot. It's found all over in pretty much every religion. Christians, witches, everyone from the beginning of time."

"But what's it mean? It was on that book too, right in the center."

At the mention of the book, Luke looked away from her. "Oh, lots of different things. But to us, it represents the four realms."

Tilly knew the four realms from the informational packets she got at the start of every job. The World, Hell, Heaven, with Between intersecting all of them.

"We use it to communicate with each other when we're in the World," Luke went on. "When it's on a door, it means that place is kind of like a safe house."

She clutched her glass, fear shooting through her. "Wait. We're not in Between?"

Luke cleared his throat. "Well . . . yes and no. This is a club linked to the Black Market, so there's some complicated magic going on to keep this place connected to Between but with access in the World as well."

"Are we in the World or not?" The fear hardened in her stomach, quickly moving toward anger.

He cringed. "Yes, technically."

She leaped up, her glass shattering in her grip. Instinctively, she spared a glance at her hand. No blood. No pain. *Of course. Why would there be? You're dead, Tilly.* She never wanted the release of tears as much as she wanted in that moment.

Luke held up his hands. "Wait, let me explain."

"You lied and I'm skating on thin ice around here as it is." She pushed her way out of the small room and back into the cacophony of the main area. Luke was right on her heels.

"You can't be monitored here," he insisted. "Tilly, listen to me for a sec."

He grabbed at her arm, but she pulled away and pushed through the crowd, frantically looking for the exit. People jostled her as they swayed in a manic trance. She no longer saw Luke behind her.

She needed to get back to Between before anyone noticed she was gone. If they hadn't already noticed. *They're going to send me to Hell.* Suddenly, she could feel the heat on the platform again, see the flames past the freakish three-headed dog. And that was just the entrance. Her scar was on fire, the invisible string tugging again.

A girl whipped her head around as Tilly bumped into her. Tilly mumbled an apology, but the girl smiled. She was about Tilly's age, but shorter and with spiky purple hair. She wore all black with heavy dark eyeliner. She reached out and stroked Tilly's cheek with an awe incomprehensible to Tilly. "You look like you need a drink," she said, and soon produced one as if by magic.

Tilly tried to wave her away, but she shoved the drink into Tilly's hand, her own elfish hands wrapping around Tilly's and bringing the glass up to Tilly's face. This wasn't the champagne she'd had with Luke; this was a tall glass, and the drink inside was a swirling tornado of reds. She could smell the liquid inside, a heady, redolent smell that reminded her of good times and Christmas and first kisses. It was mesmerizing somehow, pulling her in. Everything good was inside this glass. The liquid swirled and she could almost hear a whisper, as if it were speaking to her, assuring her one sip, just one, would make all her problems disappear. She knew she needed to find the exit, but could no longer remember what the urgency was. *Just one sip.* Before she knew what she was doing, she lifted her hand and gulped down the drink.

From somewhere behind her Luke yelled, "Tilly, no!"

VII.

Tilly wasn't worried about a thing. The drink had warmed her, starting from her stomach and radiating out in a blanket of peace and calm, followed closely by a floating euphoria. She'd forgotten all about Luke, all about his deception and the possibility of Hell. The only urgency she felt was that of dancing.

She'd begun to sway, lazily, drunkenly. The glass disappeared from her hand; who had taken it, she didn't know and didn't care. Other people moved languidly around her forming a mass of writhing souls, a mating dance of sorts, like an orgy of twisting, rubbing snakes. More drinks appeared in her hand and she swallowed them down. How many had she had? She didn't care, couldn't care. All she wanted to do was dance.

Her body felt ethereal for the first time since she'd died. It was as if she were a wisp of invisible energy, like heat around a fire, as if a strong gust of wind could blow her away at any moment, as if she could finally become nothing. It was liberating.

The purple-haired girl was back, dancing with her. Tilly

stared into her kohl-lined eyes and thought she was the most beautiful girl she'd ever seen. She thought she loved the girl and she also thought she hated her. She wanted to snuff her from existence, but also wanted to *be* her. She wanted to meld her body, her ethereal, peaceful wisp of existence, into this girl's and be one for all eternity. She found herself staring at the girl's lips, thin but sensual. The girl was smiling a faraway kind of smile. She was magical and Tilly wanted nothing more in that moment than to press her own lips against the purple-haired girl's. Leaning forward, but continuing to sway to the beat of the music, her lips finally made contact. It was a sloppy kiss, uneven and gyrating as both girls swayed out of sync. But it was wonderful all the same. Tilly closed her eyes, falling into the kiss, into the girl. She thought this was it, that she would finally, gratefully, float away and become nothing. Or become everything. Become one with the universe, learn all there is to learn, and never worry about anything ever again. The feeling was not unlike what she felt floating in that dark space after she'd died, the tunnel, where she'd felt like she was standing on a precipice, a crevasse at the end of the world, and if she'd take one more step, if she just had the courage to leap, she'd . . .

The moment was gone abruptly. Tilly's eyes shot open and she found herself staring into the vacant eyes of the purple-haired girl. The girl was no longer smiling, no longer swaying to the music. She stared through Tilly, into the void of the universe behind her. Tilly kept up her swaying, but something was niggling at the back of her brain. Something like concern, but she couldn't quite grasp the floating thought.

The whites of the girl's eyes showed and she plummeted to the floor, unmoving. Still dancing, Tilly gazed down at her for a long moment. The longer she looked, the more she wondered why she was looking to begin with. A second later, she forgot who the girl was, forgot the blissful feeling of the kiss. She stayed where she was, swaying, always swaying, her arms up and moving through the air like lazy tentacles.

Two gruff-looking men appeared and calmly removed the purple-haired girl. The girl's head lolled to the side as they hoisted her up and away through the crowd. Tilly closed her eyes again and swayed.

THE KNOCK EXPLODED on the door in a frantic staccato, startling Naveen, who'd been near sleep.

"Open up, Naveen!"

Sleep forgotten, Naveen's heart hammered in his chest. He was across his small room in a flash. Luke's eyes were wide with fear when Naveen yanked open the door.

"I need your help," he almost screamed. "She's had some ambrosia."

Naveen's eyes flared red. His stomach plummeted in anger and fear. Instinctively, one hand grabbed for his pendant while the other rose halfway to Luke's shoulder. Luke took a startled step back, his eyes widening even further. His mouth slackened with shock and he wore a look of such betrayal that Naveen immediately clenched his fist and dropped his hands. He swallowed dryly.

"I—" he started, but Luke only shook his head violently.

"No time for that," Luke said. "We need to get Tilly."

NAVEEN KNEW Luke still had many dealings with people immersed in the Black Market, despite the warnings he'd given him when he'd still been under his wing. Luke would be Luke. Naveen hadn't been to one of the Black Market clubs since he'd had to drag Luke out of one decades ago. It took days to dry Luke out and even longer to get him set straight again. He had thought Luke had the good sense to stay away from the clubs, and from ambrosia, after that. Apparently not.

He hadn't told any of his later protégés about the clubs or the Market. He didn't want them getting involved in that mess. It wasn't right. And more than a few souls he'd trained had found themselves sent to Hell for disobeying orders or for not showing up to work at all. All because of the Black Market.

But Tilly had ended up in the club regardless of his efforts to shield her. Nothing he ever did turned out how it should. It was much better before, centuries ago, when he was doing what he was made to do.

They stormed out of the port. Luke was stepping quickly, almost at a jog, while Naveen stomped along behind him, staring at the back of his blond head and imagining each step was stomping Luke's head in. As they passed the people in line, he gave them a disgusted sneer. They ignored him.

The bouncer smirked. "It's a new riddle, now," he said. "You won't get this one." Then he caught sight of Naveen and his smile vanished. His gaze dropped to the floor. "I'm sorry. I didn't realize he was with you."

Naveen didn't answer the man or acknowledge his presence. He breezed by him and yanked open the red door.

The crowd was packed inside and it was too dim to see anything properly. Naveen grabbed the nearest redhead and spun her around. Not Tilly. The girl's eyes were glazed and she giggled in a squeaky high pitch as she tried to kiss him. He pushed her away and continued his search.

"I left her over this way," Luke yelled, pointing toward the center of the room.

"You shouldn't have *left her* anywhere!" Naveen shot back. Naveen scanned the crowd frantically as he wished for a glimpse of her wild hair. Throngs of souls writhing against one another, reminiscent of Hell. Though these people were decidedly more satisfied with their current situation, even if they were in their own personal kind of hell. With each new person he spun around—*Not Tilly*—he became more frantic and more angry. His rage grew to a level he hadn't felt in years. The pendant hung heavy around his neck and his fingers itched to grab it, to bring ruination to this building, to these souls. He fought it down, shook it off. Underneath, a current of sure dread vibrated through his core. She was lost to him now, he kept thinking. She was lost, and he had failed.

For the first time in eons, he thought of praying, but knew it would do no good. God had stopped listening long ago. And He definitely would not be willing to do any favors for Naveen.

The souls crowded him, jostling, kissing, groping. It was suffocating. Dim light cast a shadow over the mess and disorder he knew was underneath all this revelry. He kept a sharp eye out for a shock of red, hoping no one had already carried her off to some den where she could nod or—*No, don't think about that.*

There. He finally caught sight of her, a lone beacon of red surrounded by men rubbing themselves up against her. He pushed his way through and knocked the stoned suiters out of the way. Tilly's eyes were closed; her mouth hung open. She was drooling. But she was still moving, still swaying to the never-ending music. Not too far gone to save, then.

He called her name repeatedly, but she wouldn't open her eyes. Luke appeared at his side.

"I can't believe you brought her here," Naveen said. He began patting Tilly's face. "Wake up, Tilly, come on now. Wake up!"

"It's not like I meant for her to drink the cocktails," Luke mumbled at his side. Naveen hated the childish petulance in his voice. "I only wanted to show her a good time."

Naveen steeled himself, brought his hand back and swung it quickly at Tilly's cheek. Her eyes finally opened, slowly. They were glazed, but he saw a spark of recognition in them. Or maybe he imagined it.

He bent, grabbed Tilly around the waist, and hoisted her limp body over his shoulders.

"If she's addicted," he spat at Luke, "I will end you."

At least Luke had the capacity of shame to lower his head like a scolded puppy as he followed Naveen out of the club.

SHE COUGHED, rousing slowly from sleep. Rubbed her eyes. The moon was high and full outside her window. "Mommy?" Coughed again. Something smelled wrong, like when her dad burned the turkey that one Thanksgiving and he had to spray all that foam all over the kitchen.

A sliver of light spilled into her room from under the closed door and Tilly wondered how the moon was able to shine from the hallway too. Then she remembered Mommy had been happy again before Daddy had put Tilly to bed. Mommy did that sometimes, skittered from one room to another, cleaning and singing with all the lights on. That must be what was going on: Mommy was just happy again.

But there was something wrong with that light. It was thick somehow, swaying, moving, reaching toward her. Sleep finally banished from her brain, she realized what it was. There was a fire like they'd talked about in the family meetings. "Mommy!" she said, more frantically. She swung her feet to the floor, her toes hitting the cold wood. "Daddy!"

Another cough came, this one turning into a choke, then a fit. She was struggling to breathe now. "Daddy!" Her voice was hoarse. She stumbled to the door, groped for the metal knob. Her wrist touched something that felt like a stinging bite and she jerked her hand back with a yelp. Panic crawled up her throat, aiding the smoke in choking her. She retreated to the far corner of her room, sat down, and drew her knees to her chest. Tears bit the corners of her eyes and slid down her red cheeks.

She was suddenly sure she was going to die, just like her Grandma June had last year. Would they put her in a box too? Would Mommy and Daddy cry while the preacher man talked about ashes and dust? She didn't want that, didn't want her parents to cry. Mommy cried enough already and Daddy was always mad. Another coughing fit overcame her. She felt dizzy.

There was a noise outside. A scratching, then a bang. Tilly jumped and smooshed herself further into the corner. A monster was coming, a monster from the hell her Grandma had always talked about. *If you're not a good girl, Matilda, the monsters will come straight out of hell and take you down there to burn for all eternity, you know that don't you?*

"But Grandma, I'm already burning," she muttered. Her eyes wanted to close badly. Had the monsters come while she was sleeping? Had she done something terribly bad? Was this hell?

Her window exploded inwards, spraying glass all over her bed, the place that had always been safe and warm and protected her from the monsters that lurked in closets and hid under beds just waiting to nibble off a toe. She tried to shriek, but her throat was so dry all that came out was a wispy croak.

"Matilda!"

Tilly's heart lurched. A balding head popped through the broken window. The head swung back and forth. She mewled and the head snapped in her direction and she could finally see it was no monster, only Daddy. "Oh thank God," Daddy said. His head disappeared again and a wave of terror opened Tilly's eyes wide. He'd left her. "Daaaadddyyyyy!" she cried.

"One second, baby." He sounded so far away. But a moment later, a blanket flew through the window and fluttered down on the sill. Then Daddy's head was back. "I need you to come to the window, honey, can you do that?" An arm reached through, the fingers gesturing to her. She shook her head. She was tired, so tired. "Matilda!" her dad barked. "Come here now!" She still didn't move. Her dad tried to pull himself further into the room. "Shit!" he screamed and jerked back. The moonlight showed a black line of something slithering down Daddy's arm.

Tilly summoned all her energy. Daddy was getting mad and she didn't want him to be mad. She swung her legs around and began crawling across the floor . . .

And then she was standing at the gates of Hell again, looking up at the heads staked atop that menacing barrier. She was older and no longer clothed in a child's nightgown. Everything was the same as earlier that day, save one thing.

This time, her mother's head was there, red hair floating around her face like Medusa's snakes, her mouth pulled back in a silent scream.

"Your mother killed herself, Tilly," a female voice whispered in her ear. She could feel the breath tickle her neck, but couldn't make herself turn to look at the woman speaking. Her eyes only wanted to stare up at her mother's decapitated head.

"She started that fire. She tried to kill you too." The voice cackled and Tilly's flesh crawled.

"I THOUGHT you were done with the clubs. With the Black Market." Naveen's arms were crossed as he stared at the sleeping girl on the futon.

She'd passed out on Naveen's shoulder before they'd even gotten her to her room and had slept deeply for hours. The past hour, though, she'd taken to jerking fitfully and moaning in her sleep. A soul coming down from ambrosia wasn't a pleasant experience. She'd be lucky if she got away with a few bad dreams and that was all. It was the waking nightmares that drove people back to the clubs, back to the drink.

"I'm done with ambrosia," Luke said. "The clubs are harmless."

Naveen cut a glare at him.

"They are! You can have a good time in one of them without, you know." He gestured at Tilly. Her face had scrunched up in a grimace as she slept.

"You people aren't even supposed to have the stuff."

"You people? Look who's all high and mighty. You're a hypocrite, you know that?"

94

Naveen felt rage rising again; his hand itched to grab his pendant. Luke stood his ground this time, his jaw set. In his mind's eye, Naveen saw himself smashing that jaw, smashing that pretty face the women adored.

Tilly grunted, then whined; her eyes cracked open a slit, then drifted shut again.

"You're lucky I've always liked you," Naveen told Luke. He shook Tilly's shoulder.

"Why don't we leave her be for a while?" Luke asked.

"She doesn't escort to Heaven," Naveen snapped. "She has souls to collect when she works." He sneered. "Unless you're going to take over for her today."

Panic filled Luke's face and he quickly looked away from Naveen.

"That's what I thought," Naveen said under his breath. He shook Tilly again. Naveen grunted in frustration. "Come on, Tilly, let's get up and moving."

Tilly's eyes suddenly shot open and she bolted upright so fast, Naveen almost fell backwards trying to get out of her way. Her eyes were wide with terror and her lips trembled. She looked like something was lodged in her throat, like she was trying to hold it back.

And then she screamed.

WHEN DEATH HAD SEEN Naveen carrying Tilly tossed over his shoulder, he almost laughed. And he would have had he not been within earshot of the trio. Naveen's face had been the definition of fury. Death knew that face well, had been on the receiving end of that anger on more than one occasion. And he acted just about like the poor blond kid bringing up the rear. Who was he, anyway? Death hoped he wasn't going to be another complication.

When he returned to his office—thankfully devoid of Eris for the time being—he did laugh, long and hard. More than he had in eons. He could picture what had happened: the poor screw up of a girl decided to go get bombed at one of the clubs and Naveen caught her. Remembering the anger on Naveen's face brought another wave of laughter.

But it ended abruptly when he thought about the dreams.

Souls under the influence of ambrosia were apt to dream a little too much. And a little too vividly.

But most worrying was that the dreams were a little too *truthful.*

She could remember.

He doubted it, but it was possible.

But then again, who would believe a junky? Because that's what she was bound to become. Maybe already was.

It would be Death's word against hers. She a screwup about to be damned and he a member of management on the verge of reincarnation. Probably no one would bother looking into her claims.

But Naveen might believe her. He liked the girl. He might insist God investigate, and while there was no love lost there, it was possible God might comply.

More than possible.

"Dammit!" He reached over his desk, yanked open the drawer and removed the prophecy. He spread it out on the desk surface, seething down at it, looking once again for some kind of loophole to save himself.

NAVEEN HAD to smack Tilly to make her stop screaming. He didn't like doing it, but no amount of telling her to calm down was working. Luke, always helpful, stood in the corner looking shell-shocked.

She stopped screaming just as abruptly as she'd started. Her eyes still held that glazed look of the ambrosia junky and Naveen didn't like the way she was looking at him. Looking through him was more like it. She was elsewhere, seeing other things, disturbing things. He shot a murderous look at Luke. This was exactly what he'd been afraid of.

"Tilly? Talk to me."

"My mother, she was . . . her head. It was *impaled*." A shudder wracked her.

"It was just a dream," Naveen said. "Brought on by the ambrosia."

"No, it was . . . " She paused, finally meeting his eyes. "Wait, the *what*?"

"The ambrosia," Luke mumbled from the corner.

Tilly's eyes narrowed at Luke. "*You.*"

Luke held his hands up in a gesture of surrender and began apologizing profusely. Tilly ignored him. "Did they see me, Naveen? I didn't know, I swear I didn't. Please tell me I'm not going to Hell." She dug at the scar at her wrist with the desperation of a fox in a trap trying to chew its own leg off.

"I told you, there's no monitoring at the club," Luke tried. She glowered back at him.

Naveen tried to remind himself that he liked Luke, had always liked him. But the kid really needed to shut up. Every time he opened his mouth, Naveen wanted to bludgeon him, and judging by the look on Tilly's face, his talking wasn't doing him any favors there either.

"There shouldn't *be* a club," Naveen said through gritted

teeth. He wanted to go back to the club and shut it down himself. Shut down the whole Black Market system while he was at it. Those souls had places to be. But so did Tilly, and she was the one he needed to worry about. It was getting late and he needed to end this right now before Tilly was sent to Hell permanently. He took a deep breath to calm himself. "But that's a conversation for a different day. Right now, we have to go."

TILLY STUMBLED along beside Naveen on the way to the Dome. Luke shambled along a few steps behind. Why they couldn't port, she didn't ask, but suspected she was being punished for the club.

She was already being punished, though. Her scar itched with a voracity she hadn't felt while in Between; only in Hell. Her head, somehow, pounded. Her mouth was dry, cottony, and she struggled to concentrate. She had some vague notion of the fear she'd felt the day before, right before going to Hell, but it wasn't fully surfacing. It couldn't. Not over the urge to go back to the club, to have another one of those swirling red drinks. To forget. To be free.

Naveen's face still wore a fury she'd never seen there. He kept glancing at her sidelong as they walked in silence. They were almost to the Dome when he sighed and said, "Ambrosia belongs to the gods and you'd do well to remember that."

She waved a dismissive hand at him. "I've heard of ambrosia. Gods got all drunk off the stuff. Real great for all the parties they had." She thought of the book in her room and the stories she'd read there. Some real rip-roaring times those gods had.

Naveen shot her a look full of disdain. "Yes, and humans can't handle it. It's a rather powerful drug to them."

"Real popular in Hell," Luke chimed in. When Naveen shot a glare over his shoulder, Luke added, "Or so I've heard."

She'd read that, too. There were all kinds of stories warning about the effects of ambrosia on humans. A lot of them were familiar myths, but slightly twisted. Icarus deciding to fly was supposedly a stoned decision. "Yeah, I read all about it."

Naveen snorted. "I would imagine the books in the World have all kinds of interesting things to say about the gods."

"Read about it here, actually."

He halted. She stopped too and faced him, enjoying the shock on his face. His attitude was grating on her nerves, making her hangover worse, and she was glad to have said something to knock that smugness off his face.

Naveen had paled. She tried to think of why that should bother her, but couldn't concentrate over the itch of her scar. Damn, it was like bugs were in there, biting, scratching, wanting to tear their way out. She clenched her fists to keep from digging.

"What do you mean, you read about it here?" Naveen demanded.

"I'm going to go to work," Luke muttered. He went to pass, but Naveen shot out an arm and gripped Luke's bicep. His fingertips dug in, wrinkling his pressed shirt.

"You're not going anywhere," Naveen said.

"I didn't give her the book, so why are you bothering me?" Luke whined.

"What book?" Naveen roared. He looked from Tilly to Luke and back again. Tilly thought she saw red flame in his eyes, but shook off the idea as a side effect of the ambrosia.

"Let Luke get out of here. I don't want to look at his face right now anyway."

He did, slowly. Luke took off toward the Dome and disappeared inside a moment later.

"What book?" Naveen repeated, his voice much lower this time. She could see he was struggling to keep himself under control.

He had questions, mainly about how she'd come across it. He wasn't happy when she told him she didn't know who would give her such a thing. He asked what all she'd read, and she gave him a rundown of various stories, focusing on the God of Death and how she thought all the gods could go shove it if that's how they acted. He clenched his jaw at that.

"That book doesn't belong to you," he said.

"The hell it doesn't! Possession is nine-tenths of the law."

"You know *nothing* about law," he said, then turned on his heel and stomped toward the Dome.

VIII.

When she got inside—reluctantly; she'd seriously considered running away, just wandering the streets forever—Naveen's demeanor was drastically different. He'd reverted to his mentor state and was all business. They waited for a name to scroll past in the Escort Dome as Naveen went through a list of things Tilly needed to remember while performing her duties. It annoyed her how easily he could flip a switch like that—angry to neutral and back again—with such ease. *Dangerous*, her mother's voice said in her mind. Then, another woman, *She tried to kill you too*. Tilly shook her head and tried to concentrate on what Naveen was saying, but the image of her mother's impaled head kept surfacing. The image mixed with her imaginings of the God of Death: him, faceless and blood soaked, cackling as he hacked off her mother's head and wiggled it down onto a sharp stake.

But her mother's head was not on display beside the gates of Hell. Tilly would have noticed already. Yesterday . . . she'd just been to Hell yesterday and her mother hadn't been there. Right?

She killed herself.

Suicide meant damnation, right? She dug at her scar, no longer caring if it was possible to rip her flesh right off whatever sort of body she had now. Someone was moaning, high-pitched, almost a scream. Flames leapt in front of Tilly's eyes. A swirling tornado of red whipped through her sight line, stopped, turned, and barreled back at her. It would eat her, swallow her up, and she'd be lost forever.

"Tilly!" Naveen was shaking her, concern etching his dark face.

The moaning stopped. The flames, the tornado, gone.

Tilly looked around. The Dome was silent, dozens of slack-jawed faces staring at Tilly.

She looked at Naveen, who still held her shoulders, his face inches from hers. His eyes glittered with tears. "Are you okay?" he whispered. She could see his carotid arteries pounding erratically. *I can see his pulse . . .*

"Tilly!" A more violent, desperate whisper. "Are you okay?"

Slowly, she tore her eyes from his neck. Nodded. His Adam's apple slid down and back up and she was sure it was real spit he was swallowing.

Real saliva. Real tears.

Real *blood*.

Naveen let go of her shoulders abruptly and stepped back. "Back to work," he told the rubberneckers. Muttering amongst themselves, they complied.

Tilly stared at Naveen for a long moment. He didn't meet her gaze, but watched the names scrolling along the tops of the ports, waiting for a red one to appear.

The ambrosia was still affecting her, causing her thoughts to be slippery and murky. She hadn't seen what she'd thought, that was all. Her mind just wanted to see those things. It expected them. Like when she went to Grandma June's funeral and saw her in the coffin. She *knew* the woman couldn't have been breathing because the dead simply *did not breathe*, but the longer she stared, the more she was sure she saw that thin, breastless chest rising and falling, rising and falling.

Naveen's chest was rising and falling.

Stop it! He's dead. Same as you.

Same as your mother.

The flames threatened to fill her vision again. *Your mother killed herself, Tilly.* She dug at her scar hard enough to feel her fingernails, even in the dull of Between, and they retreated.

Tilly found her voice, but it was thin. "Do suicides go straight to Hell?"

"What?"

"Like in the Bible. Suicides are damned, correct? No excuses. No chances to explain yourself. Just flames."

Naveen still wouldn't look her in the eye, but he nodded.

"Is there a list somewhere of the damned?"

Now he did look at her. "Yes," he said slowly.

"I'd like to see it."

"Impossible," he said with a shake of the head.

"But—"

"Time to go," he interrupted. He was pointing at the red letters frantically scrolling above a nearby port.

Richard Goodman.

THEY EMERGED on a sidewalk with a smattering of slow-walking pedestrians, heads down, reminding Tilly eerily of the damned waiting at the gates of Hell. One lone convenience store on the corner had a sign in the window proclaiming BANANAS! as if they were a novelty item.

Tilly scanned the streets, looking for a shooting or a car wreck, an Acolyte of Death, anything indicative of someone dying soon. She wanted to get this over with as soon as possible so she could go back to badgering Naveen about her mother. If she really couldn't see the list of the damned, maybe he could help her investigate in some other way. She'd seen him at the disciplinary hearing; he obviously wielded some sort of power around here.

There was nothing on the streets. No dark cloak whipping through a port. No dead body. No one running and looking terrified like there had been when they'd picked up Hector.

She turned, expecting Naveen to be standing right behind her, but he was gone. Unease pricked at her. She spun in a circle. No Naveen. The unease quickly turned to panic. Her vision tunneled, a red tinge covering everything around her. She ran.

The red tornado was chasing her. She didn't dare look behind to see, but she knew it was there all the same, wanting her, needing her. She tried to scream for Naveen, but her voice had left her and what came out was nothing more than a wheezing puff.

She skidded around a corner and ducked into an alley. Bracing herself, she peeked into the street. No tornado. Nothing was chasing her at all. Squinting her eyes shut tight, she willed herself calm.

"There you are," Naveen said. Tilly's eyes snapped open and she turned toward his voice. He was standing beside a soul wearing dirty rags. Nearby was the soul's body, wrapped in a thin, worn blanket, snuggled into the fetal position under a holey blue tarp. Naveen waved her over.

"As I was saying," the soul said, "there we were, surrounded by Charlie, just waiting for death to find us. Before I left, my mother—I still lived at home, you see, I was only a couple months past eighteen when I was sent over—my mother said to keep my head down. So that's what I did. At that point I didn't care if I was a coward or not. All I could think about was getting home to the farm, and to the sweet girl I'd left behind, so I dropped to the ground and covered my head in the fetal position." Tilly came to a halt several feet away from the chatting men, and the man gave her a nod while scratching at his unkempt beard with dirty fingers before continuing. "The next thing I know, I'm being carried away by a medic. Shot in the leg, I was. I guess the pinkos thought I was dead and left me be." A haunted look came over his face, and he was no longer there on the street, but staring into a jungle only he could see. "Not many of us got out alive, not many at all."

Tilly had been staring at the corpse as the man she assumed was Richard Goodman finished his story. The body's face was frozen in a grin. She'd heard of people dying with a smile on their face, but never thought it was something that could truly happen. Was it possible to have a happy death alone on the cold ground?

Richard sighed heavily and said, "I'm ready to go now."

Tilly felt Naveen's cool hand on hers as he slipped the pendant into her grasp. "I think you can handle this one on your own," he whispered.

The magic pulsed under her thumb, calling to her. She stared down at the bead. The longer she stared, the more it looked like the red was swirling. Swirling magic in a swirling mini tornado. She shook her head, stabbed her thumb into the center of the bead, effectively cutting off the sensation. The magic jumped to meet her. She had pulled it into her body and held it there a moment. There was something just on the other side of that magic veil, something that reached out to her, wanting to grab her with its tentacles. Naveen was watching her carefully. His smooth black brows had met and his mouth turned down in a concerned frown. She released the magic and let it flow back out of her body. A port opened at her feet, the churning cool blue a sharp contrast to the red of the bead.

Tilly froze. She thought of the heat, the flames, the screaming. Could she really go back? She looked up to see Richard staring at her with pity in his eyes. He gave her a wan smile. She straightened. She could do this. It was nothing compared to what Richard had been through, and there he was, pitying her. She gestured for Richard to go first, as Naveen had taught her the day before. He gave no argument and jumped through the port with his head held high. She followed him through, Naveen close behind.

As they waited in line, Richard continued to regale them with tales of the war: cheerful stories about camaraderie and the funny things his buddies did. Tilly suspected he was purposely trying to distract her with something happy to keep her mind off where they were. There was something grandfatherly about Richard Goodman. The thought wrenched her heart. *Was* he a grandfather? Who was he leaving behind?

Or maybe he was trying to ease his own fear. Either way, Tilly was glad for the stories. It kept her mind—and her gaze—on Richard instead of the hideous gates in front of them. She wanted to look at those spikes at the top, wanted to see if her mother's head was there, pinned like a butterfly in a collection, mouth open in a scream. But she didn't. She couldn't. Her mother had not killed herself. She'd died in a house fire. A tragic accident, but an accident nonetheless.

And she certainly hadn't tried to kill Tilly, her only daughter.

So Tilly didn't look. She just listened to Richard's stories, smiling in the right places, asking questions in the right places. And ignoring the burning tug coming from her scar.

Naveen was quiet at her side. His eyes darted around constantly, but Tilly noticed he never fully looked at the gates either.

A port opened near them and two souls tumbled out in a twisting mass of limbs. The damned woman swung and kicked and gnashed her teeth. Her Escort dodged and weaved. Naveen was on them both in a flash, his right arm around the woman's throat while his left pulled her left arm up and back in a sick angle behind her. The woman continued to gyrate. Then Naveen whispered something in her ear. Her eyes went wide and she paled. It was like all the fight had literally drained out of her, escaping through her high heels and absorbing into the oozing muck on the platform. Naveen returned to Tilly's side, but said nothing. Richard—*Shit, I'd forgotten about Richard!*—was also quiet for a long time. Tilly wondered why he hadn't tried to run during the commotion. But then, there really wasn't any place to run.

As they approached the booth, Richard said, "I was the last one of my unit alive, you know." The pain in his voice was intense and heartbreaking. Tilly fought the urge to comfort him. There was a reason he was damned, she reminded herself. She needed to toughen up if she was to deal with anything near what that woman had been doing. She couldn't get a reputation for being soft.

Martha sneered at them, drool leaking down what was left of her chin. "Name?"

Richard cleared his throat and gave his name and rank

in a commanding voice. Tilly was in awe of his lack of fear. She couldn't believe this man had played dead in a war zone.

Martha scanned her list and checked him off. "Richard Goodman, gluttony and cowardice."

Tilly waited for the rest of the charges, but there were none. Gluttony and cowardice. That was all.

Richard turned to Naveen and saluted. "Goodbye, dear boy. Have a good death." Then, before Tilly could react, he was lost in the never-ending line moving between Cerberus's legs and through the gates of Hell.

A tear rolled down Tilly's overheated cheek and she reached to touch it. She pulled her hand away and stared at the salty liquid. The ability to cry: another thing Naveen forgot to mention about Hell.

"WHY HASN'T she figured it out yet?" Eris whined. "They should be separated. She should hate him by now."

Death rubbed his temples. "You're giving me a headache." The truth was, she was right. But he'd never expected the book to work anyway. Not in the way he wanted. His endgame wasn't just to separate Tilly and Naveen. No, he needed Tilly gone. For good.

Something a little more drastic was in order. Something that would give Naveen no choice but to tell Tilly the truth. And then Tilly would be without Naveen's protection—and his love. Then the prophecy couldn't come true and no one would look into her claims even if she did remember her death.

"Be patient. I've been given permission to try out a new experiment of sorts." And if that didn't work, Death had one more trick up his sleeve. It might cost him a chance at a new life, but at least he'd get to keep this one.

Eris's eyes widened. She clapped her hands in excitement. "Do tell."

He told her his new plan.

"But they'll still be *together*! You told me I would have him back at the end of this."

"I said no such thing. Quite frankly, Eris, I couldn't care less if he ever looks in your direction again."

Her hand flew to her pendant. "You bastard."

He was beside her the next instant, his hand hovering an inch from her perfectly toned arm. "Think that tiny thing can muster something up before I touch you?" She slowly lowered her hand and he grinned. She never knew how to kill someone with magic; only two other people knew how to do that. Eris was useless arm candy and always had been. "Let's not forget whose hands the power is in these days, my dear Eris."

"Gluttony and cowardice?" Tilly yelled. "You've got to be kidding." They'd arrived back at the Dome and were waiting for the next name.

Naveen gave her a confused look.

"How are those sins?" He didn't answer her, just looked away. "Answer me!"

"Can't you just do what you're told without questioning every little thing?" he snapped. "You're this close to going through those gates yourself, or did you forget that?"

"You know what? That's bullshit too. I didn't actually *do* anything, except be really shitty at random jobs. Jobs that seem pretty useless to me anyway!" Once again, the other

Escorts in the Dome had stopped to stare and whisper about Tilly. *Getting a reputation as a crazy*, she thought wryly. Well, that was just fine. She raised her voice to address the crowd: "Do any of us actually need to be here? If they can magick up a stupid tunnel to plop us here, why can't they do the same for all the other souls? Did you people ever think this is all just a con, just busy work? Keep your head down, do your job, or *poof*, to Hell with you!"

"Tilly, you need to be quiet."

"Fuck off, Naveen. This is all bullshit!" She started to laugh. "All of it!" The laugh quickly turned uncontrollable. Naveen shuffled her through the gaping Escorts and under the EXIT sign.

"Get ahold of yourself!" he said once they were outside. He looked around furtively. "There are people who wouldn't take too kindly to you mouthing off like that."

This brought a fresh round of crazy laughter from Tilly. "Spies?" she managed to say. "Spies?! That's just too much." More laughter. Naveen looked appalled. Which didn't help.

"Richard was damned—" Naveen started.

Tilly suddenly stopped laughing and narrowed her eyes at him. "Richard was damned for saving himself in a fucking war," she said. "Isn't life supposed to be precious? Doesn't it say that somewhere? Cowardice isn't even one of the Commandments!"

"No, but,"—Naveen paused, took a breath, readying himself for recitation—"Revelation 21:8 says: 'But the cowardly, the unbelieving, the vile, the murderers, the sexually immoral, blah, blah, blah—they will be consigned to the fiery lake of burning sulfur.'"

"Let's pretend for a moment that that's not a bunch of bullshit. What about the gluttony? He wasn't fat."

"He died of alcoholism."

She stared at him, her mouth agape. "That's a disease," she said flatly. "We're damning people for being sick now?"

Naveen shrugged, not meeting her eyes.

They stood in silence for a beat while Tilly tried to come up with an argument.

"Surely he was sorry," she said lamely.

"He felt bad, yes, but never truly repented," Naveen said with a sigh. "He couldn't bring himself to be sorry for saving himself. He was only sorry that saving himself came at the cost of his fellow soldiers' lives. And he saw drink as a way of forgetting. That's not repentance."

Tilly threw up her arms in frustration. "How can you go along with this?"

"Trust me, I didn't write the Bible and I wasn't consulted on the rules," Naveen said, his voice low and menacing. "I don't have a choice. I'm stuck here, same as you. Someone threw me here to rot for all eternity, and there is *nothing I can do about it!*"

All of a sudden, a flare of red exploded into his irises. Tilly took a step back. *Dangerous!* her mother's voice screamed in her head.

Naveen's jaw was clenched and he was stalking toward her, one step forward for each of her steps back.

"Do you understand yet?" he said.

"What are you?" Tilly whispered.

A slow clap started behind them.

IX.

He shouldn't have done it. Naveen knew Tilly was right to have questions. Who wouldn't? He should have kept his want and his anger under control. Seeing her shocked look when she asked that question stuck a dagger in his belly.

What are you?

It was a good question. What was he anymore?

Going down there, going to Hell, wasn't good for him. Too many memories. Too much temptation. His anger engorged every time he felt that heat, saw what Lucifer had done.

And now Death turning up like a bad penny. Another memory better left buried.

"This is just perfect." The left side of Death's mouth ticked up, amused.

"Perfect for what?" Naveen said. Tilly's face had gone slack and she stared at the ground. Her mind was probably going back through what she'd read in that damn book. She'd figure it out. Part of him was scared of how she'd react to the knowledge. But a larger part was relieved that she'd finally know and he could move on with his life. Business as usual.

"Let's step inside and I'll explain everything," Death said. "You're really going to love this." He reached a hand toward Tilly. Naveen stepped between them and Death's hand dropped to his side, clenching into a fist.

"What are you doing?" Naveen demanded. Death couldn't touch people. That was not allowed unless their time was up. And that was only in the World. To touch someone in Between—or in any of the other realms—would be tantamount to high treason. That was one thing everyone had agreed on eons ago: no matter how terrible the soul, erasing them from existence would never be allowed.

Death gave Naveen a look that was all innocence. "Nothing at all, *master*."

Tilly inhaled sharply. Naveen glared at Death, who was smiling again.

"Shall we?" Death asked with a nod toward the Dome entrance.

HIS EYES HAD TURNED RED. There was no mistaking it. It was not a hallucination or some sort of leftover phantom from a bad ambrosia trip.

His eyes had turned red and he'd been . . .

. . . menacing.

He'd never been that way before. He'd been sullen, quiet, withdrawn. But never menacing. He was Naveen. He was her mentor. He was everything to her here, the only soul she knew, really knew.

Turns out she didn't know him at all.

They were in the Dome now. Tilly didn't remember

walking in. Death was saying something about an experiment and everyone in the room was jeering and shouting at him. The ports were all lit up, names insistently scrolling along the top. No one moved to take care of the souls. With a start, Tilly realized Naveen was standing beside her, almost touching her arm. She sidestepped.

"With the immense workload of both the Escorts and my Acolytes," Death said, "we need to streamline the system. Escorts will now be culling souls as well as taking them to their respective places of retirement."

Tilly heard him, but didn't quite register what he was saying. Her mind kept circling back to the book in her room. To the stories of the God of Death. She kept redirecting her thoughts, snapping them away from the sacrifices and unnecessary slaughter. If Naveen was some sort of god, that didn't mean he was *that* god. There were others. And not just the original seven; there had been more, many more. The gods had made more with magic. They'd married and had children. There were scores of gods.

But her mind kept turning toward the God of Death.

Slowly, Tilly became aware the room had quieted. She came back to the here and now and looked around. Luke stood next to Death, looking sick.

"No need to look so glum," Death told him. "You're simply helping out my Acolytes. And me. It doesn't hurt to be on my good side, you know." He winked. Luke looked pleadingly at the silent crowd circling around the pair.

"I'll help you." Naveen's voice was quiet, but firm.

Death laughed. "Oh, dear Naveen, did you really think this wasn't going to involve you?"

Tilly saw Naveen's fists clenching and unclenching at his side.

"Oh dear me, no. You have to be involved, Naveen. As does your little protégé."

Naveen shook his head slowly and stepped forward.

Menacing. Dangerous.

"You will *not* involve Tilly in this." He moved so he was in her line of sight, blocking her from Death.

Death's teeth flashed. Tilly couldn't tell if it was a snarl or a smile. "I don't see why not. It makes perfect sense. An Escort to Heaven, and Escort to Hell." He paused to take in the crowd. His gaze eventually landed on Naveen. "And you can cull the souls."

For a moment, Tilly thought he was speaking to her. She started to say she wouldn't be able to kill anyone, no matter what they'd done, and then she realized who Death meant.

"Naveen wouldn't kill anyone," was what she said instead. Her voice was weak, but she'd said it. It had popped out before she had time to think of what she was saying.

Death roared with laughter. Naveen's head hung. Luke looked sicker than ever. The names scrolling above the ports began flashing, insistent that someone respond to their call. Tilly's scar flared.

"Oh, that's precious," Death said when he'd recovered. "She must really be in love with you, Naveen, to not believe even her own eyes."

Tilly took a step forward—she wanted to pummel that smug face—but Naveen was already moving. He stormed toward Death, hand on his pendant. Tilly could feel the magic pulsing through the air. She felt like she might be able to reach out and grab it, even without touching the pendant. The Dome seemed to bulge, then retract, like it was breathing. Unperturbed, Death simply raised a hand and hovered it over Luke's shoulder. Naveen stopped in his tracks and Death laughed again.

"You've gotten too close to these souls," he told Naveen. "I'm really doing you a favor, reminding you who you really are."

"You don't have the authority to do this!" Naveen roared.

Death cocked his head to the side. "*He* does, though. This is with his full approval. You can take it up with him if you like." That infuriating grin again. "If you can get in, that is."

The names above the ports flashed faster, angrier. It irritated Tilly to look at them. Why was no one doing anything about those poor people? What if they wandered away from their bodies and got lost? What if they just . . . disappeared?

Naveen was practically luminescent with rage. His whole body shook. Tilly imagined the pulse at his throat, thrum, thrum, thrumming away.

He's a god.

She'd been running around with a god for weeks. She had a crush on a god.

Then why doesn't he do something?

Her scar screamed. She looked at the names, the red flashing, flashing, flashing. She imagined she could hear the souls crying out in torment. They didn't know what happened. They were confused. They needed help.

"Naveen," she said. When he didn't turn around, she said it louder: "Naveen!"

"I know!" he snapped at her. He clutched his pendant and a portal opened at his feet. To Death, he said, "We're not done, you bastard."

Death just grinned in response as Naveen grabbed both Tilly and Luke by the arm and pulled them through the port.

The next second, they were in a barn watching a farmer muck out stalls. Tilly guessed the man was in his sixties, seventy not far off, and he had a belly the size of a woman nearing birth. He flicked his pitchfork and another load of dung-laden straw came flying at their faces.

"I can honestly say," Luke mumbled, "that at this moment, I'm glad to be dead." The excrement stopped, as if by magic, right before it hit them and fell harmlessly to the floor. If the trajectory of the flung poop seemed unusual to the farmer, he didn't show it.

"I don't understand," Tilly said as she looked around the barn for the person they were here to collect. The only occupant was the farmer, his face red with effort. "Why didn't we go through one of the open ports in the Dome?"

"There's no need for that," Luke said.

"Why not?" she asked. Luke, looking miserable, didn't answer.

The farmer stopped, leaned on his pitchfork, and pulled a handkerchief from the back pocket of his overalls. A phone rang. He pulled a cell out of his front pocket, smiled, and answered. "Hello, darlin' . . . yeah, I'll be up for supper in a minute, I'm almost done . . . we'll eat in front of the boob tube . . . pecan pie? You're a woman after my own heart . . . I'll see you in a few." He hung up and slid the phone back in his pocket. He swiped the handkerchief around his face a couple times, took a few deep breaths, then went back to work.

Realization hit Tilly like a bomb. They hadn't used the open ports in the Dome because those ports led to souls that were already culled and waiting. The human bodies on the other side of those ports were already dead.

Naveen's jaw was set and he was staring at the man. He slowly walked toward him. Tilly jerked her head toward Luke. "Do something," she pleaded.

Luke looked at her with pity. "There's nothing to do." He turned his back to the scene unfolding in front of them.

Naveen had reached the man, who, oblivious to what was about to happen, kept toiling away. "Look away, Tilly," Naveen said, his voice a breathy growl.

"You're not going to kill this man, are you?" When she didn't get a response, she tried again, her voice rising toward hysteria: "Naveen? Are you?"

Naveen slowly turned to look at Tilly. Something flashed in his eyes. Fear? Sadness? "I have to. Now look away. I don't want you to watch me do this."

Luke grabbed Tilly's shoulders and spun her toward the barn wall. She buried her face in his chest as he held her tight.

She heard the old man's breath speed up and become ragged. He grunted a few times. The pitchfork kept sliding into the muck, making a sickening sucking sound.

At the last minute, Tilly pulled away from Luke, turning to make one more plea to Naveen. They could fight this. There had to be somebody to complain to. They could get reassigned. They could go back to normal.

Naveen had one hand on the old man's chest. The man dropped his pitchfork and clutched his heart, his breath coming quick and shallow. His eyes opened wide and he groaned in pain. Then he dropped to the ground.

Tilly screamed. Naveen jerked his head toward the noise. The look on his face was indescribable. He wasn't sad. He wasn't angry. His lips were slightly parted and his dark eyes crackled red and with something Tilly had never seen there: pleasure. He liked what he'd just done.

He *liked* it.

She dropped to her knees and didn't stop screaming.

LUKE WAS YELLING, Tilly was yelling, but Naveen couldn't hear. He couldn't hear anything. He was too wrapped up in the rush of death, of killing a living soul. His head was soaring, his mouth salivating, his pulse pounding. He felt *good*. It was a high he hadn't experienced in a long, long time, but it was familiar. Like coming home.

His eyesight tunneled, like he was looking at the scene in front of him from a great distance. Luke trying to restrain or comfort Tilly. The soul of the farmer hovering nearby, a look of vague concern and confusion on his face. All of it surreal.

Gradually, his adrenaline slowed and the hammering of his own pulse in his ears subsided, replaced by Luke's urgent calls to Tilly, who had swapped her incessant screaming with a catatonic state.

"Let me help." His tongue was thick in his mouth and his words were slow and slightly slurred. He stumbled over to the pair.

Luke glared up at Naveen. "I think you've done enough," he barked. "You should've told her before you did it. Told her everything. She wasn't prepared for this."

Naveen stared impotently as Luke patted Tilly's face and urged her to come back to them. She wasn't responding.

Luke picked her up, ever so gently, and Naveen felt a resurgence of emotion, this time jealousy instead of euphoria. He should be the one taking care of Tilly. She was his responsibility, his protégé. Luke's hands didn't have the right to be on her; his eyes didn't have the right to be looking at her like that, so softly, with so much tenderness.

He looked at the farmer's body slumped on the ground amid the shit and straw. He hated himself. He hated what he was. Most of all, he hated that he liked it, that it filled him in a way nothing else could.

Would Tilly hate him now? That would make things simpler.

"I'm taking her back to her room," Luke said, interrupting Naveen's thoughts.

Naveen shook his head. His elation over killing was completely gone now, replaced with a gut-wrenching guilt. "No. I'll do it," he said. "You can take the soul to Heaven."

Luke's hesitation was written plainly on his face. He looked at Tilly's lax head in his arms, then back at Naveen.

Naveen clenched his jaw. "I'm taking her," he insisted. His tone left no room for argument. Luke reluctantly placed Tilly back on the hay-strewn barn floor and ported out with the farmer. Naveen approached Tilly's body slowly, his eyes stinging. What had he done?

DEATH WHISTLED as he entered his office. Even if this plan didn't work and causing a rift between Tilly and Naveen didn't negate the prophecy, he still felt immensely satisfied with what he'd just accomplished. He'd wanted to bring Naveen down a peg for eons. Naveen deserved to be brought low for what he'd done.

Dying is supposed to be easy. There are a million things said about it: it's just like falling asleep; your friends and family are there to greet you; a winged beauty of an angel guides you to the pearly gates and paradise. Even the old cultures believed you'd roam great hunting grounds or your spirit would pass into another body and live again.

For Death, none of this was true.

So many years had passed since, he no longer remembered what he was doing before he died. Or who his family was, where he lived, or what his actual name was, if he ever had one.

He remembered the pain, though. It was the most awful pain he'd ever experienced, a sharp stabbing from everywhere at once. It was gone as abruptly as it had come, and everything seemed to be back to normal.

Except for the doppelgänger lying at his feet.

A young girl was shaking the lifeless body on the ground, crying in her frustration. He called out to her, but she didn't hear.

Then he reached for her.

He laid his hand on her shoulder and she immediately stopped moving, her eyes rolling back in her head. Then she slumped away from him, her body lying near his.

He withdrew in horror.

More people came. He reached out to at least half a dozen of them before he realized it was his touch causing them to fall to the ground, unmoving. He cried watching the rest of them as they clustered around the pile of motionless bodies, confusion and fear etched on their faces. Loneliness was already taking a strong hold on his soul. A thought hit him suddenly, giving him hope. The people he touched should be here with him. That was how it had worked for him, after all. He was lifeless in one body, but perfectly fine —if invisible—in the other.

But there were no doubles standing near him. Where had they gone?

He spent those first few decades wandering the countryside, searching for those lost souls. He never found them.

He tried not to touch anyone along the way, but sometimes it was unavoidable. They would walk into him when he wasn't paying attention. Sometimes he would experiment, touching whole villages to see if he could spot where the souls went. It was always the same: they would float out of the body and disappear in the blink of an eye. He tried following them, to no avail. He was stuck.

And all the while, a hard knot of jealousy was tightening inside him. Why should these other people get to live, to interact with each other? Why did every other soul leave here when he touched them? Why was he different?

One day, depressed and miserable, he sat in a quiet spot near a river, watching a young family on the other bank. They frolicked in the water, laughing and splashing each other. They were happy, and it disgusted him. He turned his face to the sun, wondering if he should touch them and rid himself of the misery of their presence. It would be so easy to cross the river and brush his hand over their shoulders.

"Hello," a voice said. The sun darkened as someone moved in front of his view. The person's head was haloed in bright light, but he could still see the smile. Then the man squatted and Death could see him better.

His tan skin and dark hair were flawless. Beautiful, even. But there was a darkness in those eyes, a fever of sorts. "I'd forgotten I'd made you," the man said, still smiling.

And that was how Death had met Naveen.

The time that followed was often a spree of senseless killing, punctuated by lulls of calm while Naveen retired to the underworld and rested his overtaxed body. Death reveled in the killing, then. He'd been so jealous of the living for so long, it was pure joy to take that breath of life from their weak bodies. He relished the power. He'd finally found happiness in his wretched existence.

And then the coup had happened and Naveen had done nothing to stop it. No, Naveen wasn't *able* to do anything about it. The all-powerful God of Death was nothing but a hedonistic loser who couldn't even stand up to his little brother.

But now, Death would have his life back. Soon, if everything went according to plan. God had promised him it would be soon. Finally, he had earned his reward.

He sat down at his desk, opened the drawer to read the prophecy one more time, to see if a rift between Naveen and Tilly would save the plans Death had worked so long and so hard for. The drawer was empty. He shoved his hand inside and frantically swept it around.

The prophecy was gone.

X.

Tilly was just shy of nineteen. It was spring, almost summer, and she was coming home from college for the first time. She'd skipped coming home for the holiday breaks, opting to go to friends' houses or abroad instead. She couldn't stand being home anymore. Not with the Bimbo. Not with the new baby.

She stood on the doorstep, looking in through the side window. Her father sat on the floor with the baby, who was now old enough to be taking his first wobbly steps. This shocked Tilly a bit. She'd only seen the kid once: a picture of him as a newborn. Posted on the Internet. Her dad apparently couldn't be bothered to send her one. Then again, she couldn't be bothered to come see him, so she supposed they were even.

She watched her dad play with the baby for several minutes. Then the Bimbo came in with a plate of something. They laughed together and made faces at the baby.

A happy little family, Tilly thought. How disgustingly inappropriate.

She stormed through the door and went straight to her room. The baby started wailing at the sudden noise.

"Matilda?" her dad called after her. His shoes thumped on the wooden stairs as he followed her up.

She stopped in shock in the doorway of her room, dropping her suitcase and backpack in a heap beside her. The room, once a deep purple, was now a pale light blue, with framed paintings of cartoonish giraffes and elephants hanging on the walls. Stuffed toys, a playpen, and a crib took up most of the space. A small rollaway bed had been set up in the corner.

"Matilda Jean," her dad scolded from behind, "you scared the living hell out of us. Ever heard of knocking?"

She turned to him. He was smiling, obviously pleased to see her, and not at all serious about the knocking. He looked good. He'd lost weight, and his face had a few new smile lines. He was happy. Happier than he'd ever been when she was a child. Happier than he'd ever been with her mom.

It disgusted her. Rage boiled up inside. "What have you done with my stuff?" she demanded.

Her dad kept smiling. "You went away, Matilda. We had to move on."

"I was at college! I didn't move out!"

"You went away," he repeated. "But we're so glad to have you back. You weren't supposed to go."

"What are you talking about? You helped me fill out the applications!"

"You weren't supposed to go," he repeated. "You were supposed to stay here. You weren't supposed to die." The grin remained plastered on his face, making him seem fake, plastic.

Tilly's heart raced.

"Dad, you're not making any sense." She said it slowly,

deliberately pronouncing each syllable with all the concern of someone who was witnessing a loved one's mental break.

"You weren't supposed to die." A new voice, coming from inside her room. She spun around. It was the little girl. The one who had winked at her on the streets. The one who couldn't have possibly seen her. The girl was sitting in the center of the room, wearing an outdated frilly pink dress and playing with an old stuffed bear of Tilly's. She looked up at Tilly and smiled. "Not yet, anyway."

Tilly took a couple steps back, held out her hands as if warding off a rabid animal. "I don't know what's going on here. This isn't how it went!"

A thick gray mist filled the room and the little girl vanished. When the mist cleared, the bedroom had disappeared and Tilly stood in a sunflower field. The flowers reached for the sky, taller than Tilly, so that the only thing she could see was the white fluffy clouds floating in the bright blue above her. Birds chirped and the breeze was sweet. She wore a thin white cotton dress, and the warm sun kissed her bare shoulders. She wandered through the field aimlessly, completely at peace.

A humming sound began. It had a singsong quality, like a child playing. Tilly smiled and quickly walked through the flowers, trying to find the source of the sound. It got louder, pulsing through the air. Tilly laughed and ran, her long hair flowing behind her. She wanted to play, too. Every time she got close, the sound moved and increased, until it was coming from everywhere, surrounding her. Until it was coming from inside her.

The humming stopped as abruptly as it started. In its place, a child's voice. Tilly stopped to listen.

"Once there was a girl, not much older than a child. A prophecy was foretold about this girl: she would grow to do great things, would grow to save mankind. But an Other had different ideas and the girl entered the Between before her time. The Other was satisfied, and ordered the erasure of all mention of the prophecy, thinking it was changed, that everything would continue as it had. But the Other was wrong. True prophecies can never be changed. They evolve, but the end is still the same.

"You are that girl, Tilly. Hear this, and remember."

The dream faded and, as she started to wake, Tilly was left with one persistent impression:

You weren't supposed to die.

"Look at me, Tilly. Look at me!"

Her eyes opened slowly. For a moment she looked at peace, but then her face darkened. She pushed Naveen away and recoiled. He couldn't blame her; he would probably be scared, too, if he were in her place. Especially since she'd obviously read so much about him in that stupid book.

"Did you kill me?" Her voice was barely audible.

Now it was Naveen's turn to recoil. "What? I—"

"Did you kill me?!" Fear swam beneath the look of rage on her face. It killed Naveen to see it there.

He swallowed and shook his head. "No."

"I don't believe you."

"Tilly, I haven't culled a soul in eons."

She barked a mirthless laugh. "'Culled a soul.' Is that what you call it? Is that what you think you did to that poor old man today?"

He was silent, unsure what to say. Luke was right; he should've told her who he was long ago. It would be infinitely harder for him to explain now.

"The sacrifices, the torture . . . taking people before their time!" Her voice hitched. "How could you?"

"It's not what you think," he tried, shaking his head. She wasn't listening. She'd moved from the futon and was slowly backing away from him, arms clasped around herself. Panic rose in his chest. He just needed her to understand. She could hate him after that, but he needed her to know the truth. And the easiest way to do that was to take her away from here, to take her back to where it all began. He would let her in, let her see, more than he'd ever let anyone before. Then she could judge. He reached for his pendant, then lunged at her.

HORNS HONKED and exhaust fumes hung heavy in the air. Buildings rose around them: stone that had seen centuries of sunrises. Laundry hung from balconies. Loud chatter spilled from open windows. People milled about on the sidewalks, forming a mass as impenetrable as the stationary traffic on the street.

Tilly, stunned from the sudden port, let Naveen tug her through the crowd and into a nearby side street. It was an open market, and quieter than the main avenue, but not by much. Instead of honking cars, market-goers chattered away at the stall owners, haggling over the cost of this necklace, that piece of fruit.

Naveen was looking around. His face was taut. "We should be able to see the Nile from here," he mumbled. He was still holding her arm, tightly. Finally coming to her senses, she struggled against him. He loosened his grip, but didn't let go. He locked eyes with her, a pleading look. "I'll let go if you promise not to run. I just want you to understand."

She looked at his pendant. He caught the glance and gave a wan smile as he took it from around his neck and kept it gripped in his hand. He let go of her arm. She didn't move from his side. There was no point in running when she didn't have a way of escape. She would stay put until whoever was supposedly monitoring her showed up to drag her back—hopefully not straight to Hell.

"I know you don't trust me right now . . ."

She squinted at him. He sighed and ran his hand through his hair. "Okay, here it is. You've already figured out that I am the God of Death. Or was. Or something. There was a coup some years ago—"

"I know that part. It was in the book." She'd read about how there were seven original gods and goddesses, and one got a big head and decided he needed to rule all—the God of Wisdom, if she remembered correctly. He gathered a few other gods and took over, forcing his siblings into the world between worlds. "Get to the part where you explain why you think it was okay to demand sacrifices."

"Dammit, Tilly!" He threw up his hands. "Eris and Death—"

"Eris? The woman from the disciplinary hearing? What's she got to do with this? What does anyone else have to do with this?"

He looked pained. He took a deep breath. Numbly, Tilly realized it was real air going into his lungs. He was really breathing. He was a god and he was alive.

"Eris was my wife," he said.

Tilly couldn't help but laugh. It was a sharp sound bordering on a screech.

"Can I just start at the beginning?"

For a long moment, she watched his chest move up and down. She purposely stopped hers. It made no difference. She could go on standing there without breath for eternity. He was not like her. Not dead. Never dead.

He was still waiting for her to agree to hear him out. The seconds ticked by. She weighed her options. She could try to run, but had no way to get back to Between. And she wasn't sure she wanted to run, anyway. Her instincts had been right: Naveen was a dangerous man. Better to stay and calmly listen to whatever story he wanted to spin while she waited for someone to come. She sighed and nodded. They wandered the streets as he spoke, the sea of people parting as they passed.

He told her about his life before, when he lived in Egypt as a child, before it was even known as Egypt. His family traveled with the seasons, making do with what they could find or hunt.

"My mother liked to sit on the banks of the Nile at night, staring at the moon. Just staring up, sometimes talking, like she was hearing the moon speak to her. She would sing me songs at night, about the beginning of the world, about how the sun and the moon had made all the creatures. She had great respect for the moon, and I often think that's why I was chosen."

At the mention of his mother, Tilly got a flash of her own. Her mother was driving a convertible, and they were both laughing as the wind blew through their matching curls.

"I woke up one morning and wandered around in a sort of trance. I felt like something was pulling at me, right here." He pointed at his chest. Tilly's scar burned for a second, as if in sympathy. "By nightfall, I couldn't fight the feeling anymore and I started walking. I remember it was a full moon, but other than that, the trip is a blur. I arrived at a tree, the biggest I'd ever seen. It stretched up into the sky. I couldn't see the top. There were six others waiting there. No one said anything. One by one we approached the tree, touched it." He gave a little shudder of appreciation. "It was like lightning shooting through my body—not painful, but more like my soul was singing. I was euphoric. Then the trance broke and I had all this knowledge. Around the tree trunk were all these little red beads, and we each took one. We instantly knew how to use them." He paused to watch two women fighting over the quality of fruit at a nearby stall. Tilly waited. When he continued, his face was darker, pinched.

"We mostly stayed in the World in the beginning. We had gone to the other realms, of course, but we still liked being around people. But we were different and everyone could sense that. We were harassed day and night—people asking for favors, mostly. For their daughters to find good husbands, for good hunting, for an enemy to die. We migrated from town to town, sometimes leaving of our own accord, sometimes kicked out. If something went wrong, they blamed us. If someone died, I was blamed." He exhaled slowly. "Eventually we decided to leave the World and stay in the other realms permanently."

She stared at him, incredulous. Was that it? He thought this little story about the moon choosing him against his will and how he was bullied would make everything okay again?

"I know how that book makes me look. The culture back then . . . it was different. People believed if they sacrificed a few virgins, I would save the village from whatever plague was coming through."

"You're telling me you're a god and you couldn't save a

little village from the plague?"

"No! That's what I'm trying to tell you. A plague extinguishing a village is fate. All I did was watch over the souls once they were dead and cull souls destined to die. And just like now, the good people went to spend eternity in the Realm of the Gods, known as Heaven now, and the bad went to the underworld, where I watched over them."

"So, same stupid system, different government," Tilly said.

"Not quite," he muttered. "I had tribunals set up so souls could defend themselves during judgment. I might have gone a little overboard sometimes, but I wasn't a monster."

She wasn't sure what to believe. The book or Naveen? His version seemed reasonable, but of course that's how he would tell it.

"And how does Death play into all this?"

He looked away, his shoulders sagging. "Death was a mistake. One of many I've made over the course of my life." Turning back to her, he added, "I didn't cull your soul. I haven't . . . that is, today was the first time I've taken a soul in millennia."

She did believe that. The look on his face as the farmer died was the look of a junky finally having a fix after being sober for years. And now his eyes held the shame of that fall off the wagon.

He looked down and unclenched his fist, revealing the pendant. "One more thing, about the book. You shouldn't have it. It's been missing for a long time, and I don't know why someone would've given it to you. But you should hand it over to me so I can return it to its proper home."

Tilly made a face. "I don't see why a bunch of old stories —especially lies, if you're to be believed—would be so important."

"It's not the stories. It's the prophecies." He opened the portal.

DEATH WATCHED Naveen and Tilly on the monitor. He'd enjoyed the little show, reveling in Tilly's refusal to forgive Naveen. But then Naveen mentioned the prophecies. She was too close. With the prophecy missing, he couldn't take any chances. He would have to go to God, see if he could convince him that Naveen and the girl were a threat. Get permission to get rid of them both, once and for all.

LUKE WAS WAITING for them when they ported back to Tilly's room. "Where have you guys been?" he asked. "I've been waiting here forever. I got the soul to Heaven and . . ." He looked from Naveen to Tilly. "You told her?" he asked Naveen. "Everything?" Naveen nodded.

Tilly glared at him. "You knew?" Luke winced. "You know what, whatever. I don't even care anymore. Just get out. Both of you." She wasn't really angry with Luke. At least not at that moment. She was distracted by Naveen's mention of prophecies and the book. She desperately wanted to spend the rest of the night poring through the pages, trying to find the prophecy mentioned in her dream. If there was such a thing. She didn't know whether putting any stock into something a child said in a dream was worth her time.

Naveen shook his head. "We've got work to do."

Of course. No rest for the wicked. Tilly closed her eyes and heard the port open. Luke whispered in her ear, "Just don't watch him."

XI.

They'd collected over twenty souls, most assigned to Hell, but a few to Heaven. Naveen had been quiet while he worked, and Tilly made sure to avert her eyes every time he reached out his hand to touch someone. Luke joked continuously, keeping the crowd of newly dead entertained.

They were at the site of a car wreck in the now-familiar city Tilly recognized as her home, but she still couldn't quite remember her time there. A bus had rolled over close to downtown. The soul tally was eight.

Naveen was finishing up when Tilly saw the little girl. She was standing on the sidewalk half a block away. While everyone else was watching the mayhem—cell phones pulled out to document every little thing—the girl was watching the collection of the souls. She caught Tilly's eye and smiled, gesturing with her index finger for Tilly to come closer.

Tilly looked around for Naveen and Luke. Luke was regaling the newly dead with some story and Naveen still had three souls to collect. Everything looked under control, so she slunk away and approached the girl.

They stared for a few moments, each taking the other in. The girl's eyes were a beautiful deep brown, soulful. Her skin was flawless except for a fading two-inch scar on her right cheekbone. Tilly pictured her older, a beauty and heartbreaker. For some reason, the image filled her with sadness.

The girl was the first to speak. "Hello, Tilly. I've been waiting for you."

It was the same voice from her dream. "What's your name?" she asked lamely.

The girl laughed. She was missing a molar on the upper left side, the tip of an adult tooth barely showing through the gum. "Phoebe," she said. "Phoebe Walker." She watched Tilly intently, her head cocked slightly to one side, waiting for the next question.

Out of the corner of her eye, Tilly saw several people point at Phoebe, whisper, then move away. All they saw was a little girl talking to the air. Tilly felt sorry for her. How difficult it must be to know things, to see things no one else can. Did her parents know? Did they believe her? Did she have any friends?

"Where are your parents?" Tilly asked, as she quickly swept her eyes over the crowd.

"My dad is at home, passed out." She said this matter-of-factly, without emotion. "He's a drug addict," she added, sensing Tilly's question.

"And your mother?" Tilly was afraid to know the answer.

"She died giving birth to me," Phoebe said, again without emotion. "That's how it is with oracles—that's what I am, you know. The mother must die to bring us into the world. We're tainted that way. Tainted with the other realms.

It's the only way I can see what I see. It's the only way I can see you."

Tilly's heart wrenched. Phoebe was about the same age she had been when her own mother had died. She knew how hard it was. "My mother's dead, too," she said.

"I know."

They stood looking at each other, bonding over the loss. It seemed that time had slowed, like they were standing in a soap bubble, floating along the street where no one and nothing could touch them.

Phoebe glanced over Tilly's shoulder and the bubble burst. "He's done."

Tilly looked over her shoulder, her eyes finding Naveen immediately. He was looking at her, some untold emotion written on his face. Anger? Fear? He strode toward her. Tilly had a sudden, irrational fear that he was going to take Phoebe's soul. She moved in front of her, facing Naveen, a wall of protection for Phoebe.

Phoebe sensed her thoughts again. "He's not going to take me," she said. "Not today, anyway." She put her small hand on Tilly's arm and gently turned her around. "I'll see you soon."

"When?" Tilly asked.

"When I die." She shrugged and grinned. "Maybe before." She spun around on her heel and skipped down a nearby alley.

Tilly felt Naveen approach her from behind. "Who was that?" he asked. His voice held none of the emotion she'd seen on his face seconds earlier. He seemed more in awe than anything. "She could see you?"

Tilly nodded.

"An oracle," Naveen muttered. "Haven't seen one of those in ages."

Tilly watched Phoebe go, wondering at her last words.

"Guys!" Luke called. "The souls are getting restless. I think it's time to go!"

THEIR FIRST STOP would be Hell. That didn't gain Naveen any friends in the group of culled souls, but it couldn't be helped. It was less risky because it gave the damned souls less of a chance to escape. The few that were Heaven-bound would have to stay close to Luke on the platform of Hell and they'd be fine. The side trip might even make them appreciate Heaven more when they did get there.

Naveen had opened the portal and was in the process of herding the souls like cattle. Luke was at the front, Tilly in the middle. He brought up the rear in case they had a runner. He was exhausted and wanted this day to be over. Culling was like a high—the more he did it, the quicker the high wore off and the more he wanted to do. It was getting harder to control himself, and as much as he hated going to Hell, he was glad for this small reprieve in their day. The smell of sulfur filled his nostrils as he ported and he felt a wave of nausea and hate for Lucifer.

Luke wasn't doing well. He turned away from the gates, looking out over the gurgling River Styx to the black abyss beyond. The handful of Heaven-bound souls huddled around him, as if for protection. Tilly walked over and put a hand on his back. "Are you all right?" she asked.

"We've got stuff to do," Naveen said. "We don't have time to deal with a blubbering Escort."

Tilly shot him a look.

"I'm fine," Luke said, trying to smile. The movement of his mouth made him gag and he turned away quickly. Tilly rubbed his back as he dry heaved. When he was finished, he looked at her apologetically. "Not exactly sexy, huh?" he joked.

Tilly smiled at him.

"Apparently I have to take care of everything around here," Naveen said. He began herding the damned toward Martha's booth. He heard Tilly say something under her breath as she hurried to catch up to him. He felt bad for snapping at her, but he couldn't help himself. Culling took him away from himself, from the person he wanted to be.

"Well, well, this is a fine group you've got today," Martha said. The good side of her face smiled. The motion pulled on the skin of the melted half, making the smile look more like a grimace. Knowing Martha as he did, Naveen could guarantee that was the look she was going for.

Tilly rattled off the names of the damned as Martha checked them in.

"We're missing one," Martha told Naveen when the last soul had shuffled past.

"What?"

"Yeah, you're supposed to have a Thomas Friedman," Martha said, reading from her clipboard, "in for adultery and a few more minor sins."

Naveen glared at Tilly. "I told you not to misplace a soul."

"Yeah, like I'm the only one here to blame," she shot back.

Naveen gave a frustrated sigh. "Let's find this guy and get out of here. Where's the last place you saw him?"

Tilly looked around hopelessly.

Martha drummed her fingers. "You're holding up the line," she said.

Naveen shot her a withering look and Martha cowered.

"I'll just go see if we left him with Luke," Tilly said as she hurried off.

Naveen rolled his eyes. "Trainees," he said to Martha as he turned to follow Tilly.

"Not like it was before, is it?" she called after him.

No, it's definitely not, he thought.

A few of the souls were crying, tugging at Luke's arms, asking him to get them out of there. One woman was irate, screaming at him, saying he tricked her and she was supposed to be in Heaven. Luke looked at a loss. He kept opening and closing his mouth, as if he wanted to say something but couldn't think of the words. He'd obviously never had to deal with souls that were anything but happy. But at least he no longer looked ready to vomit.

"I don't think this is going to work in the long run," Tilly said to Naveen.

"We'll come up with something else, then. I didn't realize your boyfriend was so ill-equipped for the job."

Tilly shot him a look. "He's not my boyfriend."

"Whatever," Naveen spat. He turned to Luke. "Do you have a Thomas Friedman here?"

Luke looked distraught as he cast around wildly. Naveen didn't think he knew how many souls he was supposed to be babysitting.

"I . . . I don't know," Luke stammered.

Tilly pointed at a short bald man cowering behind an older woman. The man averted his eyes quickly. "What's your name?" she asked him.

He pointed to himself. "Me?" he asked.

Naveen marched over to him and grabbed his polo collar. "Name," he demanded.

"Um . . . Brian . . ." he looked around, "Gate. Gateston. Brian Gateston."

Luke's eyes widened in panic. "I don't think we were supposed to pick up a Brian Gateston," he said. "Oh God, did we kill someone we weren't supposed to?"

"No, you idiot," Naveen said, still firmly gripping the man who claimed to be Brian, "this is Thomas Friedman. He made up a name . . . oh never mind." He dragged and shoved a kicking and screaming Thomas Friedman/Brian Gateston to Martha's booth, leaving Tilly and Luke behind. He couldn't help but think this would all be easier if he just took care of everything himself. A sort of return to the old ways.

He shoved the soul against the booth. Martha, being the sociopath that she was, looked at the man as if she wanted to eat him. She stood and whistled to Cerberus. The three-headed dog lumbered toward her. She pointed to Thomas and Cerberus bent one of his massive heads down and grabbed the soul between his teeth. Thomas flailed and screamed as the dog tossed him in the air, then caught him with one of his other heads.

Naveen swallowed, hating himself.

HEAVEN.

When Tilly emerged from the port, she was overwhelmed with the smell of lilacs. Thousands of lilacs, all stirred by a light, airy spring breeze. She deliberately kept her eyes shut as she exited the portal, wanting to take in every scent and feeling before she added the visual stimulation. She wanted to treasure this moment. She wanted the suspense to last.

The breeze tickled her eyelashes. Sunlight kissed her cheeks. It was the perfect temperature: not too hot, not too cold. She smiled, glad she was able to feel. Even if she couldn't stay, these little trips in the course of doing her job would be a welcome reprieve.

She could hear people milling about, some giggling, but the noises were hushed, as if pillows were absorbing the sound. She pictured children frolicking and adults lounging on their own personal clouds. She pictured butterflies and rainbows and cherubs dancing weightless in the skies. She pictured harps playing independently of musicians, their strings sounding the most beautiful music. All that would be inside the gates, of course. But maybe she would catch a glimpse. And surely she would be able to see Saint Peter with his long, flowing white robes standing outside a pearly gate, people smiling as they greeted their long-lost relatives.

Relatives. Would hers be here? Would her mother be here?

Your mother killed herself.

The moment of peace shattered and Tilly's eyes snapped open. The light was blinding after the depths of Hell, and it took a minute for her eyes to adjust.

When they did, her heart sank.

She was standing on a platform identical in design to the one in Hell, minus the sticky muck. No people floating on clouds, no cherubs, no harps, no relatives lined up at the gates to greet the newly dead.

The gate was there, though, but it wasn't pearly. It was gold. Painted gold, actually. Tilly could see the plain bronze where the gold paint was flaking off. The gate stood as tall as the one in Hell and stretched for eternity in both directions, disappearing into the clouds. The clouds themselves weren't pure white—they had a tinge of gray to them, like old socks that need bleaching.

A single booth stood outside the gate, identical to the

one Martha spent her eternity in, if a little cleaner. It was painted white with a placard sign hanging on cords on the front. The sign read PLEASE CHECK IN.

A line of people shuffled past the booth. A short line. Unlike Hell, this line was neat and ordered, each person waiting his or her turn. An old man sat inside, chewing gum and looking bored. He was wearing a Hawaiian t-shirt covered by a blue smock. His face was clean-shaven, and his longish hair was curly and unkempt under a trucker cap.

Tilly and the rest of her group waited in line. As they approached the booth, Tilly saw that his smock had a name tag pinned to it. It said HI! MY NAME IS and scribbled in black Sharpie was the name SEYMOUR BUTZ. Tilly balked.

None of this seemed to be affecting the rest of her group. The souls were smiling, probably just glad to be out of Hell. Naveen was impassive and Luke wore a grin so wide Tilly wondered how he wasn't in pain.

The first soul, an older woman, approached the booth. Mr. Butz blew a bubble and some of the gum stuck to his chin. He didn't notice. "Hi. Welcome to Heaven," he said dryly. "Please state your name and the names of any relatives you think are here."

The older woman cleared her throat and pronounced her name slowly. "Ruth Richmond. That's R-I-C—"

"Got ya," the man said, making a check mark on his clipboard. "Next."

Ruth looked about to protest, but the next soul had already moved to the booth. She shrugged and continued toward the gate. Tilly wondered at the question of relatives. How could they remember anyone when everyone in Between arrived without a clue who they were? Maybe the souls assigned to Heaven were allowed to keep their memories.

"Who is that guy?" Tilly asked Luke, pointing to the booth. She whispered, not wanting to make too much noise in such a quiet place.

"Oh, that's Peter," Luke said, louder than Tilly would've preferred. "He's a gas. Aren't ya, Pete?" he called.

The man grinned and waved at Luke, who waved back. "Old Pete's been guarding this gate for eons."

"You mean Saint Peter?" Tilly asked. She had a hard time believing the man before her—who was now leaning over in his chair scratching at some body part that Tilly didn't want to think about—could be a saint.

"That's the one." Luke beamed. He sauntered over to the booth to chat with his old pal.

"Not what you expected, is it?" Naveen asked.

She shook her head.

"Heaven isn't as popular anymore, so they don't see the need to keep up appearances."

"No kidding," she muttered.

Tilly felt his presence before she saw him. Something felt off. Was it her imagination, or did a shadow seem to fall over the platform? A shiver crept down her spine and she turned toward the gate. Walking out as if he owned the place was Death. He was frowning, head down and fists clenched at his sides. He glanced up and saw Tilly and Naveen. With effort, he composed his mouth into his standard grin and walked over to them.

"Hello there, Naveen," Death said when he reached them. "How's the little experiment coming? Enjoying yourself?"

Naveen stared straight ahead, ignoring him.

"What do you want?" Tilly asked.

Death looked surprised she'd spoken. "Well, hello, dearie, I didn't see you standing there." He slid his eyes over Tilly's body, as if he were searching for something. Tilly imagined she could feel hands touching her wherever he looked and she shuddered.

"What are you doing here?" Naveen asked.

Death tore his eyes away from Tilly, slowly, as if she fascinated him and it was torture to look away. "Oh, I just got out of a meeting with your brother," he said. "He says to say hello." Death let out a low chuckle.

"I highly doubt that."

"I wouldn't if I were you," Death said. "He thinks about you a lot. Asks how you're doing. What you're doing." His eyes bounced off Tilly again, then back to Naveen. "Nothing too interesting, I hope?"

"Just my job," Naveen said. He'd taken to staring at the gate again. The last soul they'd brought was checked in. "Looks like I'd better get back to it."

"Such a shame. I so enjoy our little chats." Death shot one more glance at Tilly, a flash of anger crossing his eyes, then ported.

XII.

Eris was waiting in Naveen's room when he arrived home. She was clutching a piece of paper, her face pained and uncertain. She gave him a halfhearted, distracted smile as he entered, so unlike her usual confident smirk that he second-guessed throwing her out immediately.

"What are you doing here?"

She looked down at the paper. A look of hate tightened her features. "Do you love her?"

Naveen knew exactly who she was talking about, but decided to play dumb. "Love who?"

Her eyes blazed red and she shook the paper—now wrinkled in her tight grip—at him. "Don't lie to me, Naveen."

He held out his hand, but she refused to give him the paper. "You obviously think you've got something important there, so let's get to the point so you can get the hell out of my room."

Taking a deep breath, she clenched her jaw and handed it over quickly, almost as if she were glad to have it out of her hands. Naveen smoothed it out and read the few lines scrawled there.

"Where did you get this?"

She shrugged and said, "Stole it from Death." She looked nervous: eyes darting around, worrying at her fingers. If he'd ever known her to cry, he would've expected it now.

He read through the lines again.

A powerful girl, scarred by fire and loved by death's old guard, will be thrust to the forefront of a new coup. She will have to choose between darkness and light, sacrifice and selfishness, love and hate, life and death. If she succumbs to the fire, hope is lost and all souls are damned. If she rises above, Death will be defeated and the old ways restored.

"This could refer to anyone," he said.

"It was the last in the book."

He'd suspected it was Eris who'd given Tilly the book and now his suspicions were confirmed. He couldn't quite understand the logic behind Eris's decision to give it to her —surely jealousy wasn't the main reason—but the whys didn't matter. The damage was already done.

"A return to the old ways," she was saying. "We have a chance to rule again." Her face was a mask of an internal struggle: a stiff smile, sad eyes. "Together," she added, whispered.

He thrust the paper back in her direction. "You know these things are purposely vague. It doesn't mean anything."

She didn't take the prophecy, just stared at him. He opened the door and stood back. "Besides, I wouldn't sit beside you again if my life depended on it."

She stomped to the door, paused beside him. "Maybe it won't be your life that will depend on it." She eyed him for a moment, then left.

He still held the prophecy in his hand. He read through it again. And again. It couldn't be talking about Tilly or him. He didn't love her. The idea was ridiculous. He couldn't even fathom what it would be like to love someone platonically again, let alone romantically. No. Love—at least for him—was impossible.

LUKE HAD ATTACHED himself to Tilly, insisting on walking with her when she'd said she needed to clear her head. She'd tried to make excuses, but there were really none to be made. She was stuck with his incessant chatter. She supposed he was trying to make up with her, after the club incident. Or perhaps trying to comfort her after the day they'd had. Or maybe he just needed comfort himself.

She halfheartedly went along with it—nodding in the appropriate places and saying the polite things—but her mind was on her mother. She found that the more she concentrated, the more snippets of memory returned. Her mother was wild, fun. She bought Tilly expensive things impulsively, took her to amusement parks, let her eat chocolate for breakfast. Tilly's dad always seemed to be scowling in the background, upset and glaring when they returned from their adventures. Loudly whispered fights from the bedroom where he threw around the word "irresponsible" and told her she needed help.

Tilly was contemplating how hard it would be to sneak into Heaven—she wanted a moment with her mother, as she'd truly come to believe that's where she must reside; there was no way a woman who loved life that much could be damned—when she realized Luke was no longer beside her. She turned. He was standing a few yards behind, grin-

147

ning at something down an alley. He nodded toward it. "Let's go," he said.

Tilly looked, but couldn't see anything. She knew what she should see—another bland and deserted alley with buildings rising from each side—but it was as if her eyes were sliding off whatever was there.

"Go where?" She squinted, but still couldn't bring her eyes to focus.

Luke grabbed her hand. "You'll see."

Her curiosity overcame the wariness brought on by memories of the last time she went anywhere with this boy, and she followed. As they approached whatever it was, she found if she avoided looking directly at the alley—instead casting her gaze slightly to the side—she could catch a faint shimmer in the corner of her eye line.

There was a change in the air, an unseen energy, like electricity before a storm. Luke paused, grinned again as he looked ahead, waved. Then an arm reached out of nowhere and pulled them forward through a thick but malleable barrier; it was similar to going through a port, but not quite as disorienting.

"Welcome to the Black Market," Luke said when they emerged on the other side.

The scene before them was bizarre, like a carnival. The alley was stuffed with tents and makeshift market stalls. Souls rambled about, busy wheeling and dealing with stall owners. Shrunken heads hung in the stall nearest them, the merchant calling, "Shrunken heads! Buy one, get one!" as they walked past.

"Are we still in Between?" Tilly asked as a haggard old woman lurched at her, brandishing chicken feet and a jar of teeth. She jerked back and Luke pushed the woman away.

"Yes," he answered. "This camp pops around, disguises

itself with magic. It's constantly on the move so the souls don't get caught and sent to Hell. People around here aren't exactly mainstream." The woman was back, this time offering a dead snake and a rabbit's foot. Sensing she wasn't going to go away easily, Luke reached into his pocket and pulled out a few of the red beads he'd tipped Carl with at the club. He exchanged the beads for the foot and the woman happily left, counting her loot.

"Why do you keep giving those beads to people?" Tilly asked.

"Currency," he said. "And they're not really beads. They're pieces of the Tree of Life."

"The tree that Naveen told me about? The one that connects the realms?"

He nodded.

"Is that allowed?"

"Technically? No."

A peg-legged woman wearing nothing but a bra and panties approached Luke and wrapped a red feather boa around his neck. She kissed his cheek, leaving a shockingly red smudge behind, and whispered something in his ear. He ducked out of the boa, holding her hands apologetically. "Not today, doll," he said to her.

Tilly's face must've shown her shock. He cleared his throat and chuckled sheepishly. "I may have been here a few times before."

Tilly smirked and rolled her eyes.

He stopped to talk to a young boy of about six. He asked him something Tilly couldn't hear over the sound of three women singing. She stopped and watched the women, entranced with their song. A small group of men lounged at their feet, looking up at them longingly. The women weren't speaking in any language she'd ever heard, but their voices conveyed deep longing and sorrow. It was a beautiful song.

Luke returned to her side. "Who are they?" she asked him, not taking her eyes off the crooning trio.

"Ah," he said, "the Sirens. You don't want to listen to them too long." He grabbed her by the shoulders and guided her down the alley, pointing out tchotchkes along the way. Tilly noticed a large tent at the end of the alley. "What's in there?" she asked, pointing.

Luke grinned. "The lady's got adventurous tastes."

A large man covered in tribal tattoos stood sentinel in front of the tent. Luke told Tilly to stay put and approached the man. They whispered something to each other and Luke pulled out a handful of the red beads and placed them in the man's hand. The man turned and lifted the tent flap, gesturing for them to enter.

Luke waved Tilly forward.

It was pitch black inside the tent, even more so when the flap descended. Tilly heard shuffling in the darkness and she tensed. She reached for Luke but felt only air. Her protests stuck in her throat as terror gripped her.

Then she heard the soft hiss of a match and a tall pillar candle was lit. The dim lighting illuminated the figures of three old women, one hunched over what looked like a spinning wheel while the others sat on their heels beside her. All of them had their backs to the door. Luke lit a few more candles and the room came into full view.

The dirt floor was covered in strings of various lengths that gleamed when the light caught them. Several piles of the strings were strewn about the room, shimmering like mounds of slithering snakes. The woman at the spinning wheel kept spinning, ignoring Tilly and Luke's intrusion. Every so often, she would stop and the woman sitting to her right would measure the string; afterward, the woman on the left would reach up with a large pair of shears and cut it, throwing the severed bit onto the floor.

Luke cleared his throat and the woman on the right turned to look at them. Tilly gasped. The woman was ancient, her skin so wrinkled it was impossible to discern any bones in her face. But the most shocking part of her appearance was her eyes. Or lack thereof. Her eye sockets were empty, more wrinkled skin filling them.

The lack of sight didn't seem to bother the woman, as she looked directly at Luke, then shifted her head to look at Tilly, as if she really could see them. "We have visitors," she said, her voice scratchy and hoarse like she hadn't spoken in some time.

The other two women turned toward them as well. None of them had any eyes. The woman with the shears stared directly at Tilly as she said, "Ah, the girl of fire. We know what you're here for." Her voice sounded exactly the same as the first woman's.

Tilly opened her mouth to respond, but was interrupted by the spinning woman. "The girl must die," she said.

Tilly cut her eyes to Luke, but he only frowned in confusion. "I don't know what girl you mean," Tilly said. She wondered if the women were senile and, if so, how to go about getting out of this conversation—and the tent—as quickly as possible.

Each woman spoke in turn, one sentence apiece:

"You know."

"The little oracle."

"Just like you, girl of fire."

"Before your time."

"So young."

They clucked their tongues at each other.

"But we've already cut her string."

They weren't making any sense. Were they talking about her or about Phoebe? "Before my time?"

One of them stuck a hand down into the nearest pile, plucked out a short string and held it up as evidence. The string was different than the majority. It shined more, and if the light caught it just right, there was a tinge of red.

"This is the girl's life," she said. The trio turned back to their work, as if they had explained everything.

The string was only a couple inches long. "Who are these women?"

"They're the Fates," Luke said. "They spin lives."

Tilly tried speaking to the women again. "What did you mean, about me?"

"Doesn't matter."

"Your fate was rewritten upon your death."

"The oracle's death is the catalyst."

Tilly's fists clenched. "The catalyst for what?"

A trio of chuckles. Then they spoke to each other in a round.

"She doesn't know."

"Probably better that way."

"Fire will call to her, regardless."

The tattooed tent guard opened the flap and stood behind them. "Time's up," he growled. The guard grabbed both of them by the arm and wheeled them toward the entrance.

"Wait," Tilly said. The guard paused. "When? When will she die?"

The women had gone back to spinning and didn't seem to hear her question. After several seconds of silence, the guard pushed them toward the door yet again.

Just before the flap closed behind them, Tilly heard all three women say, "Tomorrow."

"WHAT THE HELL WAS THAT?" Tilly screeched. They were back in the deserted streets of Between and Tilly was glad. The Black Market held an eerie air of desperation that she didn't like. Luke didn't answer; he looked deep in thought. "I'll tell you what that was," Tilly continued. "Nuts. That's what. They're nuts."

"I wouldn't be so sure," Luke muttered.

Tilly scoffed. "First off, Phoebe is a child, Luke. A child. She's not going to die. And second . . ." She trailed off. She was going to say something about her own death, but realized she didn't have anything to say. Hadn't Phoebe herself told her she'd died before her time? But that was a dream.

"Children die," Luke said simply. "One of my sisters was about Phoebe's age when she died."

Tilly shut her mouth tight.

"I'm not going to let Naveen take her soul," she said finally.

Luke pursed his lips and gave her a look.

"I'm not! Whatever it is her death is supposed to catalyze, it can just wait."

"You can't fight fate, Tilly."

"Watch me."

XIII.

Tilly kept trying to get Naveen alone to talk the next day, but he was more standoffish than usual. He refused to look at her and answered her in short bursts of few words. She was frustrated with him, but too busy to have it out with him in the middle of a street. They'd had some particularly rowdy souls that morning, and it was all she and Luke could do to keep them under control.

As the day wore on and they came nowhere near taking the souls of any little girls, Tilly began to relax. Maybe the old women were nuts. Then another thought hit her: what if it wasn't Naveen who would be sent to cull her soul? What if the Acolytes, or Death himself, did it? There would be no way of her knowing if that were the case.

Naveen had just taken the souls of two old ladies—best friends for over seventy years—who died next to each other in the hospital. Both had pneumonia. One died from the disease, and the other died from a broken heart a few minutes later. They had been friends for so long, they looked almost exactly alike, like when married couples begin to take on each other's mannerisms. Tilly couldn't tell them apart.

The women were regaling Luke and Tilly with a particularly raunchy story about Woodstock—which Luke was disturbingly fascinated with—when Naveen twitched and opened another portal. Tilly was beginning to understand his silence and twitching: he must be tapped in somehow, must know when someone was going to die.

Like she had every time he'd opened a port that day, she froze in momentary panic. She had no idea how to stop Naveen if Phoebe waited on the other side of the portal.

The trio plus the old ladies emerged in a rundown apartment building. Babies wailed through the paper-thin walls, and the one yellowed hall light flickered in an unsteady beat. The carpet was worn and a hideous green color one of the ladies called puke green, which the other took offense to because she'd had the same carpet in her house for years. As the ladies argued good-naturedly, they all made their way down the narrow hallway. Tilly relaxed a bit. She liked listening to the ladies' banter; it was calming.

They came to a door with a brass 1C tacked onto the front of it, but the C had fallen sideways like an upside-down horseshoe. They stood outside the door for a few minutes. The whole building seemed to hush, as though it was holding its breath, waiting for what would come next. Even the old ladies were quiet, their halfhearted argument forgotten in the tension of the moment. Naveen took a deep breath, and Tilly saw his hands shaking. Her nerves returned. She was about to ask him what was wrong when he suddenly opened the door and walked through.

The apartment was dingy and dark, tattered blinds drawn over the small windows. The air was stale and smelled of something sweet and sour, like vomit. Tilly watched dust motes float in the pins of light making their way through the blinds. There was a couch in the center of the room that looked like it had been salvaged from a dumpster. In front of the couch was a coffee table, every inch of which was covered in empty beer cans and what Tilly assumed was drug paraphernalia. The floor wasn't much better: a clear path in the mess allowed access to the small kitchenette, the bathroom, and a closed door that probably led to a bedroom. A man dressed in jeans and nothing else lay on the couch, passed out, the old television on and tuned to cartoons. He was deathly thin and had a large tattoo of a scythe on his chest.

Tilly was so relieved, she almost smiled. They had to be here for this man. There was no one else in sight.

"Hello, Tilly," a small voice said from the doorway. "I've been wondering when you would come back."

Tilly slowly turned to face the little girl. Phoebe was smiling as if this was purely a social visit from a long-lost friend and not the end of her short life. Tilly looked into those dark eyes, those eyes that saw so much, that seemed as if they belonged to a much older, much wiser person. Tilly's mind raced. She had to act now, before Naveen had a chance to move.

Phoebe's smile waned and she shook her head, slowly. "You will let me die, Tilly," she said softly. She moved into the room, calmly walking toward the windows. She stopped to peck her snoring father on the cheek. Tires squealed in the distance.

"Naveen, you can't do this," Tilly said, turning to him. She was about to say something else, but stopped. He was crying, silently but profusely. She moved to his side, placed a hand on his arm. "You don't have to do this," she whispered. He closed his eyes.

The screeching tires got closer. There was a sharp pop followed by several more. Everyone's eyes snapped to Phoebe. Then time seemed to slow. One window shattered and the blind flew off. Phoebe never flinched, but kept her eyes locked on Tilly's. She smiled, then her knees buckled and she began a slow descent to the floor.

Time sped up again. Naveen moved quickly, but not as quick as Tilly: she was at Phoebe's side before she hit the floor. She leaned over her, scanning her body, trying to piece together what just happened. Phoebe looked fine—no longer smiling, but otherwise fine.

Phoebe's father finally woke up and half-fell off the couch before catching himself with one hand on the coffee table, sending beer cans scattering. He mumbled and rubbed his eyes.

Naveen kneeled on Phoebe's other side and went to place his hand on her chest, but Tilly slapped it away. She glared at him. "There's nothing wrong with her," she said, low and menacing.

"She was shot, Tilly."

Tilly's brows furrowed. She frantically searched Phoebe's body again, but couldn't find the injury.

Phoebe coughed and a few drops of blood speckled her mouth. Then blood began to pool through her oversized shirt. Tilly immediately stuck her hands on the wound, trying to press down on her stomach, forgetting she had no power to touch anything without a pendant.

The man was screaming in the background, having finally noticed his bleeding daughter.

"I can save her," Tilly said. She couldn't produce any pressure, and the bloodstain grew larger.

Naveen shook his head. "No, you can't." He tried to put his hand on Phoebe again, but Tilly blocked him with her body. She leaned over Phoebe, almost laying on her, trying to protect her from Naveen and put pressure on the wound at the same time.

"She's suffering, Tilly," Naveen said. "You have to let me take her soul."

Tilly shook her head violently. "No," she said firmly. "You can't take her."

She looked into Phoebe's pain-ridden eyes. Phoebe gave a weak smile. "It's how it's supposed to be," she whispered, a drop of blood sliding out of the corner of her mouth and down her cheek. A cheek that still had a hint of baby fat.

"No," Tilly said again, less sure of herself now. Why couldn't she hear sirens? Didn't someone call an ambulance? Luke came up behind her and grabbed her by the shoulders, gently lifting her from Phoebe's side. "No!" she screamed.

"You have to let Naveen do his job," Luke said in her ear.

Tilly turned to Luke, burying her head in his chest. She watched Naveen out of the corner of her eye as he nodded then slowly placed his hand on Phoebe. Phoebe took one last gulp of air, then let it out in a peaceful and relieved sigh. Tilly screamed and beat her fists on Luke's chest.

Phoebe's soul rose from her body in an airy transcendence. She had a soft glow about her as she rose like an angel out of her physical self. She stood over her body, looking down with a nonchalance Tilly couldn't muster. Phoebe reached out and put a small hand on Tilly's shoulder. "It's over now," she said, her smile returned to her face.

Tilly grabbed her, pulled her into a hug. Phoebe indulged her for a minute, then wiggled away.

"Naveen, I'd like to be the one to escort her to Heaven," Tilly said in a small, drained voice.

Phoebe's smile evaporated and Naveen winced.

"What?" Tilly demanded. "Why can't I do it?"

"Tilly," Naveen said slowly, "Phoebe isn't going to Heaven."

Tilly scowled. "I don't understand. If she were going to Between, a tunnel would've picked her up and we wouldn't need to . . ." She trailed off as the implication of Naveen's words dawned on her.

"I'm going to Hell, Tilly," Phoebe said.

"What do you mean, she's going to Hell?" Tilly cried.

Naveen only shook his head.

The old ladies were in the room now, fawning over Phoebe. They chittered around her, admiring her beauty and lamenting her young death. In the background, Phoebe's father was beside himself, howling on the floor by his daughter. The ambulance still hadn't shown up. Tilly didn't know if he hadn't called, or if they were just taking their sweet time.

"But she's ten years old!" Tilly exclaimed. "What could a ten-year-old possibly do that would get them sent to Hell?"

Phoebe politely shrunk away from the women and approached Tilly. "I stole," she said simply. "Quite a bit, actually."

"You stole?" Tilly asked incredulously.

Phoebe nodded.

"Stole what?"

"Food, mostly," she said, shrugging. "Some money. You saw my dad. He's never been much of a provider. I don't think he ever got over my mother's death. He talks about her sometimes when he's stoned." She gazed at her father, who was still sobbing over her body, sadness and pity filling her eyes. For her part, Tilly could feel no pity for this man.

Tilly swung around to confront Naveen. "A little girl trying to feed herself gets sent to Hell? For what, surviving?"

Naveen's jaw was clenched, but he didn't respond.

"Can't you do something?" Tilly was on the verge of hysterics. "You're the God of Death! Put her back in her body or something!"

"I can't do that."

Tilly glared at him, fire in her eyes and her fists balled at her sides. She wanted to pummel Naveen until he was unrecognizable. She set her jaw. "We've got to go to Heaven to drop off the ladies. We'll just sneak her in there."

Again Naveen shook his head, but Luke was the one who spoke. "She'd never get past Peter. He might seem like a senile old fool, but he's sharp as a tack. He'll catch her for sure."

Tilly threw up her hands. "We'll take her to Between with us, then."

Naveen sighed. "We can't do that either, Tilly. Lucifer knows how many souls are collected every day. There's a tally of them. Pretty much all Lu does is sit in the palace, looking at the tallies and feeling smug about a job well done."

"The old prat," one of the ladies mumbled.

"Someone will notice if one's missing," Naveen added.

Tilly's mind was going a mile a minute. How could she keep Phoebe out of Hell? "Well, we'll just—"

"Tilly," Naveen interrupted. "We won't be doing anything except putting these souls where they're assigned. That's it. That's all we can do." He inhaled deeply. "Now let's go." He said it firmly, but his voice cracked at the end. He cleared his throat. "Luke, you take the ladies to Heaven."

"Um, excuse me," one of the ladies said, holding up an index finger, "but we would like to see Hell, if that's possible."

"You want to go to Hell?" Luke asked.

The other lady piped up. "Well not to stay, of course," she said, chuckling a little. "We've traveled quite a bit in our time—pride ourselves in being worldly, actually." She threw a glance at her companion.

"We like seeing new places," the first lady said, finishing her friend's thought. "Now we'll be otherworldly!" Both women laughed as if the statement were the funniest thing ever uttered. Naveen, Tilly, and Luke looked on, unamused. Phoebe giggled.

"They're funny," Phoebe said. "I think I'd like them to come with me."

Tilly glanced at Naveen, then quickly looked away. She was furious with him for not doing anything to save Phoebe from the depths of Hell. She didn't know what she wanted him to do, but trying something would be nice.

Naveen sighed. "Suit yourself," he said. "Ladies, we're going to Hell."

The two old women cheered and clapped their arthritic hand like they'd been told they were going on a free cruise.

THE LINE TO get into Hell was especially long. Despite his previous adverse reaction to the environs of Hell, Luke chose to accompany them out of respect for Phoebe. He stood rigidly in line beside the rest of the group, his face scrunched in a look of utter discomfort.

The old women were having a blast, acting more like they were in a tour group to see the sights than standing on the platform to Hell. "Look there, Bernice," one said, pointing to the heads impaled on the wall's spires.

"Oh, Violet, I wonder what you have to do wrong to get stuck up there," Bernice whispered with a hint of excitement.

They chatted with the neighboring souls, wanting to know what they were "in for." Some people refused to acknowledge their presence, but a few answered their inquiries. Tilly stared straight ahead, but kept her ears open to the stories.

"Apparently I coveted my neighbor's wife," one man said. "Once, a long time ago. I never did anything about it, barely ever talked to the woman. But I suppose it was some pretty intense coveting."

Another said, "I'm gay," and left it at that. The ladies gave him a sympathetic nod before moving on.

A woman chimed in. "I had an abortion when I was thirteen. My cousin raped me."

Soon a bunch of people gathered around the women, clamoring for their stories to be heard. All of them thought their punishment didn't fit the crime.

"I lied to my boss. Quite a bit."

"I worshiped money. Not like got down on my knees and prayed to a big pile of it. But I liked it. A lot."

"I had sex before marriage. I married the woman, and she's the only one I ever touched, but we still did it before we were wed."

"I was a Wiccan."

"I blasphemed."

"I was mad at my parents for beating me."

"I was proud of my work."

"I got divorced."

The list went on, and the women ate up the gossip,

nodding like bobbleheads and offering sympathetic responses. Phoebe listened as well, her mouth open in awe at some of the stories.

As Tilly listened, she got angry. She couldn't help but compare these people's stories to Richard Goodman's. Some of the sins were ridiculous. Some couldn't be controlled, unless the person lived in a convent or under a rock. Some only happened one time, years ago. It seemed unfair that these people committed one sin and were sentenced to eternity in the fiery pits. Sure, some of them weren't sorry, but some, like Phoebe, did what they had to in order to survive. Was it really sin to survive?

The line moved slowly. "How did you guys get to go to Heaven?" Tilly asked the old women. "I got the impression Woodstock wasn't exactly the rowdiest time you've ever had."

"Oh, we went to church every Sunday and gave confession. You have to ask for forgiveness for your sins, you know." The woman nodded her head with a look of intense seriousness.

"So I've heard," Tilly mumbled. If only all these people had asked for forgiveness. Or if they could get the chance to explain their actions. Like when Naveen was running things.

They were almost at the gate. Tilly could see Martha's half-melted face as she hurriedly checked off names.

"Naveen," Tilly said slowly, an idea forming in her head, "does Lucifer know who is coming through the gates on any given day?" He'd said there was a list of the damned.

Naveen furrowed his brows. "That's what the list is for," he said, gesturing at Martha.

"Yes, I know, but does Lucifer care who it is? Or just that it's a soul?"

"Lu only worries about the tallies. The list of the names

163

is kept somewhere, but no one really checks it after Martha and Charon let the soul in."

Tilly nodded, a plan forming in her mind and a knot in her stomach. Could she really do this? She looked at Phoebe, watched her giggle at something the old women were saying. She made up her mind. This had to be done.

"I'd like to check her in myself," she told Naveen. He gave her an odd look and opened his mouth, but Tilly didn't let him speak. "This is just something I have to do. On my own." Her tone was firm, leaving no room for argument.

Naveen nodded slowly.

NAVEEN STOOD BACK as Tilly and Phoebe moved forward toward the booth. He didn't like this. An uncomfortable feeling was growing between his shoulder blades. A tightening of sorts.

Something was wrong.

What was she doing?

PHOEBE PUT her arm around Tilly's waist as they waited in line. Tilly draped hers over the girl's shoulders and smiled down at her. "I'm a little scared," Phoebe admitted. "It's very hot here."

Tilly's smile trembled slightly. She was terrified. "Don't be scared, Phoebe." She leaned down and whispered in her ear, "I have a plan." Phoebe looked up at her with surprise and Tilly gave her a wink. They'd reached the booth. "I need you to stay back with the old women, okay?"

Phoebe looked at her with confusion, but nodded and

went to stand beside Bernice. Or was it Violet? Tilly still couldn't tell them apart. The women didn't know what was supposed to happen, so they didn't question it.

"Name," Martha droned. She didn't look up from her clipboard.

"Phoebe Walker," Tilly said, loud and clear, her voice thankfully not betraying the turmoil in her stomach.

"Theft," Martha said. She checked Tilly off, then finally looked her in the face. Her mouth dropped open, but Tilly fixed her with a determined stare and shook her head slightly. Martha's face lit up with a slobbery grin and she shrugged. "You know where to go," she said.

Tilly took a deep breath and stepped toward the throng trying to enter Hell's gates.

XIV.

Naveen watched Tilly send Phoebe away. Realization dawned on him. He pushed through the crowd calling Tilly's name. She looked back once, then hurried toward the gate. The crowd kept her from getting too far, and Naveen caught up with her. He grabbed her arm.

"Just what do you think you're doing?"

She spun toward him, her eyes flashing. "What's got to be done," she said. She wrenched her arm free and turned back to the gate.

This isn't happening, Naveen thought. *No. She can't do this.*

"You can't go in there, Naveen," Martha called. He ignored her. His chest was tight and he couldn't breathe. He lost sight of Tilly in the crowd.

Then she was in front of him again, her eyes brimming with tears. Relief rushed through his body. So she decided against this ridiculous plan, after all.

She brought up one hand as if she was going to caress his cheek, then thought better of it, dropping her arm before she touched him. Then the moment was gone. The throng of people pushed Tilly toward the gates like a wave. He reached for her, but she'd been sucked into the crowd. Panic crawled up from his stomach and choked him. He pushed his way forward, ignoring Martha's continuous screeches telling him to stay out, that he wasn't allowed in.

He couldn't port her out of there once she crossed through the gate. He needed to find her now.

TILLY STARED at the gates of Hell, letting the tears roll down her face, where they evaporated in the heat before they even reached her chin. The throng pushed and shoved. Someone jabbed her in the kidneys and she doubled over. The noise was deafening. Her body pulsed with it; her mind roared. She couldn't hear anything over the constant screaming. She imagined her very cells vibrating with the commotion, imagined she would vibrate apart and be left in a pile of ash before she even stepped foot inside.

Was it just her imagination, or was it getting hotter? She paused outside the threshold, taking a deep breath of hot, sulfur-filled air. She thought of Phoebe. She was confident Naveen would take her to Between with him. There, she would replace Tilly. She doubted anyone would even notice.

She took another breath, then stepped across the threshold into Hell.

MANIACAL LAUGHTER ECHOED over the screams of the damned. Straight from the Citadel, Naveen assumed. So Lucifer was watching.

Naveen's heart raced and he redoubled his efforts. He

kept pushing forward. Souls fell to the muck around him. He stepped on them, scrambled over them, smashed their heads into the sticky platform and just kept going.

He could see Cerberus's front paws now, and he thought he caught a glimpse of Tilly's red hair among the crowd. He called out for her. And then took one more step.

A port instantly opened at his feet and Lucifer sprang out, eyes boring straight into Naveen's. "And what do you think you're doing here, Uncle?"

THE HEAT BLASTED her in the face. People screamed all around her. Her skin felt as if it were melting off and her eyeballs sizzled inside their sockets. The giant three-headed dog snarled and drooled on her, the sole welcome in the land of the damned. His slobber crackled on her skin, threatening to burn through it. A scream caught in her throat as she pawed at the drool, trying to get it off her. The dog grinned above her, snorting his rank breath in her face. She fought the urge to vomit and whirled away from him, looking for the exit. She couldn't do this. She'd been mistaken. She wasn't strong enough to spend eternity here. There had to be another way to keep Phoebe out of here. The dog blocked her way, and even if he hadn't, the throng of souls pushing their way through the gates left no opening for escape. She was pushed back, further from the gates, from Naveen, from the relative safety of Between.

She cursed as she fell, knocked down by the maniacal crowd. The ground here was covered in more of the sticky goo that was on the platform. Her face smacked into it with a splat. An explosion rocked the ground under her as feet trampled her back. A loud roar went up. Was it a cheer?

Tilly didn't know, and couldn't concentrate. The feet were coming faster now, harder as they stomped on her back, driving the breath from her lungs. She began to panic. She sucked in great lungfuls of air every chance she could, but more goo than air got in. Her mouth was now filled with the stuff. Was this to be her eternity? Never ending trampling as she choked on the viscous fluids on the ground?

Drawing on all her strength, she wrenched her arm from underneath her body and wildly flung it straight up in the hopes that someone, anyone, would grab her hand and help her up. The tears came faster now as she struggled to breathe. Her arm faltered and she slowly lowered it, giving into her fate.

Right before her arm hit the ground, someone grabbed it, dragging her forward. The strain was almost too much for her shoulder; she could feel the joint separating as whatever kind soul trying to help pulled her from the crowd, but she didn't care about the pain. She almost laughed with relief as she was tugged into a small gap in the souls, a gap just big enough for her to pull her knees under herself and get up into a crouching position. She desperately dug at her mouth, retching and coughing as she tried to get the slime out. Gradually, she could breathe again and she wiped the tears from her eyes.

She was looking at the bare feet of a woman, her rescuer, the toes digging into the goo. Tilly's eyes slid upward, taking in the woman's filthy legs and tattered, knee-length white cotton nightgown. The breath went out of her again as her gaze settled on the woman's face. The wild red hair. The icy green eyes staring back at her, so like her own. If it weren't for the scar tissue covering most of her body, she could've been Tilly's twin.

The noise of Hell receded as Tilly stared at this woman.

This woman who shouldn't be here, couldn't be here. This woman who was smiling with such joy, Tilly forgot for a moment where she was.

"Hello, silly Tilly," the woman said, her voice cracking with emotion.

"Mom?"

The woman gave a choked sob and reached for Tilly. Tilly tried to stand, to be enveloped in her mother's embrace, but just as they were about to touch, she was blinded by a white light. Then the heat was gone, all in a rush, so quickly Tilly almost shivered with the relief of it.

The light receded and Tilly looked around. Her mother was gone. And she was standing on a gray-tinged cloud with a cherub cheerfully strumming a lyre on the next cloud over.

PARADISO

The seven became the God of the Sky, the Goddess of Home and Hearth, the Goddess of Love, the God of War, the God of the Sea, the God of Wisdom, and the God of Death.

The gods left the mortal realm of the World and inhabited an immortal realm, accessed through the sacred tree. They hid the tree with magic so no others could follow behind.

The gods formed a pantheon of rulers who watched the humans from the other realm. When it came to decision-making, no one god had more power than any other. They ruled peacefully and in harmony for eons. They visited the World often, taking on different forms depending on their mood. They gave the people knowledge and assistance when they were so inclined, and destroyed them when they were not.

Each culture had its own stories and beliefs about those divine beings. Very few of those beliefs were true. Nevertheless, the gods, wanting to be recognized, took the forms and names of the characters the humans had created when they visited the World.

As the years passed, the gods procreated and produced more gods and half-gods with humans. Sometimes, godlike powers would be passed down to these children, leaving them more intelligent, stronger, or more intuitive than other humans.

I.

"Let me through," Naveen told Lucifer.

His niece only smirked and reached for the overlarge pendant around her neck. Hers was easily three times the size of Naveen's, holding a bottomless pit of magic. The air crackled around them. Thunderheads appeared above their heads, rolling and churning. The souls around them ducked. Cerberus let out a howl.

Naveen reached for his own pendant, but when he felt for the magic, it wasn't there. He'd been porting too much lately, not using the Dome. His bead was depleted.

Lucifer must've realized what the problem was. Her smirk widened, her teeth bared in demonic glee. The air thickened with electricity. Naveen felt his hair move in response.

She couldn't kill him. But she could hurt him. Badly.

If he was going to fight her, he only had one defense. Thanks to the tree's supposed gift to him, he didn't need the bead to kill.

But she was his niece. He'd held her as a baby, had been there as she'd turned into a sullen, and often angry, teenager. She had gone insane long ago, but she was still blood.

Suddenly, Lucifer's brow furrowed and she cocked her head to the side as if listening. Lightening shot from the thunderheads in rapid succession, striking the souls again and again, as she let out a howl of rage. Lucifer spun on her heel, the lightning still crashing down around her, and darted through the gates.

Naveen scrambled backwards, calling for Luke. He didn't want to leave Tilly, but he was ill prepared to take on Lucifer. He'd regroup, get a new bead, and come back. Find her. Get her out of there. And then yell at her for the rest of eternity for doing something so stupid.

He was on his feet and running when a torrent of searing hot wind picked up. The storm of Lucifer's raged on behind him. The souls screamed in agony and fear.

He felt a tightening in the air. Cerberus howled again, then threw himself to the ground with a booming thump that shook the platform and caused Naveen to stumble. A second later, the air released its tension in a whoosh that knocked him completely off his feet. Bright white light lit the murky air of Hell in a blinding flash.

Naveen's world swam. His ears rang.

Luke was beside him, screaming something, but Naveen heard only a muffled sound. The two old women appeared, now looking far from excited to be on their little tour of Hell. They clutched Phoebe between them. Other souls and escorts stumbled around them, falling, scrambling to leave.

Naveen's head pounded, but his hearing was slowly coming back. He wished it hadn't. All he could hear was the deafening shrieks of a pissed devil. He was vaguely aware of a portal opening nearby, of a line of souls jumping through, of Luke handing the old women to another Escort and ushering Phoebe toward the escape. "Tilly," Naveen tried to say. He wasn't sure if it was audible, but Luke shook his head and said something that looked like, "Not now," before pushing him through the port.

DEATH WAS on a rampage in the World, harvesting souls with maniacal glee, when an Angel arrived to summon him to the Palace. He considered ignoring the order, something he'd never done before, regardless of who was in charge. It would serve God right, after how he'd treated Death's request to rid the afterlife of Naveen and his little girlfriend. The anger God showed at the idea was unprecedented, almost causing Death to cower. He hadn't, of course; it wasn't in his nature to fear anyone, even the gods.

The Angel was visibly irritated, insistent. Death ripped another soul out of an old woman with a ferocity that made the Angel turn away in disgust. Yet still the winged kiss-ass didn't leave. It was very important, he said. God needed his help.

The audacity. Anger flamed in Death's chest and he reached for the Angel. The Angel was too quick, launching into the air before Death's fingers could brush his arm. He returned Death's furious look with one of his own.

"You will come," he said. "It's an order." Then he was gone.

Death ported around the World a few more times, culling with relish, before he finally answered God's call.

When he'd finished the meeting, he emerged from the Palace smirking. He'd been right: Naveen and Tilly were causing trouble. If only God had listened to him earlier, he could have prevented this from happening—and he didn't let that fact slip by unacknowledged.

Lucifer, the perpetual brat, was upset about the soul count. Tilly's little stunt had left Hell short a soul, and it would have to be replaced. God had argued, citing the self-sacrifice clause in the rules, but Lucifer would have none of it. She wanted this soul, for some particular reason, and God didn't have the patience to argue.

Death's orders were to bring Naveen and the little human, Phoebe, to the Palace. God was finally in agreement with Death about Naveen, and was hoping Phoebe's soul would quench Lucifer's anger. Death doubted it would; he knew Lucifer had seen the prophecy. She'd been the one with the book for the past few centuries, after all. Tilly's soul was the important one. But before he could decide if he wanted to impart this knowledge on God, he was offered a reward in exchange for his services. It was what he'd wanted from day one.

Reincarnation.

TILLY STARED at the mostly naked baby sitting on the cloud next to her as she slowly realized she must be in Heaven. The baby was smiling brightly, playing the same few notes repeatedly on the lyre, wearing only a scrap of white cloth for modesty.

What happened to Hell? Where was her mother? She glanced down at her clothing—clean, Hellish goop gone.

"Hello?" she tried. "Do you know why I'm here?" She spoke in a soft, soothing voice, not wanting to scare the creature away. The baby didn't acknowledge her question, just stared at her with its plastered-on grin and kept playing the tune. *Maybe it can't talk*, she reasoned. *It is a baby, after all.*

"Shoo, you idiotic thing," a gruff voice said. "Get out of here."

The baby gave one last strum on the harp, then spread its tiny wings and flew away. Like a bumblebee, it seemed impossible that it could fly.

Tilly looked over the side of her cloud to see a very short, balding man waddling toward her. He was only slightly taller than he was round. "Annoying, aren't they?" he asked. He was wearing a white toga cinched with a golden rope around his plump belly.

"Cherubs?" Tilly asked.

The small man rolled his eyes. "That wasn't a cherub," he said. "That was what they call a putto. Commonly mistaken for cherubs."

Tilly slid off her cloud, which was a more awkward process than she would've preferred. Every time she put weight on one side, the cloud would puff up on the other. It was like being on a waterbed. The man watched her, bemused, with one eyebrow cocked and a slight upturn in one corner of his mouth. Once safely on the ground, she realized she stood at least a foot taller than the winged creature before her. "Are *you* a cherub?"

The bemused look evaporated. The man snorted and puffed out his chest while fluffing his wings in an irritated fashion. "I am not, thank you very much. I'm an angel. Cherubs have more wings and four heads. Ridiculous, if you ask me. You never know which head to look at when you're talking to them. Not that you would want to talk to them— they're meaner than a junkyard dog." He shook his head as he produced a small notebook from his toga. "You're Tilly, right?"

She nodded.

He stuck out a plump hand and Tilly had to bend over to shake it. "I'm Edgar, your Angel in Waiting. I'm here to put you in the right section of Heaven."

"I'm confused," Tilly said. "I was just in Hell, and now I'm here . . ."

"Yes, yes. The self-sacrifice clause. You took someone else's place in Hell; therefore, you are saved. Automatically. No questions asked." He looked down at his notebook again, mumbling, "Lucky you."

Tilly shook her head emphatically. "No."

Edgar scrunched up his face without looking at her. "I'm sorry? What do you mean, 'no'?"

"I saw my mother. In Hell. I have to get back to her. Do you have a pendant I can borrow? Or maybe there's an open port around here?" She swung her head around, but all she saw was an unending sea of gray-tinged clouds floating slightly above a mist-covered ground. In the distance she thought she could see something glittering in the sky. Something tall, a tower of some sort, but a second later a passing cloud blocked her view.

She looked back down to find Edgar squinting at her with his mouth gaping. "You're serious. You *want* to go back to Hell?"

"More like have to go back. I have to get my mother. She doesn't deserve . . ." She trailed off. Had her mother really killed herself? *She tried to kill you, too.* She shook off the thought. "I need to get back to Hell."

Edgar wasn't listening. He was shuffling through the small notebook and mumbling to himself.

"Did you hear me?"

"Oh, I heard you. Very unusual request. Unheard of in fact. I'm not sure what to do about it." He reached the end of the notebook, then started back at the beginning, flipping through its entirety once more. "Well, there's nothing in here," he said, snapping the book shut. "That means it can't be done. If you'll follow me, I'll lead you to your eternal home." He spun, flapped his wings, and levitated a few inches off the ground, hovering at Tilly's height.

Tilly clenched her fists. "Is there someone else I can talk to about this?"

"I'm afraid not. Please follow me."

She grabbed him by his arms. His feet swung erratically and his wings flapped at her face as he squirmed against her, but given her size, she had the upper hand. "Unhand me!" He tried to bite and kick her, but she easily held him out of reach.

"I need to talk to someone in charge," she insisted. "You will take me to speak with someone or I will squash you like the little bug you are."

He calmed, glaring at her and clenching his jaw. "I will take you to the Palace," he said through gritted teeth. "But don't expect to be granted an audience. No one ever gets an audience with Him." He looked forlornly at the ground. It was such a pathetic look, she felt a tinge of pity. She placed him on the ground, gently. He immediately kicked her in the shin. She winced, then bent to rub the injury as he crossed his arms over his chest and harrumphed.

"That's what you get for manhandling me. You'll think twice next time."

"WHAT HAVE YOU DONE WITH HIM?"

Death sighed. He was going to have to post an Acolyte outside his office door to keep this woman out.

"Who?"

"You know damn well who!" Eris screamed. "That home-wrecker is in Hell, and Naveen should be back here."

Death started. Naveen should have returned to Between by now, like the good little employee he'd become since his fall from power. "What makes you think I've done anything with him?"

Eris threw up her hands. "Everyone's talking about it. How Lucifer is on the warpath about her stupid souls and God wants Naveen."

Death sank into his chair. "What about the little girl?"

She paced, absently rubbing her pendant, and didn't answer.

"The girl is important. Is she here?"

"How the hell am I supposed to know? I don't care about some little brat—I just want my husband."

He cradled his head in his hands. It was one thing to lose Naveen, but to lose the girl? Lucifer would not be happy. Which meant God would not be happy. Which meant Death could kiss his reincarnation goodbye. His mind spun, weighing the possibilities. Where would Naveen have taken her?

He was vaguely aware of Eris's incessant talking. He waved a hand to silence her. "Keep looking. He's got to be here somewhere."

She retreated, throwing curses his way. He'd put a tail on her; there was no way she'd let him have Naveen even if she did find him.

Alone again, he told himself this wasn't a problem. There were only so many places Naveen could have taken the girl. The World wasn't an option: too easy to monitor. Heaven had security to keep unwelcome human souls out. So that left two realms—really, only one, since he doubted

Naveen would be hiding out in Hell. Not after his precious Tilly had sacrificed herself to keep the girl out of there.

He had to be in Between.

Somewhere.

NAVEEN SAT OUTSIDE A TENT, scanning the crowd of escapees, ex-deities, and fantastical creatures that made up the population of the Black Market. Phoebe was inside the tent, having insisted on taking a nap almost as soon as they arrived. Naveen couldn't understand how she could sleep at a time like this.

There had always been a Black Market, even when he ruled the underworld. It was much less populated then: only a few misfit souls. Now it was a whole system of underground living—multiple hidden bubbles inside Between, connections to clubs and other buildings in the World. He'd even heard there was a sort of underground railroad in Heaven and Hell, spiriting magic, souls, and ambrosia in and out. It was chaos, a representation of how out of control the afterlife had become.

He hated it here, and hated that Luke had thought of coming here as they'd ported. Of course he would. An addict was always an addict, weren't they? And Luke had had some intense times here.

To make matters worse, no one was giving up any beads. Even Luke's smooth tongue wasn't loosening the misfits' grip on their magic. The only thing they were giving up was a bunch of gossip. Namely that Death had placed some sort of bounty on Naveen's head.

Luke slid down next to Naveen, arms wrapped around his knees. "They agreed to let us stay for a while, but they're worried. If someone finds us here, they're all screwed."

"I need to go back."

Luke opened his mouth to protest.

"Shut up and listen. I'll leave you both here, and I'll go back and clear up whatever Death's issue is. Then Phoebe will be safe."

Luke shook his head. "Death's after her, too."

"That's impossible. Tilly took her place."

"I don't know why, but everyone's saying Death's looking for both of you. He's practically got an army of Acolytes sniffing around every corner in Between. And then there's the rebellion going on in Hell."

Naveen raised his eyebrows. "What rebellion?"

"Something about a prophecy," Luke continued. "Everyone's going nuts down there, I guess. It's making the folks around here nervous."

A powerful girl, scarred by fire and loved by death's old guard, will be thrust to the forefront of a new coup . . .

He had to get back to Hell. Somehow.

But for now, he needed to make sure Phoebe was safe. Tilly had sacrificed herself for the little girl, and Naveen could only imagine the reaming he'd get if he abandoned her now.

He sighed. "I guess we don't really have a choice. We'll stay here for now."

"HOW LONG UNTIL WE GET THERE?" Tilly had been walking for what seemed like hours, with nothing to look at but dingy clouds. She was getting impatient. Edgar hadn't said a word since he'd chastised her for grabbing him. And all she received now was an irritated grunt. She watched his stout body float in front of her, dipping violently when his small wings stilled. She smirked. "Your wings don't seem to be the right size for your body," she teased.

Edgar spun in the air, slightly unbalanced and awkward. He glared as he struggled to keep himself upright and in one spot. "Is that how you thank someone who is doing you a favor?" he demanded.

She shrugged. "I don't particularly see it as a favor when you said your job is to take me where I need to be."

"This is Heaven. There are no *jobs*." He rolled his lips as if he had an unpleasant taste in his mouth. "How archaic. Jobs, work. No, no. We don't do that here." He abruptly stopped the intermittent flapping of his wings and lowered himself to the ground. He harrumphed as he began walking. Tilly wondered if he had tired himself out trying to fly.

"What do you call what you're doing then?"

"Volunteering," Edgar said over his shoulder. "Community service. Giving alms. Whatever you want to call it."

Tilly took small steps to ensure she stayed behind Edgar. She didn't think his fragile ego would take too kindly to her passing him up. And she didn't know where she was, but given the repetitive state of her surroundings, she wasn't sure Edgar knew where they were either. "Sounds like work to me," she mumbled. The comment was ignored.

Her mind spun as she walked. She wondered where Naveen was at this moment. Had he gotten Phoebe back to Between? Was she all right? Was *he* all right? His eyes had been wide with panic when she'd last seen him. She wished she'd had the nerve to finish what she'd started in that moment: a goodbye kiss.

Would he try to come for her, in Hell? Maybe her mother would greet him and explain what happened.

Maybe he could get her mother out of there. Tilly hoped by the time she got to wherever Edgar was taking her and convinced whomever she needed to let her back into Hell, the situation would be resolved. If she was honest with herself, she didn't know what she was going to do if it wasn't. Break her mother out? She doubted that would be possible. She could try to convince someone to let her go, but who? Lucifer? The idea sent shivers up her spine.

But I will if I have to. The fact remained that her mother didn't deserve to be damned.

Muffled barking interrupted her thoughts. The clouds around her were beginning to thin, allowing a slightly less obstructed view of her surroundings. Up ahead, she saw a massive field covered in thick grass a shade of green so beautiful and brilliant it almost hurt to look at. The clouds didn't sit low to the ground in this area, but were high in the deep blue sky, floating like perfect white marshmallows.

She smiled as she stopped to stare at the stunning beauty. But her smile disappeared a few moments later as she realized there was something odd about what she was looking at. The clouds weren't floating, but stationary, as if a child had glued cotton balls to blue construction paper.

"Well, come on then," Edgar growled. He was standing at the edge of the field, about to put his sandal-clad foot on the unnaturally green grass.

As soon as his foot hit the ground, he was swarmed. Dogs of every shape, size, and breed pounced on him, forming a wiggling pile of fur and drool. Edgar screamed from the center as Tilly watched in astonishment.

"Brutes!" he cried. "Get off me! I command you! Help me, you idiotic girl!"

Tilly briefly considered leaving him there to be licked for all eternity, but decided against it. She waded through the dog pile, reaching her arms toward the center as she kept her chin up and her eyes closed in defense against any wayward tongues. Feathers brushed her hand, but they were lost a second later when a Labrador's behind knocked into her hip and sent her sprawling.

"Hurry, girl! I'm about to drown in slobber!"

Tilly tucked her arms tightly against her torso and rolled away from the dogs. Luckily, they seemed more interested in the grumpy angel than a full-sized human, and she was able to stand without being clobbered by too many canines. She was, however, head-butted by a goat as she scrambled to her feet. It snorted and then ran around in circles, kicking up its heels. Her eyes followed it as it skipped off.

Rolling hills of grass stretched in every direction except the way they had come. Animals of all sorts dotted the landscape. Dogs ran in packs, playfully nipping at the heels of cats, who would sometimes turn and chase the dogs, yowling with delight. Goats chewed lazily at the grass, which, upon closer inspection, Tilly realized wasn't grass at all, but a sort of plastic turf, as fake as the clouds in the sky. Chickens squawked and an assortment of songbirds flitted about as a chorus of parrots asked for crackers. Every time they asked, a cracker would magically appear at their feet. Cresting the nearest hill was a clear plastic ball, about the size of a small car, filled to the brim with hamsters and guinea pigs, all frantically working their little legs in unison as they rolled. She could have sworn she heard them laughing as they careened down the hill.

In the distance, Tilly could make out a barn and silo painted a burnt red with white trim. Not far from the barn was the matching farmhouse, complete with a tire swinging from the branches of the huge oak tree in the front yard.

Behind her, Tilly heard several sharp flaps and a few

playful growls as teeth snapped together without meeting the target. She spun to see that Edgar had saved himself, and was now struggling to hover just out of the dogs' reach. He lost his balance for a moment, allowing one of the larger dogs to grab his leg and pull him down. The dog immediately began humping him as Edgar frantically flapped his wings, successfully scattering the other dogs with the motion and finally freeing himself of the frisky one attached to him. He floated above the dogs' heads and launched into a lecture on rudeness. The animals spent a few moments jumping and nipping at his heels, then they all abruptly ran away, bored with a toy that wouldn't allow them to chew on his wings.

"Thank you so much for all your help," Edgar said with exaggerated sweetness. He took a look around before settling on the ground again and shaking out his feathers.

"I tried," Tilly said with a shrug. She turned to look at the buildings in the distance once more.

Edgar continued drying himself, mumbling something about knowing better than to walk as he did so.

"What is this place?" Tilly asked. A Pomeranian barreled up to her and used her legs as a springboard to switch directions.

"The Farm Upstate," Edgar said as he launched himself back into the safety of the air. "The first level of Heaven. And one I obviously loathe coming to." He glared at a herd of geese as they flew around him. They honked in greeting as they passed. The wind from their powerful wings knocked him off kilter.

"You've got to be kidding." Tilly scanned the hundreds of pets surrounding them, frolicking in the fake grass. One mutt—a probable mix of beagle and a Lab—reminded her of a childhood pet. She stared as the mutt ran round another dog, yipping a high-pitched, ear-shattering noise. She remembered her own dog, Roxy, who arrived as a puppy, but had disappeared to "the farm upstate" within the first few years of her life. Her dad had said her mother was fragile and couldn't be concerned with taking care of another creature in the house, especially one as hyper as Roxy. But he'd promised he'd found her a nice home with nice people at the farm. Now she wondered if he'd really bothered to find the dog another home, or if poor Roxy had met a more sinister fate.

The memory was there in her brain as if it had always been. There was no flashing interruption bordering on hallucination. It was simply *there*. Tilly wondered at the new sensation. As she thought about her dog, other memories floated back. Simple things like her dad fixing breakfast, recess at school, her mom's long naps in the middle of the day. It was all coming back, slowly, but with more ease than it ever had before. Luke had told her she'd remember everything eventually. Had she been dead long enough now, or was there something about Heaven that was conducive to remembrance?

An itching feeling emerged between her shoulder blades, the kind of sensation a person gets when someone is staring daggers into their back. She wheeled around, expecting to see someone directly behind her, but no one was there.

Edgar was halfway across the field, his bobbing body headed toward the farmhouse. Tilly shook off her unease and ran to catch up, dodging animals as she went. As awkward as it was to watch Edgar fly, it was much better than going along in the glacial pace that came with his walking.

Edgar alighted on the farmhouse porch and shuffled to

the door. Tilly bounded up the steps after him, but as soon as her foot hit the top step, the floor gave out.

"You'll have to pay to replace that," Edgar lectured as he opened the door. He had to kick it a few times, as there weren't any real hinges attached and the crease where the hinges should have been was not worn enough for smooth opening. Tilly extricated herself from the flooring, realizing everything there was cardboard, or something akin to it. Behind the door, where she expected to see a front hallway, a living room, or some semblance of a house, was only another barrier of gray clouds. The buildings were fake, their facades braced like subpar props from a school play.

"None of it is real," she murmured in disbelief.

Edgar snorted. "Well, of course not. What did you expect, your granny to greet you with a homemade pie as soon as we opened the door?" He shook his head while Tilly tiptoed across the cardboard porch to avoid another fall. "What do mangy mutts need with a real farmhouse anyway, eh?"

He was right, of course, but Tilly couldn't help feeling that this was wrong in some way. Heaven was supposed to be paradise, and filling any of it—even an area meant for pets—with fakery seemed analogous to lying.

She followed Edgar through the false front door, turning back to look once more at the happy animals running in the field. They looked at peace, happy with their eternity.

Why, then, did she feel sorry for them?

NAVEEN SLEPT for the first time in ages. He'd come in to check on Phoebe and had sat down for just a moment. That was the last thing he remembered. When he woke, he jumped from the bundle of rags he'd been sleeping on and frantically looked around.

The tent was empty.

His heart lurched as he wrenched back the tent flap. He pushed his way through the crowd of peg-legged peddlers and souls so high on ambrosia their eyes had turned milky and they'd gone blind. He called Phoebe's name again and again, panic seeping into his voice. The worst came to mind: Lucifer coming in the night, stealing her away to Hell. He reached for the pendant at his neck, ready to port to Hell and save her. Somehow.

But the pendant wasn't there. He was confused for a second before he remembered he'd relinquished it on his arrival. In the blur between seeing Tilly enter Hell's gates and coming here, he'd forgotten that the payment for allowing them to stay in the Black Market had been all the magic they possessed. He hadn't argued since his bead was useless anyway.

Laughter. The sweet, lilting, innocent laughter of a little girl coming from the direction of the Fates' tent. He shoved his way through the throng, ignoring the "Watch it!"s and "Hey"s that surrounded him. They should be the ones moving out of the way. Didn't they realize who he was?

She was sitting outside the tent, cross-legged, playing with the strings of life at her feet. The Fates stood around her, smiling down with their blind wizened faces, a trio of adopted grandmothers. Phoebe saw him approach and grinned up at him, her eyes dancing with the uninhibited joy only a child can muster. His whole body relaxed. She was fine.

He said nothing as he took his place beside her; the Fates didn't acknowledge him, but he knew they were aware of his presence. They were aware of everything.

After a few minutes of watching Phoebe play with the lifelines—a fact that somewhat disturbed him as he wondered whose lives she was messing with—Phoebe said, "We're waiting on Luke; then I'll tell you what you need to do." Her tone was nonchalant, as if they'd previously discussed this, as if he'd asked her for a solution to the problem. He didn't know whether to feel awe or resentment at her announcement.

Luke strolled out of a nearby tent, followed by a djinn and a harpy. He shoved something in his pocket. When he caught Naveen's gaze, he said something over his shoulder, too low for Naveen to hear. The djinn and harpy nodded and walked away, laughing.

Aggravation tensed Naveen's chest as Luke approached him. They had a serious problem to work through, and there he was doing God knows what in that tent.

Luke reached down and ruffled Phoebe's hair. She giggled and pulled away, play slapping his arm. Naveen couldn't help but feel a little put out by the scene: Phoebe and Luke teasing each other, the crones watching with joy, the milling crowd of souls unattached from their assigned places. He felt as if he were drifting in a wide expanse of ocean, all alone, watching as a party yacht full of people scooted by, all of them ignoring him.

He cleared his throat and threw a stern look at Luke. Phoebe mimicked him, her face falling into mock seriousness as she made a show of clearing her throat. Luke stifled a laugh. Great, now they were poking fun at him. He clenched his fists and reminded himself that Phoebe was only a child.

"Oh, come off it, Naveen," Luke said. "Our girl here has already come up with a plan."

Phoebe nodded, her mock seriousness turning real. "I'm

going to dream," she said, simply, as if that explained everything. She went back to playing with the strings as Naveen looked on, bewildered.

"We have to see Morpheus," Luke explained, "so Phoebe can contact Tilly."

Phoebe nodded sadly, her attention still on the ground. "I tried to do it last night," she mumbled, "but it didn't work. I need help."

Naveen shook his head. "What we need to concentrate on is making sure Phoebe is safe and working our way back to Between." He waved his arm around. "We can't stay here forever."

"We're going to make sure Tilly is okay," Phoebe insisted.

"I'll make sure Tilly is okay as soon as I make sure you're safe." Naveen said this in his softest, kid-friendliest voice, but he'd never been good with children. And he apparently wasn't any better now, as Phoebe crossed her arms and pouted.

"I'm *going* to talk to Tilly!" she said.

Naveen looked at Luke in exasperation, then the Fates. No one was listening to him. "It's a waste of time, honey," he said, trying on his convincing voice again as he kneeled beside Phoebe.

She frowned up at him. "She saved me."

Naveen's heart broke. Luke glared down at him and even the Fates had set their jaws, their gaping eye sockets fixed on his face. "Fine," he said, sighing. "We'll go see Morpheus."

A PERMEABLE BARRIER like a thick smoky cloud separated the Farm Upstate from the next level of Heaven. As Tilly passed through it, she was overcome with a thousand angelic voices, singing in a language she couldn't quite understand. The sound reverberated through her, making her tingle. Their song was magnificent and mesmerizing.

They stood at the back of the gathering. Wings and naked muscular backs stretched for miles to either side of them. The angels bowed their heads while they sang and they swayed slightly as a group. The only other movement was from the licking flames in their wings.

The flames didn't look like normal fire: not orange, but more of a coral color at their base, with varying shades of pastels. The burning, if that's what it could be called, didn't threaten or consume anything. The flames were simply part of the wings themselves, almost indistinguishable from the individual feathers. Tilly brushed her fingers against the nearest one, jerking her hand back as soon as she grazed it, expecting pain to follow. It didn't, so she stuck her hand out again, this time holding it there longer and eventually letting her fingers wiggle in the flaming rainbow. She chuckled. The flames tickled. The angel whom she was touching glared out of the side of his eye and shrugged her off. He never broke from singing.

Tilly quickly withdrew her hand, embarrassed by her lack of control. She looked around for Edgar, finally catching a glimpse of him pushing his way through the much taller angels several feet away. She hurried after him and grabbed his pudgy arm. "Why don't we wait until the song is over, then ask them to move?"

Edgar pushed out a huff of air. "The song will never be over. All these imbeciles do with their eternal existence is sing their praises to God." He shoved the leg of a nearby angel. "Can you imagine? Singing for eternity?" He pulled out of Tilly's grasp and continued barreling through the chorus, his small hands clamped firmly over his ears. Tilly followed. They walked for at least a mile, which was slow going for all the bodies they had to push past. No one seemed to care they were there, nor were they even slightly accommodating in letting them by. The angels kept their heads bowed and sang their hearts out.

All the while, Tilly kept waiting for the song to end. As far as she could tell, the angels weren't singing the same tune on repeat, as there was no discernible break in the lyrics. Rather, it was literally a never-ending song.

By the time they broke through yet another cloud barrier, the awe had worn off and Tilly feared she would never be able to get the song out of her head.

They emerged in a field of tall amber grass and Tilly sighed in relief. She could hear the faint chatter of a million voices, but the infernal singing was gone. "Are we almost there?" she asked. A feeling of pure peace washed over her, but was gone a second later, and the normal impatient feeling returned.

"You wish," he replied, taking flight to look over the waving grassland.

"We have to be," she insisted. "If all those angels were singing to God, he's got to be close by."

Edgar chortled. "Would you want to listen to that all day? God put those suck-ups all the way out here so He didn't have to listen to them."

"This isn't funny!" Tilly exploded.

Edgar's smile evaporated.

"I need to get back to Hell, to my mother!" She took a deep breath. "I need to . . ." Another curious sense of peace filled her and she forgot what she was saying for a second. When she remembered, it didn't seem so important anymore. She shook her head.

"Something wrong?" Edgar asked. He studied her closely, a small upturn to his lips.

"I'm not sure," she said, her voice slightly slurred. Slowly, a grin spread across her face. Edgar returned the gesture with relief. "Where are we?" she asked dreamily.

"Let me show you." Edgar pulled out his notebook for a moment, checked something, and then flitted away, gesturing for her to follow. She complied, a feeling of delight brimming inside her chest. She moseyed after him, dawdling to run her hands through the knee-high grass or to stare at the other people when she came across them. The residents of this area were many, but spread out across the wide expanse so they weren't crowding each other. Everyone seemed to have their own area of land, complete with their own small hut surrounded by a small clearing of trim green grass. They chatted lazily with their neighbors, their soft voices carrying weirdly in this open field; a whisper could be heard a mile away.

Sometimes Tilly would remember that she was following someone and looked around for Edgar, expecting to be chastised, but she only found him smiling as he watched her. He was much more at ease here, wherever here was.

Eventually, Edgar descended. He looked around, nodded his head in satisfaction, and said, "We're here."

"Here?"

"Yep. This is your assigned area." He waved his hand with a flourish toward a squat hut with a rounded thatched roof and dried mud walls. "And this is your house."

Tilly clapped in delight and rushed to enter. Her very own house. It was such a simple construction, and yet she'd never seen anything more beautiful, nor been happier. It was perfect. She beamed at Edgar. "Thank you so much. It's great." She grabbed him and enveloped him in a bone-crushing hug, planting a big wet kiss in the center of his bald head.

Edgar looked uncomfortable when she released him. His face turned a bright shade of pink as he cleared his throat, his eyes darting around, not meeting her gaze. "Yes, well. I'm sure you'll be quite happy here. Now I must be off."

II.

Morpheus was the God of Dreams and Naveen's grandnephew four times removed or something like that. He couldn't keep track. Blood relation or not, in Naveen's opinion, he was useless, a royal screwup who liked to monkey around inside humans' heads for his own amusement. He especially hated it when Morpheus would take the forms of peoples' loved ones in dreams, making them believe they were visited by souls passed, being watched over.

It didn't help matters that he traditionally lived in a cave all by himself, surrounded by poppies, rarely emerging. What can one accomplish by napping all day?

Morpheus had set himself up outside the walls of Hell, ostracizing himself from his fellow deities long ago. He was such a recluse that Naveen wasn't even sure if Morpheus was aware of the coup and the new order.

Remembering where Morpheus lived, Naveen saw a chance to forget this plan and get on with more important things. "There's the problem of getting there, however," he told Luke, gesturing at his naked neck. "We don't have any magic."

Luke's brows knitted for a moment in confusion before he realized what Naveen meant. "Oh," he chuckled, "he doesn't live down there anymore." He pointed off in the distance. "He's got himself a nice setup over that way. Secluded. Just how he likes it."

"Well, why did you have to wait for me, then? You could've already been there and back."

A sheepish look passed over Luke's face. "Um, well, I had to secure the payment . . ."

Naveen suddenly knew what Luke had shoved into his pocket earlier—a vial of ambrosia. He opened his mouth to protest, but Luke cut him off, holding up a hand. "He might not want it. I've just heard rumors that since moving out of Hell, he's become a bit of an addict. You're the backup." He said the last sentence lightly, almost happily, as if it was supposed to make Naveen feel better.

Naveen glanced at Phoebe, noticing she'd given up playing and was listening to the conversation with intense interest, her eyes wide with hope.

"There aren't exactly many gods running around here," Luke continued, still in convincing mode, "so he might just forget the payment and let us in because you're with us."

Supposedly only gods could get in to see Morpheus. Naveen had never tested the theory, despite living next door to the man for eons. He glared at Luke. "And what will you do with it if I get us in?"

Luke looked hurt. "You know I'm done with that."

"Then you'll get rid of it."

He nodded. Naveen would've believed him if he hadn't swallowed hard while nodding, but he decided to let it go for now. He just wanted to get this little field trip over with.

Morpheus's tent was situated as far from the rest of the Black Market as magic would allow. He'd set up a crude little fence around it. Naveen almost laughed at the weak security measure. In Hell, Morpheus had had two bodies of water to keep people out: the Rivers of Forgetfulness and Oblivion. They were more like moats than rivers, but otherwise lived up to their names. If someone happened to have enough luck to get through those, they faced two large guards at the entrance to his cave: monsters who had the uncanny ability to read peoples' worst fears and appear as such. The creatures were one of the reasons Naveen had never visited the dream god: he was never keen on seeing what his most base fear was.

As they approached, Phoebe held back for a moment, looking warily at the tent. Not for the first time, Naveen considered asserting some authority and turning them back. But she composed herself quickly and marched up to the opening like she owned the place. Naveen couldn't help but feel a sort of parental pride in her bravery.

A hazy blue light lit the inside of the tent. Naveen couldn't figure out the origin of the light. It was like perpetual twilight, fitting for the king of dreams. Morpheus rose from a low chaise lounge as they entered; it was the only object in the room. His hair stuck up in all directions, permanent bedhead, and he wore a pair of dark pants that looked suspiciously like pajamas. Draped over his shoulders was a long navy blue cloak covered in stars that shimmered as he moved. It was all a little too on the nose for Naveen.

"God of the Dead," he drawled. Everything the man said sounded as if he were half asleep, a trait that made any conversation of significant length torturous. "Welcome." He gestured around as if there were other furnishings or people in the room. Naveen wondered if in Morpheus's eyes, there were.

"Doesn't look like we'll need payment," Luke whispered in Naveen's ear.

Morpheus paused, swaying a bit, his head nodding toward his chest. Naveen snapped his fingers and he jerked. "Yes, God of the Dead, welcome."

"We've already been through that," Naveen said. "We need your help."

Morpheus nodded his head slowly, his eyes big and vacant like a cow's, either trying to stay awake or concentrate.

Phoebe stepped forward. "Mr. Morpheus," she said, "I need to use dreams to talk to someone."

Morpheus looked around the room, his eyes slightly wider in what Naveen assumed was panic. Or at least as panicked as this man could get. "Do you hear that?" Morpheus mumbled to no one in particular.

Naveen rolled his eyes. This was useless.

Phoebe waved her hands. "I'm down here."

"Oh, a little one!" Morpheus laughed with malicious glee. "Your lot make my job worthwhile. So easy to frighten." He nodded approvingly.

Phoebe glanced back at Naveen, a plea written on her face.

"Look, Morpheus," Naveen said, "this girl is an oracle and needs help communicating with someone in Hell."

Morpheus' eyes got even bigger—almost as wide as a normal waking person—and he looked at Phoebe with a newfound respect.

"She's been able to send messages through dreams before, but she can't do it now for some reason."

"Obviously," Morpheus said. "She's dead." He slowly

walked to his chaise and dramatically reclined, throwing an arm over his eyes.

"What do you mean?" Naveen asked, impatience creeping into his voice. He sensed he needed to keep Morpheus talking or the idiot would fall asleep.

He yawned. "An oracle can communicate through dreams only while she lives. I'm the only one who can do it in the other realms." His mouth curled in a smile of smug satisfaction.

"Well, then you'll have to do it," Luke snapped.

"I don't take assignments." Another yawn. "Especially from the likes of you."

"You will from the likes of *me*," Naveen said.

Morpheus raised his arm a bit, just enough to look askance at Naveen. "Very well, God of Death. I didn't have much to do today, anyway." He dropped his arm again and shifted on the chaise. "Name, please."

SHE RECOGNIZED HIM IMMEDIATELY. The wavy black hair, the tunic, the stance that exuded authority. He was standing by a wide expanse of a river, tossing rocks, their loud *plop* sounding methodically across the empty plains.

She called his name, or at least thought she did. He didn't turn around. "Naveen!" she tried again. No sound came from her mouth. She began to run, a loping gait that felt surreal, as if someone had hit the slow-motion button during playback. She giggled, and he finally turned, a wide and welcoming smile broad on his dark face. His arms opened and she flew into them, relishing their closeness, the scent of him—spice and heat. He kissed the top of her head, and she was surprised but pleased. She pulled away gently, blushing.

He took a look around, the smile never leaving his face. She'd never seen him smile so much.

"You don't seem to be doing too bad here," he said.

"It's Heaven, Naveen," she thought, twirling around in the tall grass. "Isn't it wonderful?" She stopped abruptly. "But you already know that, don't you?" An embarrassed giggle. "You've been here before!"

Naveen reached for her once more, grabbing her hands in his. He kissed her palms, one at a time. Tilly watched, entranced by his lips.

"Are you happy?" he asked.

She could only nod.

"Good." He turned to walk away, heading straight for the river.

When he had waded in up to his knees, she called out to him. She begged him to stay, but his only response was to smile and shake his head. Desperate, she waded in after him and threw her arms around his neck. She kissed him, lightly at first, then deeper, more urgent. He seemed surprised, but didn't pull away, quickly recovering from his shock and returning the kiss with vigor.

"Put it on lockdown!" Death bellowed. "No one in or out."

The two Acolytes in front of him shared a confused glance. "But sir, the souls will be stuck in the World," the braver one said. A woman. How he was tiring of women.

"The souls can wait," he spat, giving her a glare that would have wilted flowers. She hung her head immediately. He caught Eris sneering in the corner, her face a maniacal mask of pleasure. She always did like seeing someone reprimanded, the sadist.

He dismissed the Acolytes and sank into his chair. How could finding two souls be so difficult? Especially when one was as well-known as the former God of Death?

"We're going to have to get some help," he muttered as he ran his hands over his face.

Eris cocked an eyebrow. "Will they do it?"

Death shrugged. "God wants this done, and those idiots would rip themselves limb from limb if that's what God wanted. I don't think it would be too hard to convince them." They would probably jump at the chance; Archangels didn't have much to do nowadays. God probably wouldn't even notice they were gone.

"And what about Tilly?" Eris examined her nails, pretending to be nonchalant, but Death knew she was waiting for his answer with bated breath. She wanted Tilly gone just as much as he did, if for different reasons. She really needn't worry; he hadn't forgotten about Tilly. He just wasn't sure how to find her in Heaven without alerting someone who would ask a lot of questions.

"Did you have something in mind?"

She gave him a sidelong look and an impish grin. "As I'm sure you know, Michael and I have a bit of a past. I'm sure I could convince him to help us out."

She tossed her hair over her shoulder and tried out her best smoldering look. It wasn't bad. If Death were interested in that kind of thing, she would be at the top of his list. His mouth ticked upward. He knew there was a reason he kept her around. He just wished he could be there when the commander of God's Army dropped down on the unsuspecting Tilly.

WHEN MORPHEUS WOKE, he was grinning.

"Well?"

"You gave me the wrong address, but with my excess of skill, I was able to find her regardless." He looked at Naveen smugly, waiting for praise.

"What do you mean?"

He scoffed. "The girl isn't in Hell. She's in Heaven. I may have taken liberties with your visage, by the way, God of the Dead." He winked at Naveen. "You didn't tell me she had such a thing for you."

Naveen clenched his jaw, hoping that whatever Morpheus meant by that last statement was relatively harmless. He didn't need Morpheus encouraging Tilly's little crush. But it was more than that. He realized with dismay that he was a little jealous, as well.

A tightness in his chest he hadn't realized was there loosened as Morpheus relayed the contents of the dream. He felt like he could finally breathe again. "You're sure she's in Heaven?" he asked when he was finished.

"Of course. Now if you'll excuse me . . ." Morpheus reclined again and was asleep in seconds.

It made sense: Tilly had sacrificed herself in order to save Phoebe. The self-sacrifice clause was the only failsafe for a soul in the afterlife. He was relieved Tilly was okay. And also a little disappointed he would never see her again. Just like Hell, he couldn't cross the gates of Heaven.

The relief was short lived. Tilly may be out of trouble, but Phoebe wasn't. Lucifer was missing a soul. She'd never been a fan of the clause, always insisting on a replacement for the few souls who used the loophole.

That was why Death was searching for Phoebe. Naveen

looked down at the little girl as they made their way back to the Market proper. She was smiling. He frowned. Tilly hadn't wanted her to go to Hell. And Naveen was determined to see that she didn't end up there.

When they returned from Morpheus's tent, the Market was frantic—creatures and souls gathered, all talking animatedly. They hushed when the trio approached.

"What's going on?"

A tall man stepped forward. "Between is on lockdown," he said. "Death and his Acolytes are scouring the streets. They're close."

The bottom fell out of Naveen's stomach.

THE KISS still on her lips and the sadness of watching Naveen go still heavy in her heart, Tilly opened her eyes to laughter all around. It took her a moment to realize she'd been dreaming.

In reality, she was propped on a wooden stool in the corner of a large, rectangular room reminiscent of a log cabin. The floors and the walls were made of faded wood planks and the roof was domed and thatched with a tight interweaving of dried grass. Crude windows punched through the walls every ten feet or so, the openings uneven and mismatched and covered with some sort of transparent cloth. Large banquet tables ran the length of the building, which was so long, it was impossible to stand at one end and see the other. Meats, cheeses, and pastries covered every square inch of table, untouched. Along the walls, and shoved in every spare space to be found, were kegs. Hundreds and hundreds of kegs.

The room was packed. There were men seated at the

tables, tilting mugs toward their wobbly heads. Some of them wore furs, some armor, some uniforms. All of them wore a sad smile, trying to hide a haunted look, one that only appears in the eyes of men who have seen battle.

About fifty yards away, a large group of men and women were gathered in a circle, laughing and jeering at whatever was the centerpiece.

Tilly rose from the stool and tiptoed around a keg, looking for the exit. How did she get here? The last thing she remembered was saying goodbye to Edgar and entering her hut.

She paused, trying to remember why she'd been okay with abandoning her quest in order to stay in a crappy little hut in the middle of a field.

"Ah, she's awake!"

Tilly spun in the direction of the voice. A woman wearing camouflage pants and a tucked-in tan tee with her golden hair pulled back in a severe bun approached, grinning ear to ear. "Welcome," the woman said.

A man in a Roman helmet staggered by, trying to balance a pyramid of mugs. The woman grabbed two from the top and handed one to Tilly. Not wanting to be rude, Tilly took it with an awkward smile. She looked at the contents and gagged a little. The liquid looked and smelled like frothy orange-colored piss with flecks of something black floating around.

"Where am I?" Tilly asked. "How did I get here?"

The woman grinned and gave a sweeping gesture with one arm. "Valhalla. The resting place of warriors. You were brought here." Something squealed from the center of the circular mob and the woman quickly chugged her drink and wiped the foam from her mouth with the back of her hand. "Gotta go," she said, and rejoined her companions.

"Wait, who brought . . ." Tilly started, but the woman had already disappeared into the crowd. Tilly plopped her still-full mug down in front of a man sitting at the nearest table. He looked up at her with a crooked smile of gratitude. She nodded at him, but had to look away as he drank the foul stuff.

There was no door in sight. She thought about walking the length of the room. But that would require pushing through gobs of people for who knows how long. She wanted to get out as soon as possible. Would it be possible to squeeze through one of the windows? She approached the nearest one, eyeballing the width and comparing it to her hips. If she shimmied just right, she might be able to make it through. Grabbing a corner of the cloth covering the opening, she tugged.

The tip of a sword appeared at her neck. She froze.

"You don't want to do that, love." Her eyes followed the blade to its owner's face. He was a young man, with long hair and an even longer beard. A shaved man, dressed in a loincloth and sporting more piercings than Tilly could count, stood beside him.

"W-why not?" Tilly stammered. The man leered and shared a look with the man beside him. They both looked Tilly up and down, their gaze sliding slowly over her body. Her fear evaporated and was replaced with irritation. She swatted the sword away from her neck. She was already dead. What could it do to her?

"Unhand me, you brute!" a familiar voice called from the center of the crowd. Was that Edgar? She pushed through the two men in front of her, giving the bearded one a glare as she passed. He hooted in laughter.

"Edgar?" she called.

"Tilly! Oh, thank God. Save me from these imbeciles!"

What was he doing here? She specifically remembered saying goodbye to him and watching him fly away. She shoved through the crowd. Edgar was the centerpiece, strung up by his round little ankles, dangling over a cauldron of boiling water, his toga flopping around his head. A muscular man was systematically plucking feathers from his wings and dropping them into the water. Edgar jerked every time one was removed, swinging slightly away, only to swing straight back to the man's waiting hands.

"Edgar! Get him down from there!" Tilly demanded.

The crowd laughed. "But we caught us an angel," someone called.

"Yeah, we're gonna have some fun!"

"Boiled angel for dinner!"

A cacophony of laughter exploded through the room. Tilly looked around in disbelief. "Get him down," she insisted. "Now."

The uniformed woman from earlier appeared at her side. "Now why would you want that after he tried to trick you?"

"Tried to trick me? Edgar was taking me to see God." Even as the words came out of her mouth, she knew they weren't true. He'd led her to the hut, not to God. Then he'd left her there.

Edgar nodded vigorously and batted the toga out of his face as he swung. "See, see, I was helping her!"

Jeers abounded.

The uniformed woman put her arm around Tilly's shoulder. "Let me show you something," she said. She led Tilly to a window. "Look out there."

Tilly obliged, but saw nothing she wasn't already aware of: the grass, the huts, the people lazing about. "What am I supposed to be seeing?"

"Look closer. Pay attention."

She sighed, but looked. At first she saw nothing unusual, but upon closer inspection, the serene scene began to degrade. There were dead spots in the grass. The huts were crude and falling apart. The people who had seemed so peaceful and chatty weren't interacting with their neighbors, but lying around babbling to no one, to the air.

She looked back at the woman, her eyes wide with surprise. The woman nodded. "It's the pollen," she said.

"They're drugged?"

"Yes and no. The pollen induces a sort of calm. Peace, if you will. The Fields are the most populated area in Heaven, and a certain amount of control is needed to keep the masses happy."

Tilly thought of the drinks in the club Luke had taken her to, how she could have easily been lost to the drugged cocktail. This was eerily similar. "They'll just be numb and stupid forever?"

"They're not numb, exactly. They're at peace. There's a difference. These people still have thoughts, but they're not worried about anything anymore. Nothing seems important or urgent."

Tilly stomped back to Edgar. "Were you ever going to take me to see God?"

He slumped as much as one can while dangling upside down. "I wanted you to realize you didn't need to see God. If you just stayed in the Fields, where you belong, you would be at peace. Happy for eternity. Isn't that what Heaven is about?"

The room had gone silent, everyone's eyes on Tilly. They had a mournful look about them, as if what Edgar said was what they'd all hoped for and been denied.

"I want to get to Hell, and to do that I have to see God,"

Tilly said. A wave of murmurs floated through the crowd. "You told me you would take me to Him. You lied." She spun away from him and crossed her arms. "I would like to leave, please," she said to no one in particular.

"You can't just leave me here!" Edgar whined. "They're going to boil me!"

"You're already dead, Edgar," Tilly said.

He huffed. "That doesn't mean it won't feel unpleasant."

She stepped forward and the crowd parted to let her pass.

"And what are they going to do with me afterward?" Edgar called after her. "Torture is what this is, you know. You wouldn't let an innocent person be tortured! I know that from your file. You saved that little girl from going to Hell!"

Tilly was at his side in an instant. "You don't know anything," she spat. She couldn't save Phoebe. From Hell, maybe—hopefully—but not from death. And she couldn't save her mother the first time around, and now that Tilly knew where her mother was, she didn't know how to save her now. She couldn't save anybody, not when she was up against a room full of trained warriors, and not when she was up against the system of the afterlife.

Edgar looked at her, his face contorted in fear. She softened. Could she really leave him defenseless like this? And she still needed to get to God. She gritted her teeth and closed her eyes.

"Get him down."

The room thundered with boos and curses.

"Now, calm down," the uniformed woman said to the crowd. "She has a right to him, too. After all, she was the one wronged by him." She turned back to Tilly and lowered her voice. "The problem is, we have a certain way of doing things around here . . ." Her eyes darted around, a little glee lighting them up.

"What's that?"

"You'll have to duel for him."

"YOU HAVE GOT to be kidding! Duel? I don't know how to duel." Tilly threw up her hands. "And like you said, he wronged me, so I get him."

"We caught him, though," the woman said. "It's kind of complex. On one hand, the law says finders, keepers. On the other, there's an ancient right to defend your honor and seek retribution. It's a tricky situation, really."

Finders, keepers? Were they serious? Tilly rubbed her temples. Might as well get this over with. "Who do I have to duel?" she said with a sigh.

The woman grinned, the crowd picking up a chant around her. Tilly couldn't make out the words, as it all sounded slurred to her. The crowd parted in front of her like Moses parting the Red Sea, and a very large, very muscular, very drunk man stumbled forward. A violent map of jagged scars lined his body. He smiled crookedly, then drunk-walked toward her, grabbing someone's unattended drink off a nearby table and downing it in one gulp. He swayed in place for a moment, his eyelids fluttering, threatening to close. Letting out a large belch, he lurched in Tilly's direction, groping absently over his shoulder. After a few swipes, he still hadn't connected with what he had thought was in the sheath strapped to his back, and he stopped to frown. He tried to crane his neck around to look at the sheath, but that only succeeded in sending him into a wheeling circle until bystanders steadied him.

Someone handed him a sword, and he nodded with satisfaction.

Fear pulsed through Tilly. She was vaguely aware of a sword placed in her hand, the way a person is aware they are standing in a dreamscape but are unable to wake up. The heft of the weapon put her off balance. She adjusted her stance, widening the gap between her feet; it helped, but barely. She doubted she would be able to lift the massive weapon off the ground, let alone use it to defend herself.

All the while, the crowd roared with cheers and the drunken warrior continued his wobbly trek in her direction. Time had slowed almost to a stop in Tilly's mind, making each of the giant's steps comical to watch. She smiled nervously, turning to look at Edgar's dangling body. Edgar looked worriedly between her and the large man.

"Watch out!" he screamed.

She turned her head just in time to watch the giant swing his sword, the thick steel arcing through the air with the tried-and-true motion of years of practice. She jerked her head back as the sword passed by her, too late to avoid being hit, but it didn't matter. The man had misjudged the distance left between himself and his target and missed Tilly by a couple feet. The momentum of the sword pulled him to the side and down, sending him reeling. He flipped around in the air, falling backward. Tilly had time to register the surprised look on his face before the back of his head hit a bench. He laid on the floor groaning.

The crowd stared at their fallen warrior in shocked silence. Tilly stood stock still, stunned.

Edgar whooped, breaking everyone's trance. "You won!" he called repeatedly.

The crowd turned its attention to Tilly, confusion on most faces, amusement written on some. The uniformed woman cleared her throat. "Well, I guess you can have your angel back," she said. Everyone nodded, then dispersed, the noise level once again rising as they retold the story to each other, exaggerating to make the incident sound less like a drunken man falling and more like Tilly had risen up to slay Goliath.

Edgar wiggled impatiently. "Get me down," he whined.

In a daze, Tilly untied him. He flopped to the ground ungracefully, flapping his wings as he tried to avoid the impact. He looked like a sparrow with a broken wing.

They headed for a door at the opposite end of the hall, Edgar flying well out of reach and Tilly running through the events of the day in her mind. It all seemed ridiculous: Valhalla, dueling, pollen that drugged everyone into a peaceful stupor. "Wait," she said, jumping to grab Edgar's ankle. He squeaked in panic until he realized who had him. "I can't go out there." She nodded toward the door. "The pollen."

Edgar gave an exasperated sigh. "I told you, you'll be at peace in the Fields. Why can't you just accept your fate?"

"My fate?" Anger flamed in her chest and she laughed— a hard sound void of any mirth. "I wasn't supposed to be here to begin with." Phoebe's little face popped into her mind. "Fate can change. I've already proven that." She let go of his ankle and he bobbed in the air like a cork in water. "Now here's what's going to happen. You're going to take me to see God. No more tricks, no more lies. But first, you're going to give me your toga."

Edgar looked mortified.

"Don't make me take it from you."

"But I'll be naked!"

"After the stunt you pulled, I'm not sure I care," Tilly said.

His look hardened. Tilly sighed inwardly. Fine, she thought, we'll do this the hard way. She looked at the ground, hoping he would think she was reconsidering. Then she jumped, placed one foot on a pile of kegs and pushed off, launching herself in his direction, her arms spread wide. He turned and flapped his wings once, but it was too late; she was already on him. They fell to the ground, Tilly landing on top, feathers and spit flying as she tried to wrestle his clothes from him. He was squirmy, writhing and spitting like a cat. The edge of a wing slapped her in the face; a feather poked her eye. She jerked back, one hand still gripping the toga, the other covering her injured eye. Edgar took the opportunity to scoot away, wings flapping wildly as he took flight. A loud rip sounded and Tilly grinned.

In her right fist, she held a swath of cloth. She waved it at Edgar teasingly. He immediately looked down at his much shorter toga and cringed. He was still covered, but looked significantly less dignified, if a man in a toga can be considered dignified in the first place.

"I look like I should be walking the streets," he whined, trying in vain to cover his hairy thighs.

Tilly laughed as she fashioned her prize into a makeshift mask, tying it loosely around her mouth and nose, but making sure it gripped her chin and cheekbones. Satisfied, she stood. "Now we can go."

"Not so fast," a voice said behind her. The uniformed woman approached and held out a hank of rope. She nodded in Edgar's direction. "To keep your pet from straying."

Tilly thanked her and took the proffered rope. Edgar's face fell, but after taking a look around and noticing they were once again the center of attention, he acquiesced. Tilly knotted one end of the rope around his ankle and wrapped the other end around her wrist. "What about the door?" she asked the woman. "Won't opening it let the pollen in?"

The woman nodded. "Yes, but if you do it quickly, only a little will get in and it will disperse before it does too much damage." She smiled sadly. "Besides, some of our guys here like a little dose of it now and then. Makes them forget some of the stuff they've seen. If only for a second."

"Why don't you all just leave then?"

The woman cocked an eyebrow. "The same reason you don't want to forget. No one wants to be manipulated."

They shook hands and Tilly thanked her and wished her a happy eternity. She felt idiotic saying it, but what else do you say to a dead warrior living in Valhalla?

"Good luck," the woman said, then spun on a heel and picked up a mug. As they opened the door and slipped out as quickly as possible, Tilly couldn't help but think the alcohol was performing the same function as the pollen; either way, peace and forgetting was the goal. But, she reasoned, at least those in Valhalla had a choice in the matter.

THEY STOOD at the edge of the Black Market, looking through the thin membrane of magic surrounding the place. Looking through it was disorienting; the view was unfocused and a bit wavy, like looking through a glass of water.

The bland streets of Between stretched before them. No fewer than half a dozen Acolytes patrolled the streets, looking in every nook and cranny for the two lost souls they were to bring to their master. And those were just the ones they could see from where they stood; there would be dozens more scouring every corner of Between. Eventually, one of them would figure out that the giant area they couldn't quite keep their eyes on—the area which held the Black Market—was cloaked by magic. Then they would have them.

"You can no longer stay here." The man in front of Naveen stood with his jaw set and arms crossed, as an intimidating posture as he could muster, helped by the long, jagged scar running down the side of his face like the peak of a mountain chain. By the looks of him, Naveen assumed he was one of the many escapees from Hell that sought sanctuary among the degenerates in this place.

Luke had been trying to negotiate with the residents of the Black Market for several minutes while Phoebe played with the threads of life outside the Fates' tent. The group was divided. Some couldn't fathom letting Death get his claws into Phoebe, but the overwhelming majority feared for themselves, anxious about being discovered while harboring fugitives, especially since most of them were fugitives themselves. They had a good thing going here, away from the bureaucracy that governed the afterlife, doing whatever they pleased. Then there were the escapees, who would be sent straight back to Hell if they were caught. That obviously wasn't an option for them.

For his own part, Naveen was fine with leaving, but he didn't see how he could take Phoebe with him: it just wasn't safe for her. Not until Naveen had a chance to figure this whole thing out, to fix it. After Tilly's sacrifice, he wasn't about to let Lucifer get hold of the little girl.

"Your best bet," the man continued, "would be to turn yourself in."

"Let's just port out of here," Luke said. "Move the whole

joint. You guys do it all the time. I don't see what the problem is. We can keep porting until this dies down."

"We don't have enough magic. Zia is overdue with the supply and we can't go anywhere until she gets back."

They continued arguing, but Naveen wasn't listening; he was mulling over the options in his mind. They weren't far from the Escort Dome. Could they make it before an Acolyte spotted them? But where could they go from there? They'd catch him faster in the World than they would in Between. And even if they managed to keep from getting caught in the World, he had no magic. They would have to run like common mortals on the lam, hiding in dark places and constantly moving. It would be impossible.

The argument rose to a crescendo.

"Enough."

Naveen, along with everyone else, looked toward the voice: the Fates had joined them, Phoebe following in their wake.

"We will hide the girl here," one said.

Her sisters followed her in a round of voices.

"While the god goes to Hell."

"And the blond one follows."

Naveen scowled at them. All three turned their heads, their empty eye sockets trained on his face. "I'm not going to Hell," he said.

"Yes, you are."

"You must."

"It is already decided."

"She will need your help."

"You just said you're keeping her here," Naveen snapped. "You don't know what you're talking about, spouting off nonsense like the crazy old women you are."

"Not Phoebe."

"The other girl."

"The one with the fiery hair."

Naveen sighed and ran his hands over his face. "Tilly is in Heaven, not Hell."

"Not for long."

"Fire has touched her."

"Once fire gets a taste, it will call to you forever."

"She won't be able to resist."

"She will return to Hell."

"And you will return with her."

"It is already decided."

Simultaneously, all three turned and returned to their tent.

"I'm a god," Naveen called after them. "Your little strings have no effect on me!"

"Fate doesn't go away just because you're not in the World." Phoebe gazed up at Naveen with a hardness in her eyes, as if he had disappointed her on some deep level. It was a look far beyond her years. "Everyone has their part to play, dead or alive, god or human." The next words out of her mouth sounded more like the child she was: "Tilly saved me. Now you have to go save her."

She walked toward him slowly, frowning. He held out his arms to comfort her and to explain that Tilly wasn't in any danger. But when she came within reach, instead of hugging him, she held her arms straight out, elbows locked, and pushed him through the thin veil of magic keeping the Black Market hidden.

He had just enough time to register what had happened, and to see Luke stumble out beside him, before he locked eyes with a patrolling Acolyte. A malicious grin spread across the Acolyte's face. Then he called out to his brethren and barreled toward them.

Walking through the Fields with Edgar attached to her reminded Tilly of the weekends spent flying a kite when she was young. She'd had a large one in the shape of a dragon. She loved to watch the sun glinting off the myriad of colors that made up the dragon's back. The shimmering made it seem as if the dragon were alive, snaking its way through the air as it hunted the tiny people below. Her dad would fly it with her, running beside her in the field cheering her on while her mom would set up a picnic. A lump formed in her throat at the memory. Funny, she thought now, that she could only remember her mom being there once. She knew her dad had taken her often, so where was her mom?

She stopped abruptly, the rope tugging Edgar's ankle. He harrumphed as he fell toward the ground and began a litany of complaints. "Be quiet," she commanded. Her ears strained. She could have sworn she'd heard a rustling in the grass a moment ago. The hair on her neck stood up as she swept her gaze over the tall reeds. There was a nearby hut about a hundred yards off with a woman singing and dancing in circles at its entrance. That couldn't be it, though. The sound she'd heard was much closer, only a few yards away. "Edgar," she whispered, "get up there and tell me if anyone is following us."

Mumbled complaints began again, but he complied. He spun in the air with a dramatic sigh. "I see no one, boss."

Tilly rolled her eyes at the sarcasm. She readjusted the toga-mask on her face. *No one is there*, she told herself. *Stop being so paranoid.* But if no one was following them, why couldn't she shake the feeling of eyes boring into her back? She started walking again, but kept her ears open. They weren't far from the next barrier. They could run if necessary, maybe lose whoever it was in the transition. She shook her head, trying to clear her thoughts. No one would have a reason to follow them.

Even so, she picked up the pace. They were almost there now. Edgar continued his mumbled monologue from the air. She ignored most of it, only able to hear bits and pieces anyway, but he caught her attention when he referenced her being brought to Valhalla. "What did you say?" she called up.

"I said I'd like to get a hold of whoever plucked you from your hut," he growled back. "I could be back relaxing on my cloud if it weren't for her."

"Her? Do you know who it was?"

He snorted. "If I did, I would be throttling her right now."

Tilly smirked at the bravado. The thought of Edgar being able to throttle anybody was ridiculous. She'd already taken him down several times now.

"The savages in Valhalla kept referring to her as a her," he continued, "so that's how I know it was a woman. They seemed to be quite fond of her."

Tilly mentally kicked herself for forgetting to ask someone in Valhalla who had brought her there. Was it possible this mysterious woman was the one following them now? If there *was* anyone following them. Her attention turned back to listening, and Edgar was mercifully quiet, having finally run out of complaints.

She looked up at the clouds. In the distance, rising above the foggy barrier in front of her, she could see the glittering tower she had seen on entry. It was clearer now, a spire of gold shimmering in the light. Her brow furrowed and she looked behind her. Where was the light coming from? She hadn't seen the sun since she'd arrived. She struggled to calculate how long it had been since she'd been sucked out of Hell. Surely more than a day. Did she miss nighttime in her drugged stupor, or did Heaven's lands never darken? She squinted at the tower and realized it wasn't reflecting light: light was emanating from it. "That's where God is," she blurted.

"You are a little genius, aren't you?" Edgar said, laughing cruelly.

She yanked the rope, hard.

He lost his balance briefly and glared, trying to stay aloft while reaching down to rub his ankle. "If you're expecting me to put in a good word for you when we get to the Palace, you've got another thing coming."

"Just get me there, you giant bumblebee."

He sucked in his stomach and opened his mouth to retort, but they'd reached the barrier and Tilly went through before he had the chance.

"RUN!" Naveen yelled unnecessarily: Luke had already broken into a sprint. Naveen caught up easily, but quickly realized they were going in the opposite direction of the Port Dome. He tried to reach out and tug Luke in the right direction, but Luke shrugged him off and kept surging forward.

There were more than a dozen Acolytes in hot pursuit, a new one added every few seconds. Every turn they took brought them up against another agent of Death, but Luke never slowed, easily dodging and ducking into alleyways. Naveen would have been impressed with his street skills if he weren't taking them farther away from the Dome with every turn. He thought about splitting up, turning left and making a large loop back to where he wanted to be. Maybe the Acolytes would chase Luke for a while and allow Naveen to escape. If they caught Luke, it wouldn't matter, as he wasn't who they wanted.

Just when he was about to shear off in another direction, Luke skidded to a halt in front of a door with a faint triquetra etched into it. The shock of the change in pace temporarily confused Naveen and he hesitated. Luke quickly did an intricate knock and the door swung open. Luke grabbed Naveen by the arm and pulled him through, slamming the door behind him. Acolytes banged on the other side.

They were off again, this time weaving through sparsely lit tunnels. It wasn't long before a large crash echoed through the tunnels and Naveen knew the Acolytes had successfully managed to break down the door. They kept running. With all the turns, Naveen quickly lost all sense of direction, but whenever they came to a crossroads, Luke never stopped to consider which path to take. Naveen heard calls coming from behind them as the Acolytes split up to search the tunnels. They were getting closer.

They made a sharp turn and ran a few feet down yet another tunnel before Naveen realized it was a dead end. He called out to Luke, who hadn't changed pace. They needed to turn around before the Acolytes trapped them.

Luke shouted something in Latin and a port materialized at the end of the tunnel. They dove through to a long room with a red carpet running down the center. It was empty, save for two men—one large and black and one bald and squirrely—arguing over a clipboard. Their faces dropped in surprise when Luke and Naveen tumbled out of the port and onto the floor.

"Seal the room!" Luke yelled. The bald one didn't hesitate, rushing through the red door at his back. Naveen assumed he switched something inside the door, because the few ports that were open in the room closed a few seconds later.

When the man returned, his face was a mask of contempt. "Just what in the hell have you done now, Luke?"

WHEN DEATH ARRIVED, his Acolytes were huddled in a mass of black robes around a side door to one of the buildings in Between, all of them trying to hide behind the person in front of them. The door was broken, hanging on one hinge.

No one spoke, and no one met his eye.

Naveen and the little girl were nowhere to be seen.

He rolled his shoulders while he waited for someone to speak up. He already knew where they had disappeared to. The triquetra carved into the doorway told him that. Those idiot souls thought they could have secret hideaways without him knowing. He knew about all of them: locations, proprietors, regulars. Until now, he'd had no reason to bust them. He'd have to methodically search each and every one until Naveen showed up.

Despite the knowledge, he wanted an Acolyte to tell him what happened. He was getting angrier by the second. And impatient. It shouldn't take this long to find a god and a little girl. And he wanted—*needed*—someone to punish.

A brave Acolyte cleared his throat and stepped forward. Death was mildly surprised and proud at the same time. The man was a relatively new Acolyte; he hadn't had enough experience with Death to know he should feel fear.

"Sir, we lost the suspects."

Death almost laughed. This particular soul must have been a cop in life. He pursed his lips to contain the chuckle. The Acolyte took the gesture to mean anger and words began to tumble out of his mouth in an attempt to explain. But Death already knew what had happened, so he didn't listen. He simply nodded continuously as he slowly crept up on the man. The Acolyte was still talking as Death reached out a skeletal arm and placed his hand, gently, on the caped shoulder of his protégé.

The man disappeared, zapped into nothingness.

Shocked gasps all around. Death hadn't used that particular skill in quite some time, and he doubted most of the Acolytes before him knew that eternal life wasn't a guarantee. Not by a long shot.

He studied his nails as he spoke: "I trust this was a sufficient warning. I can always make more Acolytes."

THE BARRIER into the next area was one unlike Tilly had yet experienced. It wasn't the smooth transition, like passing through a particularly dense bank of fog, that it had been before. This felt like she was pushing her body through a viscous liquid, the molecules fighting back a little as she melted into them, then solidified on the other side.

She looked behind her and immediately realized why. This side of the barrier was a wall: smooth gray stone that looked carved from one giant piece. Even the floor and ceiling had no seams, meeting the walls with a slight curve. It looked as if someone had hallowed out an enormous piece of concrete.

Edgar's tether was still immersed in the wall. Tilly sighed and tugged until he popped through like a balloon. He was becoming more difficult as time went on. Who was doing the leading here, him or her?

He landed by her side, crossed his arms and glared around the room.

They were in a circular atrium, void of any décor or people. Passageways radiated from the center at angles, reminiscent of spokes on a wagon wheel. No breaks in the stone, no windows or doors. A faint odor of unused space hung in the air. A murky light lit the corridors, bright enough to see by, but only just. It reminded Tilly of the security lighting stores used when they closed for the night. It gave her the willies.

"Where is everyone?" She whispered the question, but it echoed off the walls, a thousand other Tillys lending their voices to a round in an eerie song.

In response, Edgar huffed and waddled forward, his soft-soled sandals making much more noise than they should have with their padding. He hesitated after a couple steps when Tilly didn't follow, looking over his shoulder uneasily.

"We should keep moving," he said, his eyes begging her not to argue.

His discomfort didn't help the growing knot of fear in

Tilly's stomach, but she followed after him, her imagination going wild. Monsters jumping out of hiding places in the corridors. Another band of misfits wanting to duel her. Fallen angels spitting fire and brimstone. Whoever—or whatever—had been following them using this deserted place as a prime opportunity to strike.

She hadn't seen anyone come through the barrier with them, but that didn't mean whoever it was didn't pass them up in the Fields and got here first. They probably had plenty of time to pick a nice hiding spot from which to jump at the most opportune moment. The idea that she was currently in Heaven, and that surely something couldn't attack them in paradise, didn't help ease her fear. She'd long ago learned her expectations of the afterlife were mere speculation.

When she reached the entrance to the nearest corridor, she paused, staring straight ahead. Was there something moving in her periphery? Her spine stiffened. She forced herself to stand still, concentrating every inch of her being into trying to make out the shape in the corner of her eye. She resolved to look, but quickly, like a child trying to catch sight of the monster in the closet. She poised to strike or give chase or run—whichever the situation required. Then she jerked her head toward the opening.

And saw nothing.

Nothing but the same stone and pale light that persisted in the atrium. There weren't even any shadows. Just a short hallway leading to another round room with a large orb placed in the center on a pedestal.

She chuckled to herself. How childish, seeing boogeymen around every corner. Although she could hardly be blamed for her runaway imagination, given the dozens of souls she'd escorted to Hell in the past several weeks, and then being in Hell herself, however briefly. She wondered absently if she had post-traumatic stress disorder.

"What is this place, Edgar?" She didn't bother to whisper this time, and her voice boomed off the walls.

He jerked at the sound, whipping around with his hand on his heart. "Don't do that!"

Tilly smiled to herself as she turned down the hallway, Edgar protesting behind her.

The orb was smooth glass, a murky storm of swirling gasses floating inside. Tilly circled it, ignoring Edgar's insistence on leaving. "If you'd tell me what this place is for, we could leave much quicker." She stood in front of the orb, tilting her head back and forth, watching the gasses change colors as she did so.

Edgar sighed. "It's the Observatory," he said quickly. "Souls come here to check up on the living they left behind. Can we go now? I'd like to get back to my cloud at some point."

Tilly's stomach lurched. "I can look in on people?"

Edgar nodded impatiently. "But you don't have anyone to check in on, do you? Your mom's in Hell. Remember your mom? The reason you're lugging me around Heaven?"

"Dad," Tilly murmured, thinking of kites and ties. The gasses swirled faster as she stared, increasing their pace exponentially. All of a sudden, they exploded outward and evaporated, leaving behind a fuzzy scene in the orb.

It was a bedroom. More specifically, her bedroom. The one she'd grown up in. The one that had been converted into a baby's room the last time she saw it. Now it lay empty, devoid of not only her things, but her baby brother's as well. The closet door was flung open, a couple bare hangers on the rod. Her father sat against the back wall, staring toward the door, a large bottle of liquor sitting between his splayed legs. He drank deeply as she watched. He was in a holey tee and sweats, both in need of a good wash. His hair was grease-slicked away from his face and he had a short, unkempt beard. He looked a decade older than she remembered him.

At the angle the orb was showing her, his glassy eyes seemed to be looking right at her. "What's he looking at?" In response to her question, the angle changed, showing her a closed door with black hash marks lining one side. Her height over the years. She'd forgotten that was there.

The door swung open and her stepmother's face appeared. Tilly noticed with some satisfaction that her normally shiny, perfect blonde hair was looking a little dull, she'd put on a few pounds, and her face was puffy, tear-stained, eyes raw from crying.

"We're leaving now," she said, her voice hoarse. "Think you can get it together long enough to come say goodbye to your son?"

The angle changed again, this time so Tilly could see both her father and his wife. Her dad's head lolled to his chest and he mumbled something slurred and inaudible. Her stepmother sighed and dropped her head too. "I wish you would see someone. You haven't been the same since Tilly . . ." She paused, unable to say it.

Her father's face jerked up. "We've already been through this," he growled, all traces of drunkenness gone from his voice. "I did see someone. Several someones. They didn't help."

"They were helping, though!" Tilly's stepmom's voice was high and shrill with emotion, exasperation. "You went back to work for a while . . ." She trailed off again when she caught the look of pure hatred in her husband's eyes. Tilly got the impression they'd had this argument many, many times. Her stepmother sighed. "I just don't know what happened."

Her father gripped the bottle tightly, his knuckles turning white. "My daughter threw herself off a bridge, is what happened," he said through gritted teeth. "My wife killed herself and then my daughter followed in her footsteps. And you expect me to pretend none of it happened."

Tilly felt sick.

"I'm your wife," her stepmom said, the whisper accompanied by a fresh round of tears. The woman held her stomach protectively, looking down at it in sorrow. Tilly realized with shock that her stepmother was pregnant again.

She couldn't watch anymore. She looked away and the mist in the orb immediately came back, mercifully erasing the scene it had displayed. Her heart ached with sadness for her father, what he'd become, the pain he was feeling. The pain she'd caused him. She clamped her eyes shut, willing the image of her ruined father from her mind.

"You're infinitely more interesting than you've led me to believe," Edgar murmured at her side.

IV.

Tilly walked in a daze down the hall and back into the atrium as Edgar prattled on at her side. Her mother had killed herself after all. Why someone would choose to do that in a house fire was a mystery.

And she tried to kill you, too.

Had she? If she'd meant to start that fire . . . was it possible she'd forgotten Tilly was in the house?

You know better than that.

"The thing of utmost interest is why you're here at all," Edgar was saying.

Tilly snapped back to the present. "What?"

"You should have been sent straight to Hell if you killed yourself," he said by way of explanation. Tilly didn't like his tone, as if he were discussing a scientific theory and not her untimely death, which she still couldn't remember. And she definitely couldn't fathom why she would've killed herself.

Edgar pulled out his notebook, rifled through it for a few seconds. "Here we go." He shoved the book toward her face, pointing to the center of the page.

Tilly focused, skimmed the page. As far as she could

tell, it was a list of everything that got a soul sent to Hell. And right where Edgar's chubby index finger pointed was the word *suicide*. Seeing the word written made her shudder.

He snapped the book shut and nodded with a smug look on his face. "You should have gone to Hell," he reiterated. "Obviously some sort of clerical error." His brow furrowed. "A mistake on an Acolyte's part, a tunnel malfunction, any number of things, really." He smiled. "But don't worry. We'll get it straightened out. I'm happy to take you to see God now."

They'd reached the other side of the atrium. A corridor wider than the rest yawned before them. Edgar paused at the entrance. He pointed up to the bit of toga still wrapped around Tilly's face. "As much as I love seeing you look ridiculous," he said, "there's no need for you to wear that anymore. The pollen only exists in the Fields."

Tilly cocked an eyebrow, unsure if he was telling the truth. He could be lying, trying to get her to remove the mask so he could take her back to her assigned hut. But then, he did seem morbidly excited about the idea of righting the wrong of her being in Heaven. She decided to risk it and pulled the mask down, letting it hang around her neck like a kerchief. She waited for even an inkling of peace to wash over her, a deep part of her wishing it would. She got nothing. The worries and confusion still reigned in her mind. She sighed inwardly. She was beginning to see the appeal of a peaceful stupor.

A KNOCK SOUNDED on Death's door. "I told you I didn't want to be disturbed," he bellowed.

The door opened anyway and one of his Acolytes stepped through.

Death gripped his desk, fury rising in his chest. An Acolyte ignoring his command was unheard of. "Just what do you think you're doing?"

"Sir, forgive me," the Acolyte said, his head bowed and his hands folded in front of him. "But you said you didn't want to be disturbed except if we found a lead."

Death stood abruptly, his fury giving way to excitement. "Well? Where is he?"

"It's not the god, sir"—Death flinched. Why did everyone still insist on referring to Naveen as a god?—"it's the girl. Tilly. You told us to keep tabs on anything having to do with her family . . ."

Death circled his hand in a get-on-with-it motion.

"And we've discovered that her father was accessed in the Observatory."

Death's mouth twitched. "How long ago?"

"Not more than half an hour."

The Acolyte turned to go.

"Wait," Death said. "Send me a copy of the Observatory feed."

The Acolyte nodded and closed the door behind him.

"Got you," Death said to the air, his mouth twisting into a sinister grin.

EDGAR WAS NOW FULLY ENJOYING his role as tour guide. "Of course I am not affected by the pollen," he was saying. "Not like other souls, anyway. One of the perks of being an angel. It's a nice reward for all the work I had to do to become one. There was a test and everything."

233

They'd passed through the corridor leading them out of the Observatory and into another atrium, more brightly lit but identical in architecture to the last, minus the corridors shooting off in all directions. Instead, conical speakers jutted from the walls at three-foot intervals. Each speaker had an angel's ear pressed against it. The angels were furiously taking notes on a clipboard.

"And this," Edgar said with a theatrical sweep of his short arm, "is Prayer Services." He bent to scratch at the rope tied around his ankle. "Incidentally, do you think we could remove this?"

Tilly glared at him.

"No? Okay, then. Doesn't hurt to ask." He cleared his throat and began an oratory in a voice more suited to addressing a large lecture hall. "As I was saying, this is Prayer Services. Here you find devices"—he gestured to a nearby angel—"to listen to people's prayers. The angels here take the prayers down. Someone comes from the Palace every so often to collect them and present them to the big man." He pointed to the center of the room, where a pile of papers the size of a small house sat. "Oops," he chuckled. "Looks like they haven't come to pick them up in a while." They continued to cross the room as Edgar continued his lesson. "At the beginning, God came here every day, but as the population grew, so did the number of prayers. It all became a little too much, so the angels took over. Someone filters them at the Palace." He glanced at Tilly, who was giving him a half-angry, half-baffled look. "I assure you, all the important ones get to God."

"I don't think some random angel should have the right to decide what prayers are important and what prayers aren't," Tilly said. If Edgar heard, he didn't acknowledge. Instead he launched into an explanation of the ins and outs of clerical jobs—or "volunteer work," as he called it—which Tilly fully ignored.

Instead, she focused on memories of her mother.

What she found, after a few moments of consideration, was the most prominent memories of her mom weren't of her mom, but rather her dad's reaction to something his wife had done.

She remembered running upstairs to her parents' room with toast and orange juice perched precariously on a breakfast tray, only to be turned away at the door by her dad. *Another one of Mom's headaches; best leave her be.*

She could recall her mom getting ready to go out, putting makeup on herself and Tilly; too much makeup. They would go to some interesting place with lots of people where her mother would laugh and dance wildly, forgetting Tilly in a corner. Then her dad would show up and take them home.

Other times, they would go on all-day shopping trips, a girls' day, coming home with their sedan stuffed to the brim with packages from upscale stores. Her mom would be ecstatic, singing loudly along with the radio, driving fast with the windows rolled down. Her dad would always return the goodies early the next morning.

She remembered late-night arguments, her mother screaming hysterically while her dad spoke in a calm voice. Glass breaking, thuds against the wall. Then crying. A headache would inevitably put her mother on bed rest for at least a day after the crying.

Her mom had been fun, erratic, moody, impulsive. The more she remembered, the sadder she became. Something had been off with her mother's mental stability, that much was obvious. But she still couldn't believe she'd tried to kill her own daughter.

DEATH FINISHED WATCHING Tilly's drunken father and turned off the feed, a sinking feeling of dread settling in his stomach. *Damn that man*, he thought. What luck, Tilly seeing this feed. When her father just happened to be whining about all the women in his life offing themselves. It was only a matter of time, now, before she figured out something was amiss. Before she began to wonder why she wasn't sent directly to Hell.

She should be in the Fields. Why was she in the Observatory? No one went there anymore. She had to be heading for the Palace. If she figured it out before she made it there, and if God granted her permission to enter, which was unlikely, but still . . .

Questions would be raised. The Fates would probably be summoned to the Palace. And those old bats wouldn't protect him. He'd thought it was odd they hadn't gone to God already, even after he'd promised to leave their precious Black Market alone. Then he'd realized they'd wanted him to kill Tilly, to kill all the souls he'd killed before he found her. They wanted the prophecy to come true. They'd probably laughed at him after they'd caught him snooping through the lifelines, pilfering those that shined more than the others, knowing those were the most powerful humans, the ones who had god blood in them somewhere. They knew all about him. All about the souls he'd culled and then made disappear into oblivion.

All about how Tilly's soul somehow fought back and his magic had failed him.

The bitches were culpable too, were they not? They'd let him go about his business, after all. They didn't try to stop him.

He inhaled deeply, willing himself calm. No matter. He knew where Tilly was now. Michael would find her quickly and dispense of this nuisance once and for all.

"WELL?" The stout man's shiny dome burned crimson with anger as he stomped over to Naveen and Luke. They both struggled to their feet as they tried to catch their breath. Naveen recognized his surroundings now: they were in the underground club where Tilly had had ambrosia. Which meant they were in the World. Which meant they were being monitored. Naveen guessed they had five minutes at best before the Acolytes swarmed the place. He started the countdown in his head and hoped whatever this little man did to "seal the room" could hold up to Death's minions.

"Luke, if you don't tell me right now why you've made me shut down my club I swear I'll have Carl string you up and I'll use you as a puppet to entertain my guests for the rest of eternity."

Naveen looked at the large man still guarding the door, who was now grinning and pounding his fist into his hand.

Four minutes, thirty seconds.

"Oh, come off it, Vernon," Luke said. He swung his arm around. "It's not like anyone is here anyway."

Vernon clamped his lips together so hard they became a thin white line. "I suppose you have something to do with that as well," he said.

"Yes and no." Luke's eyes swung to Naveen's for a moment. "We need your help."

Vernon let out a hard laugh. "Open the ports back up, Carl," he called over his shoulder.

"No!" Naveen and Luke yelled simultaneously.

Naveen took a deep breath and quickly explained their situation. Vernon kept a poker face as he listened, only breaking it for a second when he realized he had no customers because Between was on lockdown.

When Naveen finished, Vernon shrugged and spit on the velvet carpet, rubbing the glob in with his toe. "I don't see what this has to do with me."

Naveen looked at Luke for explanation, as he was also in the dark on this point.

Two minutes.

"We're going to need beads," Luke explained.

Vernon laughed again, this time with real mirth as if he'd just heard the funniest joke he'd ever been told.

"We don't have time for this," Naveen told Luke. "They'll be here at any moment." His head reeled as he tried to think of their next move.

"Do you think I would have actually let you stay if I thought Acolytes might be busting down my doors?" Vernon clicked his tongue. "You underestimate me, God of the Dead. My club is a safe haven. Little brother can't see you here."

Naveen was dubious, but this was Luke's world, not his. And Luke didn't seem concerned.

Vernon turned away.

"Where are you going?"

"You know I don't give beads away, Luke." He continued to the red door. "Everything has a price."

"And I've got it," Luke said.

Vernon stopped and backtracked, curiosity widening his eyes. Naveen was disgusted; what a greedy little man.

Luke reached deep into his pocket and produced the vial of drugs he hadn't needed to bribe Morpheus. The mixture might be part of Vernon's business, but it was hard to come by.

Vernon glanced at the liquid, then took a long, hard look at the both of them. He suddenly grinned and nodded, putting his arm around Luke as if welcoming a long-lost friend. "Come with me," he said and led them through the red door and into the empty club.

Unlike the first time Naveen had been here, the club was brightly lit and no music blared from hidden speakers. He guessed there was no need for ambiance if there were no customers. With the lights turned up, Naveen could see the dilapidated state of the room: the chairs were mismatched and wobbly; the floor was cracked, sticky, and littered with trash; the chandeliers that swung above their heads weren't metal with burning candles, but plastic with LED lights that looked like candles. Wires ran along the walls every which way, tangling together like snakes mating. The thought *fire hazard* ran through Naveen's head before he remembered most of Vernon's clients were dead already.

Vernon led them to the back of a club and into a small, closet-sized room filled to the brim with file boxes and random detritus. In the center was a desk and Vernon slid into the squeaky, rusted out chair behind it and rummaged through the drawers. Naveen and Luke scrunched together uncomfortably so they could fit in the room as well.

Vernon mumbled to himself as he tossed papers and junk out of the drawers and across the room. Naveen couldn't help repeating the words *hurry up* on a loop in his brain. He still wasn't sure Acolytes wouldn't burst in at any moment.

Finally, Vernon let out an "Ah ha!" and held out his hand to Luke. In his palm sat the smallest bead Naveen had ever seen. There couldn't be much magic in it; maybe enough for one port, but even that seemed doubtful. It definitely didn't hold enough magic to get to Hell, which was where Phoebe said they should go, even if Naveen didn't see the point.

From the look on Luke's face, he was surprised at the size as well. "What's that supposed to be?"

Vernon grinned wickedly before adopting a faux-serious look. "This is the size of the bead you get for the amount of payment you've brought me."

"You're joshing," Luke snorted. "This is quality stuff." He shook the vial in front of Vernon's nose.

The wicked grin was back along with an amused glint in his eye. "It seems to me you have no choice. You're not exactly in a position to negotiate."

Anger burned in Naveen's veins and he reached for Vernon's throat. He had the satisfaction of watching the little man's face contort in fear right before a loud alarm resonated through the club. He dropped his hands and looked around wildly. Vernon was already pushing past them and busting out of the room, cursing under his breath. Something about faulty wiring.

Shouts and sounds of a fight came from the other side of the entrance.

"How did they get in?" Vernon shouted. He fixed Luke with an accusing glare.

The red door swung open. Instead of the dark-robed Acolytes that Naveen expected, three figures of blazing light strolled through the opening.

"Archangels," Vernon breathed.

Naveen lost no time. He grabbed Vernon's clenched fist and pried it open. Vernon didn't put up a fight, as he was staring in shock at the entities in the doorway of his club. The bead rolled to the floor. Naveen was on it in an instant. He opened the port, desperately wracking his brain to come up with a place to go, a friendly place in the World. He couldn't think of anyone that would be able to help them.

The swirling sound of the port opening shook Vernon from his stupor. "My payment!" he whined.

Naveen wondered at the convoluted priorities Vernon held dear.

Luke threw him the vial as they jumped through the port and three angry Archangels bore down on them.

TILLY STOOD on the bank of a wide river, the quick-moving water crystal clear. The banks were packed with dense foliage: enormous twisting trees, a blanket of bright colored flowers. The overwhelming color made her feel she'd been walking through a monochromatic scene up until she left Prayer Services. Behind her was nothing but more thick forest, stretched out as if they'd always been walking through it and hadn't just passed through a barrier.

On the opposite bank was a golden wall emanating a light so bright Tilly couldn't look directly at it. Peeking above the wall was the sparkling spire, and now she was closer, Tilly could see a triquetra carved into the side. She smiled to herself; this was closer to what she'd had in mind the first day she'd arrived in Heaven with Luke and Naveen.

Tilly moved closer to the river. The widest part ran past her, like a moat, but directly across was a tributary that branched off toward the wall, where it ran straight through two golden gates standing wide open. She looked left and right, trying to spot a way across—a boat, a bridge. No such luck.

Edgar cleared his throat. "Excuse me," he said, pointing

at the rope wrapped around his leg, "but I'm not going into the Palace like a pet on a leash. Very undignified."

Already in view of the Palace, Tilly had no problem letting Edgar go. She quickly untied his leg and tossed the rope.

"So how do we get in?"

He ruffled his feathers and alighted, giving her a smug look.

"Well, unless you've got some fairy dust in that short little toga of yours, I can't exactly join you."

"A simple leap of faith will do," he responded before flying toward the gates.

"I hate riddles!" she screamed after him, but he didn't turn back. She paced the bank, mulling the idea of a leap of faith in her mind. If she jumped, would she sprout wings? Would a cloud magically appear under her to ferry her into the city? Was she supposed to pray? Was the river an illusion?

She stuck her foot in the water, hesitantly. A fish leapt up, startling her into jerking her foot back out. Not an illusion, then. She sighed. Edgar was now out of view.

A sound broke through the gentle rippling of the water. A loud horn, like a bugle, off in the forest. It was followed by several shouts. Before she had time to register what was happening, someone crashed through the woods behind her and shoved her, hard. She flew through the air, landing with a plop in the river, sinking quickly.

And all of a sudden she was drowning.

NAVEEN HADN'T BEEN able to help himself: the last person he'd thought of as he'd opened the port had been Tilly. Her grin and wild hair popped into his mind unbidden at the last second. He couldn't get a lock on anyone else.

They materialized in the living room of a house, blinds drawn, lights off. The only illumination came from a television set. The sound was turned down and a man was sitting on the couch in the center of the room, nursing a beer, staring unseeingly at the screen.

The bead lay impotent on the floor. Naveen snatched it up, hopeful it held enough magic to port them somewhere more useful.

It still retained an inkling, but not enough.

Naveen cursed. He had no idea where they were. Death could show up at any second.

"Where are we?" Luke whispered at his side as they approached the back of the couch.

He didn't respond. He was distracted on a skittering sound in the corner. He strained his eyes but couldn't see the source of the sound. Probably a rat. Was that a faint smell of sulfur?

"Archangels," Luke continued, his voice disbelieving. "What do we do now? Could we go to God?"

The man on the couch flipped the channels absently. Every channel was showing the same footage: the Pope speaking in front of a crowd of thousands.

Luke prattled on about how they would get to God until Naveen held up a hand to silence him.

"He won't help us," he said. "Who do you think the Archangels work for?"

The man settled on a station. This channel had a split screen, showing clips of mayhem around the world. Shootouts with cops and looting. Mass prayer sessions, tears streaming down the penitent faces. It took several moments for what he was seeing to sink in, right before a ticker flashed across the bottom of the screen announcing today to be the third day of no deaths reported globally.

He inhaled sharply as he watched the cops shoot a criminal, only for the guy to stand up and laugh in their faces. People were walking away from car crashes, beating each other in the head, bleeding out. But no one died.

"All Death's Acolytes are after us," he muttered.

Luke was watching intently. "They think it's the End of Days."

"Maybe it is," said a voice on the other side of the couch.

The man in front of them groaned in agony as a figure slithered up his body.

Naveen tensed, knowing immediately what it was. The smell of sulfur should have tipped him off earlier.

The demon's movements were sloth-like and jerky as he climbed to the man's shoulders and propped his head on the back of the couch. As he moved, the man began crying, silently at first, then with increasingly violent sobs.

Luke cringed and shrank away, moving to the far corner of the room, near the TV and away from the demon's gaze.

The demon grinned, if that's what it could be called. His mouth was slit at the sides, forming overly exaggerated lips curled down in a frown, the wounds still fresh looking and seeping with blood-tinged puss. He had three eyes: two where one could expect them, and one in the center of his craggy forehead. His skin was leathery and clung to his body, reminiscent of a mummy. A sub-demon, Naveen knew—one that possessed, but had no real powers.

"What brings you here, God of Death?" the demon asked. His voice was like claws across a chalkboard. "Come to watch the apocalypse, I suppose." He took a sucking, slobbery breath in through his gaping mouth. "Such a shame, to have all this come to an end right when I've found this lovely specimen to ruin."

He ran a clawed hand through the man's hair, eliciting a moan from the poor human. The man chugged the rest of his beer, then rummaged in the couch cushions until he produced a half-empty bottle of liquor. He took a hearty swig before settling down into his sobbing once more.

"Did you happen to think of Tilly when you opened the port?" Luke asked.

Naveen shot him a questioning look.

Luke nodded at the ruined man on the couch. "This guy looks an awful lot like her. Her dad, maybe?"

Naveen moved to look at the man. The demon never took his eyes off him, adjusting his small body to straddle the back of the man's neck. The image was eerily like a young child riding on the shoulders of a father.

The man's face twisted in agony. Snot ran from his nose to his chin. Dark circles framed his eyes. Every so often his head would snap slightly to the side, his mouth opening and closing quickly in a weird gnashing motion as if he knew there was a parasite attached to him and wanted to bite it off, like a dog snipping a tick from its skin. He was deathly pale, and Naveen wondered if the man would be dead if the Acolytes were doing their jobs. The demon kept up a murmured monologue into the man's ear.

When the man looked in his direction, Tilly's eyes stared back at him. At the moment they lacked the spark of light that blazed in hers, but this was definitely her father. Given the little amount of magic the bead had to work with, this must have been the closest to Tilly it could get them.

Anger flared in his chest. Hadn't Tilly been through enough without Lucifer sending this minion to torment her father?

"What's your name, demon?" Naveen demanded. He needed control of the demon and knowing its name was the only way to get it.

The demon shook his index finger. "Ah, ah, ah. You're not going to get me that easily."

How many minutes had it been? Death had to have a lock on them by now. He needed the demon's name. Immediately.

His mind churned as he tried to remember some demon names. He spat out a few, but it was no use: the demon simply laughed in his face. There were millions of sub-demons, and only the human host would know the demon's name. By the looks of this man, he was most likely too far gone to know even his own name.

Luke whined beside him: "Maybe we should run."

Naveen squeezed the bead in his hand. Maybe there was enough. If this really was her father, maybe he could get through.

The demon was watching him intently as he concentrated on the bead, drawing out what little bit of magic it had, sucking it dry. No godlike figure for him today, no crown or blue skin, no jewelry. He would have to appear as himself. Hopefully that would be enough to shock this man into lucidity.

When he became visible, the demon shrieked, causing Tilly's father to cry out. But those green eyes were on Naveen. Good. He had his attention.

He walked steadily to the man's side, aware of the time limit, but also unwilling to frighten this already addled mind. He knelt. The demon clutched at the man's head, fervently yelling in his ear. Tilly's dad closed his eyes as the agony rocked him. Naveen reached out and held his hands.

"Listen to me," he said, his voice calm but loud. He

246

hoped the man could hear him over the demon. "I need the name of the demon who tortures you."

The man's head lolled.

Naveen gripped his hands tighter. "Tilly."

The man opened his eyes slightly. Naveen sighed in relief. He might not be too far gone after all.

"Tilly was your daughter. Remember?"

An almost imperceptible nod. The demon shrieked louder.

"I know Tilly. I've been with her since she died. Concentrate on her. Her smile. That wild hair."

"Matilda," the man whispered.

Naveen nodded. "Yes. Your daughter. Concentrate." He could feel the magic wearing off. They were out of time. "I need the name."

"Matilda," he repeated. "Suicide."

"Not that name," Naveen said impatiently. "The name of your torturer. The name of the person whispering in your ear these past weeks. The name of the demon on your back!"

The man's eyes closed again. He convulsed and the demon yelled out in ecstasy. "I'm winning!" the demon shrieked and laughed maniacally.

"The name of the demon!" Naveen bellowed, now inches from the man's face.

His mouth moved sporadically but no sound came out. Naveen leaned in closer, the man's breath hot on his ear. "Say it again. For Tilly's sake, say it! Say it!"

The magic wore off; Naveen was invisible once more. He cursed, but kept his ear by the man's head.

The man's lips moved a second later and Naveen smiled.

"Isozal." Naveen said the name loud and clear.

The demon convulsed against the man's neck and dug in

with his claws. Hatred burned red in all three eyes. Tilly's dad screamed.

"Get off that man and open a port," Naveen commanded.

"Um. Do you have a plan?" Luke whispered.

Naveen did. It was possibly a stupid plan, but it was really his only option.

The demon slid off the man slowly, wailing all the while. Tilly's dad immediately sat up and looked around frantically. Not finding anyone in the room with him, he looked down at the bottle still in his hand. A disgusted look slid onto his face and he threw the bottle across the room.

"Where shall we go, *master*?" Isozal hissed.

"Oh, you're going home."

Another wail rose from the demon. A more muted sound came from Luke. Then the demon began retching and coughing, his body convulsing with the effort, like a cat vomiting a hairball. Finally, a stream of green bile flowed from his mouth, and with it, a bead. He opened a port. At almost the exact moment, another port opened across the room.

"Move, now!" Naveen yelled, grabbing Luke and pushing him into the swirling mass. He caught a glimpse of a black cloak as he descended, and hoped beyond hope Death would spare Tilly's father in his wrath.

FOR A SECOND, she sank. There was something peaceful about the water, something familiar about looking up through its depths, seeing light at the top, so far away —unreachable.

Then she panicked, thrashed her limbs, tugged the choking bit of toga from around her neck. Fish swarmed around her and something nibbled at a toe. She screamed and continued to sink, further and further down, past where the bottom should have been. A knot of dread formed in her stomach when she realized there was no bottom.

Then the fish swarmed and formed a tornado around her, buoying her to the top, their tails tickling her as they passed. She burst through the top and floated. The water seemed to be cradling her, guiding her body toward the tributary, and therefore the gates. She laughed a bit at herself, looked around in embarrassment, hoping no one had seen her panic. At the tree line, she caught a dark ponytail disappearing into the woods. She frowned, remembering the hard shove to her back.

She reclined on the water, her hands crossed behind her head, and floated past the gates and into the city beyond. A neat line of perfectly manicured trees lined the river as it flowed further into the city, banked by the famed streets paved of gold.

Everything here was gold and shining brightly. Buildings lined the streets, some of them sporting a rather large queue at the door. The buildings were largely bureaucratic, judging by the signs above the doors: things like WING APPLICATIONS and TOGA REPLACEMENT. Tilly supposed Edgar would want to stop for a new toga on the way out.

Ahead, the river split, forming a circle around an enormous fruiting bush. Around the bush was a large and bustling courtyard, again paved in gold. Behind the bush was the spire, rising up in all its glory and looking much more intimidating than it had from afar.

Instead of taking her around the bush, her ride ended abruptly when the river rose in a small wave and deposited her straight onto the gold brick. Her clothes were miraculously dry.

"Took you long enough." Edgar shuffled up to her.

"I needed a little push," she said wryly. His brow furrowed in confusion, but she waved him off. "So this is the Palace, huh?" She glanced around the courtyard, taking note of the shops lining it. The courtyard was clearly the tourist trap of Heaven. The shops advertised all manner of souvenirs, from Jesus bobbleheads to pieces of gold supposedly taken from the Throne itself. Tilly wondered if everything was free, or if there was some sort of currency she should be aware of.

Edgar pointed toward the spire. "That's where you're going," he said. He gestured for her to follow.

"What's with the bush?" she asked as they passed. It was bigger than she'd initially thought, the diameter easily the length of a good-sized yacht.

"Bush?" Edgar laughed and shook his head. "That's the Tree of Life. Well, the top of it anyway. You know, magical tasty fruit?"

"The beads."

Edgar nodded. "Quite off-limits if you don't have the right credentials. Have to keep the sneaks away. Can't quite figure out how they keep getting in."

He pointed at a humanoid creature circling the treetop. It was the size of a large man, but had claws for hands—which somehow managed to hold a flaming sword—and two sets of wings, one set wrapped around its lower body and the other set poised as if ready to take flight any moment. A man's face glared at her from atop the creature's shoulders, but she could see three more necks bobbing around the first, each sporting a different head. She picked out the face of a lion, an eagle, and something that looked like a cow.

"That, by the way," Edgar said in a huffy voice, "is a cherub."

"I'm sorry I ever called you one," Tilly said, tearing her eyes from the hideous creature in front of her.

The Palace loomed before them. At least two dozen steps led up to two massive gold doors. Carved in the center were the scales of justice. The doors were shut tight, an air of forbidden ground around them. Two Angelic Guards stood flanking the Palace doors. Tilly was glad to see they only had one head apiece, but was a little nervous about their wings, which were made entirely of fire—fire that looked much more menacing than that of the singing angels' wings.

Edgar approached the angels slowly, bent at the waist as he walked. He kept tugging at his shortened toga. Tilly wondered if she should bow as well, but settled on lowering her gaze to the ground.

"My charge humbly asks for permission to enter." Edgar pushed Tilly forward.

She glared back at him, then snuck a glimpse at the nearest angel. His face was stone as he glared back at her. She immediately dropped her eyes. "Uh . . . Tilly to see God?" she said, her voice commanding much less respect than she would have liked.

"Denied," came a growl. She wasn't sure which angel had spoken, or if they had spoken simultaneously.

Tilly raised her head and looked back and forth at the two sentinels. They had adjusted their gaze to look over her head and out at the courtyard. "It's really very important," she tried again. "You see, I think there's been a mistake, and—"

"She's supposed to be in Hell," Edgar interrupted. "She's a suicide."

Tilly elbowed him. "I'm not," she said through gritted teeth. Of all the memories to return, her death still wasn't one of them, but she couldn't believe she'd killed herself.

"The mistake involves my mother," she said louder. "I need to speak with God."

One Guard swung his eyes slowly to meet hers. She swallowed, hard. "Denied," he repeated.

"Well," Edgar chirped behind her, "that's that, then. Off we go." He grabbed her arm and tugged. "So sorry to disturb you gentlemen." Then under his breath: "Tilly, let's go."

She yanked her arm from his grasp. "I'm not leaving until I see God," she said firmly.

"God's not seeing people today," Edgar retorted.

She crossed her arms. "I thought you wanted to correct the clerical error of my being here."

"Look," he sighed. "I told you this was a fool's errand anyway. The truth is God doesn't see people most days." He paused. "Or really ever."

Tilly marched over to the top step and plopped down. "I'm not leaving until I get a chance to state my case."

Edgar shot a nervous look at the Guards, then pleaded with her, but she held her ground.

"Women," Edgar snorted. "The most obstinate creatures ever created." He threw his chubby arms in the air. "I'm not staying here."

Tilly glared at him.

"I'm really not. I did what you asked. I led you to the Palace."

"You've done your duty, then."

Edgar looked hurt for a moment. Then he set his jaw. "Fine,

then." He turned to go. "Tilly," he said over his shoulder, "good luck." Then he flew away. She couldn't help but feel slightly sad as she watched his bobbing body struggle through the air.

TILLY PACED in front of the sentinels, explaining her story. When she'd finished, she stopped and looked at them. They continued to stand statue still, as if there were no one in front of them. She sighed and started her story again. She thought she caught one quirking an eyebrow. Good. Maybe she was getting somewhere.

"You're never going to get in." A woman's voice, light and airy.

Tilly spun to see a woman standing off to the side of the steps, trying to hide, her arms crossed and amusement tugging at the corners of her mouth. She wore all-black, militaristic-looking clothes that were tight on her lean and muscular body, with a makeshift mask tied around her neck. She carried a small black sack in one hand; it looked empty. Two sword hilts jutted out over her shoulders, each featuring a mean-looking handguard in the shape of a crescent moon.

Two souls giggled as they exited a shop across the courtyard, and the woman turned, revealing the rest of the swords—strapped crisscrossed on her back, each with a slight hook at the end—and a long black ponytail Tilly recognized.

The woman turned back to meet Tilly's gaze. "So you're the one everyone's been talking about."

"So you're the one who pushed me into the river," Tilly shot back.

The woman's eyebrows arched briefly, a hint of surprise. "Naveen will be happy to hear you're okay."

"You know Naveen?" Tilly descended the stairs.

"For centuries now," the woman said with a wry smile.

Questions tumbled out of Tilly's mouth: "How is he? Where is he? Is Phoebe safe?"

The woman held up her hand. "I don't have time for that right now." She tugged on a leather strap at her neck, pulling a pendant out from beneath her shirt. She glanced around quickly to make sure she wasn't being watched. The cherub was on the other side of the treetop and the Guards at the door were staring off into space, as usual. Everyone else was too busy shopping.

She placed her thumb on the center of the pendant and closed her eyes, mumbling something under her breath. She morphed into a four-winged, four-headed creature. The lion's head sneered at Tilly, showing a row of angry teeth, then walked calmly over to the treetop and began filling the bag with fruit.

Tilly looked around wildly. Should she alert someone? The fruit was off-limits and she didn't know this woman.

Before she had a chance to decide, bugles sounded in the distance. The cherub/woman's four heads snapped in the direction of the noise, then to Tilly. She took one last glance at the tree, longing and regret showing on the human face. Then she morphed back into her human form, walking quickly but calmly back to Tilly's side.

"We've got to go," she whispered as she cinched the half-filled bag of fruit around her waist.

"What are you talking about?" The bugles sounded again. "Are they coming for you?"

The woman exhaled a hard laugh. "A little birdie told

me they're looking for you." She grabbed Tilly's forearm and pulled her away from the courtyard and around the Palace.

"Me? Why would they be looking for me?" This woman wasn't making sense. It wasn't Tilly who had just stolen fruit from a tree no one was supposed to go near. And surely she wasn't being hunted for asking to see God. If that were the case, the sentinels at the door would've grabbed her.

"I'm not sure," the woman said, "but they've been on your tail for a while now. And when Michael is after you, you run."

"Michael who?"

Shouts and bugles again, this time much closer. The cherub guarding the tree stopped his rounds and looked in their direction. Catching sight of them, his eagle head sounded the alarm with a high-pitched screech.

The woman dropped Tilly's forearm. "Run!"

Tilly hesitated, not trusting this strange woman in the slightest. A new sound broke through the air, one she didn't recognize immediately. She stood confused, her eyes searching for the source. Then she understood: it was the sound of very large wings, flapping furiously toward her.

She bolted.

V.

"He said 'suicide'," Luke said. "That makes no sense."

They were trudging up a mountain in what looked like West Virginia. Demons couldn't port directly to the gates of Hell, as that would cause too much temptation for them. All those scared souls waiting to get in were catnip to beings created to torture, and Lucifer preferred the souls to be inside the gates before the torture began.

Instead, demons traveled between the World and Hell through thin spots in the World's defenses. There was a sort of clocking in and clocking out process through these areas so Lucifer always knew where the minions were. They were also popular ways of escaping Hell if a soul was lucky enough and couldn't get to the Black Market. Sometimes these places were known to humans to be magical in some way and used in ceremonial rites, but more often they were seen as cursed and avoided. Those residing in other realms referred to each one as Hell on Earth.

Isozal hop-slid along, walking on all fours in an odd sideways gait. He hadn't said much since they'd emerged from the port, sulking over Naveen having complete control over him. All he told them was there was a cave a hundred yards through the woods that was the closest Hell on Earth.

"The man was delusional," Naveen said. "If Tilly had committed suicide, she would've gone straight to Hell, not ended up in Between under my watch."

They were getting closer to the cave, and now they could see hordes of demons and souls streaming down the mountain. Naveen tensed. There shouldn't be this much activity and definitely not this many escapees. Something was obviously going wrong in Hell. Or maybe Lucifer was taking advantage of the chaos Death's preoccupation was causing. Naveen considered trying to wrangle a couple souls to return them, a kind of offering to Lucifer, but they didn't have time.

"It's just odd," Luke said, "that even a delusional man would associate suicide with his daughter. That's all."

Naveen had to agree, but they had more pressing matters to deal with than the ravings of a man who'd lost his daughter and then had a demon riding his back for who knows how long.

Isozal had started whimpering and fell behind.

"Move faster," Naveen said.

The whimpering got louder.

"Oh, come now, you're a demon," he mocked. "You should love Hell."

Isozal glared but sped up nonetheless. He couldn't help obeying his new master. "Just wait until we get to Hell," he spat. "I'll rain fire down on you! I'll have Lucifer rip out your insides and dangle them in your face! I'll—"

"Right," Naveen said, laughing. "I'm sure you'll be much bigger and badder down there. You and Lucifer must be best friends. That's why we found you nowhere near the throne, clinging to a man's back, urging him to drink himself to death."

Isozal clamped his mouth shut, but so much hate was coming off him it was almost palpable.

They approached the entrance of the cave—which wasn't much more than a crack in the side of the mountain —pushing through the outpouring of demons and damned alike. Luke was trembling. Naveen couldn't blame him; a sense of relief mixed with anxiety caused his own stomach to roil. He was getting away from Death, yes, but he had no idea if Lucifer would help them. He hoped the Archangel's entrance into the fray would be enough to convince the ruler of the damned to be on his side, but Lucifer was a notoriously bad ally. Always had been, even before being cast down. And there was no love lost between the two of them. Naveen had been exiled from going further than the gates ever since the coup. Lucifer always worried he would return and take Hell back, so magic kept him out. He had to have a sponsor, a sort of go-between that was welcomed in order to enter. It tricked the system. Or it was supposed to. He'd never actually tried the loophole. He was just hoping the demon could get him in.

He thought of Phoebe and her command: go save Tilly. Should that actually be the first priority? He felt like he should secure Phoebe's future first. There was no way to know if Tilly was in Hell yet. Or if she ever would be. He couldn't even fathom how she would have made her way from Heaven to Hell to begin with. Or why she would want to.

Isozel pointed at the entrance to Hell, then began moving toward it. Naveen, quick as lightning, reached out and grabbed him by the arm.

"Not so fast," he said. "You've got to hold on to us. You know I can't go in on my own."

They lined up like schoolchildren playing red rover. Naveen took a deep, shaky breath. He was about to go home. He just hoped he'd be able to—and would want to—leave the place when the time came.

THEY ROUNDED THE PALACE, panic crawling up Tilly's chest. Her eyes swung around, looking for an exit or a hiding place. All eyes had turned to the two fugitives and no one was offering a welcoming look.

Suddenly Tilly remembered the pendant around the woman's neck. "Port!" she called to her companion. "Your pendant! We can port!"

"Not enough juice for that!" was the response.

Ahead, the golden paved streets gave way to a wide expanse of charred ground. The light there was murkier, untouched somehow by the Palace's radiance, except for a weird bluish patch of light in the center. The field was completely deserted.

Except for the three cherubim blocking their path.

Tilly skidded to a halt. The cherubim crouched and raised their claws, all twelve heads snarling at Tilly and her companion.

The woman reached up and gripped her sword hilts, pulling them smoothly from their sheaths. She didn't break stride. "Go!" she yelled. She jumped at the same time the cherubim did, all four of them colliding in the air. They landed with a thud, the woman's swords slicing through the air, the cherubim screeching and growling.

The wingbeats were closer now. Tilly turned to look. A

half dozen fiery angels were zeroed in on her position, and closing fast. She turned back to the brawl in front of her, unsure what to do. The woman punched a cherub in the face with the handguard of one sword, then crouched and kicked her leg out with practiced precision. One cherub dropped, hard, but was up a second later. The woman's eyes locked with Tilly's. "The port," she yelled. "Get to the port!"

It was only a second before Tilly realized that must be what the blue light was. She darted around the cherubim, her legs pumping fast. The port was too far away. She was never going to make it. She kept running, but risked a glance back to see how the woman was faring and saw her yank the pendant from around her neck. She rubbed it, chanting something loudly, then threw it to the ground. It burst in a small explosion, and a swarm of angry owls formed out of the debris. There were hundreds of them. The owls immediately set upon the cherubim, clawing and pecking.

The distraction allowed the woman to extricate herself from the fight. She barreled toward Tilly, again yelling at her to run. Tilly redoubled her efforts. She wasn't far from the port now. The sound of screeching filled the air.

Ten yards. Five.

A loud whoosh of air hit Tilly's back and pitched her forward onto the ground. She rolled onto her back and crab walked away from the source.

The angel above her burned bright. Hair so blond it was almost white flowed around his face. His skin crawled with translucent flames, giving him an ethereal look. A golden breastplate covered his chest. Above him, wing-shaped infernos pumped furiously as he prepared to land at Tilly's feet.

Tilly looked over her shoulder. The port was a few feet

away. She turned back and locked eyes with the angel, his a fiery orange red, burning with anger. He was almost on her now and was lowering himself to the ground.

The woman leapt on his back and hit him on the back of the head with the hilt of her sword. He went down. Using his back as a springboard, the woman launched herself at Tilly, landing on top of her. She gripped Tilly in a bear hug and rolled them both to the port.

Just before they went through, Tilly saw the angel stand, literal streams of smoke coming out of his nose in his fury.

The port dropped them from a height. They free fell for several dozen feet before landing in a pile of muck. The heat that burned Tilly's lungs was familiar.

She was back in Hell, exactly where she wanted to be.

DEATH STORMED into his office and slammed the door. He bellowed at the walls. He'd missed Naveen again. How was that possible? And now there was a demon involved. Naveen would have no trouble getting to Hell. And the little girl wasn't with him. Why? If she were, that problem would resolve itself. Lucifer's missing soul showing back up in Hell on her own accord. Simple. But of course it couldn't be that easy.

He flipped on his monitor, looking for Naveen. He might still be able to catch him if he moved fast enough. He smashed the monitor when he saw the back end of the God of Death going through Hell on Earth.

His office door opened with a bang. He swung around, ready with a reprimand, but bit down on his tongue when Michael strolled in.

"Well?" Death said. "Please tell me you found Tilly."

Michael shook his head. "She got away. But I brought you a consolation prize." He looked over his shoulder and nodded. Two more angels entered, each holding the arm of a squirming, spitting little man. They plopped him down in front of Death. The man rearranged his short toga and ruffled his wing feathers while glaring at his captors.

"He says his name is Edgar," Michael said.

Death scowled at the Archangel. "And just what am I supposed to do with him?"

"He was with the girl before she got away."

The diminutive angel mumbled something under his breath about Tilly being the death of him. Then he held his head up high and met Death's eyes, a haughty gesture that made Death want to squash him like a bug. Death reached down and grabbed him by the throat. It would be easy to make this little man disappear—and he *so* wanted to—but he couldn't risk it. Not with Michael as a witness.

"Where is she?" he hissed. He had the satisfaction of watching Edgar's face dissolve into fear.

"They've gone to Hell," Michael said in the background. "Through the open portal in the Battlefield."

Death kept a hold of the rotund angel but turned his attention to Michael. "They?"

"They," Michael said. He was frowning. "You didn't tell me an ex-goddess was with her. I didn't sign up for that."

Death struggled to keep his features under control. This was news to him, but he didn't want Michael to know he was in the dark. It was bad enough that he couldn't capture Naveen and Phoebe for God. He didn't need this oversized meathead reporting any more incompetence. Instead he said, "Well, go get them."

Michael's lip curled in distaste. "I refuse to descend into the fiery depths. I've done as much as I'm going to do for you. You'll have to get them yourself." He moved to the corner of the room and crossed his arms, settling in to watch.

Death cursed, then he turned his attention back to the spawn in his hands. He sat him down gently, every muscle in his body tensed in the effort to keep from pummeling him.

"Why would Tilly go to Hell?" he asked, his voice holding a false cheer.

Edgar harrumphed. "Because she's an idiot. Do you know what she's put me through the past several days?" He launched into a story filled with petty grievances.

Death's composure broke. He was on Edgar in a second. "You're going to tell me right now why she would want to return to Hell or I'm going to rip your wings off."

Edgar was stunned into silence.

Death grabbed a wing, yanked and twisted. Even in Between, that had to hurt.

Edgar yelped. "Okay!" he screamed. "Okay. Put me down and I'll tell you."

Death complied and Edgar took a deep breath.

Death was smiling by the end of the story.

"Can I go now?" Edgar whined. "Please, I just want to leave here."

Death waved a dismissive hand. He would have liked to have sent the little idiot to oblivion, but he couldn't afford to do so with Michael standing watch.

Besides, he had better things to do: Tilly's precious mommy was in Hell and the idiotic girl thought she could do something about it. He could definitely use that to his advantage.

DEATH WAS GRANTED an audience with Lucifer almost immediately. The Demonic Guard at the door claimed he'd been expected for some time now, which was surprising. But at least he wouldn't have to charm his way into the inner chambers. Charm was never his strong suit.

Lesser demons—ones too crazy to be of much use—skittered in the corners as Death approached the great metal double doors leading to Lucifer's private chambers. He took a deep breath and immediately regretted it; the smell of sulfur choked him. The Guard swung the doors open and a giddiness filled Death. The situation had worked out perfectly for him. Tilly and Naveen were in the same place and Hell was unobserved by God. That made it much easier to get rid of Tilly for good. And of course, with Lucifer's help, he could convince Naveen to give up Phoebe's location. All he had to do was get Lucifer on his side.

Candles in skull-shaped sconces lit the room he entered. A roaring fireplace lined the entirety of the back wall. A throne with two giant horns sprouting out the top and otherwise engraved with flames sat in the center of the room, a large baboon perched on one arm. It screamed and bared its fangs at Death. The doors to the room slammed shut.

"I've been expecting you," a smooth voice said from behind him. It was a voice that could cause even the most pious person to kill and fornicate. A voice that told countless lies over the eons, manipulating every mortal whose ears had the misfortune of hearing it directly.

He turned.

Lucifer stood before him, pale with straight black hair that flowed to her waist. She was dressed in a blood red pantsuit, a large medallion holding a bead around her neck. Tribal tattoos snaked around her chest and up her neck, like flames licking toward her chin. He imagined she was covered with them. Her eyes glittered in the candlelight, shining like obsidian. The baboon rushed toward her and she absently petted it while she studied Death with a lazy, half-lidded stare.

A shuffling in the corner behind her caught Death's attention. Naveen and Luke stepped out of the shadows, both glaring at him.

Death silently cursed, but allowed a small smile to play across his lips. *Act like this doesn't bother you*, he told himself. *They might not have had time to recruit her to their side.*

"Well, Lucifer," Death said to the woman, "I see you already have company."

INFERNO

Unhappiness reigned in the heart of one god. He thought he was more intelligent than his siblings, and therefore he should rule alone.

He gathered others, lower gods and half-gods, and convinced them to rebel. He promised them high ranks in the new order.

He waited until his siblings had gone to the World for a celebration in their honor. The rebel god chose this moment for his coup. He swiftly took over the realm and locked the entrance to the Realm of the Gods to all except his cohorts. When the remaining gods returned to the sacred tree to reenter their realm, they found they could not. Instead, they were forced into another realm, the one between worlds, and the living never heard from them again.

Without the presence of the gods in the World, the people began to forget them and turned to the new god as their leader. Eventually, most people in the World followed only one god. Some still worship the old order, but there is no one left to hear their prayers.

I

As soon as Naveen and Luke had stepped through the fissure between Hell and the World, they were taken into custody. Isozal—beholden to Lucifer instead of Naveen now that they were in Hell—danced around as the Demon Guards took Naveen and Luke into custody, mocking and spitting and singing praises to his master. One of the Guards eventually got annoyed and backhanded the little demon, sending him flying. Isozal sprang up immediately, spat out a few teeth, and resumed his celebration as he skittered away from the troop, off to cause havoc elsewhere, Naveen assumed. He might even try to return to Earth and possess some other poor soul.

Lucifer had been expecting them. Naveen wasn't surprised; he knew Lucifer was aware of each and every soul in her kingdom. An intruder would not go unnoticed for long.

The Guards had led them to what used to be Naveen's home. Above, the red-tinged clouds hung low, just showing the blackened, gnarled roots of the tree of life. The Citadel jutted up from the center of a bloodred moat like shards of glass in an open wound. Its smooth surfaces glinted in the light of a billion fires, giving the impression of smoldering coals, as if the building itself was afire. The walls were angular, sharp looking. From the outside, nothing about the building's construction made sense: towers sprung from nowhere, walls ended abruptly. It was an architect's first draft, an amalgam of random ideas that were never supposed to be brought to fruition. When Naveen was still in charge, the building was simpler, more functional. Now it was more representative of the addled mind that ruled Hell. Naveen doubted whether a good majority of the building was functional at all.

The Guards had taken them directly through the foyer and into the throne room. A wave of longing had washed over Naveen when he'd entered. Lucifer had kept this room the same. It was a circular chamber paved entirely with black marble. Twin silver thrones stood in the room's center. The one on the right was empty. Lucifer reclined in the one on the left—Naveen's traditional seat. She stroked the baboon perched next to her as she watched her visitors arrive. She dismissed the guards with an upward jerk of her head.

"I don't normally receive visitors," Lucifer said. She rose and circled the pair. Naveen watched Luke's face closely. He was gritting his teeth, his fists clenched at his side. Naveen was impressed. Given the previous visits to Hell, he'd fully expected Luke to have run in panic by now. "Especially from family. And twice in the span of a few hours? What an honor, dear uncle."

Naveen had opened his mouth to speak, but Lucifer raised a hand and pointed to the side. "If you'd kindly move over there. Not all the guests have arrived."

They did as she asked, Luke shooting Naveen a questioning look.

Not thirty seconds later a knock had sounded at the door and Death was admitted.

Now Naveen stared at his nemesis. His instinct told him to run. He wasn't safe here to begin with, let alone with Death standing before him. But there was nowhere to run to. Death and Lucifer blocked the only exit, and even if they could get past, Guards would be on them in seconds.

Naveen saw Death's hand twitch at his side right before his old friend lunged.

He was quicker than Naveen remembered. There was no time to react before Death tackled him. Luke yelled and dove on top of the pair, beating his fists on Death's back. Naveen stayed perfectly still, not wanting to give Death a reason to do anything stupid. Out of the corner of his eye, Naveen saw Lucifer calmly return to her throne. The baboon jumped up and down, screaming its excitement.

"Get him off of me or I'll get rid of him," Death spat.

Luke's blows stopped and he recoiled. Naveen nodded at him over Death's shoulder. Luke extricated himself completely, but Naveen noticed his hands were still balled.

Death stood and dragged Naveen up with him. He kept a hold on Naveen's collar. Maniacal glee shone from his blue eyes. "One down," he said.

Lucifer gave a bored sigh. "What's this now?"

Death kept one fist wrapped around Naveen's shirt as he turned to face her. "I'm taking Naveen with me. God wants to see him."

Lucifer exploded out of her throne. She was inches away from Death's face in seconds. Death's surprise gave Naveen the chance he needed, and he pulled away from Death's grasp.

"Do not mention him in my presence!" Spit flew from her mouth and landed on Death's face. He reached to wipe it off and Lucifer grabbed him by the neck. She seemed to get larger, her eyes burning with fury. "No one leaves here! No one! Not unless I say so!" She released Death and spun in a circle while letting out a guttural roar. "Do you hear me, old man?" she screamed at the ceiling. "This is my domain and in my domain, I rule!" She shook her fists above her head.

The baboon circled the room in a canter, howling ecstatically. The demons outside the door answered him in kind.

Lucifer whipped her head toward Death. She cackled briefly, then was silent. The demons and baboon quieted with her. She narrowed her eyes. "What is it you want? Other than to steal my souls, that is."

"There is a girl here who is not supposed to be," Death said.

"And one who's supposed to be but isn't," Lucifer shot back. "And you, Naveen? Are you here to usurp me?" She laughed again, a hard, grating sound that sent chills up Naveen's spine.

"I'm here for a girl as well."

The walls vibrated, like a mild earthquake.

Lucifer rolled her eyes at the wall and muttered something under her breath. "Yes, Tilly, Tilly, *Tilly*." She paced the room, absently rubbing the pendant at her neck. "This girl is becoming quite the headache for me, as you can see." She waved her hand at the walls, as if there was something there to see. The prophecy popped into Naveen's head: *thrust to the forefront of a new coup . . .* He thought of the escaping souls, the chaos outside. Hell was rising up. Lucifer was losing control. And Lucifer out of control was never a good thing.

Lucifer abruptly stopped pacing. "Well," she said, her voice taking on a chipper tone, "I'm just going to have to go meet this Tilly. Finally." She looked at each of them in turn, as if expecting praise for her idea.

"Guards!"

The two large demons who'd escorted Naveen and Luke into the palace appeared at the door.

"Make sure these imbeciles don't kill each other." Opening a portal, she cooed at her baboon, "You want to go on a little trip, my darling?"

TILLY ROLLED onto her back and gazed up at the open port, the only source of light in the dark sky above. She was back in Hell, but her brief feeling of satisfaction was slowly turning into fear as the heat burned her throat. She was covered in the muck. Her clothes clung to her, the wet making her feel like she was being steamed in the heat.

The woman she'd fallen with was already standing and sheathing her swords. Then she opened the sack and looked inside. Her face fell in disappointment. "Ruined. Damn." She tossed the bag to the side and looked around warily. "We've got to move," she said. "Find a port out of here."

Tilly struggled to extricate herself from the squelching muck. It had a strong hold on her and, like quicksand, was working hard to pull her under. The woman held out a hand.

"The name's Zia, by the way," she said once Tilly was upright.

"Tilly."

Zia nodded, a smirk on her face. "I'm aware."

A roar sounded in the distance, followed by an explosion, and Tilly ducked her head.

"Not near," Zia said. Despite her words, she looked worriedly in the direction of the noise. "This area is kind of off-limits, given its history and all."

"Its history?" Tilly tried to brush the mess off her clothes, but it smeared. It smelled like bloody shit. She gave up and looked around, noting that they were in the center of a crater, not terribly deep but wide. No one else was around.

"The Fall," Zia explained, pointing up at the open port in the sky. "When Lucifer rebelled, God threw her down from Heaven with such force it left an open port. Since this is the original site of her exile, it's not a real popular hangout."

"Lucifer is a woman?"

Zia chuckled. "Yep. A disappointing daughter, bent on the exact opposite of light and decency." She waved her hand around, indicating their surroundings.

Tilly took it all in for a moment. She couldn't see the gate or the walls from here. What she could see in her immediate vicinity was a barren landscape covered in the viscous goop she'd come to know all too well. Geysers of steam were every twenty yards or so, set up like a sinister game of whack-a-mole, burping fire every few minutes. In the distance she could see mountains arranged in a circle. There was one opening, but it had some sort of black fog blocking it. Even from this distance, though, she could hear the screaming from the damned souls.

Her mother was one of those souls.

Zia smoothed her ponytail, squeezing the mud from its length as best she could. When she finished, she said, "We really do have to get moving."

Tilly took a look at the mountains in the distance and

shuddered. As much as she wanted to find her mother, staying here, far away from all those damned, held some appeal. She looked down at the scar on her wrist. Deep down, she didn't believe her mother had tried to kill her. Her eyes stung with tears. She had to move on. She had to find her mother.

She nodded her head in the direction of the mountains. "Let's go."

A swirling portal appeared ten feet before them. Tilly's stomach flipped. The sight of an open portal had become so associated with Naveen that she couldn't help but think he would be the one to emerge. He must have heard about her mother somehow, and now he was here to save her. He'd help her find her mother and set everything right.

She'd so fully convinced herself of Naveen's imminent arrival in the few seconds between the portal opening and the dark head emerging that she was already rushing forward to greet him.

But it wasn't his face that followed the black hair: it was a woman's, her black eyes flashing, her mouth set in a hard line, lips the deep brown red of dried blood. A baboon launched out of the portal and landed at the woman's side with a shriek.

"Speak of the devil," Zia mumbled.

Tilly took a reflexive step back as the portal snapped shut behind the woman.

Lucifer glanced at the portal in the sky. She winced, and seemed to shy away from it, ducking a bit. She cocked her head to one side, letting her eyes roam up and down Tilly's body. The baboon circled Tilly and Zia, sniffing.

"So you're Tilly."

Lucifer's voice was so smooth, it was as if it slithered across the space between them, caressing Tilly's body and

277

wheedling its way into her ears. She felt violated and her head panged sharply. She opened her mouth to speak, but her voice caught in her throat. She choked a little.

"Don't worry, Luci," Zia said. "We're just passing through. We'll be out of your hair before you know it. If you're in a charitable mood, I wouldn't say no to borrowing that." She gestured to the large pendant at Lucifer's neck.

Without taking her eyes off Tilly, Lucifer said, "For being the Goddess of Knowledge, you're not too bright, Zia."

Zia shrugged. "Worth the try."

"Why are you here?"

Tilly knew the question was for her, but she was still having trouble finding her voice. Lucifer closed her eyes and rolled her neck with a sick crunching. The baboon sidled up beside Tilly, bared its fangs, and bit down on her leg. The pain was instant and intense. He locked his jaws as Tilly screamed and tried to shake her leg free. Zia's hands flew to the swords on her back.

Lucifer laughed, a sharp, barking sound. "You really think you're a match for me, Cousin." She caressed the pendant at her neck. "I believe you're out of power."

Zia hesitated and Lucifer sneered. She held up a hand.

"Enough."

The baboon immediately released. Tilly bent to press a hand to her wounds and was amazed to find blood pouring out of holes in her skin. The blood ran in thick tributaries down to the muck and mixed with it. The muck seemed to lap it up like it was food.

"You'll heal," Lucifer said. "There's an eternity of injury and healing here. One of my proudest accomplishments. Now, I'll ask again, and this time don't try my patience. Why are you here?"

The scream had loosened Tilly's vocal cords. "For my

mother." She stood and met Lucifer's eyes. The task proved difficult, as one look at those dark holes made her want to run away screaming, but she managed to keep from shirking away. She could sense Zia fidgeting at her side.

Lucifer raised an eyebrow. "Your mother belongs to me. And I think you know that."

Tilly felt dizzy and her eyes lost focus. The heat made her want to vomit. "She was unstable. Or something. She had to be."

"Your mother started that fire," Lucifer continued. "She hated her life and wanted out. She tried to take you out, too, you know."

"Liar."

Lucifer barked a laugh, then shrugged. "I've been called worse."

Another explosion shook the ground. Cheers followed. Lucifer gritted her teeth until the tendons in her tattooed neck rose like snakes. Tilly's hand inadvertently went to the scar on her wrist. Lucifer noticed, stared at the scar for a moment.

"'Scarred by fire,'" she whispered. She met Tilly's eyes and cocked her head to the side, squinting. All at once, her face relaxed and a smile appeared. She snapped her fingers. "I'll make you a deal."

"Don't listen to her," Zia urged in Tilly's ear. "Whatever she's going to say will not end well for you."

"I'll give you your mother's soul, if you do one thing for me in return."

"Tilly . . ." Zia warned.

"What is it?" Tilly managed to whisper. "What do you want?"

Lucifer studied her nails. They were long and curved under at the tips, painted the same crimson as her pantsuit.

"It's simple. All you have to do is make it to the center of Hell. To my Citadel." She looked up with a half smile. "Of course, along the way, you'll need to crush that." She pointed a thumb over her shoulder. Another crash sounded as if on cue.

Tilly looked past Lucifer to the mountains in the distance. Souls she couldn't see hooted and screamed in riotous fury.

"You're to blame for that," Lucifer said.

"I don't understand."

"Of course you don't. But it's your fault, nonetheless. Those imbeciles see you as some sort of savior. All because of that ridiculous oracle."

Phoebe's innocent face flashed behind Tilly's eyes. What did Phoebe have to do with this?

"That and your refusal to stay in Heaven." Lucifer sniffed. "Although I really can't say I blame you there." Her eyes took Tilly in again, a curious approval written there that made Tilly feel simultaneously proud and ashamed.

"Regardless, you've given them something I simply cannot tolerate." Lucifer shuddered. "Hope. They have hope now because of you and they've gone wild. I can't keep them inside my gates. They're escaping to the World; they're rioting here." Her nose wrinkled in distaste.

Zia smirked. "I thought your goal was to take over the World, Luci."

Lucifer's head snapped toward Zia. Her eyes burned with hatred. "I will when I'm *ready*. When I've got my army, when there's absolutely no way *he* can win—" she cast a menacing glance up at the portal swirling in the sky—"then, and only then, will I take my place as ruler of all."

"You would be a lot happier if you weren't such a fan of melodrama."

"Don't forget where you are, Zia," Lucifer seethed. "You're not invincible down here."

Zia's smirk faltered.

"Your choice," Lucifer said as she opened a portal. "What will it be?"

Tilly didn't hesitate. She nodded once.

Lucifer smiled. "I'll be waiting." She vanished through the port and her baboon gave one last shriek before it followed.

Zia rushed at the port, but it winked closed before she got to it. She sighed and returned to pick up the discarded bag of ruined fruit. "I guess we'll need this now."

DEATH AND NAVEEN glared at each other. The two Demon Guards stood nearby, keeping a watchful eye on the pair.

"Why do you hate Tilly so much?" Naveen asked. He knew Death had been in possession of the prophecy, had read the words "Death will be defeated." But prophecy vagaries were no reason to hate the way he hated Tilly. After all, there had been many prophecies over the eons that hadn't been interpreted correctly. Something else had to be the root cause.

Death feigned innocence. "Why would I waste any time hating an insignificant mortal? I'm simply doing the job God asked me to do."

"It's because I . . ." He hesitated. "It's because I care for her. You want to get your revenge?"

Death smiled thinly. "As much as I would love to pay you back for the *kindness* you showed me by making me *this*, I really have more important goals at the moment."

Lucifer appeared. She looked more serene than when

she'd left. Downright happy, even. The portal snapped shut as soon as the baboon came through.

"Where's Tilly?" Naveen asked. He'd expected Lucifer to bring her back. Why else go to her?

"Never you mind, Naveen. I have a job for you." She nodded to a Guard, who immediately grabbed Luke from behind. Luke yelped. The other Guard left the room for a moment, returning with a giant wrought iron birdcage, flat bottomed with spikes poking every which way. Luke was shoved inside. There was barely enough room for him, and when he struggled stakes impaled him. He yelped in pain, then held very still.

Naveen clenched his fists. "What are you doing?"

"Your friend will stay here while you go get the girl."

For a moment, Naveen thought Lucifer hadn't found Tilly, which was why Tilly hadn't returned with her. He'd worried Lucifer would use her magic to kill Tilly on the spot, sending her to the blackness of oblivion, never to return. Relief washed over him. A split second later, his relief was replaced with nausea as he realized who Lucifer must mean.

"I don't know where she is."

Lucifer *tsk*ed. "Now, now, Naveen. You can't lie to the queen of lies."

Naveen ground his teeth together. Death crossed his arms and smirked.

"Tilly is here, though," Naveen said. "You've got your soul."

"Let's call Tilly a bonus." She closed her eyes and swayed. She smiled like she was savoring something delicious. "A particularly useful bonus."

Death looked sharply at Lucifer, but didn't say anything.

"I need the girl," Lucifer continued. "The oracle. I'm

entitled to her, and you will provide me with her soul." Her eyes cut to Death. "Which is something that has been denied me thus far."

"And if I don't?" Naveen said.

Lucifer's eyes burned a bright red, but otherwise she remained composed. "Don't think I don't know about your relationship with these people," she said. "The blond one and *Tilly*. They're both in my domain at the moment, Naveen. You wouldn't want them to disappear, would you? Have you forgotten that I have that ability? I can get rid of your friends with a simple touch on the shoulder if I want. It would be no trouble. I would even enjoy it."

"You can't give her Phoebe," Luke called from his cage. He moved slightly when speaking, and another spike jabbed him. A demon jumped at the cage and bared its fangs. Luke closed his eyes and whispered some sort of chant under his breath. Naveen hoped it wasn't a prayer. It would take a lot more than a threat to a mere mortal soul for God to help anyone in Hell.

Naveen's heart raced as he watched Luke try to avoid the demon's forked tongue by pressing himself as far against the spikes as he could. Blood poured from the wounds, blossoming crimson on his white shirt. He wanted to rush at the demon, break Luke out of the cage. But he couldn't. He wore a perfect mask of disinterest. Lucifer was watching him closely. "I think you're overestimating my connection to the humans," he told her. Death snorted in the background.

"Oh, I don't think so," Lucifer said. "You've gotten soft, living with them all these years." Her hand shot to the pendant resting on her collarbone. "I could also kill you right now, Naveen. Would you like to see where your soul would end up? I'm betting right here." She waved her arms around and cackled. "You'd be back home, like you always wanted. But I would own you."

There was a long pause. Naveen wasn't sure what would happen to him if she killed him. He wasn't technically dead, but a god had never been killed before. He might wink out of existence altogether. Or he might become a mortal soul. No one knew, and the fear of the unknown was what Lucifer was counting on.

Naveen had no intention of handing Phoebe over to Lucifer. There was something going on here that he couldn't quite grasp. Lucifer was a little too interested in Phoebe for Naveen's taste, and he had no idea what she meant by Tilly being a useful bonus. No, he wouldn't be a part of whatever she had planned by returning to Hell with Phoebe.

He also didn't intend to permanently abandon Luke and Tilly. He needed a plan. And he needed help.

"Well?" Lucifer asked.

For the moment, he had no choice. He nodded.

Luke roared from his cage. "No!"

Lucifer's mouth twitched and her eyes returned to their normal black color. "Good boy."

II.

"There's really only one easy way to get to the center of Hell," Zia was saying as they trudged toward the mountains.

Tilly wasn't listening. She was mesmerized by the river of lava to their left. It rushed along like rapids, its oranges and reds slapping the banks and cresting in small waves. More than a few souls stood at the edges, staring in as if hypnotized. Every few minutes one of them would jump in, swallowed immediately.

But that wasn't what was fascinating Tilly. What caught her attention was the humming that seemed to be coming from the river. She'd been hearing it for a while now. If Zia heard, she didn't seem bothered by it. Although Tilly doubted Zia could hear much over her incessant talking. Everything had to be fully explained, every plan hashed out. She had the habit of saying "logically" at least once every few sentences. After a while, Zia became white noise, her voice fading into the background as the humming from the river became louder.

"Are you listening?"

Tilly rubbed her scar and nodded.

Zia sighed in exasperation. "I was saying we need to keep a lookout for condors. Any birds, really. But if we see some, I can call them down and they'll take us to the center." She looked down at the bag of smashed fruit with longing. "If these were beads, I could call them from here. Better yet, just port out of here."

The river hummed.

"Flying wasn't part of the deal," Tilly mumbled, staring at the river and digging at her wrist. It had started tingling about the time the river started humming. It wasn't unpleasant, not like her other trips to Hell, just different. Almost as if one spot on her skin had fallen asleep. She felt her nails breach skin and pulled her fingers away quickly.

Zia grabbed her by the shoulders. "Look at me. Don't listen to it."

She tore her eyes from the river. "What is it?"

"It's not just physical tortures in Hell. Just keep listening to me, and you'll be fine. Ignore everything else. And I mean everything."

A wind whipped up out of nowhere, strong and stinging.

"We're getting close to the monks," Zia said. "This isn't going to feel pleasant."

The wind got stronger. Their vision was compromised. The wind was so forceful, it dried out the muck on the ground and slung it around, causing a dust storm. The further they walked, the more sediment swirled around them. It stung their arms, leaving a million tiny cuts. They hung their heads and held their arms in front of their faces. Tilly couldn't talk; when she opened her mouth, dust filled it immediately and choked her. She wanted to turn around, to go back to the river. Its call hadn't faded in the storm.

Rather, it was louder, as if someone turned up the volume to ensure it could be heard over the wind.

Tilly's foot hit something hard and she stumbled forward. She hit the ground.

"Meet the monks," Zia shouted.

Tilly had tripped over a man sitting cross-legged on the ground. At least, she assumed it was a man; it was more skeleton than flesh. His eyes were gone, as was most of his face, blown off by the storm. The only fleshy parts were hidden under his tattered clothing, which was so bloody, Tilly couldn't tell if she was looking at skin or meat. A wave of nausea overcame her and she dry heaved. Dust lodged in her throat and she panicked, tearing at her neck with her fingernails. Her fingertips broke through skin and brushed muscle.

The wind stopped abruptly, the dust settled. Tilly spit the sediment from her mouth as best she could. Her fingers found her neck once again. It was healed, no sign of the self-inflicted scratches. If it wasn't for the blood covering her hands, she would have doubted she was injured to begin with.

Now that she could see properly, she noticed the rows of skeletons, all lined up and seated in the same meditating pose. Most were buried in the sand to some level, some with just their heads peeping through.

As she watched, their bodies began to regrow. Muscles slung over bones, skin over muscles, clothes over skin, until they were once again whole and unmarred.

Zia came to stand beside Tilly. "The deep state of meditation allows their minds to travel from here. Lucifer can't stand it, so they're destined to have their flesh blown away over and over. Not that they care. I don't think any of them have opened their eyes for centuries."

She'd barely spoken the last syllable before the man directly in front of them snapped his eyelids open. Tilly yelped and skittered backward.

"Had to make a liar out of me," Zia said.

The man offered a thin smile. His eyes were glassy and unfocused, the look of someone who'd just woken up after a long nap. "Welcome, visitors. I offer you the opportunity to join us. Forget your troubles. Travel in time and space. Make your own eternity."

"Oh, a travel brochure. How nice." Zia tugged Tilly to her feet. "We should get moving."

The man's head turned slightly and he locked eyes with Tilly. "Tilly, join us."

The humming in her ears got louder.

"It's not safe for you to continue. We have been to the future. Failure and heartache is all it holds for you. It's time to let everything go. Your life, your death, your anger. Let it go and join us in our escape."

It had to be a trick, something Lucifer set up to keep Tilly from reaching her mother.

"I'm getting really tired of everyone telling me what my future holds," she said.

The other skeletons opened their eyes. "Join us," they said in unison. "Let it go, Tilly. Join us."

The humming became a voice. She could have sworn it was calling her name. She looked to the river. She could no longer see the physical form, just an orange glow on the horizon. A waterspout had formed, sucking up some of the lava. It swirled faster as she watched, eventually moving to the shore. She glanced at Zia, who was looking in the same direction, frowning.

The monks continued their chant as the wind picked up

again. Zia and Tilly turned sharply and jogged away, dodging chanting skulls as they went.

The tingling in Tilly's scar increased to the edge of pain.

A VOLCANO of emotions bubbled in Death's chest. Damn Naveen for beating him to Hell, to Lucifer. He didn't know what was said before he arrived, but clearly some deal had been struck. Death knew of no other reason Lucifer would even entertain Naveen in her presence, let alone allow him to leave unharmed. Even if it was to find the girl.

Damn the girl, too. He was so close to reincarnation, and she was the only thing standing in his way. He should have been able to find her. He'd failed, and now Naveen would look like the hero, as usual. He was always the star, Naveen, God of Death. He had gotten the accolades, the cult worship, the sacrifices, while Death did the hard work. In the end, the disparity was the downfall of their short friendship. Naveen would say the hatred was due to Death's greed, his need for power, his obsession with killing. But Death knew better. Naveen had wanted the same things, once. He was the one who changed, not Death.

Death watched the blond one in the cage. He knew there was some shared history between him and Naveen, but was it enough for Naveen to sacrifice the little girl to save him?

Lucifer was petting that hideous baboon again, cooing at it like it was her child. He stood watching her awkwardly, not sure if he was dismissed. This trip was not going as planned.

He decided to leave as well. He wanted to see if he could find the girl before Naveen brought her back. He needed the redemption of bringing her in himself, as he was unsure if

God would follow through on his promise of reincarnation if he wasn't the one to return her to Lucifer. He'd come back to take care of Tilly later. She didn't have anyone to spill his secret to right now, anyway. If she remembered at all.

He turned to the door, hoping to sneak out unnoticed.

"I'd like to make a deal with you," Lucifer said. She looked at him coyly as she nuzzled the baboon.

Death froze. Making a deal with Lucifer almost always ended badly for everyone but Lucifer.

"Oh, come now," she said, seeing the expression on his face, "it's been so long since I've had a good game. You wouldn't deny me this, would you?"

"You don't have anything I want."

She raised a jet-black eyebrow. "Oh no? I have the girl."

"Then why did you send Naveen—"

"Not *that* girl, you imbecile." She rose and discarded the baboon in one fluid motion. It hit the ground hard and glared at her, then took up residence in the vacant throne. "The other one. The one you killed. The one you really want to get your hands on." She watched Death closely, smirked when she saw his face fall.

"I've killed many people," he said, trying and failing to keep his voice from faltering.

"Never before their time. Not before your little frantic foray a few months ago, at least."

Death didn't speak. He didn't move. He cursed himself inwardly for not having control when he found the prophecy. He shouldn't have gone around killing those with special lifelines. Or at least he should've made sure the Fates hadn't caught him. And now Lucifer knew and she would use that knowledge to her full advantage.

And dear gods, the blond one was in the room. Death's

stomach ached. His reincarnation was going down the drain rapidly.

"Don't worry, I'm not going to tell *him*," she said, rolling her eyes. "I'm sure that would ruin your chances of living again. Although why you would want to live as a human when you have the power you do is beyond my comprehension."

She paced the room, pretending to study her nails. "Did you know she knows how to wield magic like a god, without being taught? It's a unique power these days. Not so much godly blood in the mortals now. She'll be very useful to me."

So this was the deal, then. He would leave Tilly alone so Lucifer could have her. That was not an option.

"You're wondering how to make this deal with me, yet still eliminate her." She laughed, a rough crazy sound.

The blond was watching their every move, latched onto their words like a leech.

"We should probably move this conversation elsewhere," Death warned, nodding his head in the direction of the cage.

Lucifer waved her hand dismissively. "He's not going anywhere." She was close enough in her pacing the room to whisper into Death's ear: "And even if he does, he can't stop my plan."

She pulled back, a sly grin on her porcelain features. Tucking her arm into his, she led him in her processional around the room. The baboon watched him warily from the throne.

"I've made a deal with her, as well," Lucifer explained. "She will come here and I will give her mother's soul to her."

Death stopped and narrowed his eyes at her.

She chuckled. "I've made sure she'll be insane by the time she gets here. She won't even remember why she's here. Not that I plan to find her mother for her even if she does. And when she arrives, all hope will be snuffed out. Those idiots rebelling outside will go insane right along with her, and she will lead them in the battle against the angels and the prophecy will be fulfilled!"

Death recited the prophecy in his head once more. *A powerful girl, scarred by fire and loved by death's old guard, will be thrust to the forefront of a new coup. She will have to choose between darkness and light, sacrifice and selfishness, love and hate, life and death. If she succumbs to the fire, hope is lost and all souls are damned. If she rises above, Death will be defeated and the old ways restored.*

Was Lucifer purposely ignoring everything but the first line? Or was it possible he'd interpreted it incorrectly?

She lowered her voice again. "There won't be a reason for you to kill her. Again. She won't care about what you did to her."

She told a guard to watch the prisoner and guided Death from the throne room. Her baboon followed like a lost puppy.

There wasn't much to Lucifer's home besides the throne room, which was the only bit she'd salvaged from the old palace. The rest was haphazard and nonsensical, matching the outside of the building and Lucifer's deranged mind. Most of the hallways went nowhere, or somehow led outside or back to the foyer outside the throne room.

"And what do I get out of this?" Death asked. She had led him down a dead-end hall and they were doubling back. He wondered if she was as lost in her own home as everyone else.

"Other than assurances that she will no longer be a problem for you?"

"It won't matter if she is a problem for me if you're plan-ning on taking over the World," he said. "There won't be a world for me to be reincarnated into."

"There *will* be a world. Just under different management. You will live again, Death. That I promise."

Death considered. A promise from Lucifer was rare, and was often like a genie granting wishes: the result might be drastically different from what the wish maker had intended.

Her plan was already in motion, and he could think of no way to stop her. He wasn't sure if he wanted to. It seemed her machinations on the World revolved around Tilly losing her mind and becoming a zombie of evil like all the other demons in this fiery pit. God wouldn't listen to a demon any more than he would listen to the devil herself. Even if she'd misread the prophecy, Lucifer was right about one thing: if her plan succeeded, Tilly would no longer be a problem for him. And if not, he'd just vanquish the girl as originally planned.

"What do I have to do for this deal?"

Lucifer tossed her head back and cackled, spinning swiftly in a circle. "My dear Death, all you have to do is what you've wanted all along." She stopped abruptly, fixing him with a wide-eyed, serious gaze. "Try to get rid of her."

NAVEEN PORTED to the Disciplinary Building, thinking it would be safer that way, in case he was followed. He planned to roam the streets of the Between for a bit, lose whomever might have seen him port in, and then make his way to the Black Market. If it was still there.

He stared at the massive building, thinking of Tilly, of how scared she'd been that day, the day that started all this.

Maybe he should have let her go to Hell like Death and Eris had wanted. Maybe it would have been easier on them all. She would never have met Phoebe; he would never have had to cull a soul again. He wouldn't have this itch under his skin to cull more and more.

Tilly seemed to be destined for Hell anyway, if the past few days had taught him anything. No matter what she did —or what he did—she always seemed to end up back in the fire.

He roamed for hours, dodging behind buildings and into alleys every time he saw the black cloak of an Acolyte. They seemed calmer now, no longer frantic in their search for the Black Market. It made him nervous: had they already found it? There were still too many of them around, though, so they must still be searching. He wondered if the World was still in chaos, if anyone was dying.

Half-baked plans flitted in and out of his mind, not one of them without a major flaw that would either get someone sent to the black abyss or play into Lucifer's hand somehow. He wondered if God knew what was happening. He understood his brother wouldn't care what happened to him, but he should be interested in what Lucifer was doing. Then again, it seemed he wasn't interested in much of anything that had to do with humans lately.

He was around the corner from where he'd left the Black Market. It was either still there, Zia still missing with the magic she was supposed to return with, or it was gone. Naveen was banking on it still being right where he left it. He still didn't have a plan, but was hoping the Fates would be able to weigh in.

He took one last look around. No Acolytes, no one he recognized. He exhaled and turned the corner. His eyes slid off the area in front of him. Still there, then.

He walked forward until a small hand reached out and pulled him inside the protective shield.

"Naveen!" Phoebe hugged him tight around his midsection. She was laughing with a childlike giddiness that bordered on hysteria. "I was so worried!" She pulled away, looked up at him with a mile-wide grin. Then she looked behind him and her face fell. "Where's Tilly? And Luke?"

"I—" Naveen began.

"He has returned."

"Without the girl."

"That was expected."

"Still."

"Disappointing."

The Fates had come up behind Phoebe, their bodies forming a protective barrier around her. Everyone nearby noticed the new arrival and moved in to see what the fuss was about.

"Does he have any beads?" someone shouted.

Naveen shook his head. There was a collective groan. Some of the onlookers wandered away, no longer interested if Naveen couldn't secure their protection or escape.

"What happened?" Phoebe said.

Naveen explained. Her face contorted more with every sentence. By the time he was finished, she looked broken-hearted.

"I'm sorry, Phoebe," Naveen whispered. "I've failed you. I've failed everyone." Coming back to the Black Market had been a mistake. He brought destruction and heartbreak everywhere he went. He needed to leave now.

Phoebe straightened and wiped her tears with balled fists. "What's the plan?" Her face was full of expectation. It was the same expression he'd seen on Tilly's face the day

295

she'd asked him if he could do anything about her sentencing.

A hot flash of anger shot through him. Why did all these people expect him to fix everything? He didn't ask for this responsibility, and he certainly didn't want it. He took a deep breath. "I don't have one."

"You have to have a plan. The prophecy says—"

"The prophecy is wrong! You're wrong!"

Phoebe looked up at him with a look of such betrayal that all the anger melted out of him.

"Phoebe," he started, but she pivoted on her heel and sprinted away, ducking inside the Fates' tent.

All three Fates shook their blind heads at him.

"Unless you three have a plan, you're not helping," he snapped at them as he pushed past and followed Phoebe.

He would comfort her. Maybe they could go on the run together, away from these Black Market people. They'd be less likely to be found that way. They could forget about everything and just disappear. She'd be heartbroken, but he didn't see a way around that. Eventually she would forget. Kids were supposed to be resilient. Of course, he'd have to find some beads along the way, but that could be dealt with. Probably.

He had the tent flap in his hand when a murmur cascaded through the crowd. He craned his neck to see what the commotion was. The crowd was pulling someone inside. Zia must be back. Good. He would need to bargain with her for beads later if he and Phoebe were going to go out on their own.

A bright blond head bobbed through the crowd. "Naveen! Where is he? Naveen!"

"What the . . .?"

Luke burst through, his eyes wide, shirt bloody from his now-healed wounds. "There you are!"

Phoebe tumbled out of the tent and rushed Luke, tackling him to the ground. A slew of words escaped her mouth, so fast they were almost indecipherable. What Naveen did understand was that she was begging Luke to do something about Tilly, as Naveen was seemingly unwilling to.

Luke pulled her off him and struggled to stand up. He only made it to kneeling before Phoebe had her arms around his neck. He gave in and hugged her back. "That's what I'm here for, little lady." He hushed her. "Naveen, I know what Lucifer's plan is."

III.

They trudged on, passing few souls. The ones they did, Zia knew by name. None of them were communicative, all concentrated on enduring their individual tortures. These were the men and women Naveen had sentenced. Zia explained the punishments as they passed. Tantalus reaching for fruit he could never get. Sisyphus rolling a giant rock uphill for eternity. Tityos strapped to the side of a hill for vultures to feast on. Zia pitched a fit over this one, mumbling that if she had beads she could summon the vultures to carry them to the center. She tried calling out to them anyway, but they were so involved in their meal, they ignored her.

As they walked, Tilly's anger grew. So this was what Naveen saw as justice. The more she thought about him sitting on some throne, doling out punishments to those below, the louder the whispers got. By the time they reached the mountains, she could barely hear Zia over the grating voices. It was as if her brain was a chalkboard someone kept scraping claws over.

Come to us. You're no use here; you can't make it. It wouldn't matter if you did. No one cares about you, Tilly. No one is going to help you. No one wants you. Your mother chose to go to Hell rather than spend one more moment with you. She chose to try to kill you . . .

Out of the corner of her eye, she saw a glimpse of the tornado. It was following her, not moving as a tornado should. It skipped and hopped around, ducking and hiding when it wanted, appearing in full view only when Zia turned away. Every time she saw it, it was bigger.

They were almost out of what Zia called the Badlands. She always laughed when she said it, but Tilly didn't get the joke. She didn't find anything funny at the moment, and was finding it harder to remember why she ever would have laughed.

They were approaching the main area of Hell, encircled by the mountains, where Lucifer preferred to keep her souls —closer to the center, where she could keep a better eye on them. Or rather, her princes and demons could. Zia had explained that Lucifer actually did very few managerial tasks; she mainly sat in her throne room muttering to herself. In reality, Hell was managed by her seven princes— each with his own wedge of Hell, and each with his own legions of demons. The princes had fallen with Lucifer and the demons used to be regular souls who'd gone crazy when faced with an eternity in Hell. Zia really did not stop talking.

Ahead, mountains jutted up violently, as if they had formed all at once, someone stabbing them through the ground like spikes. Lava ran down the sides in thick ribbons. The tops burped flames and thick black smoke every so often. These were the mountains Tilly had seen from the platform.

The mountains formed a ring of fire around the souls. Where Tilly stood, there was a break, a missing mountain, allowing entrance to the masses. The only problem was the entrance was blocked by a low, vibrating black cloud. To the right, in the base of one of the volcanoes, was a cave.

"We'll go through there," Zia said, pointing to the cave.

Tilly shook her head. "I'm supposed to go through and quell the rebellion."

"Logically, the cave is a better choice, as we won't have to go through Beelzebub's flies. We can avoid all the damned souls, hopefully trade this bag for some actual beads so I can call birds. Besides, the cave network leads to the center as well. Worst case scenario, we walk."

"No. I'm not going to risk my mother's soul just because you don't want to walk among people."

It's a trap. Don't listen to her. She'll lead you away from your mother.

"There's a chance even if you do go through the masses, Lucifer doesn't have your mother. Or won't give her to you. We have to think about this logically. Strategize."

"I don't want to think logically!"

Zia's jaw clenched. "Well, that's what I do. I am the Goddess of Wisdom."

"Former goddess, you conflated know-it-all."

Zia's eyes narrowed and she took a step forward.

See? She wants to fight you. She doesn't want to help. Hit her. Run away. Come to us. We're the only ones that care about you. We'll take care of you. You'll be safe inside.

Tilly tossed her head. "I'm sorry. I can't think straight in this godforsaken place."

"I told you not to listen to them."

Of course she did. She doesn't want you to hear the truth. Did you ever wonder how she knows where she's going?

"How do you know so much about Hell?" Tilly asked.

"What are they saying to you?"

"Answer the question. How do you know where to go?"

Because Lucifer told her where to take you.

"I spend quite a bit of time down here. Unfortunately."

See? Why would she spend so much time down here unless she was friends with Lucifer?

"I can't help if you won't tell me what they're saying," Zia whispered.

She put a hand on Tilly's shoulder. It was meant to be a comforting gesture, but Tilly's eyes shot to the sword hilts at her back. She needed to find a way to get away from this woman. What did she know about her, really? She was stealing from Heaven when they met. That couldn't be a trait of a good person. She glanced at the black cloud. She could vaguely see the writhing souls on the other side. It seemed the best place to lose her.

"I don't know what you're talking about," Tilly said. She shrugged Zia's hand off her shoulder. "No one is talking to me except you. And you never shut the fuck up."

Zia exhaled and closed her eyes. "Fine. We'll go through the masses. Maybe I can find someone there to trade with. My normal guy is in the caves, though." She shot a pleading look at Tilly, one last chance for her to change her mind, to bend to Zia's will.

Tilly returned the look with a stony glare. "Well, let's go then."

"How did you get here?" A hard feeling had settled into Naveen's gut as he watched Phoebe clamor all over Luke. There was no way he'd walked out of Lucifer's throne room. She would have had to let him go. But what purpose would that serve?

301

Luke grinned. "Let's just say there's not a woman in any realm I can't charm."

Phoebe giggled and finally let go of Luke's neck. He made an exaggerated show of inhaling and exhaling as if she'd been strangling him, which threw her into a fit of laughter.

"Phoebe, come here," Naveen snapped.

The smile evaporated from her face. She looked from Naveen to Luke and back again, then slowly backed away from Luke and went to stand behind Naveen.

Luke cocked his head to one side, one side of his mouth raised in a half grin. "You can't be serious. You actually think . . ." He stood abruptly, the grin evaporated. His nostrils flared. "Naveen, how long have you known me?"

"How did you get here?" Naveen repeated.

The crowd had formed a circle around the three of them. They all whispered to each other, panic written on more than a few faces.

"I can't believe this." Luke shoved his hand through his hair.

"I left you in Hell, guarded by the devil herself, Death, and two demons." Naveen's voice was even as he spoke, despite the swirling in his stomach. "You have to know how this looks."

The noise from the crowd began to crescendo. Luke held up his hands in a defensive gesture. "I broke out."

The crowd buzzed. There were a few standout shouts of disbelief.

"No! Listen," Luke insisted. "I really did." His eyes begged Naveen for help.

Naveen wanted to believe whatever came out of Luke's mouth so bad it hurt. He nodded, but kept his guard up.

Luke spoke quickly:

"After you left, Lucifer and Death got to talking, right? They had me sitting in the cage in the corner, but they didn't care if I heard. Lucifer explained her plans for Tilly and then they left me with a demon. I don't know where they went, but the other demon went with them. So there was only one demon, and you know how I had that vial of ambrosia?"

Naveen nodded. "The one you threw to Vernon in payment for the bead."

"Yeah, well, I didn't actually throw it to Vernon. It was a fake. I switched them."

Naveen thought back and remembered he'd thought the vial looked different, but hadn't thought much of it at the time.

"So I still had the ambrosia," Luke continued, "and there was only this one demon, so I figured, why not? I pulled out the vial, which was harder than it sounds with all those spikes around me, and taunted the demon with it. They love that stuff down there, you know. Anything that helps someone forget they're in Hell is obviously going to be in high demand. He or she or whatever couldn't get at the vial without opening the cage door. Claws were too big. So it opens the door and takes the whole vial down in one swig. I've never seen anyone drink so much of the stuff at once. That must've been one hell of a—"

"Luke."

"Right, sorry. So I'm free, and it's passed out on the ground, grinning like a damn fool. If you want to call whatever sharp-toothed, slobbery, open-mouthed mess that was a grin. All I had to do was reach down its throat to get its pendant." He puffed out his chest and produced a pendant. "Voilà. Back here."

Naveen stared at Luke as he mulled the information over. He wanted to believe him.

"Look, I know I haven't been the most dependable person in the past, Naveen. But you know I would never betray you."

Naveen sighed. That was true. Luke was mostly irresponsible and inconsiderate, and he rarely did anything that wasn't to his benefit, but he was loyal.

Naveen allowed himself a small smile. "Vernon probably isn't too happy with you."

Luke grinned with relief. "Yeah, I'll be banned from the club again. But that's okay. I think that life is behind me now."

Pulling the flap back on the Fates' tent, Naveen waved Luke over. "Come tell me about this plan of Lucifer's."

TILLY WOULD HAVE THOUGHT the flies were awful if she hadn't already been through the dust storm. At least the biting didn't hurt as bad as tiny shards cutting flesh to ribbons.

Zia hadn't said a word to Tilly since she'd agreed to come this way. The whispers told Tilly this was because she was trying to think of another plan to get Tilly to where Lucifer wanted her. Tilly didn't know if this was true—she didn't know what was true anymore—and she didn't care. She was concentrating on finding the right moment to ditch Zia.

"And just where do you think you're going?" a voice boomed.

Coming down the side of the mountain was a fly the size of a two-story building. Smaller flies buzzed around it, but didn't block its path. The whispers quieted, letting the cacophony of Hell crash all at once into Tilly's ears. She winced.

"Beelzebub," Zia whispered to Tilly. Then louder: "We're just passing through."

Tilly could have sworn the giant fly grinned. There was no mouth to be seen, but somehow it was giving the impression of amusement.

"You know I don't like you running drugs through my section, Zia. I prefer my souls to be mentally present when they're being tortured."

Tilly saw Zia readjust the bag at her side. "No drugs today, Bee. I'm just making sure this girl gets to the center."

The fly approached Tilly. Its feelers probed the air around her, eventually brushing her sides. They were longer than she was tall. She fought the urge to run. A million versions of herself shone back at her from its eyes.

"Lucifer's business," Zia said. She sounded nervous.

"Mmm. I'm sure. What's your name, girl?"

Tilly looked askance at Zia.

"She's not important," Zia insisted. "Like I said, we're just passing through."

Beelzebub's wings vibrated in irritation. "She must be important if Lucifer granted her access through my territory. Name. Now. Or I'll string you up and make sure all my little friends eat your flesh off you for eternity."

Tilly gave her name and the fly recoiled, standing on its hind legs. "I should string you up anyway, you little bitch." One leg gestured through the swarm of flies. "All these morons are rebelling because of you. There's a group of them marching to the center as we speak."

"And you're just sitting here?" Zia chuckled. "Some prince you are."

"I'm awaiting orders," he huffed.

"Lucifer wants her to walk through. There are your orders, you oversized bug." Zia grabbed Tilly's arm and tugged her away from Beelzebub. He called after them, but they didn't stop. Zia swatted a few of his little friends on the way, a half grin on her face.

The whispers immediately resumed when they reached the end of the swarm, louder than ever.

"She says Tilly is able to use the pendants like a god."

Luke had finished laying out Lucifer's plan. While Naveen didn't want to believe Tilly would ever become one of Lucifer's Generals, he knew what a trip through Hell would entail. Especially if Lucifer put her energy behind the tortures. There was no telling what evil was being whispered into Tilly's ears.

"Is that true, Naveen? Can she really use magic like that?"

"I've suspected for some time that she's a descendant of the gods. Distantly, of course."

If it was true, and she had a gift for magic, that meant she could wield it as a weapon. She would have the same power as the gods, the same power as Death. She could wipe souls out if she tried, sending them to the black abyss of oblivion. She would be a powerful ally for Lucifer.

"What I don't understand," Luke said, "is what Lucifer meant when she said she would finally be ready."

"She must have some plan to show the souls in Hell Tilly's downfall. Most of the souls in Hell are normal souls. It's not until after they're there for a while, after they lose hope, that they begin to go insane. If they lose it enough, they transform, become demons. Lucifer has no hope of winning a war against her father in the World with a bunch of souls that aren't on her side. If those souls see Tilly join forces with Lucifer, they will lose all hope."

"And go insane."

Naveen nodded. *If she succumbs to the fire, hope is lost and all souls are damned.*

"And then Lucifer will be ready to fight God."

Phoebe, who had been sitting to the side chewing on her fingers, spoke up. "But what would make Tilly do that? Why would she decide to join the devil?"

"That I don't know. She would have to do something that she couldn't take back. Something that she couldn't deal with, that went against her very being."

The entrance to the tent flew back. "The barrier is failing," a man said. He pointed to Luke. "We're gonna need that pendant."

EVERYTHING VISIBLE WAS MOVING. Souls writhed against each other like maggots on an open wound, screaming in terror, rage, ecstasy. Flames exploded from mountaintops, geysers, people's bodies. Lava rolled down the sides of volcanoes, pumping continuously like blood from an artery. It was the life force of Hell. A stream of souls climbed upward, for what reason, Tilly couldn't guess. The lava pummeled them. They screamed, but kept walking, falling face first into the molten mess when their legs melted away. Under it all was the steady booming of explosions, like a heartbeat. The atmosphere was thicker here, pressing in, suffocating. The air was red, a mist like blood spray. It clung to bodies, running down arms and legs in rivulets, forming a vein-like netting of red. It met with the ground and mixed into the muck to form a never-ending floor of sucking, bloody swamp. It stunk of decay and sulfur with a hint of burnt flesh.

There was something sharp looking on the horizon, jutting up through the low-hanging crimson clouds.

There were so many voices in Tilly's head, she couldn't form her own thoughts. The masses screamed; the tornado whispered.

This is where you were meant to be.

Her scar stung like it was only a few days old. She could feel the tornado nearby, but didn't dare look back at it. She worried that if she did, she wouldn't be able to stop herself from jumping straight into it, ending this nightmare.

They stood on the edge, not yet part of the sticky mass of bodies. Zia grimaced and swung her eyes over the crowd, uncertain how to proceed. Tilly didn't know either. How was she supposed to stop a rebellion?

You have to get their attention. Call out to them and they will follow.

Tilly obeyed, earning a look of confusion from Zia.

"It's best not to get too many people's attention," Zia hissed.

Tell them your name.

She ignored Zia, took a deep breath of blood-tinged air and yelled her name, one more voice into the indecipherable cacophony. To her surprise, a few of the nearest souls turned and studied her.

"It's her," one of them announced. He was a young man whose left arm had been ripped from his body. He was carrying it in his right. A stub formed at the vacant shoulder as he turned and said her name to the person next to him. Tilly's name passed from mouth to mouth, whispered in reverence. Slowly, the crowd quieted somewhat. All eyes were on Tilly.

You are a god in your own right. They worship you. You must lead them.

"Tilly," Zia said, her voice shaking a bit, "this is not a good idea."

Ignore that bitch! She's a betrayer! A liar!

A cheer rang out from the crowd. Zia reached for her swords, slid them from their sheaths with a sharp *shiiing*. A smattering of chuckles from the bystanders. "We just need to pass through," Zia said. "I'm looking to trade, as well, if anyone is interested."

A haggard old man shuffled forward. He was missing an eye and the few teeth he had left were brown. "Whatcha got there, little darlin'?" He nodded his chin toward Zia's bag. "Wouldn't happen to be some o' them sweet, sweet berries would it?"

Zia swallowed. The whispers cackled in Tilly's head. Many souls smacked their lips together, inching closer.

"We could use a little forgettin' just now," the old man said.

The souls were closing in. Tilly held out her hands. "No." They all stopped, looked at each other.

Let them have her. You don't need her, anyway.

Tilly shook her head. "Back off," she told the crowd. They complied.

The whispers threw a fit, screeching and howling, then seemed to talk to each other for once instead of Tilly.

Have to get rid of her. Can't wait any longer.

Tilly caught sight of the tornado. It was to her side, now a wide expanse of angry lava cutting a path down the nearest mountain. It was redder than before, with an added touch of a black substance that looked like tar. It threw souls out of the way as it made its way down the mountain face. It stopped at the bottom, swirling angrily, as if something were holding it back. Or it was waiting for something.

"Look," Tilly said, "I don't know why you people think I'm leading any kind of rebellion. I'm nobody. I just want to get my mother back." Didn't she? She couldn't quite remember why that was important.

Confused chatter.

"You refused to accept the little girl's fate!"

Tilly hesitated. She thought of Phoebe's sweet face, of the people she'd brought to Hell, none of them having a chance to defend themselves. The whispers interrupted her.

No one cares about you. Why should you care about anyone else? Your own mother tried to kill you! Your father found another family!

"You left Heaven to come defend us!"

"That's not true," Tilly replied. "I never meant for any of this to happen." She waved her hands around. "I can't help you. I'm not who you think I am."

Yeeesssss.

Another explosion shook the ground and a smattering of angry shouts went up. Tilly felt a presence at her back, heard a scornful laugh.

"That's right, kill their hope," Beelzebub said.

A few of the faces in front of her twitched. They looked around like they were searching for something. Opened their mouths wider and wider until their jaws popped. Their arms stretched backward, shoulder sockets twisting at an unnatural angle. They crouched, wailing. Some retched, vomiting blood and pus. Then they began to convulse, rolling in the muck and flailing.

Tilly looked at Zia, who looked back in confusion.

Beelzebub continued to laugh from behind them. The whispers joined in.

The seizing souls stopped all of a sudden, lying deathly still. Everyone in the vicinity was quiet, watching.

Then they all spasmed at once. Their abdomens split down the middle; their limbs stretched until they became thin and spidery. As if pulled by an invisible string, they were on their feet, hellish marionettes controlled by the same puppet master. Their faces looked as if they'd been burnt, barely recognizable as human. Their eyes bugged out. They screeched.

Zia tossed one of her swords to Tilly. She held the hilt uncertainly. The last time she'd wielded a sword, it had been too heavy and awkward. This one, however, was light and well balanced. It felt like an extension of herself. Zia moved close, putting her shoulder against Tilly's. No other soul moved. They were mesmerized.

"What just happened?" Tilly asked as they watched the disfigured souls. The whispers were weirdly quiet. Tilly felt like she could think again.

"They went nuts. Turned to demons."

"What do we do now?"

"Stab them."

The newly formed demons lunged, their mandibles clacking. Zia was the first to strike, sending her blade straight through an arm. It fell to the ground and flopped around. The demon shrieked and the others backed off. They formed a circle around Zia and Tilly, pacing around and around, like a pack of dogs moving in on wounded prey. The demon with the missing arm shook for a second. Then its arm regrew.

"You going to do anything about this, Bee?" Zia called out.

Beelzebub chuckled. "I think I'll just watch."

"You know Lucifer wanted Tilly to get through."

"Yes. She didn't say anything about you, though, now did she?"

Zia swore.

The demons paced faster and faster until they were a blurry ring encircling the two women. As they swirled, anger bubbled inside Tilly.

"Get ready," Zia said.

Tilly gripped the hilt, but it was slippery with the blood rain. It wobbled. She didn't see how she would be able to hold onto it in order to stab. She didn't see the point, anyway, if the demons just regrew their limbs. And then there was what Beelzebub had said: Zia didn't have to make it through. Tilly was protected. Why should she care what happened to Zia? They could rip her limbs off for eternity and it wouldn't matter to Tilly's goal.

The whispers were talking amongst themselves again.

Almost. Not quite yet. One more push.

The demons stopped all at once.

And standing directly in front of Tilly was her mother.

Tilly lowered her sword fractionally. Her mom took a step forward. The demons around her stood at the ready. "Where did you come from?" Tilly said.

Her mother opened her mouth to speak, but she didn't get a word out. Instead, Zia's sword sliced neatly through her neck. Her head rolled off and onto the ground. Her body stood for a moment, as if dumbstruck, before falling to its knees.

Tilly screamed. Her vision went fuzzy.

Zia turned to face her. "Tilly, that wasn't—"

Tilly careened forward and buried her sword into Zia's stomach, clear to the hilt.

The demons cheered, Beelzebub roared with laughter.

Zia's brows knitted. She slowly looked down at her stomach, lightly touched the hilt, then dropped to her knees just as Tilly's mother had done a moment ago.

Tilly stumbled backwards, looking at her mother's still-smiling face, then staring at her bloodstained hands. She shook.

The whispers called to her.

Good girl. Now come to us. We'll make it all better.

She turned to the tornado and started walking.

THE CROWD WAS IN AN UPROAR.

"We have to have the pendant or we'll be found!"

"Hand it over!"

"We'll take it by force if we have to!"

Phoebe hid behind Luke and Naveen outside the Fates' tent. The failing barrier was now crackling feebly instead of shimmering calmly. It wouldn't be long now until it was completely down and the fugitive souls would have nowhere to go.

"We should give it to them," Luke said.

Naveen shot him a sharp look.

"We could always get to the Port Dome."

"We'd be caught before we ever got there." Naveen could see the telltale black cloaks of the Acolytes moving in. They'd spotted the disruption in the atmosphere. It was too late to resurrect the barrier; everyone would have to port elsewhere.

"I don't think there's enough magic in that bead to transport everyone here," Naveen said.

"We can't just leave them here," said Luke. "They'll be sent to Hell."

Naveen shrugged. "That's where most of them came from anyway."

"There're escaping a messed up situation, and you know it." Luke pulled the pendant out, tossed it at the crowd. Naveen was quick and caught it midair. The crowd moved in, hissing insults.

He brandished the pendant in front of their faces. "I can end all of you right now." He meant it only as a hollow threat, but the idea of taking them all out sent a little thrill through him. *Get yourself together*. He took a deep breath.

The crowd took a collective half step back, shaking heads and whispering to each other. Naveen felt a tiny hand grab his. He looked down and Phoebe frowned at him, shook her head. He lowered the pendant. "You can't have it both ways," he told her. "We can either save Tilly or let these people go."

The barrier shuddered and then it was down. The crowd turned to face the Acolytes, who lined up in formation.

A familiar voice called out, "Naveen, my darling. Just hand over the girl, and I'll let everyone else go."

The Black Market crowd parted, all eyes on Phoebe. Eris slithered her way to the front of the Acolytes. "Except you, that is. We're going to Hell together. We'll trade the girl for a place down there."

Naveen transferred Phoebe's hand to Luke's. "Don't let go of her." He handed Phoebe the pendent, then he walked through the crowd to face his ex. "You know I'm not going to do that."

She pouted. "Then I'll just have to get her myself."

Chaos broke out. The Acolytes charged and crashed

against the fugitives. Eris hissed and dove at Naveen, pinning him to the ground.

"Naveen!" Phoebe squealed.

A group of fugitives had turned on her. Luke was doing his best to fight them off, but one was tugging hard at the pendant strings. Phoebe was losing her grasp. Eris launched herself off Naveen, but he grabbed her ankle and she fell.

"Open a port!" he yelled.

Luke reached for the pendant, managed to touch the bead despite the fugitive's arm around his neck. The swirling blue opened. Eris kicked Naveen in the face and he recoiled. She scuttled away. Naveen lost sight of her in the crowd. Phoebe was standing beside the port, screaming. Fugitives filed past her, diving through the port.

Naveen pushed himself up and through the crowd. He elbowed and punched, all the while listening to Phoebe's high-pitched cries. Luke was still swinging and kicking. Every time he got loose for a moment, he reached for Phoebe, but someone always grabbed him from behind and he'd be back in the fray. By the time Naveen reached him, Luke was on the ground, being trampled as more people realized there was an open port. He helped him up, then looked around for Phoebe. She'd been jostled further from the port, and was now huddled next to a tent, whimpering and rocking back and forth.

"Get through the port," Naveen shouted at Luke as he made his way toward the girl.

It was a stampede: fugitives pushed toward the port, shoving struggling Acolytes right along with them. Naveen pushed his way through, but it was like fighting an avalanche. He was coming closer to the edge of the port. Phoebe cried out again. A head of black hair bent near her. When she straightened, she had a firm grip on Phoebe's upper arm. The girl was flailing, but Eris wasn't deterred. Eris caught Naveen looking and waggled her fingers at him. Then she touched the pendant at her neck and was gone, taking Phoebe with her. Naveen was shoved through the port a few seconds later.

When he landed in Hell, the first thing he saw was Luke fighting off a hissing, spitting demon.

The second thing he saw was Tilly's fiery hair as she walked toward a tornado of lava.

SHE HEARD voices far behind her, muffled, as if underwater. She couldn't look back. All she could do was stare unblinkingly at the swirling mass of lava, thinking about her mother lying dead on the ground. Thinking about how it felt to drive Zia through with a sword. She laughed, once, hard. Then she did it again and again until her voice rose to a hysterical pitch. The whispers had quieted. They'd gotten what they wanted, whatever that was. There was no more need for them to coax her into the fire. She was already there.

A familiar voice cut through her thoughts. It seemed so close, as if he were speaking in her ear. *Tilly*, it said. A voice she couldn't quite place. She was almost at the tornado now.

She turned slowly. There were thousands of people around, too many to take in. But her eyes landed on one: raven-black hair, a concerned look on his face. He reached out to her, as if he could grab her hand, as if he wasn't far away. He called her name again.

"You're not real," she muttered.

Zia was up and slicing demons once again, even as the rather large wound in her stomach stitched itself together.

Zia thrust a sword hilt into Naveen's hand. He glanced at it briefly, then locked eyes with Tilly once more. *Come back*, he was saying.

"Not real." Tilly turned her back to the fight. Her scar burned and tugged her arm upward to the tornado. She brushed the outer edge. It was hot, but not as hot as the tangle of wrinkled skin on her wrist.

She heard her name once more before the tornado lurched forward, tired of waiting, and enveloped her.

She was falling. Down, down, into a bottomless pit. She thought she would fall forever, that there was no more outside world. This was it, this darkness, this heat. This despair.

The whispers started again, but this time they were outside her head. They were here, inside the tornado with her, a physical presence. She saw them out of the corner of her eye, but when she looked, they were gone. Always whispering. Tilly let them in, let their whispers encompass her brain, take her over. There was no longer any reason not to.

Images flashed in front of her eyes.

See?

Her dad fawning over his new baby.

Luke flirting with a group of girls in a club.

Eris running her fingers through Naveen's hair as he sat on a throne made of silver.

Her mother lighting a spark in the fireplace, watching it grow, then kicking a log out toward the curtains with a smug look on her face.

Phoebe giggling as she played on the floor of the Fates' tent.

Everyone had forgotten about Tilly. They'd moved on, not caring if she was there or not. She wanted to die.

Wanted to be wiped from this existence. No more Hell, no more anything.

A new image flickered, then sharpened and stayed. This one was different: she wasn't seeing it from afar like some Peeping Tom; she was in it. It was her memory.

She was standing on the side of a bridge, crying as she stared down at the dark water below. It was nighttime, the moon shining but the stars invisible behind the bright city lights. She briefly wished she could see them one last time. It had rained recently, the crisp smell still clinging to the heavy air, little puddles of water sitting in the shallow indents in the road. The metal railing was beaded with moisture as she gripped it and looked over, her hair serving as a blinder, only showing her the rushing river below. She could feel the coolness of the water from here, like it was inviting her to go for a dip.

The voice was back, in her head as it had been for weeks. "Do it," it said. "Jump."

The whispers in the tornado joined in, chanting *jump, jump, jump*. She was beginning to have a hard time telling what was real: the tornado or the bridge?

Her body on the bridge hopped over the metal railing and leaned forward on the other side, the breeze whipping her hair around her head. She closed her eyes, allowing her grip to relax a little.

She hesitated. What was she doing? Her eyes snapped open and she gripped the railing so hard her knuckles turned white.

She slowly turned, holding onto the railing for dear life. Her foot slipped on the wet concrete. She caught herself, but in the brief moment of shock, of near-death, she thought she saw someone standing there on the other side of the railing, someone with a dark hooded cloak and a very white smile.

There came a sensation of a firm hand pressing on her heart. She looked down but didn't see anything. Then the pain started. Intense, shooting pain around her chest. She couldn't breathe. Her grip loosened as her muscles screamed for air that wasn't coming.

She fell backwards into the cold water.

Just before she hit, she saw the figure again, looking over the railing, grinning with those unnaturally white teeth and laughing a low rumbling laugh.

The image was gone. She was still falling in the unnatural tornado. But now she knew. That one missing piece she'd tried so hard to remember.

Hate bubbled under her skin like a third-degree burn. She let out a scream filled with anguish. The whispers chuckled in glee.

Death had killed her. She wasn't ready and he'd snapped her life from her and then *laughed about it*.

IV.

Tilly was gone, swept away by the cyclone. There was nothing Naveen could do for her now; she would have to fight off her demons on her own.

Naveen turned and surveyed the situation before him. The displaced souls from the Market wailed as demons attacked them. Zia's swords whirled, chopping limbs from demons. An arm would fall only to be replaced by a new one a few seconds later. It was a losing battle.

Luke floundered on the ground, struggling to wriggle free from the two demons pinning him. Naveen rushed over and, with one swift, sure movement, twisted a neck until it snapped. The demon lay prone as the other one hissed while crouched over Luke. Luke took his opportunity, giving the demon a hard uppercut. It didn't kill it—couldn't kill it —but knocked it back enough for Luke to slide out from under it. Naveen helped him up.

"Where's the pendant?"

Luke showed him his left fist, which still gripped the pendant he'd used to open the port. Naveen sighed in relief and took it from him. He felt for the magic; only a tiny bit winked back at him. Not enough to port anywhere.

"Please tell me there's something left in that thing," Zia shouted as she slid a sword from a demon's abdomen.

"Not much."

She kicked another, spinning on the ground then bringing both swords up to drive them into the demon's face. "I don't need much," she said. Naveen tossed her the pendant. A demon came from nowhere and plucked it from the air right in front of Zia's face. It grinned at Naveen, brandishing its prize. Zia didn't hesitate; she crossed her swords over her body and brought them together in a scissor-like motion, beheading it. She grinned as she sheathed her swords then bent to rip the pendant from the demon's still-twitching body. "I did miss the fighting."

Me too, Naveen thought, and immediately hated himself for thinking it. He was surrounded again, Luke beside him, as they threw punches and kicks every which way. Claws and teeth ripped flesh from bone, sending searing pain through his body. Luke's arms were bloody as well, but he was fighting on. "Got a plan?" Naveen called to Zia.

She raised an eyebrow and pursed her lips. "Always." One sword was again unsheathed, stabbing at anything that came near her as she made her way to Naveen. The other hand pressed the pendant.

Nothing happened.

Naveen and Luke continued to fight off the hoard as Zia moved behind them. They formed a barrier for her so she could concentrate. They were both exhausting themselves and wouldn't be able to keep it up much longer. A demon managed to get purchase on Naveen's arm and wrenched. Naveen heard the sickening crack and saw bloody bone before he realized what had happened. The pain came a moment later. The demon was still tugging on it, trying its best to rip it from Naveen's shoulder. "Any time, Zia!" He kicked out, connecting with the demon's knee. It buckled backwards.

She shushed him. "Just a second. I'm having trouble finding them . . ." She tugged a sack from her belt and tossed it to him. "That should tide you over."

He caught it with his good arm. He was starting to feel faint. He knew he'd heal, but it would take several minutes. Demons closed in and Luke did his best to keep them back. Naveen was out of time. He pulled open the bag, holding his injured arm to his chest. He saw the red jelly-like substance of crushed fruit and smiled. Ambrosia. Stuffing a hand in, he swiped some of it out and into his mouth. He lay back for a moment, relishing the taste as he listened to Luke's failing struggle. It had been a millennium since he'd tasted the sweet nectar. He heard Luke call out in pain, then heard loud sniffing all around him. Everything quieted. The demons had caught scent of the ambrosia.

The pain in Naveen's arm lessened as demons closed in on him. He could feel the bone straightening, the skin mending itself. He would be fully healed in a few seconds. He used his good arm to grab the bag and threw it as far as he could. The demons chased after it like a dog to a bone.

He stood, flexed his fingers, moved his elbow. Everything worked. "You could've had them off you earlier with the ambrosia, my dear niece," he told Zia.

"I was saving it for a rainy day."

"You're an odd one," Naveen said.

She just smiled in return, then closed her eyes as she concentrated on the magic in the bead.

He heard the flapping before he saw them. They soared just under the blood-tinged clouds, their great wings whooshing. There were three of them, all black except for a white ring around their necks. Their heads were bald and the color of a bad sunburn. Their wingspan was easily the length of a football field.

"Come to me, my pretties," Zia cooed. She had a smug look on her face.

The condors of Hell were some of Lucifer's many pets, but even she couldn't summon them. Zia was the only one of the gods who could control birds of all forms.

Luke stumbled over, a large chunk of skin missing from his left cheek. He was hovering a hand over it, wanting to touch it but too afraid to. "How bad is it? Will I still be pretty?" His eyes held a lot of pain, but he was smiling with the good half of his face.

Naveen grunted. "You'll heal," he said as he patted him on the back.

"Get ready," Zia said.

The condors slowed, but didn't look to land. They reached their claws out as they approached, ready to pluck up their fares.

"To the Citadel!" Zia whooped once they were in the air.

Luke clung to his condor for dear life, his eyes bugging out as he looked at the ground far below. His face was already healing. Zia was giggling with glee as they zoomed along. Naveen couldn't share in her joy. He remembered Eris tugging Phoebe through the port, Tilly diving into the tornado.

She will have to choose between darkness and light . . .

His stomach clenched. He willed the birds to fly faster. There might still be time to bring Tilly back from the brink of madness. He hoped.

DEATH AND LUCIFER returned to the throne room to find a Demon Guard passed out and the cage door swinging on its hinges. Death stepped away, wanting to be out of reach when Lucifer devolved into a rage. He waited, but all she said was, "The incompetency of my Guards makes me wonder how anyone stays imprisoned here at all," and then shrugged. She called for more Guards and told them to take the useless one away. Her calm made Death wary. Either she had an impeccable plan or her tendency toward mental illness had blinded her.

Lucifer jerked her head to one side as if she were listening to something. "Damn that woman," she said as she rushed from the throne room. Death followed, but only to the doorway.

In the entrance hall he saw Eris prostrating herself on the floor, Guards surrounding her. A small child stood at her side, frozen stiff in fear. Death's heart lurched and he had the urge to rush the little girl. He had to remind himself that his goals had changed and he was no longer tasked to bring Phoebe to Lucifer. Lucifer called off the Guards. He watched her closely as she studied Phoebe, whose chin shuddered as she tried to keep from crying. Lucifer had stopped breathing, her hand to her heart. She had a look of near reverence on her face. It was bizarre.

"My lovely, powerful niece, I've brought you the girl you wanted," Eris said, her face still pointed at the floor. Her formal speech almost made Death laugh. "Perhaps you would consider letting me return home permanently. I would serve you well."

Lucifer's calm awe had vanished. She pressed her index finger lightly on her pendant and Eris flew across the room, pinned to the smooth black wall by an invisible hand. Phoebe jumped and her eyes welled.

"So you can usurp me," Lucifer hissed. She approached Eris slowly, a wolf closing in on its prey.

Eris struggled against the wall in vain. "I deserve a reward for bringing the girl." Her tone was harder than Death's would have been in her situation. He winced. Lucifer had the power to kill if she wanted and hated Eris enough to do it, goddess or not.

Lucifer laughed without mirth. Eris's defiance dissolved. "Please let me come home," she begged. "I'll do anything. Anything! I can't stand Between. Please!"

Lucifer seemed to consider, but Death knew there was no way she would let Eris live down here. It was too much of a risk.

"You may be useful yet," she said, and Eris's face lit up. She spoke to her Guards briefly and Eris was taken away.

Turning to Phoebe, she put on a saccharine smile and bent at the waist a bit. "You and I are going to have a little chat. Would that be alright?"

Phoebe sniffed then let out a small moan. Lucifer clucked her tongue. "No need to fret, my tiny oracle," she said as she placed her arm gently over Phoebe's shoulders and guided her past Death and into the throne room. "How would you like to play with a baboon?"

Lucifer's pet hissed and hopped to the top of a throne when it saw Phoebe. She stopped and shook her head. Lucifer looked confused.

"I don't like it," Phoebe said. "It has big fangs."

"Is there something else you would rather play with?" Lucifer asked through gritted teeth.

Death wondered what she was up to. He'd been told she only wanted the girl in order to keep up with her soul count, but if that were the case, she would have simply thrown Phoebe out into the masses and forgot about her.

"A puppy?" Phoebe said.

Lucifer rubbed a bead and an ink-black dog appeared on the floor at Phoebe's feet. She immediately plopped down and began petting it. Her sniffles calmed. The baboon climbed off the throne and took a few curious steps forward, but Lucifer gave it a stern look and it retreated.

Lucifer retired to her throne and watched Phoebe play with the puppy for several minutes. Death noticed her hands clenched in her lap as if she wanted to reach out and strangle the girl.

Phoebe was still sniffing every so often, but her tears had dried.

"What do you know about me?" Lucifer asked.

Phoebe kept her eyes on the puppy when she answered. "I know you're mad at your daddy for choosing your brother over you."

Lucifer's eyes clouded over and she dug her nails into her hands until Death saw blood squirting from in between her fingers.

"Is there somewhere else I can wait for Tilly to arrive?" Death asked. He really did not want to be in the room when this maniac decided to attack the girl. Children's deaths were always hardest to witness, even for him.

"Stay where you are," Lucifer snapped. Then she took a deep breath and addressed Phoebe. "Anything else?"

Phoebe shrugged.

There was a moment of silence as Lucifer struggled to keep calm.

Phoebe looked up abruptly, first at Lucifer, then at Death. "You won't win, you know." She smiled.

In the next instant, the baboon rushed over and grabbed the puppy in its mouth. Phoebe screamed.

"Now maybe you'll tell me what I want to know," Lucifer

said. Her face was calm now, serene even. She always had enjoyed torturing, Death knew. That sadistic streak was why God had chosen his son instead of her as his successor. It had never sat well with Lucifer, as she was the firstborn. Being down here, alone, had only cultivated her sadism.

Phoebe was crying again, shaking her head violently. "I don't know anything but what the prophecy says," she insisted. "I don't, I don't."

"There has to be something about the war!" Lucifer exploded out of the throne. Death took an involuntary step back. He swore under his breath. He shouldn't have come down here. It was stupid to want help from someone who was notoriously mentally off.

Lucifer raised her arms at her sides as if she were parting the Red Sea. Her eyes were glazed and she was staring into the middle distance. Death wasn't sure if she knew where she was. The baboon screeched and bounced around the room. The puppy, forgotten by its torturer, ran whining from the room.

Her voice boomed as if she were addressing troops on a battlefield. "There must be something about my rule on Earth. Tilly will lead my army to greatness. I will conquer all!" She shuddered in ecstasy. "Then he will see! He will see that I'm the better choice, the better child!"

Phoebe scooted along the wall, coming nearer to Death. Her eyes were saucers when she looked up at him. It was ironic that she thought he would protect her. He couldn't even if he wanted to. Lucifer was much more powerful than he'd ever been.

Two Demonic Guards rushed in. "The tornado approaches."

Lucifer came back to reality and smiled. "Well, let's go greet my newest general."

Phoebe was left in the custody of the guards. Lucifer and Death made their way out to what would be called a courtyard at a normal palace. Here it was a wide expanse of hardened lava, smooth and jet black. The rippled rock sloped downward slightly until it met with the blood-red moat that sat on the inside of a tall fence made of smoothed bone, lashed together with entrails. On the other side of the fence were the damned. They'd pressed in close, some of them smashed against the fence so hard that their bodies were being pulverized. All were yelling, pumping their fists. Lucifer waved and they got louder, not in admiration but indignation. These people were rioting. They expected their savior to arrive any moment. Lucifer expected hers as well. Death wasn't sure who would be correct.

They watched the tornado approach. It was massive. Had it been in the World, Death was sure it would have flattened a swath the size of Kansas. As it was, it simply bowled over the souls in its way, leaving no more destruction than a gentle wind. There was nothing to be destroyed in a place that thrived on destruction.

It cut through to the courtyard and stopped. Death saw Tilly's feet alight on the ground and the tornado pulled back as if she were a snake shedding its skin. It dissipated, retreating to the well of evil that spawned it.

Tilly was left on the smooth rock. Death inhaled sharply when he saw her. Her eyes were clouded, her face haggard. There was a sternness about her that wasn't there before, a taut look to her body that suggested she was ready to pounce at the first thing that came near her. She jerked her head to the side suddenly, then let it roll back. She wasn't far from turning.

Lucifer clapped her hands. "You're almost ready," she called to Tilly. Tilly tossed her head, like she was shaking off an unwanted thought. Her eyes cleared for a moment as she studied Lucifer.

"For what?" she said. Her voice was hoarse.

"To lead my army," Lucifer replied, and raised her arms to indicate the masses beyond the fence.

Tilly turned to look at them in bewilderment. When she looked back, her eyes locked on Death's. The cloudiness returned to her eyes. Her mouth opened slightly and she drew her lips back over her teeth and gnashed them. He heard the strike from where he stood and he felt a shock of fear.

But she turned her attention from him back to Lucifer, who was now holding a pendant out to her. She tossed it and it skittered across the rock and stopped at Tilly's feet. "You know what to do," she told Tilly.

Tilly sneered as she popped her neck to the side again.

Death stared at Lucifer's grinning face, fully realizing she'd set him up. She'd said he should try to get rid of Tilly, and now he understood what she meant by "try."

Tilly had finally remembered exactly what he'd done to her, and she was mad as hell.

THERE WAS a haze in front of Tilly's eyes and in her mind. She could see the shapes of people in front of her, but they were mostly in shadow. Sometimes their forms would clarify, and she would be able to think clearly. She saw the pendant stop at her feet, its bright red bead looking up at her like an eye. It was speaking to her, throbbing with life, with want, with anger. She picked it up. It thrummed in her hand, pulsing like a beating heart. Experimentally, she brushed her fingers over it, and was overwhelmed with the power she felt there. She'd never held a bead this big. She could do *anything* with this amount of magic. Her brain clouded again as she saw red, her chest swelling with hate.

Muffled shouts from the crowd at the fence. She heard, but didn't understand. They were chanting her name. They expected her to do something for them, but Tilly was done doing for others. There was only one thing she wanted to do now.

She raised her eyes and saw Death standing a few yards away from her.

"You can kill him," Lucifer whispered. She was also several yards away, but sounded as if she were right beside Tilly. "Feel the magic. Wipe him from existence."

Tilly did feel it. She knew she could end him. Her body twitched. She could feel her joints cracking. She convulsed.

Then she was moving forward. She didn't remember telling her legs to walk, but they were doing so just the same. She tried to stop them. Something wasn't right. She didn't feel right. She was forgetting something—something she wanted badly.

Lucifer's voice penetrated the haze once more: "That's it, Tilly. Just a few more steps and you'll be there. You'll be a god, a leader among souls. They will all follow you."

Her vision pinholed. All she could see was Death's pale face.

The crowd stopped chanting and exploded in cheers. She heard a beating sound, then Naveen's voice calling her name. It was faint over the cheering crowd.

"You're too late," Lucifer cackled. "She belongs to me now."

There was a scuffle. Tilly didn't take her eyes off Death. She let the fight fade into the recesses of her mind.

"You killed me," she said. Her voice came out all wrong;

it sounded gravelly and hesitant as if she'd forgotten how to speak. Her tongue felt heavy in her mouth. Dry and fat. Death's eyes narrowed. She was almost to him now. A few more feet. He didn't move, just waited.

A thought flashed across her mind. He could just as easily kill her. Her vision cleared for a moment and she stopped walking. She looked to the left. Demon Guards were fighting Zia, Luke and Naveen. Why were they there? She couldn't remember. Lucifer stood behind her Guards, head thrown back, laughing. There were too many Guards for the three of them. They wouldn't last long. It didn't matter anyway: they couldn't really be there. Tilly had killed Zia. She remembered seeing her fall, the hilt of her own sword protruding from her abdomen.

Tilly's eyes skimmed past, landing on the souls outside the fence. They'd quieted. All were staring at her and reaching through the bars as if they could touch her. Some were crying, some twitching in the way that meant they were turning. She couldn't help them.

Her attention returned to Death. He still hadn't moved, but was now flexing his fingers.

Yes, he would try to kill her. He didn't need a pendant to do so, and she'd never done this before. She took a half step back. Her brow furrowed and she cocked her head to the side. She was forgetting something and it was making her angry. What was wrong with her? Why couldn't she think straight?

"Well, get on with it," Death growled.

Her jaw worked, opening wide, then snapping shut. She bit off the tip of her tongue. It tasted metallic and somewhat rotten. She swallowed it. It grew back almost immediately.

There was a bang to her right as doors were thrown open. Feet pounded toward her.

Tilly swung her head around and down. She was staring at the round face of a girl whose eyes held heartbreak. The girl skidded to a halt when she saw Tilly's face.

"Tilly?"

Tilly twitched.

"What's wrong with you?" The girl's voice was small, confused.

A sharp bark of laughter escaped Tilly's throat. She jerked her head back in surprise.

Phoebe's eyes widened in fear and she took a step back. She looked from Tilly to Death and back again. Her brown eyes settled on the pendant clutched in Tilly's hand. "What are you doing, Tilly?"

"She thinks she's going to kill me," Death said. "I suppose it's only fair. I did kill her, after all."

A violent shudder began in Tilly's stomach and tore through her limbs. Her vision clouded again. She was falling, falling from the bridge. Into the cold water, pain in her chest. She rubbed the pendant, felt the power there coursing through her. She found what she needed, held onto it. She could wipe this man from existence. She took a step forward and Phoebe screeched.

"Tilly, no!"

She stopped, shook her head. The haze retreated a bit, but her mind couldn't settle. It was arguing with itself. She had to kill him. He took her life away, her real one, not whatever subpar existence she had now. "I don't have a choice."

"But you do," Phoebe said. "You've always had a choice."

Tilly took a step forward.

"You'll become just like them if you do this." Phoebe's words were rushed, panicked. She pointed at the demons.

Tilly looked again. The fighting had stopped. The

demons held fast to her three friends. Everyone—even Lucifer—was watching her with bated breath.

"Finish him," Lucifer breathed. "Do it now, and you can have your mother."

Tilly took a deep breath. Her mother. That's what she'd forgotten. She was here to get her mother. But that wasn't right either—was it? She saw a head roll off a body in her mind's eye. Zia had killed her mother.

"No I didn't," Zia shouted.

Had Tilly spoken aloud? She didn't think so, but she couldn't be sure. She couldn't be sure of anything.

"It was an imposter," Zia choked out as the demon holding her kicked her knees out from under her and shoved her face into the ground.

"Who cares anyway," Lucifer said. "Your mother was a psychotic bitch who would rather burn to death than stay with you."

Everyone spoke at once.

"Those souls need help—"

"Stay with me—"

"Kill him now—"

"Your duty—"

"The prophecy—"

Tilly pressed her hands to the sides of her head, felt the hard pendant digging in. She screamed, shocking everyone to silence. Tilly opened her eyes and looked at Naveen. "I don't know what to do," she said. His eyes turned red and he struggled with renewed vigor against the demon holding him.

"Finish it!" Lucifer screamed. Her voice crackled with hysteria. Her eyes burned scarlet and her fists clenched at her sides.

Out of the corner of her eye, Tilly saw Death reach for her. She turned to face him.

Time slowed. Death's hand inched toward her body. She stared, frozen with indecision, as the pale appendage came closer. *Move*, she told herself. *Move now*. But she couldn't.

A head of dark hair dove in front of her, blocking her from Death's touch. Tilly realized who it was too late. He fell to the ground and convulsed. Then he was still.

She dropped the pendant as her knees met the ground. She reached for his body. She couldn't breathe. She pulled him to her, held his head in her hands and looked deep into his gaping eyes, willing him to move. He didn't.

Naveen was dead.

V.

A horrible wail went up. Eris ran from the building, pushed Tilly aside and clutched Naveen to her chest. Lucifer cackled with glee in the background.

Phoebe was crying somewhere near. Tilly relished the sound of Phoebe's mourning, as she couldn't bring herself to do the same. Her scream had lodged in her chest, hardening into a hateful tumor.

She lifted her chin. Death's lips curled in a smug sneer. The hate boiled over.

Then she reached for the pendant. She was going to end this now.

Phoebe got to it first. She snatched it off the ground and put it behind her back. Her cheeks were still slick with tears, mouth pursed in a deep frown, chin dimpled.

"Give me the pendant," Tilly demanded.

Phoebe shook her head violently.

Red distorted Tilly's vision. Sounds blurred together, an ocean of static. She grabbed Phoebe around her thin neck. "Give me the damn pendant!" Phoebe's eyes widened, but she still shook her head. Tilly wrenched the girl around and wrestled the pendant from her small fist, then shoved her hard. She fell and cried out in pain.

Tilly reached into the magic as she spun on her heel. Death was no longer sneering, but staring slack jawed at something to the side. Tilly didn't see. Her vision had tunneled again and she popped her neck. She rushed him, feeling the magic flow through her. Grabbing his collar, she pulled him close, her face inches from him. He struggled, lifted his own hand to touch her.

His palm was hot when it touched her cheek. The magic coursed through her body; she wanted nothing but to repel him, to make him pay for what he'd done. His face fell in confusion. He tried again, pushing harder against her face, shoving her head backward as she clutched both him and the pendant. The magic was cresting; she could feel it bubbling up, about to explode. Death's magic met her own and there was a spark, then a loud crack. They blew apart, each flying through the air and landing hard on the ground. The damned souls roared. The fence rocked, snapped. A few more moments and they'd break through.

Death remained on the ground, stunned, as Tilly rose again, on all fours curled up like a cat. She launched herself up and forward, going for Death again.

Someone caught her around the shoulders, held her tight. She spat and kicked, but he didn't let go. She struggled against the strong arms, hissing and gnashing her teeth.

"Tilly," a calm voice whispered in her ear. "Stay with me."

She hesitated, calmed. It was impossible. She'd just watched him die, had held his lifeless body.

The hands turned her around, a firm grip still on her shoulders. Naveen's dark eyes found hers.

"He killed *you*," she said. Her head swam. She twitched.

To her surprise, he grinned. "It's about time someone did."

She shook her head violently. "I'm losing my mind. You're not really here."

He turned her to look at the body on the ground. His body. "I am, just different." She stared at his body, unable to believe. "I was a god, not a dead soul. And now I'm free."

She convulsed. Her mind felt like it was tearing in half.

"You can be free, too, Tilly," Naveen said. "Just let it go." He pulled her into his chest. "Let it go," he repeated, his voice cracking.

"Kill him!" Lucifer roared with rage.

Another sound crackled through the air: the fence had finally given way. Souls poured forth, diving into the moat.

"You can stop this, Tilly," Phoebe said.

She watched the souls climbing out of the bloody moat. She wanted them to come, wanted them to tear everyone limb from limb. Their frantic energy was contagious.

"Kill!" Lucifer repeated.

Tilly stared at Death, who was now standing, looking ready for another fight. Eris had gone to stand beside him, hate pouring from her every pore as she glared at Tilly and Naveen.

Tilly pulled away from Naveen. "He killed me," she growled. "He killed you."

"Tilly, you have a choice!" Phoebe wailed as Tilly took a step forward.

Lucifer was manic, jerkily dancing and howling like a banshee.

Naveen reached for her hand, pulled her back into him. His mouth found hers. His lips were cool, gentle. They sent a wave of calm over her, quenching the hot fire.

She felt the hate soften, loosen its hold on her heart. He kept his forehead touching hers when the kiss was over. He reached down, his fingers brushing the hand holding the pendant. She relaxed. Her thoughts cleared. She didn't want to kill anyone. She let Naveen slide the pendant from her fist.

Lucifer roared with rage. She shook her fists at the sky and stomped up and down like a toddler throwing a tantrum. Tilly pulled away from Naveen and watched the damned scramble closer, like an infestation of roaches. Lucifer ran at them, hissing and spitting, screaming that she was their ruler and they would obey her. They swarmed her, lifted her into the air. Ripped at her clothes, her hair.

In the sea of chaos, one woman stood at the moat bank, gazing serenely at Tilly. They locked eyes. Her mother. Tilly remembered the reason she was back here, the unfairness of it all, the broken system.

"Stop!" she yelled.

The crowd quieted, all eyes on her. Some of the souls were mid-change, snapping at their own shoulders.

Tilly pointed at Lucifer. "Put her down." They hesitated. "Now," she insisted. They dropped her with a thud and retreated.

"I know most of you don't believe you belong here." Tilly kept her eyes on her mom's face as she spoke. Her mom was smiling at her. "And some of you probably don't." Nods and clapping all around. "I'm going to see what I can do about that." They cheered.

A CRACK of blue light broke the sky. Everyone looked up. The port widened, stretching to let three fiery figures through—angels flying in a V formation. The damned went wild, in excitement or fear or both.

As they got closer, Tilly recognized the leader as the angel who had attacked her in Heaven. She tensed, ready to run. But then she noticed a fourth figure, bobbing erratically, and hesitated, squinting.

The three figures landed gracefully; the fourth came to a crash landing, but popped himself upright immediately and adjusted his toga. Tilly smiled—it was Edgar.

Two angels drew their swords and stood guard around their leader. The souls taunted them, but didn't come closer.

The leader looked around with his nose wrinkled in disgust. "I really don't know how you live down here, Lucifer."

"It's not like I have a choice, Michael," Lucifer spat. The Archangel smirked. Lucifer hissed at him, but backed away on all fours.

Edgar pointed furiously at Death. "There's the brute who tortured me! Arrest him this instant!"

Death stepped forward and glared at him. Edgar recoiled, hid behind Michael's leg. Michael ignored him.

"I've returned the small girl to Lucifer as promised," Death said. "And here are Naveen and the other girl. I believe my job is done."

Michael frowned. "Oh, you'll get your reward. God has something special planned for you."

"Indeed he does," Edgar said, peeking out from behind Michael. "You haven't been following the rules. Do you know how much paperwork I had to complete in order to get my wings repaired, sir? Do you? A nightmare, I tell you."

Michael gave Edgar a look. "That's not the primary reason for our descent into this pit." He wheeled to face Tilly. "You've certainly caused an uproar."

Tilly swallowed, unsure what to say. She hadn't exactly been the model dead person since she'd died. Taking Phoebe's place, breaking out of Heaven, inadvertently starting a rebellion, almost killing Death. It wasn't a good track record.

Edgar waved at her, alighting once more. He wore a smug smile on his face. "I've come to liberate you, Tilly. After that heathen"—he spat in Death's direction— "accosted my beautiful wings, I went straight to the Palace and demanded an audience with God." He was interrupted by a derisive snort from Michael. "Of course, I didn't get one," he backpedaled, "but I raised the alarm. Something wasn't right. You belonged in Hell, you know, because of your suicide—"

"I didn't kill myself," Tilly interrupted.

"Indeed! That's what I'm trying to tell you. After looking into the matter, I discovered that you were murdered, by none other than the man who attacked me. And after that—"

Michael swatted him to the ground. "Do shut up, you imbecile."

Edgar huffed and slunk away to pout, mumbling about not getting credit.

"As I was saying," Michael said, "the primary reason for our presence is you, Tilly. We were alerted to unusual activity by that little imp over there." Edgar flipped him off behind his back. "He was quite insistent on your damnation."

"Of course he was," Tilly said. She couldn't help the smile that crept across her face.

"So we looked into the matter," Michael continued. They —Tilly wasn't quite sure who "they" were; she doubted Michael had done it personally—had reviewed the recording from her supposed suicide and noticed something was off. From there, they began investigating Death's actions up to and after that point. After the raid of the Black Market, the Fates came forward and told how they'd caught Death with the lifelines. This information led to more investigating, which eventually led them to realize the Acolytes had stopped culling souls and the World was in chaos.

"It took you that long to realize that?" Tilly said with an incredulous laugh. Michael didn't find it funny and glared, a quick shot of smoke coming from his nostrils.

"We've since ordered the Acolytes to resume their duties, and the escaped souls and demons are being rounded up as we speak. The World will be back to normal within a few hours."

"That's not even the good part," Edgar said. He was so pleased with himself he would've wagged a tail if he had one.

"I'm getting to it," Michael snapped. He sighed, then turned to face the masses of damned.

Tilly interrupted. "I have something to say."

Michael's eyebrows shot up.

"I've promised these people that I would do something about the unfairness of this system." She glanced at where her mother stood, still smiling at her. "I would like to ask that . . . no, I demand that a hearing for each damned soul take place immediately. My mother—"

Michael waved an impatient hand at her. "Yes, we know all about your mother. And as I said, I'm getting to it." He gave her a stern look, one that said *shut your mouth*. Then he turned to the waiting souls.

"As many of you know," he said, his voice loud for all to hear, fire trailing from his wings as he paced, "there is a standing bet between God and Lucifer for all your souls."

The masses bellowed.

"Since the usurping of the old gods and the coming of our Lord to the throne, we have disregarded the antiquated ways and moved forward without panel judgment for your souls." Groans and cursing all around. Michael let it go for a moment, then held up his hands to silence them. "It has recently come to our Lord's attention that the magic-driven automated system, while efficient, may not be the best way to decide your eternal fate. It seems—" he glared at Lucifer "—that the ancient enemy of God and mankind alike has used this system to her advantage, gaining many more souls than she would organically under the old ways." He paused for dramatic effect. "Therefore, God, in His infinite wisdom and benevolence, will reinstate the tribunals, effective immediately."

Everyone cheered. The angels stood with smug looks, pleased to be the bearers of good news. Lucifer dove at Michael, but he whipped around at the last second and a flaming sword appeared at her neck. "There will be none of that," he growled. The other two angels restrained her. She hissed and spit and struggled, cursing them all, but they held fast.

Satisfied, Michael turned back to the fence. "All souls, regardless of when they died, who believe they deserve a chance to defend themselves against the punishment awarded them will have a chance to apply for a hearing in front of the judges."

Phoebe squealed in delight. The remaining hate sitting inside Tilly's chest melted away. Her scar stopped burning; it was once again just a marred piece of skin. She felt like crying. Phoebe would get a fair trial. So would her mother. Tilly looked for her mom in the crowd, but she'd disappeared.

Tilly looked at Naveen, expecting to see a grin on his face, but he was watching Death, who was slowly backing toward the open doors of Lucifer's palace. When he thought he was safely out of sight, he turned to run. Michael was in front of him in a second. They spoke for a few moments, but Tilly couldn't hear what was said. Death looked afraid. Then Michael put both hands on Death's shoulders and Death disintegrated.

Tilly gasped. All that, and he was killed anyway.

Once Death was gone, Michael turned to Tilly. One minute he was standing by the doors; the next he was right in front of her. She jerked and felt Naveen tense at her side. Phoebe was fascinated: she lifted a hand and gently touched the flames coming from Michael's wings. She giggled as they tickled her. "Please don't do that," Michael scolded. He frowned at her.

"Tilly," he said, turning his attention to Tilly once again. Tilly's mouth dried out. "God wanted me to inform you that He is grateful for your help. You have brought the declining state of the kingdom to His attention. And for that He is indebted to you. He has offered you reincarnation."

Tilly's mouth fell open. Tears sprang to her eyes. She thought of trees, the sun, the moon, laughter, love. Living. She could see her dad again, mend the ties there. Her baby brother would be so big by now, and she'd missed so much.

Phoebe squeezed her hand and she looked down at the girl. She was beaming up at Tilly, crying with joy. She hugged her around the middle, tightly. Tilly grinned at Naveen. He smiled back, but the corners of his eyes were turned down.

Living would mean leaving him. And it would mean leaving her mother.

She took both hands and held Phoebe's face. The little

343

girl was bouncing on the balls of her feet in her excitement. Living would mean leaving her, as well.

"You did it, Tilly," Phoebe squealed. "Just like I said you would. Didn't I say she would, Naveen?"

Naveen chuckled. "You did, indeed, little one."

"I didn't," Tilly said. "If it weren't for the two of you . . ." She trailed off. She looked at Michael. "Could we speak in private?"

Michael tilted his head, gestured for her to lead the way. She walked until she was out of earshot, and then said, "I accept the offer of reincarnation."

"God will be ple—"

She held up a finger. "But not for me."

VI.

Death awoke to bright lights and the smell of disinfectant. He wailed the high-pitched sound of a newborn. A masked man announced that it was a boy, and he felt warm tears on his face as his mother held him.

He remembered everything. Michael had told him this was how it would be. He would remember every life, every death until the end of time.

He felt his heart speed up and choked a bit. Then he couldn't breathe. There were worried voices and he was plucked from his mother's warm embrace.

This is how it would be: he would be reincarnated, taking the place of innocent souls, only to die within a year of his birth.

Over and over again.

TILLY once again stood outside the Disciplinary Building. This one was just as large and intimidating as the one in

Between had been. But this new one had the added factor of a hellish backdrop.

"You'll do fine," Naveen said from beside her.

She smiled at him doubtfully, then reached for her mother's hand and gave it a squeeze. "Ready, Mom?"

"Definitely."

She led her mom through the doors and into the judgement chamber. Naveen followed and took up a position in the back of the room among the other spectators.

Ret, Rho, and Ren sat at the bench on the other side of the room. In the early days, there had been some talk about Naveen sitting on the panel, but he'd turned it down before the discussion got too far along. He'd said dying had lifted a great weight from his shoulders, one he hadn't known he was carrying. Part of that weight had been Eris, who wanted nothing to do with him now that he wasn't an immortal god. He was finally free, granted a second chance like the souls they now escorted. And he didn't want more responsibilities. "Besides," he'd told Tilly, "being in Hell is a bit too much of a temptation for me." She supposed she understood that.

Lucifer sat on a silver throne, petting her baboon, on the left side of the room. A podium stood on the right. Tilly made her way to the podium, avoiding looking at Lucifer as much as possible. She'd grown accustomed seeing her at these hearings, but that didn't mean she wasn't unnerved by that devilish smile. And today, of all days, she didn't need to be unnerved.

"And how does your client plead, Tilly?" Ret asked.

Tilly glanced at her mother and smiled.

"Not guilty."

PHOEBE'S SOUL was reborn without much fuss after only a few hours of labor. She was healthy and perfect, letting out a short cry when she emerged and then falling silent, her face beatific and peaceful. When the baby opened her eyes for the first time, Tilly saw Phoebe there, her old soul already taking in the world around her. Her eyes seemed to lock on where Tilly stood clutching Naveen's hand. Tilly smiled. She knew the girl couldn't see her, but hoped she could feel her presence.

"We've got to get back," Luke said at her side. "I've got souls to escort."

"Well, aren't you the model resident of Between all of a sudden?" Naveen smirked.

"We really do have to get back," Tilly's mom said. She gave Tilly a quick hug and a peck on the cheek.

Her mom was doing well. The judgement panel had rightly decided a person in the middle of a bipolar manic episode wasn't to be blamed for thinking they could withstand a fire. Invincibility was a common enough delusion of the disease. She was transferred to Between and took over Tilly's old job escorting to Hell.

Lucifer ranted and raved throughout the sentencing, but at the end had grinned at Tilly. "She'll be back, you know. She belongs with me." It chilled Tilly to hear that, but she had to hope that wouldn't be the case.

"I'll see you later, silly Tilly," her mom said now and ported out with Luke.

Beside the hospital bed, Tilly was unable to take her eyes from her family. The room's lights were turned low, but the light of a full moon shone brightly through the hospital window, blessing the scene in front of her. Her father cupped his new baby's head gently and kissed his wife's forehead. He reached to pick up his son—the half brother

Tilly foolishly hadn't wanted in life—so he could see his new baby sister. They whispered amongst themselves as Naveen gently tugged Tilly's arm toward an open port. She turned to go, sad at having to leave. They were a beautiful family. She didn't regret her decision, only wished she could be there to see her siblings grow.

"You'll watch them on the monitors," Naveen said, reading her thoughts.

She smiled. It wasn't the same, but it would have to do. She was meant to be where she was, dipping her toes into the fire to give souls hope for a second chance to defend themselves.

Fate had predicted it, and she had chosen it.

THANK YOU FOR READING!

We hope you enjoyed following Tilly through the afterlife.

Authors love reviews. If you enjoyed this book, please consider leaving a review on the site of your choice.

Would you like to be the first to hear about Sarah Gribble's latest news? Please go to http://bit.ly/sarahgribble to sign up to her author newsletter. They're packed full of free stories, giveaways, and general horror and dark fantasy chatter.

ACKNOWLEDGMENTS

I'm thankful every day for my husband, who never once faltered in his support of my writing, even on those days when I couldn't muster any support for myself.

I'm also grateful for my mom (who will probably read *way* too much into the mother/daughter issues written here) for letting me read whatever I wanted when I was a kid, no questions asked. And to my dad, who told me I could be anything I wanted to be, even if he would've preferred it if I'd wanted to be a lawyer.

I'm indebted to the Write Practice writing community for more things than I can count. Every single one of you is amazing.

Special thanks to Joe Bunting and Alice Sudlow. And a very special thanks to Kim Kessler, who helped me rediscover what this story was supposed to be.

Mental health and addiction issues fill the pages of this book. If you are struggling, please don't suffer alone. If you know someone who is struggling, please don't look away. Visit samhsa.gov to get help.

ABOUT THE AUTHOR

Sarah Gribble lives in Columbus, Ohio with her husband, dog, and two cats. She enjoys hiking, camping, consuming horror in every way possible, and freaking out her readers. She's currently working on her next novel.